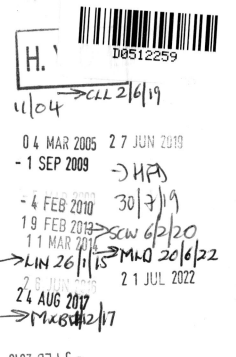

H.

D0512259

11/04 →CLL 2/6/19

0 4 MAR 2005   2 7 JUN 2019
- 1 SEP 2009   → HPA
- 4 FEB 2010   30/7/19
1 9 FEB 2013 → SCW 6/2/20
1 1 MAR 2014
→LIN 26/1/15 → MLO 20/6/22
2 6 JUN 2016   2 1 JUL 2022
2 4 AUG 2017
→MxB 12/17

- 5 FEB 2018

HYC

About the author

Mandasue Heller was born in Cheshire and moved to Manchester in 1982. She spent ten years living in the notorious Hulme Cresents, which have since become the background to her novels. She has sung in cabaret and rock groups, seventies soul cover bands and blues jam bands.

MANDASUE HELLER

Tainted Lives

CORONET BOOKS
Hodder & Stoughton

First published in Great Britain in 2004 by Hodder and Stoughton
A Division of Hodder Headline
This paperback edition first published in 2004 by Hodder and Stoughton
A Coronet paperback

A CIP catalogue record for this title is available from the British
Library

ISBN 0 340 73505 8

Typeset in Plantin Light by Palimpsest Book Production Limited,
Polmont, Stirlingshire

Printed and bound by
Mackays of Chatham Ltd, Chatham, Kent

Hodder and Stoughton
A division of Hodder Headline
338 Euston Road
London NW1 3BH

To my Nana
EVELYN HANCOX
(1908–2003)

Acknowledgements

———•◆•———

Much gratitude to all who have helped and supported me along the way, especially JUDE DAVIES (& staff of Waterstones, Deansgate).

Many thanks to MARK WYLIE (M.U.F.C).

Special acknowledgement, as ever, to:

WINGROVE WARD – for giving me time, tons of coffee, suggestions (and honesty when I'm talking rubbish). AAF.

JEAN HELLER – I learned from the best, Mum!

MICHAEL, ANDREW and AZZURA – my multi-talented children.

AVAJANE, my sister, who will one day write the book I so long to read!

Nieces and nephews, AMBER (& Kyro), MARTIN, JADE and REECE. Auntie DOREEN, PETE & ANN, LORNA, CLIFF (Chris & Glen).

NATALIE (Aaliyah) and DANIEL (Scholes) WARD.

NORMAN FAIRWEATHER (aka: Kaine Brown) – friend, and true technical wizard.

CAT LEDGER, and FAYE WEBBER (Talkback). Mighty fine agents.

NICK AUSTIN – thanks so much for your help and encouragement.

MARTINA COLE – Love and hugs to the queen from the princess.

Everyone at HODDER, especially:

My lovely publicist, EMMA LONGHURST.

BETTY-BOO SCHWARTZ – words can't express how much you mean to me. (And Mr Irrepressible!)

And my ace editor, WAYNE BROOKES . . . nobody does it better!

PROLOGUE

2003

D ucking to avoid the jagged spears of metal jutting down from the ruined door shutter, Detective Inspector West stepped into the long-abandoned Victorian swimming baths.

It was a bright day, but even with the shafts of light filtering in through the gaps between the boards covering the windows it was too dark to see clearly. And, brisk as it was outside, the temperature in here was off the scale. The chill air enveloped his face like a dead hand.

Releasing a loud breath that momentarily hovered like a cloud in front of his face, he surveyed the scene before him with narrowed eyes.

The room was empty, the fixtures and fittings scavenged or destroyed, the walls bearing the scars of where the ornate wrought-iron changing-stalls had once been securely bolted. The pool was bone dry, its pock-marked tiles stained in a ghostly reminder of where the waters had once gently lapped.

The corpse sat in a crumpled heap directly below the high-diving board, its legs oddly twisted as if it were a marionette dropped from a great height. But this was no puppet. It was a real human being, with a slip-knotted noose still biting into its snapped neck.

Making his way around the pool edge to the iron steps, West climbed carefully down into the pit and crossed to the corpse. Hunkering down before it, he gazed dispassionately at the bloodstained face. With its smashed nose, half an ear missing, its mouth locked open around a grey slug of tongue and the clouded eyes bulging, it was a gruesome sight.

Shaking his head, West wondered at the error of judgement that the two young uniforms had made in cutting it down. What on Earth had possessed them? All right, it was dark in here, but any fool could see that the carcass was stiffer than a porno dick. All they had achieved was a serious contamination of a crime scene – for which they would pay dearly, starting with a severe dressing down from the pathologist, Lynne Wilde. Brilliant and generally easygoing, she didn't suffer fools lightly and her tongue was sharper than her scalpels when faced with this brand of incompetence.

And it wouldn't end there, for they would then have to face the wrath of their formidable Chief Super – and West doubted they'd dare touch so much as an injured *dog* for fear of getting it wrong after *he*'d finished with them.

If they had only thought before leaping in, they'd have known that this was no suicide – that the hanging was just the finale of a more sinister set of events. Even a couple of greenhorns like Pratman and Bobbins – the heroic duo whom West had banished to wait outside for the forensics crew – should have spotted the blood-blackened, burnt-edged holes in the denim covering the victims' knees. Not to mention the damage to the face, and the livid bruising and strangely blood-lacking slashes on both wrists where they had been bound, then cut free post-mortem.

'Found anything, Tony?' It was Lynne Wilde.

Smiling, West straightened up and turned around. He liked Lynne. Somewhere in her fifties, she had the forceful presence of the worldly-wise woman, and the blessing of a much younger physical appearance. Quite tasty, if he was honest – and far too astute for him to feel entirely comfortable lying to her.

'Nah,' he told her. 'I doubt we'll get too much. Looks pretty pro.'

'More than can be said for our lot,' she snapped, waving her crew to carry the equipment down to the site. 'Any idea what the idiots thought they were playing at?'

Shrugging, West crossed the floor of the drained pool and climbed the steps to join her.

'Don't think they stopped to think.' He folded his arms, his expression grim. 'They were pretty panicked when I got here. Must have freaked when they saw it and dived right in – so to speak. Think they've done a lot of damage?'

'Damage?' She snorted, pulling on a latex glove with a snap. 'They might as well have committed it themselves, the bloody imbeciles! There'll be traces of them all over it. Doubt we'll find anything usable.'

Shaking his head, West frowned.

'Sticking around?' Lynne asked.

'Well, I was supposed to be somewhere.' He checked his watch. 'But if you need me . . . ?'

'I think I can manage.' She gave a half-smile, her eyes bearing the slightest hint of a twinkle now. 'Wouldn't want to keep you from anything important. I'll let you know if something develops.'

'I'll be handing it over, as it happens,' he told her. 'But I'd appreciate it if you kept me up to date. Last case, and all that.'

'Ah, yes.' Lynne smiled. 'You're on the long run to freedom any day now, aren't you?'

'Tomorrow.' West too was smiling now. 'Didn't think I'd look forward to it, but this has kind of sealed it for me.' He nodded back towards the corpse, starkly defined now by the arc lights that the crew had set up – and all the more unreal for it. 'Just think, I won't have to look at another scene like this for as long as I live. Bliss.'

'You'll miss it,' she remarked confidently. 'You'll be one of my regular visitors at the morgue before too long, if I know you. I've heard retirement doesn't quench the thirst. Once it's in your blood, you're a lost cause.'

'We'll see,' he murmured, thinking that she couldn't be more wrong. 'Good luck.'

'It'll take more than luck,' Lynne said, sighing wearily. 'I'll need a bloody miracle.'

Giving her a casual salute, West left her to salvage what she could from the mess.

Making his way outside, he strolled to his car with a lightness of step – and heart. Pausing to light a cigarette, he gave the ashen-faced uniforms a sympathetic smile, then set off to relay the good news.

PART ONE

1985

I

─────◆─────

S arah hadn't seen the man with the camera before, but she could tell at a glance that he was the same as all the rest. He even smelled the same – mouldy dog, stale beer, and too many fags. And his eyes were big and starey, telling a different story from the fake-nice words in his mouth.

'Ooh, you're a pretty girl, aren't you? Bet you're gonna break a few hearts when you're bigger. So, how old are you, darlin'?' He was licking his lips now, watching her greedily as he set up his special lights and pulled down the roll-down screen behind her.

She didn't answer. She just glared at him and folded her arms.

'Didn't you like the kitten?' he asked, peering at her through the camera, hoping to get a smile out of her by reminding her of the tiny black and white bundle that he'd brought along as bait.

Sarah's lips tightened into a knot. She'd like it if she was the one playing with it in the kitchen. But she wasn't, was she? No, her snotty little brat of a sister Karen was!

'Gonna put this on for me?' he was asking now, holding up a horrible frilly pink mess of a dress.

Snorting softly, Sarah turned her head and fixed her gaze on the closed curtains. The sunlight filtered through the hanging folds at the top where the hooks had fallen off the rail. She could hear the kids running about outside, shouting to each other to pass the ball or get out of the way. She so wanted to be out there with them. But she wasn't going anywhere till this was over.

'Come on,' the man wheedled. 'It'll look great on you, this. Don't you like it? What's wrong with it? It's got a lovely bow. Look.'

She refused to even glance at it, so he came right up to her and grinned into her face, teeth as yellow as a tea-stained cup.

'You'll have to get dressed up all the time when you're a real model, you know?'

'Don't wanna be a moggle,' she muttered, tensing at the nearness of him, the too-close stench of anticipatory sweat.

Sighing, he slapped his hands down on his knees.

'Look, kid, I've come a long way for this. Just put the dress on and stop messing me about.'

'No.'

He tried to persuade her, but when he realized she wasn't having it, he started shouting instead. She was wasting his time, he said. Wasting his petrol getting him over here for nothing. Wasting the *electric*. His special lights used a lot of electric, and the longer she refused to cooperate, the more she wasted. Did she want him to tell her mammy about the waste?

Sarah was seriously scared now, but she couldn't back down. She didn't see why she should do the job when Karen had wriggled her way out of it – *again*. If he wanted someone to wear it, he should have asked for *her*. *She*'d have put it on for a kitten. But then, why would she bother when she was already reaping the benefits without doing a thing?

It wasn't fair, and the injustice made Sarah all the more determined. Anyway, she knew exactly what would happen if she *did* put the dress on. He'd take his pictures, then he'd . . .

And she hated *that* even more than she hated the man and his stupid dress.

Giving up, he called her mother in to sort her out.

'What you playing at, you little bitch?' Maggie Mullen screeched, gripping Sarah by the arm and shaking her roughly. 'You know I need the bleedin' money!'

She raised her fist but the man stopped her just in time.

'Don't! Not her face! The bloke wants her looking sweet, not battered. Another time, maybe, but not today, eh?'

So Maggie started pinching instead, and pulling Sarah's long black hair, threatening her with what she'd get if she carried on playing funny buggers. They'd all starve if she didn't get on with it, and her mammy would die! Was that what she wanted? . . . *Was* it? . . .

Hours later, when the man had got what he wanted and gone, Sarah crept out of the bedroom. She'd stopped crying now, and she was curious to see the kitten she'd earned.

Creeping downstairs, she saw that her mother was gouched out on the couch. At least *she* was happy – now that she'd fed her veins. It remained to be seen if she'd get it together and feed her kids as well.

Tiptoeing past her, Sarah went out into the backyard.

Karen was sitting on a heap of bricks by the wall, clutching the kitten possessively. 'I've called him Joey,' she announced. 'And he really likes it.'

This really annoyed Sarah, but to save an argument she let it go. She just wanted to hold the little cat, to feel his silky fur, kiss his tiny nose and listen to his purrs.

'Let me have him,' she said, holding out her hands, smiling.

'No!' Scowling, Karen clutched Joey tighter to her chest and turned her back. 'He doesn't want you. He loveses me.'

Sarah gritted her teeth. 'All right, but you've had him long enough. It's my turn now.'

'No!'

'*Yes!*' Sarah was getting angry now, she made a grab for him. 'He's mine, Karen! The man gave him to *me!*'

'Mammy says we've got to share!' Karen squealed, ignoring the kitten's pitiful mewing as she squashed it. 'Get *off*, Sarah. You're hurting him!'

'No, I'm not – you are! You're just jealous 'cos you know he'll love me best!'

'No, he won't, you big fat liar! Let *go!*'

'*You* let go, you little bitch!'

'No! He hates you, so there! *Everyone* hates you, Sarah Mullen. Everyone! 'Specially Joey!'

'No, he *doesn't!*' Sarah was close to tears now.

'Does *so!*' Karen hissed spitefully. ''Cos you're horrible. And I'm gonna tell!'

'You wouldn't *dare!*'

'MAM . . . Sarah's hurting Joey! *MAAAAM* . . .'

Maggie woke with a start. It was Karen screaming, she'd have known that piercing tone anywhere. It was her least favourite thing about her otherwise favourite daughter. Not that she'd admit to having a favourite because you weren't meant to, but of the two, it was definitely Karen she liked most – for the most part. Except when she was screaming. With the glass-shattering shriek rattling the teeth in her gums, she could cheerfully throttle the little cow.

Hauling herself up, Maggie rubbed her gritty eyes and lumbered to the door. The screams grew louder with each step and she felt her blood pressure rising to dangerous levels. The little bitches knew that she needed to rest after a fix. Why could they never give her a minute's peace?

She hurtled out of the back door, ready to bellow the hair off their scalps, but what she saw in the yard stopped her dead in her tracks.

Gape-mouthed, she looked from Karen, still screaming fit

to bust, to Sarah, standing against the wall with a thick shard of glass in her hand, to the bloody mess on the concrete at Sarah's feet, its tiny paws flexing weakly as the blood leaked from its scrawny neck.

Time stood still. Then reality slammed home with a vengeance.

'Shut up, you!' Lurching off the step, she raced across the yard to give Karen a rough shake. 'You'll have the pigs round!'

'She stabbed him . . . she stabbed him!' Karen screamed.

Clapping a hand over her mouth, Maggie gaped at Sarah in disbelief. 'What you done, Sarah? What you bloody *done*?'

'Weren't me,' Sarah muttered, her mouth a bloodless knot. 'It was *her*.'

'She's nowhere *near* it!' Maggie yelled. 'And you're the one with the flaming glass in your hand, so don't think you're talking your way out of this one!'

Sarah knew exactly what would happen next, and that nothing she said would make any difference, but she had to at least try.

'If you don't believe me, ask *her*,' she said.

Maggie saw red – literally. A crimson curtain slipped down over her eyes and made the top of her head feel like a geyser about to blow. Hurling Karen in through the half-open back door, she rushed towards Sarah with her fists clenched.

'Ask *her*, is it? Ask *her*? Well, I'm asking *you*, lady! And you'd better have a bleeding good reason for this, or I'll strip the skin right off you!'

Sarah froze as fourteen stones of violent mother-fury thundered towards her. Then, at the very last second, she leaped out of the way.

Swerving to make a grab for her, Maggie stepped squarely onto the kitten and skidded into the wall with a house-shaking thud. Flat on her face in the mud and debris that the council laughingly called a garden, she struggled to right herself, rage causing her eyes to bulge and the breath to hiss out of her mouth in a wet spray of foam.

'Just wait till I get a grip of you, Sarah Mullen! I'm gonna bleedin' batter you!'

Edging back along the wall, Sarah trapped herself in the corner. Sinking to the floor, she curled into a tight, protective ball, whimpering, 'No, Mammy, don't! It wasn't me, honest . . . It was an accident!'

'Get up!' Maggie hissed, grabbing her by the hair. 'And shut your lying mouth, 'cos that weren't no accident, that was you being your nasty-arse self!'

Sobbing as her mother lavished blows on her head and her face, Sarah screwed her eyes shut and raised her arms to protect herself.

Letting go suddenly, Maggie staggered back a step and stared at her arm in disbelief.

'You've cut me!' she gasped. 'You've fuckin' *cut* me!' Sickened by the sight of her own blood dripping onto the ground at her feet, she sank to her knees.

Shocked, Sarah got up and took a tentative step towards her. 'I'm sorry, Mammy. I didn't mean to—'

'Get away!' Maggie yelled. 'Just get away, or I swear to God I'll kill you!'

'Mammy, please,' Sarah sobbed, keeping her distance as she desperately tried to explain. 'I didn't mean to hurt you and Joey! It was Karen's fault, honest it was! It was my turn, but she wouldn't let me have him, and—'

'Shut your *mouth*!' Spittle flew from Maggie's mouth. 'I don't want to hear your lies. I just want you *out*! You're bad, Sarah – bad, useless, an' good for nowt but trouble – just like your bastard father! Why don't you just piss off and leave me and our Karen alone!'

Tears of rage and sorrow at this rejection and injustice

streamed down Sarah's cheeks. Why was everything always her fault, while Karen the liar could never do any wrong? It just wasn't fair.

Swiping at the tears with the back of her hand, she said, 'Right, I'm going, and I'm never coming back – 'cos I *hate* you!' Turning to run, she screamed when her mother's hand shot out and grabbed her skinny leg.

'Well, I hate you an' all, d'y' hear?' Maggie snarled, digging her nails in hard. 'I hate you an' all!'

Too far gone to care now, Sarah lashed out wildly, trying to free herself from the painful grip.

Feeling a blow to the back of her neck, Maggie threw her hand up and was shocked to feel a warm wetness. Bringing the hand around to her face, she stared at her crimson-stained fingers.

'Oh, my God,' she wheezed. 'Look what you done *now*!'

Cowering behind the kitchen window, Karen saw it all. But most of all, she saw the blood. It was everywhere, and she was petrified that Sarah was going to kill Mammy, then come after her. Starting at the sound of the telephone ringing, she raced towards it and snatched it up.

'She's hurted Mammy! Sarah's hurted Mammy! There's blood, and, and—'

'I'll be there in a minute,' the man on the other end said, slowly, calmly, taking instant control. 'Now put the phone down and dial nine-nine-nine for an ambulance. Do you understand?'

'Yes.'

'Good girl. Do it right now, then open the door and wait outside till someone gets there.'

Tony West loved his job. He thrived on always being in the thick of things, relished the power. Black, white or yellow, he didn't differentiate. If someone stepped out of line, he stamped on them. Crime committed – punishment dealt. Simple.

He was in a particularly good mood right now, having received the nod to a stabbing at Maggie Mullen's house. The caller was a child, so it was unclear who the victim was, but he hoped it wasn't Maggie. Much as he'd like to see her suffer, he'd prefer it if she were the one holding the knife. Disarming her would give him the perfect opportunity to indulge in some not-so-reasonable force – payback for their last encounter, when she'd spat in his face for saving her miserable life. He should have left the fat-arsed bitch where he'd found her – flat on her back on the Princess Parkway, playing chicken with the drink-drivers.

Pulling up at the kerb, he saw a small, thin girl standing on the pavement beside the front door, her plain face a dirty mask of distress, the grime on her legs streaked white with piss – a pool of which she appeared to be standing in.

In the passenger seat, probationer Kay Porter shook her head as she unclipped her seatbelt. 'Poor little sod,' she murmured pityingly. 'Look at the state of her.'

'I've seen worse,' West said, accidentally brushing his shoulder against Kay's breasts as he leaned down to unwedge his baton from down the side of the console.

'Oh, *please*,' she hissed, pressing herself back against the door.

'What?' He was the picture of innocence. 'I didn't do anything. You wanna chill out, darlin'.'

Suppressing the urge to yell at him to stop calling her that as if she were some piece of fluff that he'd been given to amuse himself with during his working hours, Kay gritted her teeth and followed him out of the car.

'Yeah, this is mild compared to the filth you'll see round here,' West was saying now, adjusting his trousers around his six-pack-and-a-barrel gut. 'You'll think this one's dressed for a picnic with the Queen by the time you've seen a few more. Which reminds me—' He leaned towards her conspiratorially. 'Word of advice: if you ever have to give anyone a boot up the jacksy, watch where you put your foot, 'cos you don't wanna be getting shit on your lovely shiny shoes.'

Kay bit back the cutting retort that sprang to the tip of her tongue. She knew that any complaint she made would be met with derision. He was a patronizing swine. Always *explaining* everything, and making snide digs about the neatness of her uniform, as if ironing her shirt and polishing her shoes proved that she thought herself too good to get her hands dirty with 'proper' police work.

West shook his head in despair as he sauntered towards the child. Kay was doing his head in. She was such an uptight bitch. Taking everything he said the wrong way and acting like she was trapped with an animal when they were in the car together. He couldn't wait till her probation was over and he got rid of her.

Reaching the little girl, he bent down with his hands on his knees and smiled.

'This your house, pet?'

'Yeth,' she lisped around the thumb stuck firmly in her mouth.

'And what's your name?'

'Kawen Mawie Muwwen.'

'That's a nice name. And I bet you're the clever girl who called nine-nine-nine, aren't you?'

'Uh huh.'

'Good girl. Mummy inside, is she?'

'Yeth.'

The living room reeked of cabbage soup gone bad. Wrinkling her nose as she followed West inside, Kay quickly changed her expression into a sympathetic half-frown when she noticed Maggie Mullen sprawled on the couch, her left arm wrapped in a dirty, bloodied towel, being held above her head by a scruffy, gaunt-faced man.

'Fine mess this, eh, Maggie?' West strutted into the centre of the room and cast a glance of undisguised disgust around him. 'Bit gutted, actually. Got myself all geed up on the way over thinking I'd find you standing over some poor bloke with his bollocks sliced off. Still, can't have everything, can we?'

'Sorry to disappoint you.' She shot him an evil glare. 'Who asked *you* to come, anyhow? I don't need the pigs, I need an ambulance.'

'Shouldn't it be here by now?' the man holding her arm asked. 'She could bleed to death, you know.'

West narrowed his eyes. 'It'll be here. And you are . . . ?'

'Lawrence Dakin. I'm an old friend of Maggie's.'

I bet you are, thought West. *About as old as the joey you rode in on.*

'How long have you been here?' he asked brusquely.

'I didn't do this, if that's what you mean,' Dakin replied evenly, fully aware of the implication behind the question. 'I just—'

'It was my Sarah, if you must know,' Maggie cut in, immediately succumbing to a coughing fit. Slumping back when it passed, puce-faced and breathless, she waved at Kay. 'Pass us me fags, will you, love?'

Kay looked around for the cigarettes. Finding them on the floor between the cup-ring-encrusted table and the couch, she handed them over. From the corner of her eye, she glimpsed West's look of contempt at her compliance. No doubt she'd get a lecture when they left about the evils of kowtowing to the natives.

'Your Sarah?' West said. 'She another little 'un?'

'Yeah, she's seven – and evil as fuck!'

'That's a bit rich, isn't it?'

'Oh, you reckon, do you?' Maggie glared at him. 'Well, if you think *this* is bad—' she waggled her injured arm, almost sending Dakin flying across the room '—you wanna see what she done to that cat!' Shaking her head now, she moaned, 'Oh, I can't believe a kid of mine could pull a stunt like that. Honest to God, I can't.'

Clearing her throat, Kay said, 'Um, what was that about a cat?'

'Go see for yourself,' Maggie motioned with a nod towards the kitchen door. 'Only don't say I didn't warn you, 'cos it ain't pretty.'

'In a minute.' West took his notepad from his pocket. 'Let's just get the full story first.'

'Oh, no, you don't!' Maggie shook her head. 'I didn't ask for you lot, and I ain't telling you nowt. Just call it a domestic and piss off.'

'Bit late for that.' West grinned nastily. 'When a kid's involved, we can take whatever action we see fit.'

'Ah, but she's only seven, so you can't do nowt to her,' Maggie countered.

'Depends what's going on. So, like I said, let's get the full story, shall we?'

'Kiss me arse!'

Dismissing this with a wave of his hand, West said, 'Why did she do it, Maggie? Been laying into her again?'

'Again?' Maggie's mouth dropped open. 'What d'y' mean, again? I never laid a hand on her!'

West squinted disbelievingly. 'You don't seriously expect me to swallow that?'

'You can think what you like. I never touched her.'

'Yeah, whatever. Maybe we'll get a different version from her, eh?'

'You ain't got no right to question her, you bastard! I'll get me brief onto you, you see if I don't.'

Noticing Dakin squirming uncomfortably, West zoomed in on him. 'And what's your take on this, sir? You know it's an offence to conceal evidence, I'm sure.'

'What evidence?' Maggie yelped indignantly. 'I just told you I never touched her! . . . Not straight off, anyhow,' she added, looking as if she'd like to bite off her own tongue for saying it at all. 'I only defended meself when she started going psycho.'

'Ah, so you *did* hit her.' West's eyes glinted with jubilation. 'Right, where is she? What've you done to her?'

'Oh, shit!' Maggie hissed, furious with herself for falling into his trap. 'Look, I haven't done nowt, Mr West, honest. Nowt you wouldn't have done in the same situation, anyhow. Christ, what was I supposed to do? She was trying to kill me!'

'Where is she, Mrs Mullen?' Kay's voice was grave.

'*I* don't know. But don't worry, I never did nothing to her, I swear I didn't.'

'Let's have the full story, then.' West came full circle. 'The *truth*, this time.'

Using artistic licence to cover her back, Maggie reluctantly told him what had happened. When she reached the part about skidding into the wall, she had a flashback of the mess and retched, groaning, 'Oh, God help me, it'll be all over me slippers!'

They all looked at her feet. There were scraps of fur stuck to the sole of her right slipper, and something gorelike had splattered onto her ankle and dried there.

'Aw, no . . . shit, no!' she cried, kicking the offending slipper off.

Grimacing, West went to check out the backyard. Going through to the kitchen, he tried the back door. It was locked. 'You got the key for this?' he yelled.

Pulling the key from her pocket, Maggie thrust it at Dakin.

'Oi!' she called as he moved towards the door. 'You better not let her in if she's still out there, 'cos I'll do for her! I *mean* it!'

'You say she's only seven?' Disapproval rang through Kay's words.

Nobody's fool, Maggie Mullen caught it and spat it right back at her.

'Ever had a kid look you in the eye and tell you they wish you was dead, have you? 'Cos that's what *she* said to me, and all the while she's cutting me up like a flaming loony! Here, take a look at this if you don't believe me.' Hauling herself upright, she turned her head and lifted her grease-thick hair.

Kay gasped when she saw the gash on the other woman's neck. It was still bleeding: a faint pulse, sending thin rivulets of blood down the flesh and into the collar of Maggie's blouse. Sparking her radio to life, Kay put out a renewed call for the ambulance, then looked around for something to stem the flow of blood.

Slumping back, Maggie impatiently waved her away. 'I don't need nothing on it, love. It don't even hurt no more, to be honest. It's me flaming arm that's giving me gyp.'

Kay was saved from having to force the issue by the siren-blaring arrival of the ambulance. Leaving Maggie in the paramedics' capable hands, she went to see what West was up to.

Dakin was standing at the open back door watching West tiptoe across the yard towards Sarah, who was sitting rigidly against the wall, her face turned from the house.

'What's happening?' Kay asked quietly.

'I don't know.' Chin trembling, Dakin gave a jerky shrug. 'I think she's c-cutting herself.'

Shooting a glance across the yard, Kay saw the glass in the

girl's hand. It was thick and green, like the base of a smashed beer bottle. And it was darker around the edge. Blood, she surmised, probably the mother's. It didn't look as if Sarah had used it on herself – yet – but she was obviously on the verge. She had the sharpest point poised above her arm, her face dipped towards it as if willing herself to get it over with.

Sending Dakin to check on Maggie and Karen, Kay radioed the station, to tell them the state of play and to get a second ambulance sent over. She hoped to God that she was wrong, but West might just prove to be the push the girl was looking for.

Stopping ten yards from Sarah, West dropped slowly to his haunches.

'Hello, Sarah, I'm PC West. Can we talk?'

Turning her face towards him, Sarah narrowed her eyes and, slowly, deliberately, lowered the glass towards her wrist.

'Don't!' West's hand shot out of its own accord, the butterfly of dread anticipation fluttering in his stomach. '*Please* don't.'

'Why not?' Sarah's voice was barely audible, her gaze scarily steady. 'Who cares?'

'Oh, come on now.' He smiled sadly. 'Lots of people will be sad if you hurt yourself.'

'No, they won't.' It was adamant, un-self-pitying. 'No one cares about me.'

'*I* do.'

'You don't even *know* me.'

'So what? I still don't want to see you hurt yourself.'

'That ambulance for *her*?' Sarah abruptly changed the subject.

Realizing that she must have heard the siren, West nodded. 'For your mum, yeah. They're just gonna take a look at her, make sure she's all right.'

'I hope she's not.'

'Why's that, then?'

''Cos a' that!' Waving her glass-clutching hand, Sarah pointed out the smeared remains of the kitten a few feet away.

Glancing towards it, West murmured, 'Oh, I see. She do that, did she?'

With a look that clearly said she thought him an idiot, Sarah said, 'Don't pretend she didn't grass, else you wouldn't be here. I *told* her it was an accident,' she went on bitterly, 'but she don't believe me, so she can get lost. It all her fault, anyhow – hers and Karen's, and I hate 'em both!'

'Can't say I blame you.' Resting his elbows on his knees, West lowered his chin onto his fists and smiled. Sarah's eyes narrowed with suspicion. 'Look, I'll let you into a secret,' he went on, half whispering now, as if it really were their big secret. 'I hate mine, an' all.'

'Your what?' she asked cannily.

West noticed the slight lessening of tension in her shoulders. Good. She was relaxing. Her reflexes would be slowing. Just a little more and he'd be able to grab her before she could do herself any damage.

'My family.' He twisted his lip contemptuously. 'Mam, dad, sister, brother – I hate the bloody lot of 'em! Can't tell you how many times I've wished they'd all just disappear.'

Sarah chewed this over for a moment, then said, quite seriously, 'Know what you should do? You should pretend you're taking 'em out somewhere. Take 'em all to the station and wait till the train comes and shove 'em under it. That's what *I*'d do if I was growed up.'

West was stunned by the cold hard logic of the suggestion; more so by the fact that it had come from the mouth and mind of a seven-year-old child – and such a pretty one, at that. She certainly didn't take after her mother in the looks department.

Averting his gaze from her pale, troubled face, he scanned the rubbish pit of a yard, eyes squinted, mouth pursed, as though giving Sarah's suggestion real consideration. After a minute, he shook his head.

'Nah, they wouldn't go for it. They've already got me down as a tight-arse. They'd never believe it if I suddenly started being nice to 'em. Ace idea, though.' He gave her a respectful grin.

'I *always* have ace ideas,' she told him smugly. 'And my teacher says I'm the best writer in my class, too. In the whole *school*, actually. Better than *Karen*, any day!'

'I can tell.' West dipped his voice conspiratorially. 'She looks like she'd be dead untidy, your sister. Bet she can't even draw a straight line without going like this . . .' Holding up a finger, he drew a wobbly line in the air.

Sarah giggled. He pounced.

'Go easy!' Kay frowned as West manhandled Sarah in through the back door. 'She's only a kid, for Christ's sake.'

'Fuck off!' Sarah screamed, kicking out wildly as she was carried past. '*FUCK OOOOFF!*'

'See what she did to her mam, did you?' West yelled over his shoulder as he marched through the living room and out of the front door to where the second ambulance was now waiting. 'Or what she was about to do to herself? An' you don't even wanna *know* what she did to that kitten!'

Kay snapped her mouth shut. He definitely had a point; the child was a real danger to herself, right now. But what had sparked it off?

According to the mother, Sarah was *born* evil. But that was rubbish. In Kay's – admittedly limited – experience, kids *became* what they were as a result of their environment. And from what she'd seen of this child's environment so far, she didn't doubt that Sarah Mullen had probably witnessed things that no child of her age should have even been aware of, much less seen.

2

———◆◆◆———

Three weeks later, Maggie was sitting on the couch, agitatedly chain-smoking. A few feet away, Karen was playing with a tiny ginger kitten on the dust-coated carpet beneath the window. A gift from a neighbour, the kitten was a replacement for the ill-fated Joey. Runt of the litter, it was too young and fragile to have to deal with a Mullen child's idea of affection. If it were lucky, it would learn to hide before its nine chances ran out. If not . . .

The phone began to ring for the third time in an hour. Maggie ignored it. She knew that it was the Social Services calling to ask why she hadn't turned up for the meeting – again. But how could she go? The little bitch could have told them all sorts by now.

'In't you gonna get it, Mammy?' Karen moaned, squashing the kitten's belly with an unwashed foot. 'It keepses on ringing, an' it's hurting my head.'

Maggie shook her head. 'It'll stop in a bit. It's only them from the social about our Sarah.'

At the mention of her sister's name, Karen snatched up the kitten and clutched it tightly to her chest. It squealed with terror, jangling Maggie's taut nerves.

'Stop squashing that fucking cat!'

'Don't want Sarah back!' Karen's lip quivered. 'She'll hurt Bobby like she hurted my Joey!'

'No, she won't.' Maggie lit yet another cigarette, adding to the smoke blanketing the room in a suffocating blue haze. 'I won't let no one touch him. Now put him down before you strangle him.'

'Anyone home?' Dakin popped his head around the door just as the phone stopped ringing. Grinning at Karen, he produced a packet of sweets from behind his back. 'Look what I've got.'

Squealing with delight, Karen tossed the kitten aside and ran to him, snatching the sweets from his hand. 'Ta, Uncky Lorry!'

'Stop calling him that!' Maggie tutted loudly. 'How many times do I have to tell you, he *ain't* your bleeding uncle!'

'She can call me that if she wants,' Dakin said, reaching out to ruffle Karen's hair as she greedily ripped the sweets open and went back to the kitten. 'Why didn't you answer that?' he asked Maggie then, motioning with a nod towards the phone.

''Cos I didn't want to,' she muttered. 'And you know what it's about as well as I do, so don't bother saying nowt.'

Frowning, he dropped down onto the couch beside her. 'You can't keep this up, you know. They're not just going to give up because you ignore their letters and phone calls. They'll send someone round if you're not careful.'

'Let 'em!' Maggie gave a cavalier shrug. 'I don't have to open me door. They can't *make* me.'

'They can, and they will.'

'No, they can't. I know me rights. Anyhow, I don't want her back. Not after what she done.'

'If you want my opinion, I think you're making things worse for yourself,' he said. 'But if you've made your mind up, I suggest you just tell them. I'm sure they'll understand.'

'*You* deal with it, then, if you're so bloody sure,' Maggie snapped as the phone began to ring yet again. 'But you can leave me well out of it.'

'I *can't*,' Dakin snapped back. 'Just bloody *talk* to them and get it over with, will you?'

'Belt up, Lol.' She cast a warning glance Karen's way. 'The neighbours'll have it out of her in no time, the nosy bastards!'

Lowering his voice, he said, 'All right, I'll take her to the shops, then. She can't tell 'em nothing if she don't know nothing.'

'Stop *nagging* me!' Lashing out, Maggie caught him a glancing blow on the shoulder. 'You *know* I can't talk to them! What if she's said summat?'

'She won't have,' he hissed, rubbing his shoulder. 'But even if she has, you just deny it, don't you? No one's gonna believe her after what she did.'

'I can't risk it.'

'So you'd rather just sit here worrying?'

'I can't!' Maggie chewed on an already-butchered fingernail, drawing blood.

Dakin stood up. If she wouldn't take the plunge of her own accord, he'd just have to force her hand. She'd crack up if she carried on like this, and then they'd take little Karen away as well.

'I know you don't want to,' he told her, heading for the phone, 'but you've got to sort this out, so, here . . .' Lifting the receiver, he held it out to her. After a stubborn pause, she reached across the back of the couch and snatched it from him.

The caller introduced herself as Mrs Baker from Social Services, then said, 'We had a meeting, Mrs Mullen. Did you forget?'

'No. I just couldn't come.'

'But we gave you plenty of advance warning. Surely you could have contacted us if you knew that you wouldn't be able to make it.'

'It's not my fault,' Maggie whined. 'I haven't got no money for a start. And then there's my Karen to think about. It's not that easy to get a babysitter at the drop of a hat, you know.'

'Okay, fine.' A sigh. 'Well, maybe we could reschedule for later this afternoon? We'll reimburse your bus fare, if need be. And you can bring your daughter along, if that helps. Now, what time is best for you?'

'Never,' Maggie muttered, ignoring a warning frown from Dakin.

'Oh, I'm sure we'll come up with a mutually suitable time if we put our heads together,' Mrs Baker persisted breezily. 'Obviously, we need to resolve this situation as quickly as possible, but there are certain things we need to discuss before we can move forward.'

'Such as?' Maggie felt the sweat breaking out on her back. Was this the sting? Was the woman only being friendly just to lull her into a false sense of security – getting her to agree to a meet so that they could arrest her? Flicking a worried glance at Dakin, she said, 'Has that little mare been spinning tales about me?'

'Not that I'm aware of.' Mrs Baker sounded confused. 'She's very eager to return home, obviously, but we need to discuss the situation first.'

'What's to discuss?'

'I'm afraid I can't give details over the phone. There are strict regulations governing our procedures. We need to see you in person.'

'I've just told you I can't come, so either tell me now or send a letter.'

'I can't do that. I thought you underst—'

'See, this is why I didn't come to the flaming meeting,' Maggie interrupted angrily. 'I don't like being *told* I've got to come here or go there. And when I ask you to tell me, you start going on with yourself about procedures, and shit. It's like you're trying to blackmail me, or something.'

'Not at all.' Mrs Baker struggled to keep the astonishment from her voice. 'That's just the way it is.'

'For you, maybe, but I don't have to do nothing I don't want to.'

'Look, Mrs Mullen, there are certain provisos attached to Sarah's return. Now, obviously we wouldn't expect you to have to deal with this alone, so we need to set up a schedule of support involving various official bodies – family counselling, for example. So, if we could just set up another date?'

Irritated by her condescending tone, Maggie said, 'Tell you what, love, here's a pro-wotsit of me own: *keep* her, 'cos I don't *want* her back.'

'I appreciate you're a little frustrated at the moment but, with respect, Sarah's been perfectly well behaved while she's been with us, and I'm sure if you could just take an objective view of—'

'Bollocks! I know me own kid better than you, and if you ask me, you're looking up your arse if you can't see what she's really like. I had to live with her, don't forget, and if you think I'm carrying on as normal after what she done, you can forget it!'

'Mrs Mullen, please . . .'

'Oh, piss off. You're useless, you lot. Always butting into people's business and telling 'em what to do – *Oi!*'

Snatching the phone, Dakin said, 'Sorry to interrupt, Miss, but if you could just give us a minute.' Turning to Maggie then, his hand firmly covering the mouthpiece, he said, 'What d'y' think you're doing, you stupid cow? You can't talk to them like that!'

'I can talk to 'em anyhow I *like*,' she bellowed. 'What's she gonna do? Sue me?'

'There's a *few* things they could find you guilty of if they decided to make an issue of it,' he hissed, drawing his face back from the stench of stale beer and no toothbrush wafting from her mouth. 'Just stop being so flaming aggressive.'

'Fuck off! They've got no right to tell me what to do, and neither have you!'

'Stop shouting, Mammy,' Karen whined. 'You'll make Bobby piss 'isself.'

'And he'll get his bleeding neck wrung!' Maggie yelled.

Karen immediately began to wail.

'It's all right, sweetie,' Dakin told her. 'Mammy's just a bit upset. Why don't you take him into the kitchen for a bit, eh?'

'Sorry, babe,' Maggie said when Karen sloped past, sniffing back her tears. 'I'm not mad at you.'

'Shouldn't've said that 'bout Bobby,' Karen scolded sulkily. 'He's only lickle!'

'Never mind looking guilty,' Dakin said when Karen had gone. 'You'd better get this sorted before you land yourself right in it.'

'Don't see why I should,' Maggie muttered. Then, knowing he was right, she snatched the phone back and forced herself to apologize to the bossy bitch on the other end.

'Look, I'm sorry for kicking off, love, but this is really hard for me. I know you probably think I'm terrible, but I just can't cope no more. No matter what *you* say, I know she's not right in the head. What if I let her come back and she cuts our Karen? Is that what it's gonna take before something's done about her?'

'Of *course* not.' Mrs Baker was sympathetic now, heartened by the gabbled but – she believed – *sincere* flood of self-doubt from Maggie Mullen. 'Although, in our opinion, Sarah is unlikely to display such uncharacteristic violence towards either yourself or her sister in the future.'

'Ah, but that's just it. Your opinion don't really cut it

with me, 'cos you've hardly known her two minutes, have you?'

'No, but—'

'But nowt, love.' Maggie was far less aggressive now that she felt she was winning. 'Look, why don't you just keep hold of her for the time being? Sort her head out, then I'll . . .' Pausing, she sighed heavily. 'Well, we'll see where we go from there.'

Slowly, so as not to misunderstand nor be misunderstood, Mrs Baker said, 'Are you requesting that Sarah remain in care?'

'Yeah.'

'Temporarily?'

'Why . . . have I got a choice? 'Cos I'll go for permanent, if I have. Can you do that?'

'You do realize that you'll be relinquishing custody if you take this step? And that you'll be facing a much more taxing set of procedures than at present should you ever try to reverse that decision.'

'Oh, I won't change me mind.'

After a momentary pause, Mrs Baker said, 'Well, it's your decision, of course, but you will *definitely* have to attend an appointment to finalize things.'

'And that'll be it?'

'Indeed it will, so please be sure that it's what you really want.'

'Oh, it is, love. It is. So, when can we do this appointment thing?'

At Starlight Children's Home twenty minutes later, Dandi Matthews said goodbye to Rhona Baker and put the phone down. Dropping her head into her hands, she exhaled loudly, muttering 'Bitch!' under her breath.

Scraping her chair back, she left the office and wearily

mounted the stairs, dreading the effect that this news would have on the child waiting patiently in her – supposedly temporary – bedroom.

Much as she loved her job as housemother, Dandi found this particular aspect of it loathsome. She was genuinely fond of the kids in her care and hated having to give them bad news. And this was going to be particularly hard, because Sarah Mullen wasn't the usual rude, aggressive kid who'd take such a blow on the chin. She was a sweet little girl, with the face of an angel, and an air of sadness so real that you could practically taste the pain.

Dandi had no doubt that there was far more to this story than anyone realized, but they might never know for sure. Sarah certainly wasn't telling. But then, the most dreadfully abused children were also the most vehemently loyal. Especially when the abuser was the parent.

Sarah was perched on the edge of the bed, her small bag of belongings clutched tightly in her lap. She'd refused to unpack because that would have been like saying she wanted to stay. And she had no intention of doing that. Not for one second longer than she had to.

On a knife's edge all day, waiting to hear the outcome of the meeting between her mother and the Social Services, she looked up anxiously when the door opened. One look at Dandi's expression told her everything that she needed to know. Shaking her head slowly from side to side, the tears she had valiantly held at bay for three long weeks spilled onto her cheeks.

'I'm so sorry,' Dandi sat down beside her, 'but I'm afraid it's bad news.'

'I wanna go *hooome* . . .' Sarah wailed.

'I know you do, sweetheart, but it's just not possible at the moment. Your mummy's not quite ready yet.'

'Tell her I'll be good,' Sarah begged, her face alive with desperation as she grasped the front of Dandi's dress and tugged on it. 'Tell her I'm sorry for being naughty, an' I'll do what I'm told from now on! Please, Miss . . . tell her if she loves me again I'll be a really good girl!'

'Oh, Sarah, she *does* love you!' Taking Sarah's hands, Dandi squeezed them to emphasize her words. 'She loves you very much, and wants to be sure that you're getting the best possible care, but she doesn't feel able to give that to you right now.'

Stiffening, Sarah slid her hands free. 'How long have I got to stay?'

'Just until your mummy feels able to cope,' Dandi reassured her. 'But you mustn't worry, we'll make sure you have a wonderful time. We go on lots of trips, and picnics, and stuff. Oh, and you'll love Blackpool,' she went on, forcing gaiety into her voice now. 'You're just in time for this year's visit. We go on all the rides, and—'

'She's dumped me 'cos I'm bad,' Sarah murmured, ignoring Dandi's attempt at casting light into the pit of darkness.

'You are *not* bad. You're a lovely girl, and you're very, very good.'

'No, I'm not. I'm bad, an' useless, an' good for nowt but trouble. She said so.'

Blinking back the tears stinging her own eyes now, Dandi said, 'If your mummy said that, then she was *wrong*, and I can promise you she'll be feeling very sorry for it now.'

'Bet she's kept *Karen*?'

Dandi knew she was expecting an answer – confirmation or denial that her mother, who supposedly couldn't cope with her own children right now, was keeping the sister whilst giving her away. The truth would hurt her deeply, but Dandi couldn't bring herself to lie.

The hesitant silence was answer enough.

'Go away,' Sarah said, looking up at her with stark bitterness.

'Sarah, please . . . I just—'

'Go . . . *away*!' Gritting her teeth and balling her hands into fists, Sarah got to her feet and stalked proudly to the window.

Rising slowly, Dandi gazed at the child's rigid back and wished with all her heart that she could take her in her arms and magic the hurt away. But she knew that it wouldn't help. Not yet. The pain was too raw.

'I'll be in the office if you need me,' she said, going to the door. 'Any time, Sarah. I'm always around somewhere.'

Sarah's proud resolve crumbled when the door clicked shut. Climbing into the bed, she clutched the bag to her stomach and rocked to and fro, keening, as if she were a mother and the bag a cherished baby discovered dead in its cot.

By nine, a fierce storm was flexing its muscles. Lightning snaked down from the sky, and rumbling thunderclaps challenged the soundproofed double glazing to the hilt.

Concerned that Sarah might be scared, Dandi crept into the little girl's room to close the curtains and turn on the lamp. Sarah was still huddled beneath the quilt, just as she had been every other time Dandi had checked on her throughout the day. Hoping that the silence meant the child had finally stopped crying, Dandi gingerly raised the edge of the quilt to check. Sarah was asleep. Thanking the Lord, Dandi gently eased the bag from the girl's arms, covered her over, and quietly crept out.

Mark Chambers was making coffee when Dandi reached the office. She gave him a grateful smile. He'd only been with them a few months, but he was fitting in nicely. A good-looking twenty-three-year-old, he was tall and muscular, with sleek auburn hair, soft brown eyes, a gentle manner, and an infectious, boyish grin. And he made a mean brew. He was practically indispensable.

'I take it you could use one?' he asked, dropping a couple of sweeteners into her cup.

'Does a woman need good batteries?' she quipped, flopping into her chair like a rag doll. 'No biscuits for me,' she added, determined to stick to her latest diet. 'Help yourself, though. I put some nice choccy ones in earlier.'

'Don't know why you bother if you're not going to eat them,' Mark said, placing her cup on the desk blotter and sitting down. 'How was she?'

'Sleeping.' Sighing wearily, Dandi leaned her head back. 'And let's hope it's a long one. She certainly needs it.'

'It's amazing, isn't it?' Mark pursed his lips thoughtfully. 'The way some people can just . . .' Pausing, he shrugged. 'Abandon their kids like that.'

'Yeah. Especially when they're as good as Sarah.'

'She is, isn't she? I just don't understand it.'

'And you probably never will. I don't, and I've been at it fifteen years.'

'Oh, don't!' Mark groaned. 'You make yourself sound like a right old war horse.'

'That's 'cos I feel like one most of the time.' Dandi yawned long and hard. 'You'll know what I mean before you're too much older.'

'I doubt I'll ever be as old as you,' he teased, hiding a grin behind his cup.

'You'll get yours, matey.'

They fell into a peaceful silence then, sipping their drinks and pondering the evils of the world. Dandi soon gave it up. There was little she hadn't seen in the evil department, and it no longer affected her so badly that she couldn't eat or sleep. Mark, on the other hand, was a long way off jaded, and she watched him now as he struggled with the conflicting emotions: care – but not too much. It was the toughest lesson of them all, but he would master it, she was sure.

Dandi wondered then – and not for the first time – whether Mark was gay. If he was, he concealed it well. But for all his masculinity, his size and his easy, testosterone-laden gait, he was so much softer of heart than most of the men she had ever met. Not that that meant anything. He could be one of those so-called 'new' men. The type who went out of their way to explore those aspects of their personalities that *real* men would rather die than admit to – but which most women adored.

The creak of the door slowly opening interrupted her reverie. Looking up, she saw a tiny face peering in through the crack.

'What is it, Gillian?' she asked, sitting up straighter. 'Did the storm frighten you?'

Rubbing her eyes, Gillian shook her head. 'Sarah's crying again. She woked me up.'

Exchanging a weary glance with Mark, Dandi went to the door and reached for Gillian's hand.

'Don't worry, sweetheart, she's probably just having a bad dream. Let's get you back to bed.'

'Is the wind gon' break the window?' Gillian asked as Dandi led her up the stairs. 'I thinked it was gon' smash it, and it scareded me.'

'No, it won't break the window,' Dandi assured her. 'The glass is really strong, so the heat stays in and the wind stays out. Which is a good job,' she went on teasingly. 'Because the wind would mess up your hair, and I'd have to sit up *all* night brushing it again.'

'It can't get messed when it's tied up,' Gillian giggled. 'You're silly.'

'And you're very clever,' Dandi said, squeezing her hand.

'Is Sarah sad 'cos her mummy gived her away?' Gillian asked then.

Sighing, Dandi said, 'No. She's just a bit upset because she can't go home right now.' Opening the door, she ushered Gillian into her bedroom. 'Back to bed now, there's a good girl.'

Two rooms down, Mark had his ear pressed against Sarah's door.

'It's not clear,' he whispered when Dandi joined him. 'But there's definitely a noise of some sort.'

'Okay,' she murmured, 'let's take a look. I'll go first.'

'Get the dress on!' The man was getting mad. 'I'm not messin' about, kid!'

Sarah shook her head, not daring to walk out of the blazing pool of light that he'd placed her in, but determined not to give in.

'Why?' Holding the dress up he looked it over. 'What's wrong with it? Don't you think it's pretty? Look at the bow, and that nice satin rose. It's gorgeous. Why don't you just try it on?'

'No.'

'You'll have to get dressed up all the time if you wanna be a proper model,' he coaxed, grinning like a snake.

'Don't wanna be a moggle.'

'Right, that's it! No more messing . . . MAGGIIIEE . . .'

Maggie charged into the room, demanding to know what all the shouting was about.

'Sort her out.' The same-as-all-the-rest man pointed angrily at Sarah. 'She won't put the fuckin' dress on!'

'Oh, won't you now?' Maggie balled her hands into fists. 'Right, lady! You've got two seconds to get that bleedin' dress on, or else!'

'No, Mammy, I don't wanna! Don't, Mammy . . . noooo . . .'

Sarah's eyes were open, but she wasn't awake. Curled into a

defensive foetal ball in a dark corner of the room, she stared wide-eyed at an apparition that only she could see.

Moving slowly towards her, Dandi said, 'Sarah . . . wake up, my love. It's all right. You're safe now.'

'No, Mammy . . . *Please* . . .'

'Careful, you could shock her.'

Mark's voice penetrated the fog of Sarah's mind. Her head snapped back, her mouth opened wide, emitting a scream so piercing that it made Dandi's hair stand on end. Reaching out, she pulled Sarah into her arms and held her tightly, whispering soothingly until the screaming stopped.

Motioning for Mark to leave them, Dandi carried Sarah to the bed and gently laid her down. Lying beside her, she stroked Sarah's sweaty cheeks and hair until she was sure that the child was properly asleep.

Easing herself up after a while, Dandi gazed down at Sarah's face, so pale and fragile against the pillow, and prayed that the little girl's mother would never reverse the decision to give her up. No child – whatever they had done – deserved the pain that Sarah was suffering right now. And, given the little that Rhona Baker had told her about Maggie Mullen, Dandi feared that Maggie would cause Sarah a great deal more should she ever take her back.

She never even tried.

PART TWO

1993

3

———◆◆◆———

Starlight was a detached Victorian house, with a half-acre of garden, encircled by a six-foot wrought-iron security fence, mostly obscured from view by the forest of overgrown bushes and stately trees lining the perimeter. With ten bedrooms and four bathrooms, it more than adequately housed the children already resident when Sarah Mullen first arrived. Eight years on, with more arrivals than departures, it was quite a different picture.

Most rooms were now shared, but Sarah had managed to hang on to her privacy. Her room was too small for sharing, but even if it hadn't been she'd have refused. It had taken her a long time to settle, and she wasn't about to let some troubled brat come along and disrupt the fragile peace that she had achieved.

It hadn't been easy. There had been some awful moments along the way: terrible heartaches, and bouts of depression so overwhelming that she'd thought she would never recover from them. But those times had decreased as the years passed, stopping altogether on her tenth birthday when, unbeknownst to Dandi, she had accidentally-on-purpose got onto the wrong bus after school.

Arriving in Moss Side full of anxious anticipation, Sarah had made her way through the old estate, hoping against hope that her mother would welcome her with open arms and say that she had made a terrible mistake in giving her up. She'd been shocked to find her old home empty – abandoned, like she had been – its doors and windows boarded up. But she'd been pierced to the heart when a gang of scruffy kids had informed her that the 'fat slag' had 'done a moonlight' two years earlier.

Anger had quickly dampened the pain and, taking the bus back to Starlight, Sarah had made a vow never to let anyone get close enough to hurt her like that again.

It was hard sometimes, when the dreams dragged her back to that last terrible day, but she struggled on – spurred on by the knowledge that each day brought her closer to her ultimate goal: to reach the age of sixteen, leave Starlight, and stand on her own two feet at last.

And with her fifteenth birthday just weeks away, she was almost there – providing she survived that long without getting banged up for murdering Dandi.

It was just Dandi's way of showing that she cared, but Sarah found her attempts at mothering somewhat smothering. She needed to remember how old Sarah was and stop treating her like the fragile little girl that she'd been when she first arrived.

Still, only one more year to get through . . . And the rest of the six weeks' school holiday.

Waking on the Monday of the third week, Sarah stretched languidly and opened the curtains. Smiling when she saw that it was a bright day, she settled back against her pillows and began to plan her day.

A series of rapid taps at the door, followed seconds later by the irritating appearance of Dandi's smiling face, interrupted her thoughts.

'Morning, Sarah. Breakfast's ready.'

'Not hungry.'

'Oh, *really*! You'll waste away if you keep skipping meals.'

'Doubt it,' Sarah plucked at a non-existent roll of fat. 'I could last a month on this.'

'If only I should be so lucky!' Dandi patted her own wobbling belly.

'Dandi, I'm not hungry. I'll get something later.'

'Promise?'

Rolling her eyes, Sarah put her hands behind her head and gazed out of the window.

'Okay!' Dandi held up her hands. 'But I'll be checking, so make sure you do.'

'Yeah, right . . . *Bye.*'

Tutting at Sarah's dismissive tone, Dandi closed the door, then immediately reopened it, earning herself a *whatnow?* frown.

'Sorry. I just wanted to remind you that the new boy's coming today. Make sure you're around to say hello. Okay?'

'I'm going to town.'

'*Again?* What on Earth do you find to do there?'

'It's the holidays, Dandi.' Sarah gave an impatient sigh. 'I don't have to *do* anything – that's the point. Or do you just want me sitting in here all day so you can nag me?'

'You win,' Dandi conceded. 'Just try not to be too long. You know it helps them settle in if they meet everyone right away.'

Sarah groaned inwardly. They all settled in sooner or later – with or without the stupid house greeting. And if they didn't – tough! It was a dog-eat-dog world.

'I'll try,' she said. 'But can you go now, please? I'm trying to think.'

'All right, but can you at least—'

'*Dandi!*'

'Okay, okay!' Smiling, Dandi closed the door, leaving Sarah to her cherished solitude.

She wasn't concerned. Sarah had always kept herself to herself. At first because she'd needed time alone to heal, then later simply because she preferred her own company. Still, she was happy enough. That was all that mattered.

Happy, and gorgeous.

Always a pretty child, she was now a stunning teenager. Tall and slim with waist-length glossy black hair, and the most incredible eyes Dandi had ever seen: luminous green, with lashes so long and black that they should have come with a government health warning.

The girl's looks were the one reason Dandi was glad that Sarah was such a loner. She was far too young to be suffering unwanted male attentions. She'd have more than her fair share of that when she was old enough to cope with it. God forbid she should land herself in the same mess as Claire Wilson at this tender age.

Claire was a walking disaster. Just fifteen, and already five months into her third pregnancy. This was the first to survive beyond a month, but Dandi didn't rate its chances too highly if Claire didn't sort herself out – soon.

Which reminded her. Claire had an antenatal appointment at ten-thirty, but had pulled yet another disappearing act early that morning. Dandi had warned her what would happen if she did it again. It was time to put her money where her mouth was.

Going down to the office, she phoned the Mother and Baby Unit at Hillgate House. It was two months early for Claire's transfer and no doubt they would raise objections, but she didn't care. She had more important things to be getting on with than chasing Claire around. Anyway, Hillgate's staff were medically trained. They'd stand a far better chance of saving the baby should something go wrong – which was all too likely, given that Claire was showing definite signs of drug abuse.

After a ten-minute verbal tussle with her less than sympathetic counterpart at Hillgate, Dandi was frazzled. But at least she'd achieved her objective. By six that evening, Claire would be someone else's problem.

Releasing a weary breath, Dandi reached for the cigarettes

stashed at the back of her drawer. Bringing one to her lips, she hesitated, reminding herself that she was supposed to be quitting. But the need for relaxation was stronger than the fear of cancer. And as long as she wasn't corrupting the kids by doing it in front of them, she had nothing to feel guilty about.

Lighting up at the window, she drew in a luxurious lungful, then another, and another . . .

Jumping at a knock on the door, she quickly stubbed the cigarette out and wafted the smoke away. *Not guilty, my ass!*

'Yes?' she called, taking her seat.

Mark Chambers came in. Frowning at the smoke swirls defiantly riding the sunlit air at the window, he folded his arms and gave Dandi a pointed look.

'Oh, shut up!' She flapped her hand. 'It was only a drag. What's up, anyway?'

'Vinnie Walker's here.'

'Christ, he's early.' Swivelling her chair around to the window, Dandi was shocked to see a car parked outside the front door. 'Bloody hell, when did *that* come? I didn't even see it.'

'Too busy drooling over your sneaky ciggy,' Mark chided. 'Anyway, he's in the hall. I think you'd best come and take a look.'

'Is something wrong?' Concerned by his tone, Dandi stood up. 'He's not had an accident, or anything, has he?'

'No, it's nothing like that. He's just – how shall I put this – a one.'

'Meaning?'

'Meaning that he's already strutting around like he owns the place, so I don't think you need worry too much about settling him in.'

'Great, that's just what we need.' Sighing, Dandi came around the desk. 'I hoped we'd have a bit of peace now I've sorted Claire's transfer.'

'Well *done*!' Opening the door, Mark raised an approving eyebrow. 'How did you manage that?'

'Never underestimate the power of begging!' she quipped, following him out.

She immediately saw what he'd meant about Vinnie Walker.

While his social worker waited patiently on one of the chairs lining the wall beside the front door, Vinnie was stalking arrogantly around the large sunny hallway, opening doors and poking his nose into the rooms. He was tall and muscular for a fourteen-year-old, with dark blond close-cropped hair, steel-blue eyes and a strong, masculine jaw. A little cruel around the mouth, she thought, but very good-looking all the same.

Walking towards him, she extended her hand. 'Hello, Vinnie, I'm Dandi. Welcome to Starlight.'

Shoving his own hands into his pockets, Vinnie eyed her suspiciously. 'What kind of a stupid name's that?'

'Which?'

'Both.'

The social worker gave an exasperated sigh. Smiling, Dandi said, 'Why don't you go into the office with Mark and get a coffee while I show Vinnie around?'

'Thanks,' the social worker said wearily. 'I could certainly use one.'

Linking her arm through Vinnie's, Dandi led him across the hall.

'We think our name suits us, actually, Vinnie,' she told him chattily. 'Star – light.' She waved her hand through the air. 'Lovely name for a lovely home. Have you eaten, by the way? Breakfast's almost over, but there's bound to be something left if you're hungry.'

'Had a butty earlier,' he muttered, thrown by Dandi's friendly banter. He wasn't used to people being nice. They usually just shouted and told him how bad he was. Still, she'd probably drop the act when his social worker had gone. They usually did.

'How about a cup of tea?' she persisted.

Vinnie shrugged as if he couldn't care less.

In the dining-room doorway, Dandi clapped her hands together for quiet.

'Everyone, this is Vinnie Walker,' she announced. 'He's just arrived and I want you to make him feel welcome.'

Vinnie glowered at the kids seated at tables around the room, sizing them up to gauge where he would fall in the all-important pecking order. He was pleased to see that he was bigger than most. Only one lad looked anywhere near his height, but he didn't have an ounce of the muscle. Vinnie smirked to himself. It would be a doddle establishing himself as top dog.

Taking him across to that boy's table now, Dandi said, 'You can sit here while I get your drink, Vinnie. Peter will introduce everyone.'

'It's *Pete*,' the boy muttered, glaring after her as she walked away. Eyeing Vinnie then, he said, 'Pete Owens. Who are you again?'

'Vinnie Walker.'

'Right. Well, that's Jimmy . . .' Pete pointed out his tablemates in turn. 'That's Ade . . . And that little knob-head's Rob.'

'Get lost!' Rob retorted sulkily. 'I ain't no knob-head.'

'You are if I say you are!' Reaching across the table, Pete slapped his head. 'Now, belt up an' say hello.'

''Lo.'

'All right.' Nodding, Vinnie dropped into the chair beside Pete with studied nonchalance, letting them know from the off that he was in control.

'What you in for?' Pete asked.

'Murder. *You?*'

Pete was taken aback for a second, then grinned when he realized he was being had. 'Shit, man! You had me going for a minute there!'

'Shouldn't ask stupid questions then, should you?' Relaxing, Vinnie put his hands behind his head. 'So, what kind of a dump is this?'

'It ain't too bad.' Pete leaned back in his chair. 'Better than most, anyhow. You ever been in the Lodge at Langley?'

'Nah, why?'

''Cos that *is* a dump. They don't do nowt for you, and they spend all the food dosh on booze. I looked like a match when I took off, I was that thin.'

'Yeah, me too,' Jimmy joined in. 'Me dad come for a visit once, and when he saw the state of me he took me straight back home.' Pausing, he shrugged. 'He took off with his bird a week later, so they shoved me in here instead.'

'They kicked the crap out of you at Gorton,' Rob interjected bitterly. 'For stupid shit, like not making the bed right, and not eating your peas, and that.'

'For *peeing* in the bed, more like, knowing you!' Pete snorted.

'Get lost!'

'The Grange in the Moss is all right,' Jimmy went on. 'The staff are pretty cool, and the—'

'The Moss is shit!' Vinnie cut in aggressively. 'My old lady lives there, for a kick-off. And the five-o are a load of cunts.'

'Tell me about it!' Pete leaned forward animatedly. 'I got pulled once, right, and they give me a proper kicking 'cos I wouldn't tell 'em me name. They shit it when they found me picture in the missing-kids file!' He laughed nastily. 'They knew they'd cop for it, so they banged me up till the bruises had gone, then said they'd only just picked me up!'

'Sounds about right,' Vinnie said, adding slyly, 'Mind, I've never been stupid enough to let 'em get a grip of me.'

'Shit, man!' Pete feigned admiration. 'You must be well too smart for 'em!'

'Wanker!' Vinnie laughed, recognizing that he was being sent up.

'Takes one to know one.'

Thinking that it might not be so bad here after all, Vinnie asked what the score was on the bird front. He hadn't seen anything of interest yet, but he was hoping that there'd be something tasty to pass the time.

'Bag of shite, mate,' Pete told him. 'Most are too little, and the ones our age ain't worth looking at.'

'S-S-Sarah is,' Ade said, blushing furiously when Vinnie immediately focused on him.

'That r-r-right, is it?' he mimicked cruelly. 'So, who's this S-S-S-Sarah, then?'

'Leave it out, man.' Pete frowned disapprovingly. 'He can't help it.'

'I'm only messing.' Vinnie winked at the still-blushing Ade. 'So, tell us about these birds?'

Still frowning, Pete said, 'Well, there's Ruth and Fiona, but they're a right pair of dogs. Caroline's all right, but she's already hooked up. And Claire's all-right-looking, but she's well shady.'

'Fat slag, more like!' Jimmy muttered.

'Sack that!' Vinnie curled his lip. 'I hate fat birds.'

'She ain't fat, she's up the duff,' Pete explained. 'And she's—' He stopped abruptly when Dandi reappeared carrying a cup of tea. Snapping his mouth shut, he smiled up at her.

'What were you talking about?' she asked, narrowing her eyes.

'Nowt.' He shrugged innocently. 'I was just telling Vinnie what a babe you are, that's all.'

'I bet!' Dandi muttered. Handing the cup to Vinnie, she said, 'You don't mind if I leave you a little while longer, do you, only I want a quick word with your social worker. I'll show you to your room when we're finished.'

Shrugging, Vinnie said, 'These can take us, if you want?'

'Well, yes, that'd be fine.' Dandi smiled, pleased that he seemed to have accepted – and been accepted by – the others. 'You're in with Ade and Rob, for the time being. I'll pop up and see you later.'

Waiting until she was out of earshot, Vinnie asked who shared Pete's room.

'Me,' Jimmy told him. 'Why?'

''Cos you're not no more,' Vinnie said. 'I am. You can go in with them.'

'Cool with me,' Pete said. 'You all right with that, Jim?'

'Whatever,' Jimmy muttered, guessing correctly that he had no choice in the matter.

Ade breathed a silent sigh of relief. The new lad frightened him, and he'd only been here ten minutes.

'Right,' Vinnie said. 'Now that's sorted, what was you saying about this Claire bird?'

'Jeezus,' Pete snorted. 'You got the horn, or summat?'

'Nah. I just like to know what's on offer.'

'Yeah, well, don't even *think* about Claire.' Pete lowered his voice so that the kids at the surrounding tables wouldn't hear. 'She's a smack-head.'

'Yeah?' Vinnie's eyebrows rose with interest. 'Didn't think you could get it round here.'

Pulling his head back, Pete narrowed his eyes. 'No way do you do that shit, man?'

'Now and then,' Vinnie lied, giving a casual shrug. He'd never actually touched the stuff in his life. But that didn't mean he never would, and it wouldn't hurt his cred any to let these idiots *think* he was into the heavy shit.

'I'd keep that to yourself if you want to stay here,' Pete warned him. 'Dandi's right down on drugs. She'd get you banged up for that.'

'She'd have to catch me at it first,' Vinnie drawled. Then, sitting bolt upright, he pointed towards the door. 'Shit! Who's *that*?'

Following his ogling gaze, Pete saw Sarah Mullen descending the stairs. Pausing halfway, she drew her hair over her shoulder to resecure the bobble at the tail end of her thick plait.

'That's Sarah.' He grinned. 'Fit, eh?'

'You can say *that* again!' Vinnie couldn't tear his gaze away. 'She's gorgeous!'

'T-t-told you,' Ade said quietly.

'Fuck me,' Vinnie went on. 'I thought you said she wasn't worth a look? I'd give it one any day!'

Snorting dismissively, Pete said, 'Yeah, well, forget it, mate, 'cos she hardly talks to no one, never mind giving it up.'

'Not for you,' Vinnie murmured as Sarah continued on her way, disappearing from view. 'But I reckon I'd be in with a chance.'

The other lads looked at each other and laughed.

'What's so funny?' he demanded, glaring at them as he scraped his chair back.

'Nowt, mate,' Pete spluttered. 'Good luck – that's all I've got to say.'

Unaware of the excitement that she had stirred, Sarah passed by the office on her way to the front door. Catching a snatch of the conversation going on within, she paused to listen.

'You name it, Vinnie's done it,' a woman was saying. 'Theft, burglary, joyriding . . . The list is endless.'

'And just fourteen,' Dandi tut-tutted quietly. 'What a waste.'

'Mmmm, well, he's walking the wire this time, and he knows it. One more incident and he's for the chop. He only escaped remand this time because you agreed to take him on.'

'Oh, I'm sure we'll coax his better side to the surface.' Dandi sounded confident.

'If he stays around long enough,' the woman replied knowingly. 'He also has a very interesting line in absconding – usually involving stolen cars, so I'd keep all keys out of his way if I were you . . . and money, and credit cards, and—'

'Sarah!'

Starting guiltily, Sarah turned to see an unfamiliar boy rushing towards her. Guessing him to be the infamous Vinnie of the unimpressive CV, she folded her arms.

'It is Sarah, isn't it?' he asked, giving his best grin.

'Yeah.' She didn't return the smile.

'Er, right . . . Well, hi. I'm Vinnie.'

'Uh huh.'

'Yeah, Vinnie Walker.' He was flustered by her coolness. 'I've, er, just got here.'

'*And?*' She raised an eyebrow.

Sticking his hands deep into his pockets, he said, 'I just wanted to say hello.'

'Well, now you have, so . . . *bye.*'

Vinnie frowned when she turned on her heel and marched out of the door. Then he smiled as understanding sank in.

Course! She fancies me. It's obvious.

Swaggering back to the dining room, he gave his new gang the thumbs-up.

Sarah rushed to the bus stop around the corner, reaching it just as the bus trundled into view. Glancing back, she breathed a sigh of relief that the new boy hadn't followed her. The last thing she needed was a lout like him trailing after her with his tongue hanging out, drawing attention to her comings and goings.

Just wanted to say hello! Who did he think he was kidding?

The bus pulled in, its door swishing smoothly open. Stepping forward, Sarah cried out when Claire Wilson hurtled off. Grabbing at the centre bar to steady herself, she yelled, 'Watch it!'

Turning on her, Claire said, 'Get stuffed, you stupid bitch! That fat cow's gonna send the pigs after me if I'm late!'

'Never mind late, you're off your head! And I'd stay out of Dandi's way, if I was you, 'cos she's got someone from Social Services in.'

'She's grassed me up!' Claire screeched, turning in frantic circles on the pavement. 'What'm I gonna do?'

'Bloody hell, Claire, calm down!' Sarah frowned. 'It's only the new lad's social worker.'

'New lad?' Claire was confused. 'What new lad?'

'You getting on, or what?' the bus driver called out through the door. 'Only if you're not, can you get your foot off the step?'

'I'm *coming*,' Sarah snapped back at him. 'Look, Claire,' she said then, 'do yourself a favour and get your head down for a bit. I'll come and see you when I get back, if you want?'

'Whatever, Trevor,' Claire muttered, waddling away, her step jerky and uncoordinated.

Boarding the bus, Sarah went to the back seat and reached into her bag for a cigarette, wondering how the bright girl Claire had been just a few months ago had let herself sink so low. But she was so far gone now, she didn't seem to know – or care – that she was destroying herself. And what was the point of worrying about her if she wasn't worried about herself?

*   *   *

Back at the home, Vinnie was bugging Pete for information as he followed him to the bedroom. Jimmy was already there, packing his things into a rucksack.

'Want a hand?' Pete asked.

'No, he don't,' Vinnie said, pulling him aside. 'Come on, man. I've got to know about her.'

'Where d'y' want these?' Rob interrupted, carrying Vinnie's rucksack in, trailed by Ade struggling with a heavy case.

'Over there.' Vinnie waved towards the bed. 'How old is she? What's she here for? Where does she go when she goes out?'

'Jeezus!' Laughing, Pete threw his hands over his ears. 'Give it a rest, man!'

'Aw, come on,' Vinnie persisted. 'I need to know . . . *Oi*!' This directed at Ade, who was hefting the case none too gently onto the bed. 'Break any of my stuff, I'll rip your bleeding bollocks off!'

'S-s-sorry,' Ade stuttered unhappily. 'It's h-heavy.'

'Well, you've done it now, so piss off!' Vinnie snarled, motioning the smaller boy out of the room with a flick of his head. 'You an' all,' he said then, glaring at Jimmy and Rob.

'See you later, Pete,' Jimmy said, snapping the clasps on his rucksack. 'Give us a shout if I've left anything.' Frowning at Vinnie, he followed Ade and Rob out.

'Where d'y' find them idiots?' Vinnie sneered when the door had closed behind them.

'Ah, they're all right.' Throwing himself onto his bed, Pete pulled a pack of cigarettes from under the mattress and threw one to Vinnie. Opening the window, he said, 'Flick it out here or Dandi'll kick off. Fire hazard, and that.'

Smirking, Vinnie said, 'You don't half worry what *Dandi*'s gonna say, don't you? You fancy her, or summat?'

'Behave!' Pete snorted. 'She's old enough to be me Nan!'

'Bollocks. You're gagging for it.'

'Piss off.'

'Anyhow, never mind her, how old's Sarah?'

'Too old for you,' Pete smirked. 'Nearly fifteen.'

'When's her birthday?'

'Why? Gonna get her a prezzie?'

'Might.'

'Forget it.' Pete blew a smoke ring. 'Like I said before, she don't bother with no one.'

'Yeah, but she fancies me.'

'Dream on.'

'Yeah, well, you'll see. So, what else d'y' know?'

Pete shrugged. 'Hardly ever see her, she's always out. I don't know why she's here, 'cos she don't tell no one nothing. And I don't know nowt else, so don't bother asking.'

Finishing his cigarette in silence, Vinnie threw it out of the window and pursed his lips thoughtfully. If there were anything else to know about Sarah Mullen, he would find out one way or another.

Raised voices and the pounding of feet came from the corridor outside. Cocking his head, Pete said, 'Sounds like Claire's kicking off again.'

'Might as well have a nosy,' Vinnie said, heading for the door. 'Coming?'

'Nah.' Pete lay back against his pillow and laced his fingers behind his head. 'Seen it all before.'

'I'm not going!' Claire flailed her arms as she marched along the corridor with Dandi in hot pursuit. 'And you can't make me, so piss off!'

'You left me no choice,' Dandi puffed, almost trotting in an effort to catch up. 'You're a danger to yourself and the baby, and Hillgate have got the facilities to give you the care you need. Anyway, it's approved. You're going tonight – like it or not.'

'Oh, am I? We'll see about that, won't we?'

Catching up with Claire at the head of the stairs, Dandi grabbed her arm. 'Let's not be silly about this. It's for your own good.'

'Get your fucking hands *off* me!' Claire yelled, tearing her arm free. 'Touch me again and I'll say you were feeling me up, you fat freak! I *hate* you!' Lashing out, she caught Dandi a glancing blow across the cheek.

'Pack that in!' Mark yelled, running up the stairs.

'It weren't me!' Claire whined, pointing an accusing finger at Dandi. 'It was her! She was messing about with me, Mr Chambers!'

'Enough!' he barked. 'I saw exactly what happened, and Dandi did *not* touch you in an inappropriate way. Now, stop all this nonsense and go to your room and pack.'

'Fuck *you*!' Claire hissed, backing away from Mark. 'Fuck you *both*! And get out of my way or I'm gonna . . .' Pausing mid-sentence, she glanced wildly around. Then, hawking up noisily in her throat, she spat on his foot. Laughing maniacally, she pushed past him and galloped down the stairs, screaming obscenities back over her shoulder.

'Get back here!' Mark bellowed after her.

'Leave her.' Dandi patted his arm. 'She'll come back when she calms down.'

'And if she doesn't?' Scowling with disgust at the mess sliding down his shoe, he took a tissue from his pocket and wiped it off. 'You know where she'll go now, don't you? Straight back to that man she's been seeing.'

'What can I do about it?' Dandi gave a small, helpless shrug. 'I can't exactly chain her to the bed, can I?'

'No, but we can't stand by and watch her destroy herself, either. Have you checked out that address in her diary yet?'

'Yes.' Dandi sighed. 'But you were right, it was false. You can say I told you so, if you like.'

'There's got to be *some*thing we can do. How about following her?'

'There's no point. She'll be long gone by now. We'll just have to wait till she comes back then get her off to Hillgate as soon as.'

'What if she doesn't come back?'

'Then I'll call the police. Now, can we stop fretting and get on with our work?'

'You're the boss.'

'Well, do as you're told and make me a cuppa, then,' Dandi said, smiling when Mark saluted and set off down the stairs. 'I'll be down in a minute. I just want to make sure Rosie's okay.'

Turning, she jumped when she saw Vinnie loitering in his bedroom doorway. Walking towards him, she grinned sheepishly. 'I suppose you saw all that? I bet you're wondering what kind of a madhouse we're running here.'

'It's all right. I like a good scrap.'

'Mmm.' Dandi pursed her lips. 'Well, it's not exactly the ideal welcome, but I guess when you've seen the worst the rest can only be better. So,' she looked past him into the room, 'you decided to swap with Jimmy, did you?'

'Yeah.' Edging around her, Vinnie went and sat on his bed. 'Me and Pete are gonna share.'

'Oi, Dandi,' Pete called out. 'Tell him to get his shit put away, will you? He's made a right tip of it.'

'And there was me thinking you'd been burgled!' She glanced pointedly around the messy room. 'Still, I'm sure you'll have it tidy by dinner time.'

'I ain't doing it!' Pete snorted. 'That's Jimmy's job.'

'Not any more,' she reminded him. 'Was he all right about moving, by the way?'

'Yeah, he's cool.'

'Oh, well, as long as everyone's happy.' Dandi made a

mental note to double-check with Jimmy that he hadn't been bullied into the move. The two bigger lads seemed to have formed quite a team already. 'Well, I'll leave you to it, then. Show Vinnie where everything is, and tell him all the times for meals and what have you.'

Closing the door, she went along to the girls' landing to check on Rosie – Claire's eight-year old room-mate. As if the poor little thing hadn't suffered enough already, Claire's violent reaction to the news of her transfer had terrified Rosie.

Claire was so inconsiderate sometimes. But what more could they expect of her? She was a mess – a nasty, unstable mess. And if ever proof were needed that she was losing it, she'd just displayed it for all to see.

Dandi just hoped she calmed down and came back before six or Hillgate would get awkward about taking her. If she knew where Claire kept disappearing to, she'd go and get her and deliver her there personally. Anything to get the girl off her hands.

4

———◆———

Claire was on a comedown by the time she reached the
Crescents. Jumping off the bus before it had fully
stopped, she legged it head-down across the rubbish-strewn
grass fronting John Nash and launched herself into the end
stairwell. Desperate to get to Billy Norman's flat, she was
gasping for breath by the time she reached the third floor.

'Aw, for fuck's sake!' Makka Caine hissed when he answered
the door. 'Not you again! What d'y' want *now*?'

'Gotta see Billy.' Ducking under his arm, Claire ran inside
before Makka could stop her. Pausing in the living-room
doorway, she looked around for Billy among the men sprawled
around the floor. A few groaned when they saw her, the rest
just glanced at her, uninterested.

The groaners were Billy's mates who knew what a nuisance
she'd become. The rest were punters who thought nothing of
her arrival as they waited for Billy to get the shit ready. They
didn't give a damn *what* turned up – as long as it wasn't in
uniform.

Ignoring them all, Claire stepped clumsily over their legs
and made for the kitchen on the far side. Falling noisily
through the door, she yelped, 'Billy, I'm back! Giz a snog,
then, gorgeous?'

Glancing up from the heap of powder he was cutting and
dividing on the ledge, Billy kissed his missing teeth, making
a strange slurping sound. In his mid-forties, he looked older
thanks to a hefty habit. Gaunt-cheeked, with greasy hair

trailing into his eyes, a permanent stoop and enough spots to line the bottom of a fish tank. Even *he* knew he was anything but *gorgeous*.

'What d'y' want?' he growled, shoving her away as she tried to hug him. 'I told you this morning, you'd had your lot.'

'Aw, c'm on, babes.' She greedily eyed the small pile of silver-foil wraps he'd prepared. 'I only need a bit to knock the edge off. I'm bombing out, man.'

'Where's the cash?'

'Not got 'ny.' She patted her empty pockets. 'But I only wanna bit.'

Glancing back over his shoulder, Billy gave her a disgusted look. 'You're a disgrace, you,' he said, meaning it – conveniently forgetting who'd started her down this road in the first place. 'Look at the state of you, man. You're filthy, an' you stink like a fucking *badger*!'

Joining them, Makka kicked the door shut and scowled at Claire. 'Want me to get rid, Bill? I could take her down the canal an' give her a snide shove, if you want?'

'Yeah.' Claire grinned, nudging him. 'Snide shove . . . Good 'un, Makka. Make that fat cunt in the Home think I'm dead and get her off me back.'

'She thinks I'm joking,' Makka snorted. 'Christ, she's fucked up!'

Frowning, Billy grabbed Claire's shoulder and turned her roughly around. 'What's that about the Home? You'd better not have been mouthing off about me to that lot, 'cos if you have . . .'

'Course I ain't!' She clutched at his arm. 'I wouldn't do that to you, Billy. You've been dead good to me, you have. I'd never drop you in it . . . I *could*, but I wouldn't!'

Billy felt the anger churn in his stomach. The bitch had him over a barrel, and she knew it. One word from her, and he was dead meat. Sex with a minor was bad enough, for a kick-off –

and the fact that she'd told him she was seventeen would be no defence.

Then there was the gear he'd been supplying her with. And the money he'd made charging his mates for a poke of her once-tight hole. And, worse than all of that, there was that *thing* growing inside her – which he knew intuitively was his, despite the fact that it could be down to any one of the blokes who'd used her as a sperm bank. He'd be in serious strife if she opened her increasingly flapping gob, but what was he supposed to do?

'So, you gonna give us a bit, or what?' Claire licked her lips in anticipation. 'I only wanna take the edge off. An' I really need it, babes. You don't know the mess I'm in back there.'

'What mess?' Billy squinted at her. 'What you done, Claire?'

'It ain't *me*,' she whined. 'It's them! They're trying to send me to Hillgate . . . But I ain't going back.' She shook her head adamantly. 'I've had it with that lot. They can kiss me bleedin' arse!'

'What d'y' mean, you ain't going back? You've got nowhere else to go, you dozy bitch.'

'I've already gone,' she sniggered.

'You *what*?' Billy shot a poisonous glare at Makka who was laughing out loud. 'I hope that don't mean what I think it means, 'cos I'm telling you now it ain't happening. I don't need no pregnant kid fucking me life up. You can piss right off!'

'Give us a wrap first,' she begged. 'Then I'll go – if that's what you want?'

'Too right it is.' Then: 'Okay . . . I'll give you one last one. But that's it. No more. Got that?'

'All right, all right,' Claire agreed, nodding furiously. 'Come on, then . . . Gimme gimme!'

'I mean it, Claire. I don't wanna see your face round here again – *ever*!'

'You *won't*!' Her cheek muscles twitched with anticipation as Billy took a piece of foil and heaped a tiny mound of powder onto it.

'You ain't seriously giving her none?' Makka wasn't amused. 'She ain't paid, man.'

'And she ain't gonna.' Billy stood his ground. 'You heard me. It's her last, then she's out – an' she *won't* be coming back.'

'Yeah, right, like that's *really* gonna happen. She'll be back before you've got the stench of her out of the fucking flat. She's one of them birds what can't take no for an answer.'

'Didn't hear *you* saying no when I spread me legs,' Claire sniped. 'You was one of the first begging for a go, you.'

Makka turned on her angrily. 'Yeah, but we didn't know what you was like then, did we? We wouldn't have laid a finger on you if we knew what a dirty little slag you was.'

'You want to watch how you talk to me,' she threatened, her voice mean. 'I could drop you in it like *that*!' She snapped her fingers.

'An' I could break your fuckin' neck like *that*!' Makka yelled, clapping his hands together sharply, a fraction of an inch from her nose.

'Pack it in, the pair of you,' Billy hissed, conscious of the men beyond the door who didn't – and shouldn't – know the score here. They were all good for the money, but he wouldn't trust them to guard a pet ant, let alone the dirty secrets surrounding this girl.

Coming to a decision, he handed the foil and a rolled fiver straw to Claire and sat her down on a stool. 'Here, have this, then go to my room and lie down.'

'You *what*?' Makka was incredulous. 'What you playing at, man? If you let her stay, she'll never fuckin' leave.'

Pulling him to the far side of the kitchen, Billy said, 'I'm buying time, man.'

'For what?'

'I'm gonna have a chat to May.' Billy raised an eyebrow. 'Get me?'

Makka looked confused for a moment. Then he grinned as realization sank in. 'Got you.'

'Worth a try, innit?' Billy went on quietly. 'That's the third time this week she's said summat about dropping us in it, and I reckon she's capable of doin' it, an' all. Least this way there'd be no evidence.'

'So long as May keeps it zipped,' Makka warned. 'You know what a gobby slag she is.'

'Nah.' Billy shook his head. 'She ain't that thick. She knows what she'd get. Anyhow, go an' have a word with her while I get them in there sorted. I wanna clear the place out before it gets too late.'

'All right,' Makka agreed. Then he added quietly, 'But if May don't go for it, keep in mind what I said about the canal.'

'You serious?'

'Deadly! The bitch could send us down for years, man. Think what that'd be like, then tell me if you've got any better ideas.'

Billy didn't need to think about it. There was no way he was going down again. He wouldn't last a minute. If the turkey didn't kill him, the other cons would. He had one of those faces prison hard men took exception to. No, he wasn't going down again.

'Okay,' he agreed. 'I'll keep it in mind. But let's see what May's saying first. Less messy in the long run.'

'What you talking about?' Claire squeaked, going red in the face as she struggled to hold the dragon-smoke in.

'Sshhh!' Billy hissed. 'It's a secret. Feeling better now?'

'Loads.' She exhaled noisily. 'But there weren't much there, Bill. Can I have a bit more?'

Motioning Makka to the door with a nod, Billy went to Claire and pulled her to her feet. 'Later. I want you to have a lie-down first, like I said.'

Shoving her out the door and through the living room, he pushed her into the bedroom and made her lie down on his mattress. Pulling the door firmly shut, he went back to do his deals and clear the flat.

Makka came back ten minutes later. 'Sorted,' he said, giving the thumbs-up. 'I'm giving her a knock after dark.'

5

———◆———

Sarah was having a good day. Shoplifting was so much easier when the weather was nice and the town was packed. You didn't need subtlety, you just grabbed what you wanted and legged it, losing yourself in the crowd before anyone had a chance to suss what you'd done. She'd managed to get much more than usual already – and most of it real quality: Chanel and Givenchy. She'd even managed to snaffle a cool pair of Armani shades.

Taking her haul to the grotty backstreet pawnshop she used, nestled innocently among the smut stores on Tib Street, Sarah waited until Old Man Gerber had locked the door before laying it out on the counter for his appraisal. Watching as he looked it over with a greedy gleam in his eye, she smiled to herself. Seconds later, she laughed out loud when he offered her just fifty quid for the lot.

'Two hundred,' she told him firmly. 'There's a grand's worth of stuff there.'

'But it's *dodgy*,' Mr Gerber slimed, grinning toothlessly. 'And I mightn't get rid of it. It could end up in the back room with all the other shit I've got myself stuck with. You know how much I lose, taking risks like this?'

'Come off it!' she scoffed. 'You'll have it shifted before I've caught my bus.'

'Ah, but it's a buyer's market, my little sweet-cheeks.'

'Not this time, it's not. That's top gear, that.'

Tilting his head back, Mr Gerber gave a thoughtful gurn.

'All right, here's what I'll do. Seeing as you're so pretty, I'll go to a one-er. But that's the lot. Take it or leave it.'

'See ya!' Gathering her things together, Sarah made for the door.

'Catch a breath,' he called. 'Look, okay, one-fifty – but that's my limit.'

'Done!'

'My, you drive a hard bargain.' Reaching beneath the counter for his money bag, he made a meal of laying the five-pound notes on the counter one by one, grumbling, 'I don't know how I'm gonna rake this back, you know. You kill me, you kids, you really do. You'll have me in an early grave.'

Pocketing the money, Sarah smiled. 'You always say that, Mr G, but you're still here, aren't you?'

Tossing her a lewd wink, Mr Gerber leaned his elbows on the counter and raked her body with his stare, telling her in a lust-thick voice, 'That's 'cos I've got the stamina of a bull, my love. I could give *you* a ride you wouldn't forget in a hurry.' His tongue flicked in and out between his lips like a restless worm. 'Fancy giving it a shot?'

Grimacing, Sarah shook her head. Shrugging with his hands, Mr Gerber gave an *Oh, well, your loss* sigh and pressed the buzzer to release her from his dungeon – calling after her as she escaped that he had a great stack of videos if she ever changed her mind.

Shuddering with revulsion, Sarah wrapped her jacket tighter around herself and hurried back to the civilized part of town.

Most of the shops were closed now but, too hyped up to go straight home after such a good day, she decided to hang around for a while – treat herself to a burger, and maybe a trip to the Odeon. She hadn't been to the pictures for ages, but she'd made so much today that she could afford it this once. As long as that was all it was – a one-off. She'd worked too hard to fritter her money away on nonsense.

If there was one lesson that Sarah had learned from her mother, it was that you could never rely on anyone but yourself. With that in mind, she never missed an opportunity to add to her secret savings, and had shoplifted her way through two school holidays – making a fair profit, even at Mr Gerber's rip-off rates. And she hadn't stopped there, for there was plenty lying around at Starlight for the taking: petty cash from the office, unattended purses, trip funds . . .

She had no qualms about what she took from Starlight, because she didn't consider that *real* stealing. It was Council money, which meant it was intended for her. And what could Dandi say when it was her who'd drummed it into them that God only helped those who helped themselves?

Slipping into the shadow of an industrial-sized bin, Sarah peeled four fivers off the money that she'd got from Mr Gerber and stashed the rest beneath the lining of her bag before setting off to treat herself.

By eight-thirty, Dandi was at the end of her tether. Claire still hadn't come back, and to make matters worse, Hillgate had phoned to say that they'd not only given her bed away but didn't foresee another vacancy until the appointed time. Furious at the thought of being lumbered for another two months, Dandi rang the police.

'You've done the right thing,' Mark assured her. 'She's had plenty of time to sort her head out.'

'I know.' Dandi sighed guiltily. 'I just wish I hadn't had to let it get to this. I feel like a complete failure.'

'That,' he told her firmly, 'is one thing you most definitely are not!'

'Thanks.' She smiled gratefully. 'It's nice to know someone has faith in me. Don't mind if I smoke, do you?' She was already pulling a cigarette from the drawer.

'Hell, yeah!' Frowning, he folded his arms.

'Oh, don't do this to me. I'm desperate.'

'Hey – I'm joking. I'll open the window.'

'Do you *have* to?' Shivering exaggeratedly, Dandi lit the cigarette and wrapped her cardigan tighter around herself. 'It's the middle of winter, man!'

'It'll do you good.'

'I'll freeze to death.'

'Nonsense. You're just scared your lungs won't recognize that strange new substance – fresh air.'

'Sadist!'

'*Smoker*!'

There was a knock at the door, accompanied by a gaggle of arguing girly voices. Sighing, Dandi went to stub the cigarette out.

'I'll deal with it,' Mark told her. 'You stay there and relax.'

'What would I do without you?' she asked, smiling.

'Don't worry.' He grinned. 'It's going on your tab. And *boy*, will I enjoy the pay-off!'

Opening the door just enough to slip out, he pulled it firmly shut behind him. Seconds later, the shouting was replaced by giggles.

Mr Charming Chambers strikes again, Dandi thought, marvelling at his ability to relate to the obstreperous girls. If she'd had to deal with it herself she'd have probably made it worse. But that was girls for you. A female tells them off, it's a challenge to their burgeoning womanhood. But let a *man* open his mouth . . .

Hearing tyres on the gravel outside, she looked out of the window and was surprised to see a police car. It usually took a few hours to get a response out of them. But she wasn't complaining. The sooner she got this sorted, the sooner she could wipe her hands of Claire.

It was pouring with rain when Sarah left the cinema at just gone nine. A group of aftershave-soaked men ran by as she emerged onto the pavement, their huge feet splashing filthy water at her legs. Leaping back into the doorway, she weighed up her options: wait for the bus and be way later than she already was – big ear-bashing. Or invest the change from the twenty quid in a taxi and be just a bit late – slightly less of an ear-bashing.

Braving the downpour, she dashed to the edge of the pavement and hailed a black cab. Settling back in her seat, she squeezed the excess water from her hair and rehearsed her excuses for the inquisition that was sure to come.

Directing the driver to pull in at the corner, she paid the fare then waited until he'd turned and headed back to town before running around to the gates.

Sarah stopped dead when she saw the police car sitting at an angle outside the door. A cold thrill of dread ran through her. Had she been caught on one of the shop cameras? Or followed going into Gerber's with the gear? Or, worse – had Gerber himself grassed her?

No, of course he hadn't. He'd be dropping himself in it, and there was no way he'd risk that. It was more likely that Dandi had phoned them, panicking because she was late. She was in for a rollicking. But she'd rather that than the alternative – getting carted off to the cells.

Taking the money from her bag, Sarah stashed it carefully in the heart of a bush beside the gate. Then she ran up the path and let herself into the house, an innocent smile on her rain-slicked face.

*   *   *

A uniformed policeman was talking to Dandi in the hallway. Turning when Sarah entered, he said, 'This her?'

Dandi shook her head. 'No, that's Sarah, one of our other girls.'

'Sorry I'm late, it's throwing it down.' Sarah slipped her jacket off and gave it a shake. 'Everything all right, Dandi?'

'Nothing for you to worry about.' Dandi said. 'Go into the dining room with the others. I'll be through to explain in a few minutes.'

'She a friend of the missing girl?' the cop asked.

'Not particularly,' Dandi said. 'No one's really had a—'

'Missing girl?' Sarah interrupted. 'Who?'

'Claire Wilson.' The man peered closely at her face to gauge her reaction. 'You wouldn't happen to know where she is?'

'Isn't she in bed? She said she was going for a lie-down when I saw her.'

'And when was that?' He jotted something down in his notepad.

'This morning. She got off the bus I was getting on. I thought she looked tired, so I told her to get her head down for a bit – said I'd look in on her when I got back. Have you checked her room, Dandi?'

'She's not there,' Dandi admitted guiltily. 'She, er, got a bit upset and stormed out.'

'So, you don't know where she might have gone?' the policeman persisted. 'Friends, boyfriend, people she visits . . . ?'

'No idea. We don't really get on.'

'But you said you'd look in on her when you got back?'

'Yeah.'

'Why would you do that if you don't get on?'

Frowning now, Sarah said, ''Cos she looked tired, like I said. I was worried about her.'

'Why?'

'*What?*'

'I don't really think this is helping,' Dandi interrupted, sensing that Sarah was becoming irritated. 'I doubt whether Sarah knows any more than the rest of us. Claire isn't the kind of girl to confide in anyone.'

'Okay.' The cop relented. 'But if you think of anything, Sarah, be sure to let Miss Matthews know, won't you?'

'Yeah, course.' Smiling tightly, Sarah left them and went to the dining room.

A few minutes later, Dandi came in and clapped her hands for quiet.

'As you all know, Claire Wilson has gone missing, and we're very concerned about her.'

'Don't see why.' Pete snorted derisively. 'It's not like she can get in *trouble*, or anything.'

'That's not very helpful, Peter,' Dandi scolded.

'Yeah, *Peter*!' Vinnie gave him a shove. 'Be *helpful*, y' pillock!'

'Behave!' Mark told them sternly. 'This is serious!'

'Yes, *sir*!' Vinnie muttered, smirking.

Mark fixed him with an iron stare, letting him know that he had his measure and wouldn't tolerate any nonsense. Vinnie glared back for a moment, then reluctantly looked away, reminding himself that he was on a good-behaviour order. He focused on Sarah's tits instead. They looked real good in that tight—

'As I was saying,' Dandi went on. 'We're very concerned about Claire, which is why we've had to call the police in. Now, I know you've all said that you don't know where she might have gone, but I want you to really think about it, and if you come up with *any*thing, however insignificant you think it may be, please let us know immediately.'

Pete raised his hand.

'Yes, Peter?' Dandi hoped that he had something sensible to contribute.

'Just wondering if there's something we should know? I mean, you're not just worried 'cos she's up the duff, are you?'

'Yeah,' Vinnie chipped in, raising his eyes to look pointedly at Sarah's face now. 'Or is it just 'cos she's *late*?'

Tutting loudly, Sarah turned her shoulder, blocking him from view.

'There *are* other reasons,' Dandi said. 'But nothing I can go into with any of you, I'm afraid.'

'Yeah, but surely it affects us if Claire's messing with – say – *drugs*, or something?' Pete persisted. 'I mean, it ain't exactly a secret that she's always off her head, is it?'

'Whether she is or isn't is no concern of yours,' Dandi told him firmly. 'Now, I think that's enough for one night. You can all go and get ready for bed. But don't forget what I said – any ideas where Claire might be, let us know immediately.'

Ignoring the chorus of groans as the kids straggled from the room, Dandi crooked a finger at Sarah, motioning her to come to the office.

Sighing, Sarah followed her out, pausing in the doorway to shoot Vinnie a venomous glare.

Misreading it, he winked, annoying her even more than he already had.

In the office, Dandi motioned for Sarah to sit down.

'I said I was sorry for being late,' Sarah grumbled, slumping into a chair.

'What you haven't said is where you've been.' Dandi peered at her expectantly.

'Town.' Sarah shrugged, affecting boredom. 'I told you I was going. What's the big deal?'

'You're late, *that*'s the big deal! The shops closed hours ago. What have you been doing?'

'I went for a Coke with a girl from school.'

'That's one bloody long Coke!'

'We had a *few*, actually!' Sarah folded her arms. 'What's wrong with that?'

'The *time*,' Dandi snapped, concern making her voice harsher than she'd intended. '*Any*thing could have happened. I was worried.'

'Well, you needn't have been. I can look after myself, you know.'

'You might think so, but you're too young to know the dangers lurking on the street.'

Sarah gave a contemptuous snort. 'Christ, Dandi, I'm fifteen, not *five*.'

'Not yet, you're not.' Dandi pursed her lips primly. 'But even if you were, it's still too young to be wandering about on your own so far from home.'

'I was with a friend in a well-lit place with loads of people about – just like you're always telling us. What's your problem?'

'That's very naive, Sarah.' Sighing wearily, Dandi made a conscious effort to temper her tone. 'Some people hang about in those places specifically because it makes them seem less threatening.'

'Yeah, well, there was no one like that where I was.'

'Maybe not this time,' Dandi conceded. 'But if you get into the habit of going off on your own all the time, you never know what might happen.

'Anyway, enough of that.' Dandi clasped her hands together to show that she meant business. 'Given what's happened, the Board have decided to take steps to ensure this situation doesn't arise again. So, as of today, there will be a strict curfew. No more solo trips to town – you'll go with someone else, or not at all – and only if I okay it. If you do go out unaccompanied, it must be local, and if you're not back by nine, the gates will be locked and you'll be reported to the police.'

'That's not fair!' Sarah spluttered. 'You can't punish *me* for that stupid bitch taking off!'

'We're not *punishing* you,' Dandi replied calmly. 'We're protecting you. And it's not *just* you – everyone's included. You just happen to be the first one I've told.'

Pursing her lips, her nostrils flaring with annoyance, Sarah said, 'Can I go now?'

'Yes. But remember – I'm only doing this because I care. You *do* know that, don't you?'

'Mmm.'

Vinnie and Pete were leaning against the banister at the top of the stairs. When Sarah came out of the office, Vinnie followed her with his stare as she marched up the stairs. He couldn't get over how gorgeous she was. He never thought he'd meet someone like her in a Home. It was fate – it had to be.

'Didn't get you into trouble, did I?' he asked when she reached the top.

'Get lost!' she muttered, striding past with her nose in the air.

Motioning for Pete to stay put, Vinnie quickly caught up with her. 'Don't be like that. I was only messing. Where've you been all day?'

'None of your business.'

'Aw, come on . . . I'm trying to get to know you.'

'Piss off! What do I want with a muppet like you?'

'I'm all right when you get to know me.' Dipping his head, Vinnie peered up into her face, grinning cheekily. 'Honest.'

'I doubt *that*!' Stopping abruptly at the corner of the girls' landing, Sarah looked at him questioningly. 'Going somewhere?'

Hoping it was an invitation, he said, 'You want me to walk you to your room?'

'I don't *think* so! Anyway, even if I *wanted* you in my

room – which I *don't* – boys aren't allowed down here, so get lost.'

'See you tomorrow, then,' he called as she stalked away.

'In your dreams!' she retorted.

'Nah, that'll be tonight!' Grinning, he walked backwards to rejoin Pete.

'Told you you're wasting your time,' Pete said.

'That's what you think.' Vinnie smirked, heading for the bedroom with a spring in his step. 'She's just playing hard to get.'

'You reckon?' Pete shook his head. The new lad was a laugh, but he was a bit thick if he thought that Sarah Mullen was interested in him. He had *no* chance.

6

———◆———

May Cox was pissed off. It was late and she was on the edge of a teeth-rattling comedown. She was sure there was something she was supposed to be doing, but she couldn't for the life of her remember what. She couldn't even keep track of the TV programme she was supposed to be watching, never mind something she might or might not have planned.

Hugging her stick-thin frame as a bone-deep shudder passed through her, she glared at the kids fighting and yelling and rolling around on the floor in a tangle of arms and legs.

'Pack it *IN*!' she bellowed when she could stand it no longer. Swiping her snot-nosed youngest to the floor as he tried to scramble to safety on her knee, she said, 'Just shut the fuck up the lot of you, before I get the belt out!'

In the momentary lull that her threat achieved, the doorbell echoed loudly in the uncarpeted hall. Her heart catapulted into her throat. Leaping to her feet, she grabbed her eldest daughter and shoved her towards the door.

'See who it is, Tara. If it's anyone looking for money, I'm out. If it's that bitch from the social doing a sneaky drop-in, tell her to wait while you get the key. The rest of you, get your arses in gear!'

The remaining six sprang into action. They knew the drill: mess on the floor was shoved into the cupboard or behind the couch; table-top mess was swept into carrier bags and thrust behind the curtains.

Seconds later, the room was tidy enough to satisfy the Social Services bitch that May was coping. Much as May would have loved to ship the lot of them off to the council's never-return-land called 'care', she had no intention of letting it happen. She'd lose her benefits if they went, and there was no way she'd survive that. And she was fucked if she was going back on the game at her age.

'It's monkey-head Makka,' Tara said, popping her head around the door. 'Want me to tell him to fuck off?'

'Watch your bleeding mouth, you!' May warned, remembering at the mention of his name what she was meant to be doing. 'I'm nipping down Billy's gaff for a bit. Get this lot to bed while I'm out.'

'Do I have to?'

'Yeah!' Pushing Tara aside, May snatched up the plastic bag she'd left beside the door. Glancing into it, she saw that she'd forgotten something and tutted. 'Run upstairs an' get us the piss-sheet off our Leroy's bed.'

'Aw, Mam! Can't *he* do it? It'll be soaked.'

'GET UP THE BLEEDIN' *STAIRS*!' May roared, walloping Tara around the back of the head as she fled past. 'Jeezus and flaming *Mary*! . . . Can't anyone ever do what they're told round here?'

Hearing voices, Claire tried to open her eyes but they felt as if they were glued shut. Lifting her hand to prise them apart, it felt lead-heavy, as if she'd slept on it for a week.

'She's coming round,' a man muttered in the dark somewhere to her left.

'Oozzah?' she mumbled, struggling to make her tongue work.

'All right, sleeping beastie?' Makka grinned nastily when her eyes finally opened. 'I hope you feel as rough as you look.'

'Fukov!' she slurred, flapping a hand at his too-close face. 'Wurze Billa?'

'Thick bitch,' Makka sniggered. 'She can't even talk proper!'

'You said she was out cold,' May hissed accusingly. 'I ain't doin' it if she's looking at me. Sack that!'

'Stop freakin' out,' Billy murmured, peering closely at the powder turning to liquid in the spoon he was heating. 'She won't know nothing once she's had this.'

'Billa?' Claire flopped her head in the direction of his voice. 'S'pose t' go bag 'ome.'

'Don't worry about it.' Billy lifted her arm and looped his belt around it. 'You're too late, anyhow.'

'What y' doin'?' She eyed the syringe warily as he drew the smack up into it. She hated needles; they terrified her. Makka had had to sit on top of her earlier, holding her down while Billy spiked her. She didn't want to go through that again.

'Relax,' Billy crooned, giving her a toothless grin. 'You won't feel a thing.'

'Hurry up.' May licked her lips as he tapped the vein in the crook of Claire's elbow. 'I've got to be quick. I need a hit, an' the kids are on their tod.'

'Like that's owt new!'

'Fuck off! I don't have to do this, you know. I'm doing youse a favour.'

'And you're getting paid, so shut it.'

'Not enough,' she grumbled. 'And, here – I want a gram, you know. I ain't doin' it for no fiver bag.'

Billy gave an irritated nod. 'Yeah, all right. Stop pecking me bleedin' head.'

'You *do* know what you're doing, don't you?' Makka asked her, frowning. 'You ain't gonna leave it half done, or nothing?'

'Oi, smart arse, you'll be doin' it y'self if you're not careful!' May retorted indignantly.

'What's goin' on?' Claire shook her head in a vain effort to clear it. 'What's she doin', Bill?'

Leaning down, May jabbed her in the chest with a rigid finger. '*She*'s got a bleedin' name, y' cheeky cow!'

Claire's face crumpled with frustration. She wanted to punch the scruffy bitch in the mouth, but she couldn't even *think* straight, never mind get up. She was groggy and confused, couldn't make sense of the situation.

'Here we go.' Raising the syringe to eye level, Billy gave the barrel a sharp flick. 'Some nice anaesthetic to stop you screaming the gaff down.'

'Don't,' Claire whimpered, trying to pull her arm from his steely grip. 'Please, Billy . . . I don't like spikes.'

Bending forward, hands on her knees, May gave a sinister smile. 'We're cleaning you out, chuck. And it's for your own good, so button y' gob and let us get on with it before me kids trash me bleedin' house, eh?'

In a vivid flash of lucidity, Claire understood what was about to happen. She opened her mouth to scream, but her breath was stolen by the shock sensation of the needle piercing her flesh. Instantly, a rush of searing pleasure surged through her body, dissolving the thoughts and fears of a moment ago.

'Whooo-ee, look at her go!' Makka cackled as her head lolled back, a frozen expression of ecstasy drawing her mouth down into an elongated 'O' as her eyes rolled to the backs of their sockets.

Reaching down, May gripped Claire's cheeks and gave her head a waggle. Getting no response, she snapped her fingers. 'Right, let's get cracking before she comes round. Makka, get that sheet out me bag an' put it on the floor . . . Bill, you lie her on it while I get me stuff ready.'

Billy grimaced when May began to take the 'tools' from her bag. Genuinely concerned now, he said, 'Here, you ain't gonna mash her up, are you? You *have* done it before?'

May was offended. 'Course I have. Shit, man, I did me own cousin a month back. You think I'd have risked that if I didn't know what I was doing?'

'Okay. I'll take your word for it.' Holding his hands up, Billy backed towards the door with Makka right beside him.

'Where d'y' think you're skedaddling off to?' May demanded. 'You'd best get your wussy arses back in here, or I'm off – and I *mean* it!'

'Aw, man,' Billy grumbled, coming reluctantly back into the room. 'We don't know nothing about this shit.'

May narrowed her eyes. 'Listen, mate, if you think I'm doing this by meself so's I can get the full whack if it goes pear-shaped, you can think again. You got your dick dirty putting it in there, so you can get your hands dirty getting it out!'

Exchanging a sick glance with Makka, Billy said, 'All right. What d'y' want us to do?'

7

———◆———

Sarah finished her dinner before the rest of the kids and ran up to her room. Lying on her bed, she picked up the magazine that she had been reading before Dandi had called her down and stared blankly at the page. She must have read the same article three times over already, but she still didn't have a clue what it was about. She was too wound up to concentrate.

It was her fifteenth birthday and, so far, it had been crap. Sundays were the most boring days on Earth *ever*, for a start. But to cap it all the weather was dire – rain pelting the windows, the wind howling and whipping the trees into a frenzy outside.

There was nothing to do, and she hadn't even been able to escape to 'work', thanks to Dandi's stupid curfew. For a profitable lift you needed time to select a quality mark, and the confidence to pull it off without setting off every alarm from Manchester to Liverpool. These days, she had neither. She hadn't made a penny in the whole of the three weeks since Claire's disappearance and had finally given up. It wasn't worth the price of the bus fare, never mind having to account for her every step to Dandi when she got home. Sarah was sure that she wasn't alone in wishing she could throttle Claire for the trouble she'd caused.

But that wasn't the only reason she was holed up in her room right now. She was waiting for shit to happen. And, if her intuition served her right, it would definitely happen soon.

If she'd been smarter she'd have seen it coming, but things had changed so fast that she hadn't realized until it was too late.

After just a couple of weeks of trying to convince her how nice he was, how perfect a boyfriend he'd make if she'd only give him a chance, Vinnie Walker had finally got the message that she wasn't interested. But instead of backing off, he'd turned nasty; following her around the house making veiled threats, and turning the other kids against her by spreading rumours about what she'd supposedly said behind their backs.

She suspected that he'd been biding his time – waiting for the chance to pay her back for rejecting him. And this last week, she'd sensed that he was getting ready to make his move. He'd glared at her once too often, and she'd heard her name in too many hushed conversations. Whatever he was planning, she wished he'd hurry up and get it over with.

She didn't have long to wait. At just gone six, he threw her door open without knocking.

Determined to keep her wits about her – to at least *appear* as if she were on top of the situation – Sarah kept her mouth firmly shut, preferring to let him throw down the gauntlet.

Vinnie gave a triumphant sneer. She looked nervous – and so she should. After weeks of giving him the run-around, the bitch was about to learn the error of her ways. He'd had more than enough of her snotty attitude. Enough of her dirty looks. Enough of his mates laughing their bollocks off at him for getting nowhere fast!

Well, she was going to regret it now. Having broken into the office and read her personal file, he now knew the secret that she'd kept from all the other kids, and he was going to reveal her for the scum she really was.

'Oi, bitch!' he started. 'How come you're so up yourself

when you're nothing but a murderer? Don't come the innocent,' he went on when she looked momentarily confused,
''cos I *know* what you did.' Turning sideways now to include
his mates in the shock revelation, he said, 'You slashed a cat
to fuck, then turned on your own mam and sliced *her* up,
didn't you?'

Sarah almost laughed out loud. She'd been worrying about
what he was planning to do, and *this* was it? Nasty, childish
words. Shaking her head, she raised the magazine and casually
pretended to read.

Pissed off that she was ignoring him, Vinnie said, 'Oi, bitch!
I'm talking to you.'

'Sorry.' She glanced up, a hint of amusement in her eyes.
'Were you expecting an answer?'

'Don't fuck with me,' he warned, viciously elbowing the
sniggering boy behind him. 'Just admit it.'

'What's it got to do with you what I have or haven't done?'

Vinnie felt a blush creeping up his neck. He hadn't expected
her to be so calm. He'd expected her to shit it that her big
secret was out. But the bitch was laughing at him, making a
prat of him in front of his mates – again.

'I wanna know why you did it,' he snarled. 'And you'd
better tell me!'

'Or what?'

'Or I'll kick your bleedin' head in, *that*'s what!'

Resting her cheek on her fist, Sarah slowly looked Vinnie
up and down.

'What you lookin' at?' he demanded, squirming now.

'Dunno,' she mused, pursing her lips. 'They don't label shit
nowadays.'

'You what?'

'You heard,' she said, the control in her voice belying the
fear that she was pushing him too far. 'Now, if you don't
mind, I'm reading.

'It's quite good, actually,' she went on, unable to stop herself now she'd started. 'It's a letter from this lad who reckons his dick won't stop dribbling after he's had a piss. You can have a look, if you want. You might find it useful.'

'Don't, Sarah,' Pete warned, sensing that Vinnie was about to lose it.

'Oh, sorry, I forgot!' She threw a hand up to her mouth as if realizing she'd put her foot in it. 'He still wears nappies, doesn't he?'

At yet more sniggering, Vinnie turned on his friends. 'Think that's funny, do you? Well, let's see who's laughing when I've kicked the fucking shit out of the lot of you!'

'That's enough, Walker!'

Sarah breathed a sigh of relief when she heard Mark Chambers's voice. She didn't know what she would have done if Vinnie had gone for her. She could kick herself sometimes. Why could she never keep her big mouth shut?

Sending Pete and the others away but telling Vinnie to stay put, Mark drew himself up to his full height and demanded to know what was going on.

'Nowt,' Vinnie muttered, scowling at the carpet.

Looking past him to Sarah, Mark said, 'Everything all right?'

'Fine, thanks.' She nodded. 'Vinnie was just going.'

Jerking his head dismissively, Mark said, 'Right, Vinnie, move it. But don't let me catch you near the girls' rooms again, or there'll be trouble. Got that?'

Muttering 'Yeah' under his breath, Vinnie shot Sarah an evil, hooded glare and swaggered away with as much bravado as he could muster.

'Are you really all right?' Mark asked when he'd gone. 'You know you can tell me if he's bothering you. I can deal with him without him knowing you'd said anything.'

'I'm fine,' she insisted. 'He was just asking the time.'

'If you're sure?' Mark smiled, but it was obvious that he didn't believe a word. When Sarah nodded, he flapped his hands in a *what-more-can-I-do* gesture. 'You know where I am if you need me.'

'Thanks.'

When he'd gone, Sarah waited a few moments. Then she leaped up and ran to the door. Popping her head outside, she made sure that the corridor was clear, then wedged the door shut with a chair. Kneeling beside the bed, she lifted the edge of the mattress and reached into the slit she'd made in the material of the bed-base for the metal box she kept hidden there.

There were things in the box that she didn't want anyone to see. The cracked, fading Polaroid of herself at two holding baby Karen on her knee, for example. And her all-important savings.

Taking out a five-pound note, she replaced the box and smoothed the quilt over. Slipping her jacket on, she headed out, keeping a watchful eye open for Vinnie. There was no telling what he'd do now that she'd embarrassed him in front of his mates. She'd have to hide out in the café, then sneak back in at nine, in time to help Dandi put the younger girls to bed. He wouldn't dare do anything if she was with Dandi.

Running silently down the rarely used backstairs, Sarah slipped out of the kitchen door and darted across to the dense bank of hedges covering the garden wall. Pushing her way through, she edged her way along until she reached the section of railing where, some years earlier, a determined absconder had forced two bars apart, making a gap just wide enough for a medium-sized child to squeeze through. Hoisting herself up, she slipped easily through the gap and dropped down to the pavement below.

Pausing to dust herself down in the still-pouring rain, she was about to make a dash for the bus stop when a hand snaked out through the bars and grabbed her hair. Twisting to free herself, she saw that it was Vinnie. Too big to follow her through the gap, he was trying to pull her back, a furious scowl on his face.

'Let go!' she cried, digging her nails into his hand.

'Not till you've paid for grassing me up.'

Holding on to her hair to stop him tearing it out, she said, 'I didn't grass you, you idiot! I said you were asking the time.'

'You think you're too good for me, don't you?' he hissed. 'Strutting about with your nose in the air like you're something special! Well, you're not. You're just an ugly bitch!'

'Well, leave me alone if you hate me so much!'

'No way, you've pissed me off now. How come you never wanted to talk to me when I was trying to be nice, eh? Wasn't I posh enough, or summat?'

'Get lost! I don't have to talk if I don't want to.'

'Oh, yeah?'

'Yeah!'

'Right, that's it. I've had enough of this shit. I ain't gonna bother talking no more, I'm just gonna batter the bleeding face off you!'

His words drove a stake through Sarah's heart. It had been eight years, but hearing almost the exact words that her mother had used before the shit had hit the fan turned her stomach to liquid. Sinking her teeth into his hand, she tore free and ran as fast as she could.

Vinnie gave a howl of impotent rage. 'You'll have to come back sometime, and I'll be waiting, you got that? I'll be *waiting*!'

Ignoring him, Sarah ran hell-for-leather into the park across the road. Skidding and sliding her way across the sodden grass, she didn't stop until she reached the boarded-up, long-abandoned gatehouse on the far side. Vaulting over the low fence, she darted around to the back window and squeezed in past a broken slat of wood, falling onto the old kitchen floor with a thud.

Breathless, she soaked up the calm silence of the house. This had been her sanctuary, once upon a time – the place that she had run to whenever she needed time alone.

When her eyes had adjusted to the dark, Sarah made her way into the hallway. It was even darker here and she had to feel her way along the wall to find the hazardous rotted shell of a staircase. Placing her feet with care, she climbed up to the tiny attic room at the top of the house.

Stepping through the door, she peered around. It had been a while since she'd last been here, but nothing had changed. It felt the same; smelled the same; sounded the same. Musty. Dusty. Silent.

This had always been her favourite room. Still boasting glass in its window, it was a fraction warmer than the lifeless morgue that the rest of the house had become. And it afforded the best view of the park – and, if you found the right gap in the trees lining the park's entrance, most of Starlight's right side. Even if Vinnie sussed where she was, she'd see him coming in plenty of time to hide.

Smiling when she saw that the wooden packing crate she'd always used as a chair was still there, Sarah pulled it up to the window and sat down. Resting her arms on the sill, she lowered her head and closed her eyes, sighing wearily.

Sarah woke with a start. It was pitch dark – inside and out. Rubbing her eyes with the heel of her palm, she pressed her nose against the window and peered out. She couldn't see a thing other than the gnarled arms of trees silhouetted against the pewter sky and the dim twinkle of lights on the main road ahead.

Illuminating her watch face, she groaned when she saw that it was five to ten. Starlight would be well and truly locked up for the night. And Dandi had probably reported her missing. But there was no point worrying about it now. She might as well accept the fact that she was here for the night and try to make the best of it.

Shivering in the rapidly dropping temperature, she plunged her hands into her pockets and smiled when she felt the five-pound note she'd taken from her box earlier. She'd forgotten all about it. If she hurried, she'd catch the shop before it shut. A nice big bottle of cider was just what she needed to keep her warm.

Getting up, Sarah made her way carefully back down the stairs and out of the house. Glancing all around to make sure that no one was about, she climbed the back gate and ran to the shop.

She was just in time. The window shutter was already down, but the door shutter was only half-drawn. Ducking beneath it, she went inside and shivered as a warm blast of air fell down on her from a heating vent set in the ceiling above the door. Luxuriating in it for a moment, she selected her bottle, paid for it, and made her way back to the gatehouse.

Back in the attic room, she settled on a pile of dusty old newspapers and twisted the cap off the bottle. Taking a long drink, she closed her eyes and revelled in the warmth spreading through her body. Raising the bottle again she drank some more. And some more.

The drunker Sarah became, the more her thoughts turned to the nasty scene with Vinnie, rerunning every word he'd said and every reply she'd made. Mentally rewriting the script, she rehearsed it out loud between swigs, revising it each time, until she had a new, perfect version of what she *should* have said.

. . . *You're bad, Sarah . . . Bad, useless, an' good for nowt but trouble . . .*

Shocked to hear her mother's voice as clearly as if she were right there in the room, she dropped the bottle. 'Shit!' she yelped, groping blindly for it. 'Don't *do* that!'

Taking a long drink, giggling now at her own stupidity, Sarah said, 'She ain't even *here*, y'idiot! You're on your lonely-only-owny!'

... *Bad* ... *useless* ...

... *Get the dress on* ... *Now* ...

... *Good for now but trouble* ...

'Aw, fugov!' Struggling to her feet, she peered drunkenly around the blinding darkness. 'Y' di'n want me then, Mammy, so don't come lookin' f' me now!'

... *Bad* ...

'Right, tha's it!' Raising her fists, Sarah looked around for her mother. Finding nothing but emptiness to vent her anger upon, she sank to her knees, sobbing, 'Why, Mammy? Why ... ?'

When the tears subsided, she closed her swollen eyes and hugged her knees to her chest. The crying had sobered her a little, but she couldn't shake the maudlin mood taking a grip of her heart – or the memories flooding her mind.

The hatred in Mammy's eyes when she said Sarah was bad like her father ...

The man getting mad because she wouldn't put the horrible dress on ...

Poor little Joey Kitten with his squeaky little cry ...

Karen – the dirty little liar – screaming that Sarah had stabbed him ...

And the blood ... So much blood, leaking out of her Mammy like raspberry juice ...

Covering her ears, she rocked to and fro, humming loudly to drown out the haranguing, accusing voices of the past.

When they finally stopped, Sarah downed what was left of the cider and was soon as drunk as ever. But this time she was not amused, not maudlin – she was furious. With her mother for dumping her, and with herself for giving in to her emotions after holding fast for so long, but most of all with Vinnie, for chasing her out of the house and landing her in this mess.

This, more than anything, brought her to her feet and spurred her on as she made her precarious way back down the stairs and out of the house.

'You're a bastard, Vinnie Walker!' she muttered as she stumbled through the now-deserted park. 'Think y' kickin' me outta my bed, y' c'n think *again*!'

Clambering over the gates, Sarah fell to the pavement with a thud. Numb to the pain, she picked herself straight back up and lumbered across the road.

Navigating her way over the wall and through the railings was more difficult from the pavement side, but she managed it and, thrashing her way through the bushes, emerged into the garden with a jubilant yelp. She immediately shushed herself when she saw that the house was in darkness.

Tiptoeing across the lawn she tried the side door. It was locked. Giving up after a number of futile tugs, she stumbled around to the rear of the house.

Inside, Mark had activated the alarm and switched out the lights. He was heading up to bed with a glass of Scotch when he heard rustling, scraping noises. Stopping mid-stair, he leaned over the handrail and peered through the open kitchen door. Seeing the dark shadow at the window, he crept back down the stairs and placed the glass on the hall table. Creeping silently into the kitchen doorway, he strained to hear above the thudding of his heart. He hoped to God it wasn't a burglar. Big as he was, he'd never been much of a fighter. Recognizing the familiar voice muttering drunken obscenities outside the window, he breathed a shuddering sigh of relief.

Sarah!

He pondered the problem facing him now. He should really

get Dandi to deal with this, but he didn't want to disturb her. She'd had an awful night, waiting around at the hospital while one of the boys had his head stitched back together after a nasty accident. She'd had a migraine when she'd got back and had gone straight to bed.

But Mark's reluctance to wake Dandi was not just that he doubted whether she'd be in any fit state to deal with this, it was also because he felt guilty that he hadn't realized Sarah was out when he'd locked up for the night. That was really lax, and Dandi would be pissed off when she found out.

If she found out.

He didn't *have* to tell her, did he? Sarah was safe, that was the main thing. He could sort this out quickly and quietly, and no one would be any the wiser.

Going back into the hall, Mark downed his drink, deactivated the alarm and eased the door open. Stepping outside, he hissed, 'Sarah . . . stop making all that noise and come here.'

''S all right . . .' she called back. ''S only me . . .' Staggering around to the door, she raised a finger to her lips. *'Sshhh!'*

'Look at the state of you,' Mark whispered, amusement tingeing his voice. 'Come on, birthday girl. Let's get you up to bed before Dandi sees you.'

'Mushn't let Dandi shee me!' she giggled, allowing him to lead her inside. 'Oh, no! Mushn't let *her* know I'm – *Oops!*'

Catching Sarah as she fell, Mark covered her mouth with his hand and held his breath. When no one appeared after a moment, he hustled her up the stairs at an almost-run.

Opening her bedroom door, he pushed her inside and slipped in behind her, increasingly nervous about the trouble that he'd get into if he were caught. It was bad enough that he was practically carrying one of the girls to bed, but a drunken one, well after hours, with Scotch on his breath . . . It didn't bear thinking about! Pulling the quilt aside, Mark laid Sarah down and covered her up, then tiptoed towards the door.

'Mish'r Chambers!' she cried just as he reached it. 'Go'n be sick.'

'Oh, no,' he groaned. 'Don't do this to me!'

Scanning the room for a wastebin – or anything that would pass as a sick-bucket – Mark spotted an ice-cream tub filled with small bottles of nail polish on the dressing table. Tipping them out, he took it to her.

'Here, do it in this,' he whispered, pulling her upright and holding the tub beneath her chin.

Sarah retched a couple of times, but nothing came. Flopping forward onto his shoulder, she looped her arms around his neck.

'Not sick now . . . *Spinnin'*.'

Dropping the tub, he attempted to ease her back down. 'Come on, Sarah . . . lie down, there's a good girl.'

'No . . . 'S not nice,' she cried, holding onto him. 'Spinnin' round, and round, and . . .'

'Okay,' he whispered urgently. 'Okay, keep still . . . *Sshhh*.'

After a few minutes, the room settled and Sarah tilted her head back.

'D' you think I'm ugly? Vinnie says I am. D'y' think he's right?'

Choosing his words with care, Mark said, 'No, you're very pretty, Sarah. But it's time you went to sleep now. Night, night.'

'C'n shee the moon in your eyes,' she murmured, gazing up at him with a drunken grin as a sliver of moonlight filtered in through a gap in the curtain. ''S nice.'

'Thank you.' Firmly, he pushed her hands beneath the quilt. 'Now, sleep.'

'You shmell like *booooze*,' she said then, giggling as she struggled to sit up.

'Oh, shit!' he muttered. 'Just do as you're told and *lie down*, will you!'

Sarah flopped back and closed her eyes. Almost instantly, her breathing took on the slow, whispering quality of sleep. Waiting a couple of seconds to make sure she was really out for the count, Mark drew the quilt up to her chin and made a hasty escape.

Cursing himself for getting into such a potentially compromising situation, he rushed to his room and locked the door firmly behind him.

A few doors down, Vinnie smiled to himself in the dark. Unable to let go of the image of Sarah's gloating face as she'd escaped him, he'd been wide awake when she'd made it back to the house. He'd crept along to the landing window, from where he had seen everything – right up to Mark bringing her inside. He'd gone back to bed then, the plan for revenge forming in his mind like a living, breathing thing.

Now he waited a further fifteen minutes, then slipped out of bed and tiptoed onto the landing – thankful for Pete's capacity to sleep through an earthquake. Pausing briefly outside Mark's door, he listened for a moment, smiling when he heard the soft snores coming from within.

Letting himself into Sarah's room, he eased the door shut and padded softly across the carpet.

Sarah stirred when the quilt was disturbed. 'Mis'r Chambers?' she murmured, her voice thick with drink-sleep.

'Yeah, that's right,' he whispered, a triumphant grin spreading across his face as he climbed on top of her. 'Just Mr Chambers . . .'

8

———◆◆◆———

S arah felt sick. Rolling onto her back she opened her eyelids. It was morning, the room bright despite the closed curtains. A sliver of brilliant sunlight streamed through the gap and made her narrow her green eyes in pain. Wincing, she rolled across to the edge of the mattress and stared at the comforting dark blue of the carpet.

Focusing after a moment, she noticed the ice-cream tub and frowned, wondering what it was doing there. But no matter how hard she tried, she couldn't remember a thing. Closing her eyes as a surge of nausea flooded her mouth with saliva, she breathed slowly to settle her stomach and struggled to get her thoughts in order.

She'd gone to the old gatehouse to hide from Vinnie, and she'd fallen asleep. But what then?

Cider. She could still taste it. No wonder she felt so sick.

So, she'd bought the cider, then gone back to the gatehouse to drink it. But how had she got back here?

Nothing.

. . . *You're bad . . . useless* . . .

Blinding flashes of unwelcome recall made her head spin, taking her stomach with it. Reaching for the tub, Sarah threw up.

Flopping back when she'd finished she felt a sharp pain in her breast. Lifting the quilt, she looked down at herself and was shocked to see her clothes in disarray. Her bra, undone and no longer covering her breasts, was a twisted tangle around her collarbone, and her left breast was bruised with what looked suspiciously like a lovebite.

Filled with dread intuition, she looked down at the rest of her body. Her fears were confirmed when she saw her knickers wrapped loosely around one ankle. Touching herself gingerly, she winced. It was so tender down there.

Sarah knew instinctively what had happened, and the knowledge filled her with shame. How could she have done something so terrible and not even remember? She was a dirty, disgusting slut. Her mother had been right all along.

Wallowing in self-loathing, it suddenly dawned on her that whatever she *had* done, she'd done it here in her own bed. Which meant that it had to be somebody from the house. But who?

'No!' she gasped, jerking bolt upright as a vision flitted across her mind's eye.

Mark Chambers with the moon in his eyes.

She was locked out . . . He'd let her in, brought her upstairs, put her to bed . . . And then he'd . . .

No! She shook her head disbelievingly. He wouldn't.

He'd told her to do as she was told and lie down. Then he'd pulled the quilt aside and got on top of her. And he'd said 'Yeah' when she'd called his name.

Sarah covered her face with her hands, disgusted, and more ashamed than she'd ever felt in her life. How could she have done something like that?

But, hang about . . . If she'd been too drunk to remember getting back here, how could she have made him think she wanted *that*? And even if she had laid it on a plate, he should never have gone along with it. He was supposed to be looking after the kids, not having sex with them.

Kids! Oh, shit! What if he'd made her pregnant? She couldn't have a kid. She didn't want one. Not ever. And definitely not *his*. She'd have to go to a clinic and get them to test her – tell them she'd got pissed at a party and slept with someone, or something. She looked eighteen. They couldn't say anything. And she'd give a false name so that they couldn't get her into trouble.

Getting out of bed, reeling with the knowledge that a grown man had taken advantage of her – *again!* – she paced the floor, wondering what to do about it.

There was no way she could tell. Chambers would only deny it, and she'd end up being branded a liar *and* a slag. So, what *was* she going to do? Keep her mouth shut and let him get away with it?

Shit, shit, *shit!*

Anger surged through Sarah's veins. All right, so she couldn't report Chambers. But one way or another, the bastard would pay for what he'd done.

Tearing off the rest of her clothes she stuffed them into a carrier bag and stashed it behind the bed. She'd deal with that later. Right now, she just wanted to scrub all traces of Chambers from her body.

Pulling on her dressing gown, she marched to the bathroom and locked herself in. Turning the shower on full blast, she stepped beneath the icy spray and scoured every inch of her flesh with a stiff nailbrush.

Twenty minutes later, Sarah strode downstairs with her head held high. There was no way she was giving Chambers the satisfaction of seeing her shuffle around as if she had something to be ashamed of. If anyone should be ashamed, it was *him!*

Dandi was serving breakfast when Sarah entered the dining room.

'Morning,' she called, smiling as she took a couple of bowls from the trolley. 'What you having?'

'Toast,' Sarah snapped, stomping towards an empty table

at the far side of the room. Sitting down heavily, she folded her arms and glared at nothing.

Bringing a plate of buttered toast across, Dandi noticed the livid draw of the girl's lips, the sparking anger in her eyes.

'Are you all right?' she asked. 'You're not feeling ill, are you?'

'Oh, don't worry about me,' Sarah snarled. 'I'm just hunky-dory, thanks.' Snatching the plate, she stared out of the nearest window, chewing a piece of toast with taut-jawed fury.

Dandi frowned. They usually got on pretty well, but Sarah had practically bitten her head off. She'd always had a sharp tongue, but she didn't often lash Dandi with it. Doing a quick mental calculation of the older girls' period routines, Dandi realized that Sarah's was pretty close. Best not pour petrol onto the flame by bugging her, then. Satisfied that Sarah would soon be fine, Dandi left her alone.

From his own table across the room, Vinnie watched Sarah closely. It was obvious from her expression that she knew what had happened, but he needed to know if she remembered who had done it to her. She'd been so drunk that he doubted it, but he had to be sure all the same – to prepare himself in case he had to take off quickly. He knew what these girls were like for saving face. They'd say anything rather than admit they'd asked for it.

After a while, he relaxed. Sarah hadn't even glanced his way, none of the staff had approached him and there were no blaring sirens. He was in the clear.

He grinned smugly. Not so special now, was she, the stuck-up bitch. He'd shown her the perils of fucking with Vinnie Walker!

It suddenly occurred to him that she had done *exactly* that

– fucked with him – and he snorted out loud, almost choking on a mouthful of cereal.

'What's the joke?' Pete asked.

'Nowt.' He shook his head. 'Just thinking about something, that's all.'

'Yeah?' Pete grinned expectantly. 'Let us in on it, then.'

'Can't, mate.' Vinnie wiped the milk from his chin with the back of his hand. 'It's a secret.'

Composing his face into a less smug, less knowing expression, he hugged the knowledge to his heart. This was his alone – his to savour during his every waking moment, his to dream about in the long, dark nights.

'Oi!' Pete hissed, nodding towards Sarah as she strode towards the door. 'She's getting off. We going after her, or what?'

Vinnie shook his head. 'Nah, she'll keep.'

'But you said—'

'That was yesterday.' Scraping his chair back, Vinnie stood up and stretched. 'I've got better things to do now.'

'Like what?' Pete broke into a trot to keep up as Vinnie stalked purposefully out into the hall.

'Like, shut your gob and wait till there's no earwiggers about!' Vinnie pushed him towards the front door and impatiently waved the rest of the gang to catch up. 'I'm after jacking a motor, if you must know.'

'Yes!' Pete crowed, punching the air. 'Blackpool!'

'All right, but I'm driving,' Vinnie said.

'Fight you for it?' Grinning, Pete raised his fists.

'Get real!' Vinnie sneered. 'I'd wipe the floor with you.'

'Oh, yeah?'

'Yeah!'

Sarah turned onto the girls' landing and literally bumped into Mark Chambers coming the other way.

'Morning, Sarah.' He smiled tentatively. 'Feeling better?'

'Don't talk to me!' She glared at him, infuriated that he was pretending nothing was wrong.

Shocked by the vehemence of her tone, but putting it down to a hangover, Mark dipped his head towards her. 'Look, if you're worried about last night, don't be. I'm not going to report you.'

'*You* report *me*?' Sarah gasped incredulously. 'That's a good one! Think yourself lucky I haven't said anything to Dandi about what *you* did, you bastard!' Pushing past him then, she marched to her room.

Open-mouthed with shock, Mark watched her go. He couldn't believe that she'd spoken to him like that. She was normally so quiet and polite – a little distant, yes, but always civil. What had he done to warrant that outburst?

It occurred to him that he might have offended her by rushing out on her the previous night. If she was feeling this rough now, she must have felt terrible then and had probably expected him to stay and look after her. But surely she understood the risk he'd taken just by smuggling her in and not reporting her?

Hell, it was like walking a tightrope, dealing with these kids. One minute they wanted help, the next they were telling you to get lost. He'd only wanted to keep her out of trouble on her birthday – and himself, if he were honest. But he wouldn't do it again. Next time one of the girls came home in such a state, he'd wake Dandi and let her deal with it – however ill she was.

Sarah wedged her door shut to prevent Mark from following her. Not that she thought he'd dare try anything with Dandi about, but you could never be too sure with men like that.

Going to the window, she watched Vinnie and his crew making their way up the path. Aiming all of the venomous hatred festering in her heart at Vinnie's back, she thought, *Huh! Look at the big man! Thinks he's so bad, but he doesn't know the half of what goes on under his own nose! Dickhead!*

She was still thinking about him long after he'd disappeared from view, wondering what he would do if he found out what Mark Chambers had done to her. Would he laugh and say she'd deserved it, or play the hard man and offer to kick the shit out of Chambers? She doubted that. Yeah, he'd had a thing for her in the beginning, but he hated her now. Why would he bother coming to her aid?

No, this was her fight alone. No one was going to take her side, and the sooner she got used to that, the sooner she'd get herself together.

But that didn't mean she would just carry on as normal. From now on, she'd steer well clear of everyone. And if they got too close, by God she'd make them pay.

9

———◆———

Dandi was convinced that something bad must have happened to bring about such a drastic change in Sarah. In the weeks following the girl's birthday, she'd been snappy, rude, and more reclusive than ever. But no matter how many times Dandi tried to coax it from her, Sarah refused to admit that anything was wrong. Hoping one of the other staff might be able to shed some light on it, Dandi mentioned her concerns at the monthly meeting.

'I'm worried about Sarah,' she told them. 'She's not been right for a while, but she won't tell me anything. Has anyone any idea what's troubling her?'

'Puberty,' Glenda Nash, the housekeeper, stated airily. 'Girls are much worse than boys.'

Dandi disagreed. 'No, she hit that a couple of years back. Don't you remember the moods? I do. What about you, Mark?' she asked then. 'You've known her as long as I have. Haven't you noticed the change in her?'

Blushing, Mark folded his arms. 'I, em, agree she's definitely changed, but I couldn't say in what way specifically. She doesn't really speak to me, to tell the truth.'

'That's exactly what I mean.' Dandi frowned. 'She hardly talks to *any*one. She just goes about her business with that awful scowl on her face.'

'Yeah, but that's hardly cause for concern when you consider how much of a loner she's always been,' said Glenda. 'Honestly, Dandi, I really think it's normal for her age.'

Shaking her head, Dandi said, 'I hear what you're saying, but my instincts tell me this is different. Something's happened, I'm sure.'

'Sure you're not just being paranoid after the Claire thing?'

'Claire?' Carl, one of the newer members of staff, checked his notes. 'Have I met her? Her name's not on my list.'

'She left before you came,' Dandi told him. 'She had a lot of . . . problems.'

'Huh!' Glenda snorted. 'You can say *that* again.'

'Oh?' Carl was intrigued.

'She disappeared,' Dandi explained, sighing guiltily. 'Five months pregnant and messed up on drugs, and I chased her out.'

'You did not!' Mark cut in. 'You did everything you could for that girl.'

'Yeah,' Glenda agreed, nodding vigorously. 'I mean, what were you supposed to do, Dandi? Lock her in her room?'

'No, but I could have handled it a little more sensitively.'

'You did your best,' Mark said firmly. 'She'd have killed the baby if she'd carried on the way she was going.'

'She still might have,' Dandi murmured, steepling her fingers beneath her chin. 'I often wonder about that body they found.'

'Ooh, yeah,' Glenda grimaced. 'The baby in the bin bag. Awful business.'

'I saw that on the news.' Carl looked a little sick now. 'That wasn't *hers*, was it?'

'We don't know,' Dandi admitted quietly. 'We haven't heard from her since she took off.'

'What about the police?'

'She's sixteen now,' Mark told him. 'They'd have no obligation to tell us if they *had* found her.'

'That's terrible.'

'Yep, but that's the way it goes.'

'Anyway, enough of this,' Dandi said, determinedly shaking off the gloominess that she always experienced when she spoke of Claire – her biggest failure to date. 'Let's get back to the business at hand, shall we? What do we do about Sarah?'

Getting little response but shrugs, a few raised eyebrows, another blush from Mark, and an unhelpful 'Stop fretting and leave her to it' from Glenda, she gave up.

She probably *was* just being paranoid, Dandi decided. It wouldn't be the first time her fears about one thing had grown to encompass everything else. If there truly was something wrong with Sarah, she'd just have to wait until Sarah herself decided to tell her.

Sarah had no intention of telling anybody anything. The more she thought about what had happened, the more convinced she was that it wasn't her fault. Mark Chambers had used her, exactly like those bastards her mother used to bring back to the house had done.

Hiding behind a wall of aggression, she made enemies of all the other girls. The younger ones avoided her, which suited her down to the ground, but the older ones challenged her, leading to numerous fights – which Sarah invariably won; launching herself at them as if fighting the Devil himself, seeing in their faces those of everyone who'd ever done her wrong.

Even the solitude of her bedroom no longer provided refuge as her dreams became increasingly disturbed. Night after night, she was haunted by distorted versions of everything that she had experienced throughout her life, all twisted together in a macabre plot line of her own mind's making, and always ending the same way – Sarah disappearing beneath a raging sea of blood as the key players stood by, watching and laughing, united in their desire to destroy her.

She was seriously contemplating ending the misery once and for all when ten-year-old Harry Shaw arrived at Starlight and inadvertently saved her life.

With his carrot-orange hair, wire-thin limbs, invisible eyelashes and freckle-peppered skin, Harry had suffered an endless round of rejection and abuse. And his own pretty mother had started the cycle.

Repelled by the sight of him as he slithered from her loins, Amy Shaw greatly exaggerated a mild case of post-natal depression and begged the authorities to take him into care – just until she was better. Well-meaning social workers made many attempts at reuniting them, and Amy always agreed to give it a try – rather that than face their disapproval if she refused. But it was never more than a week before she sent him back, claiming she was still too depressed to take proper care of him.

Harry was six the last time Amy had him and, in a last-ditch attempt to make him more presentable, she plastered liquid foundation over his freckles and dyed his hair blond. He suffered an allergic reaction to the chemicals.

When the social worker called a week later to check on Harry's progress, she was appalled to discover him locked in a cupboard, his mother nowhere in sight. His hair had fallen out in clumps, his face was raw and swollen, he hadn't eaten for days, and he hadn't been allowed out to use the toilet. Phoning the police, the social worker had him removed – for good.

Harry adored his mother and would have endured any amount of abuse to stay with her. But he was never allowed to go back, and he had to learn to deal with it.

He was ten-going-on-forty when he arrived at Starlight after the latest in a long line of unsuccessful foster placements. Knowing now that he would always be judged on his unattractive appearance, and that bullies would always target him, he avoided close contact – with other kids, especially. But it rarely worked out the way he planned and, having found himself up against the wall more times than he could count, he had developed a self-deprecating humour. It usually worked, but he soon found out that it wasn't going to at Starlight.

In the vain hope that the polite, much bigger twelve-year-old would take Harry under his wing and give him a running start, Dandi roomed Harry with Ollie Ford. Unfortunately, she had no idea that Ollie's manners only extended as far as the staff. To the other kids, he was a nightmarish Vinnie wannabe. From the first night, he joined in gleefully as Vinnie punished the new boy for daring to be so ugly.

By the end of the first week, Harry had learned that his brand of humour flew straight over the bullies' heads and intensified their desire to hurt him, so he stopped that. And struggling spurred them on, too, so he stopped that as well, hoping that his lack of response would deprive them of whatever perverse pleasure they were getting. It didn't.

Most of the kids knew what was going on, but none was prepared to lay their head on the line and tell, because the repercussions of grassing someone like Vinnie Walker were far worse than the actual bullying.

Only Sarah had no idea. In fact, she was completely unaware of Harry's existence until a few weeks after his arrival when she happened to spot Vinnie, Pete, Ollie and Rob ambushing him as he made his way to the bathroom.

If Sarah hadn't been in such a foul temper, she might have gone about her business and left them to it. But she was, so she didn't. And it didn't matter that she didn't know Harry, because this was no act of heroism. It was simply as good an excuse as any to start an argument – with someone who actually deserved it, for a change.

Vinnie had left her alone since her birthday, but she knew he still harboured ill feeling towards her – it was obvious in the way he looked at her. Not that she gave him the satisfaction of looking back, but she could feel the skin-crawling sensation of his stare on her body, nonetheless.

Interfering in his business now was guaranteed to spark a violent reaction from him, but Sarah truly didn't care. She was in exactly the right mood to take him on – to pay him back for the misery his ego-fuelled attack had caused her. And if he tried to get heavy he'd get the shock of his life, for she wasn't the same girl he'd chased out of the house that day. These days, she carried a small, sharp penknife around with her. And if anyone deserved a taste of it, Vinnie did.

Slipping silently along the landing, Sarah pushed past Rob before he could close the bathroom door and warned him to stay quiet with a finger to her lips. With their backs to the door, the others didn't even notice her standing there.

Thrusting Harry up against the tiled wall, Vinnie held him by the throat while Ollie unbuttoned his trousers and yanked them down to his ankles, taking his underpants with them. Laughing nastily, Ollie took a piece of string from his pocket and wrapped it around the boy's tiny genitals.

Sarah couldn't believe what she was seeing when Ollie began to pull on the string. Not only was the poor kid's dick in danger of being sheared right off, it was obvious that he could barely breathe. His face was growing more scarlet by the second, and his hands were flapping like clumsy, hairless birds on the ends of his skinny wrists.

'Get off him, you bastards!' she yelled, marching towards them.

Glancing around at the sound of her voice, Vinnie grinned. 'Oh, look who's here, lads. Come to join the party, have you?'

Harry's eyes bulged alarmingly as Vinnie increased the pressure of his grip.

'Let go!' Sarah demanded, pulling on Ollie's arm. 'You're gonna kill him, you fucking morons!'

'Belt up,' Ollie snorted, pushing her away. 'We're only having a laugh!'

'A *laugh*?' she exclaimed scornfully. 'God, you're as thick as *him*!'

'What *you* gonna do about it?' Ollie leered at her breasts.

'Don't even *look* at me, you little *shit*!' she spat disgustedly.

'And I don't know why the hell *you*'re going along with this.' Sarah turned on Rob who was still hovering in the doorway. 'Jimmy and Ade had the sense to sack this lot off. How come you're still hanging about with them?'

'They're me mates,' Rob muttered, blushing deeply as he stared unhappily down at his feet. In truth, he was just too scared to face the kind of beating that Jimmy and Ade had taken for daring to leave the gang.

'Maybe I've got you all wrong, eh, Rob?' Sarah went on mercilessly. 'I thought you were all right, but maybe you like all this shit? Think it makes you look *hard*, hanging about with these brain-dead bastards, do you?'

'Watch who you're dissing, you!' Ollie scowled.

'Or what?' she demanded. 'You think I'm scared of *you*? Don't make me *laugh*! Move!' Shoving him aside, she wrenched the boy from Vinnie's grip. He fell to the floor in a gasping heap.

'Ah, look at her protecting the little mong,' Vinnie sniggered, leaning casually back against the wall. 'Love him, do you?'

'Sick bastard!' she snarled.

'Nah, babe,' he drawled, reaching out and stroking a finger down her cheek. 'You can't fool me. You might as well just admit it . . . You fancy me, don't you?'

Snatching at the finger, Sarah bent it right over onto the

back of Vinnie's hand. Staring icily into his eyes, she said, 'Touch me again, and I'll break it right off. Now fuck off before I get *really* mad!' Pushing his hand aside, she pulled the knife from her pocket and thrust it towards him. 'Know what I mean, *babe*?'

Laughing, Vinnie jumped back, his painfully throbbing finger clutched protectively to his chest. 'Come off it! What you gonna do with that . . . *peel* me?'

Pete wasn't so sure that it was a joke. In fact, Sarah looked decidedly serious. Backing out of the room, pulling Rob and Ollie with him, he said, 'Yo, Vinnie . . . leave it, man. Come on.'

Vinnie shook his head, still looking at Sarah. 'Nah, man, it's cool. She wouldn't *dare*.'

'Want to try me and see?' Her voice was low and mean. 'I mean, I've got nothing to lose, have I? It's not like I haven't done it *before*, is it?'

Something in Sarah's eyes gave Vinnie a jolt. It was the coldest, deadliest stare he'd ever seen in his life – and from a *girl*, of all things. But it was no girly look. It contained the pure essence of a woman – a truly dangerous woman.

'Sack it,' he sneered. 'I ain't gonna touch you. Even if you wasn't just a bird, you ain't worth it. Then, looking down at Harry still huddled on the floor, he cocked his finger like a loaded gun and swaggered out.

When he'd gone, Sarah locked the door and took a towel from the cupboard. Her hands were shaking as she soaked it in cold water, but it wasn't fear, it was the massive adrenalin rush that she'd experienced when confronting him with the knife. The fact that he'd backed down empowered her in a way she couldn't yet define – a way that lifted her mood considerably.

Taking the towel to Harry, she kneeled beside him and gently placed it on the welt encircling his neck.

'Are you all right?' she asked, gazing at him with concern.

'Yeah,' he croaked, too embarrassed to look her in the eye. 'Just need to catch my breath.'

Heaving a sigh of relief, Sarah sat back on her heels. 'Shit! You had me scared for a minute there. You should've seen the colour of your face! I thought you were a goner.'

'It's not often I have colour,' Harry flipped back.

Frowning, she said, 'Is that supposed to be a joke?'

'Well, you're not laughing,' he murmured, 'so I guess not.'

'No!' she snapped. ''Cos it's not *funny*! Vinnie was *throttling* you, you stupid little prick!'

Blushing beetroot as her words reminded him that his trousers were still around his ankles, Harry doubled over and dragged them up.

'Oh, God!' Sarah put her hand to her mouth. 'I didn't mean anything. I was just . . .'

''S all right.'

'No, it's not. I'm really sorry, and I *swear* I didn't look. But you just don't get it. Vinnie could have *killed* you!'

Shrugging resignedly, Harry hugged his knees to his chest. 'He's been practising long enough.'

'He's done this before?'

'And the rest.' Sighing, he pushed himself to his feet and buttoned his trousers.

Standing, Sarah looked down at him and felt the anger welling up in her breast. He looked so . . . *unfinished*. Like a waxwork waiting to have its features painted on. Vinnie was a whole lot taller and heavier. What pleasure could he get from torturing the boy? But that was Vinnie's *thing*, wasn't it? Seeking out the weak and vulnerable and making their lives miserable.

'You're Sarah, aren't you?' Harry asked her shyly. 'I saw you when I first came. Dandi shouted to you to come and say hello, but you mustn't have heard her.'

'Oh?' she murmured, not remembering. But then she wouldn't. She'd been too wrapped up in herself to notice anyone else. 'Sorry.'

'It's all right,' he said. 'Not many people want to meet me. Not exactly good to look at, am I?'

Sarah knew he meant it despite the jocular tone, and she thought it was a shame that he had so little respect for himself. He *was* ugly, there was no use denying it. But he had something about him, all the same.

'Know what?' Folding her arms, she cocked her head to the side. 'I don't see what your problem is. I think you're all right.'

Harry Shaw fell in love.

'Aw, you don't have to say that,' he murmured, pulling a face to cover his delight. 'I know I look like a bumhole. That's why my mum gave me up. But I'm glad, 'cos her cooking's shit. Anyway, I used to scare her boyfriends. They probably thought they'd catch whatever disease she must've had to give birth to me.'

'Quit with the *shit*,' Sarah scolded, frowning deeply. 'We've all had crap to deal with. Get over it! Who *are* you, any-how?'

'Harry Shaw,' he said, blushing yet again as the next words escaped of their own accord: 'You can call me Quasi, if you want.'

'I don't think so!' she snorted. 'He's got a hump the size of Vinnie's head. How old are you?'

'Ten,' he admitted, sighing heavily. 'Bet you won't want to talk to me now? No one your age ever wants to talk to little kids.'

'I don't talk to *any*one – kid or not,' she retorted. 'Not unless I want to, anyway. But I reckon you and me will get on all right.'

'Really?' He squinted disbelievingly.

'Yeah, really.' Reaching out, Sarah gave his cheek a rough tweak.

Harry couldn't look at her for a full five seconds. He'd never been spoken to like this in his life before – not even by the adults in the various homes that he'd been in over the years – and they were *supposed* to make you feel good about yourself. Dandi was the best so far, but even *she* hadn't made him feel that she really liked him and wasn't just doing her job. Sarah actually sounded like she *meant* it. It was a nice experience, but potentially dangerous – for Sarah, at least.

Deflating fast, he said, 'Look, I, er, don't think you should bother with me. People get picked on when they hang about with geeks.'

'Bollocks!' Sarah snorted. 'I just told you I don't talk to anyone. It isn't exactly gonna make a difference if they all fall out with me over you, is it?'

'Yeah, but you don't know what it's like being *this* geeky,' he muttered, thinking that she was far too pretty to understand. 'I'm not worth it – honest. I'd ignore me from now on, if I was you.'

Sarah folded her arms and pursed her lips stubbornly. 'Don't tell *me* what to do. If I want to be your friend, I will be!'

Harry grinned, but his face quickly fell when Sarah frowned.

It had just occurred to her that flaunting any kind of friendship in front of Vinnie would be like waving a red rag at a bull after what had just happened. She wasn't so much concerned about herself, but she doubted whether Harry needed any more shit.

'Er, look, on second thoughts,' she said. 'It might be best if we did ignore each other.'

'Yeah, sure, whatever,' Harry murmured, dropping the wet towel into the washing basket and heading for the door.

'Oi!' She folded her arms. 'Where you going, sulky?'

'Places to hide, people to avoid,' he quipped, shrugging morosely. 'Don't worry about it. I'll be all right.'

Shaking her head, Sarah smiled with amusement. 'I only meant in front of the others – to keep Vinnie off your back.'

'Oh, right.'

'Yeah, so you can stop pulling your face now, can't you?'

There was a knock at the door.

'Harry, are you in there?' Dandi called through.

'Er, yeah,' he answered, grimacing. 'Won't be a minute.'

'I'll wait,' Dandi said. 'But don't be long. I need to get you measured up for your uniform.'

'Oh, great!' Sarah giggled. 'How am I supposed to explain being locked in here with you?'

'Hide,' Harry hissed, pointing towards the shower cubicle. 'I'll move her away so you can sneak out. I'll, er, get her to go to my room, or something.'

'Have fun getting *measured*,' she teased, stepping into the cubicle and pulling the curtain across.

Rolling his eyes, Harry flushed the toilet for effect then went to the door. Thinking of something, he ran back to Sarah.

'When will I see you?'

'I'll catch up with you,' she said. 'Now, piss off before she kicks the door in. She probably thinks you've fallen down the loo!'

Vinnie couldn't stop thinking about Sarah. The psycho bitch had pulled a *knife* on him! What was *that* all about? And she would have used it, too. He could tell from the stare that she'd given him.

Shit, that had been a bad-assed stare. But how *sexy* was it? It reminded him of those horror films where the demon turns into a gorgeous naked woman, and just when the main man thinks he's going to get his rocks off she skins him with her teeth.

He got a hard-on every time he thought about it, but then Harry Shaw's face would appear and Vinnie's cock would droop. Not only had the ugly little mong caused Sarah to almost stab him, he'd also stopped Vinnie having a bit of fun in peace. Harry would have to be taught a lesson after lights out, to show him the error of his ways.

Vinnie wasn't sure what he was going to do with Sarah yet, but he didn't think he wanted to hurt her. In fact, he was toying with the idea of trying to win her over instead. He hadn't succeeded first time round, but they'd both grown up a lot since then. And he'd been working out a lot recently. She'd *have* to be impressed by his body. He was solid as fuck.

Yeah, he'd do that – win her over. However long it took. He'd just have to bide his time – and he was good at that.

In the meantime, Harry Shaw would suffer for getting in the way.

Harry curled into a tight ball when Vinnie, Ollie and Pete approached his bed that night. He had been expecting it.

In the pitch darkness it was impossible to see their faces, and their voices were indistinguishable. But it didn't matter who was where, or who was saying what. Their intention was unanimous.

'Think you're well smart, getting' a girl to save you, don't you?'
The quilt was yanked away.
'Bet you thought you was off the hook. Well, guess what? You ain't!'
The first punch deadened Harry's arm.
'Yeah, we're gonna do you!'
The next punch sent him flying onto the floor.
'You listening, you fucking mong?'

The kicking and stamping took the wind right out of him. *'Ugly twat! This is what you get for hiding behind a girl!'*

Harry stayed on the floor long after Vinnie and Pete had gone and Ollie had climbed into bed and fallen asleep. As the tears spilled silently down his cheeks, only one thought stopped him from going down to the kitchen, taking a knife from the drawer and slicing his own throat from ear to ear.

Sarah was his friend.

And he loved her – *really* loved her. If he could see her face and hear her voice for just five minutes a day, he would gladly endure whatever Vinnie threw at him.

IO

$\blacksquare\!\!-\!\!\cdot\!\!\cdot\!\!-\!\!\blacksquare$

Sarah and Harry became firm friends, and no one had a clue – least of all Vinnie. Had he realized, he would have intensified his attacks, not lessened them as he had done, too preoccupied with finding ways of getting closer to Sarah to bother. He still had a go when he got the urge, but if he'd known that Harry had taken what he believed to be his – Vinnie's – rightful place in Sarah's heart, he'd have killed him.

Relishing the fact that they were getting one over on the others, Sarah and Harry protected their secret vigilantly – each knowing the value of keeping close to the heart what was held most dear. What nobody knew about, nobody could take away.

Ignoring each other throughout the day, they would meet up in her room after lights out – strictly against the rules, but Harry was so insignificant that no one ever noticed him sneaking about in the dark. They talked about everything under the sun, and soon knew as much about each other's hopes and dreams as they did about their own.

It was a new experience for Sarah who had never had a real friend – not one she could really trust. And despite the difference in their ages, she trusted Harry absolutely. But, while she told him a lot, there were things that she kept back. The stuff her mother's *friends* had done, for example. Those foul, stinking bastards who had never left without taking a slice of her soul away with them. She could never tell anyone about that, let alone her dearest friend. She didn't want to see the disgust in his eyes – nor he the shame in hers.

Harry was intuitive, gleaning almost as much from what she didn't say as from what she did. But he didn't badger her. How could he, when he was just as guilty of holding out on her? He hadn't told her that Vinnie and the others still picked on him. And he never admitted how he really felt about her – and probably never would. It was enough just to be part of her life.

Which was why he was dreading Sarah's sixteenth birthday. He was terrified that when she got a flat, a job, and a fantastic life of her own, she would forget all about the ugly boy she'd left behind.

As the big day drew near and her silences grew to outweigh her talking moments, he convinced himself that she was detaching herself from him – preparing him for the big break.

With just a week to go, Harry finally plucked up the courage to ask if that was what Sarah was doing.

'Don't be such a pillock!' she snorted. 'How many times do I have to tell you that I'm not going to abandon you. I'll always make time for you. You're my best mate!'

Harry was relieved for himself, but even more concerned about her. *Something* was worrying her. He knew her too well. But if it wasn't that, what was it?

'Can I ask you something?' he said after a while, plucking at a feather that was working its way out of her quilt. 'Remember how you said you went looking for your mum that time?'

The muscles clenched in Sarah's cheeks. 'Yeah. What of it?'

'I was just thinking,' he went on, not daring to look at her and see the anger in her eyes that he could hear in her voice. 'Why don't you have another go when you get out? I would if it was me.'

'What's the point?'

Looking up, Harry gave a tiny shrug. 'I just think it's worth a try. You can't tell me you don't think about her.'

'Course I *think* about her, but it doesn't mean I want to see her. She didn't want me, so why should I?'

'You don't know that for sure. She's your mum. She won't still be blaming you for that stuff with the kitten.'

'You don't know her,' Sarah told him huffily. 'When she gets a grudge she never lets it go.'

'You don't know her that well yourself,' Harry pointed out. 'She might have changed.'

'Huh! I doubt that! She never liked me. It was always our Karen, right from the off.'

'That's another reason to do it. I *know* you think about your sister. You wouldn't keep her picture if you didn't.'

'For your information, smart arse,' she hissed, angry now because he'd hit a raw nerve, 'I kept that because it's the only photo I've got of me!'

'Bullshit! You don't fool me, Sarah Mullen!'

Jumping up, Sarah stomped across the room and got her cigarettes from her jacket pocket. Lighting up at the window, she blew a thick stream of smoke into the chilly night air.

'All right,' she said after a moment. 'Supposing I *do* want to see them – so what?'

'Do something about it.' Taking the cigarette from her fingers, Harry took a drag. 'There'll be no one to stop you. You're free to do whatever you want once you leave here.'

'And what if she don't want to see me?'

'She will.' Harry was certain. 'Why wouldn't she? You're . . . well, you're lovely.' Blushing, he handed the cigarette back.

Sarah finished it in silence and Harry watched her, wondering if he'd done the right thing in bringing the subject up. He knew about the bad dreams. They had stopped a while back, but he hoped his meddling wouldn't stir them up again.

Sarah might blame him, and he couldn't bear it if she fell out with him.

'I'm sorry,' he said. 'I had no right to say that stuff. It's none of my business. It's just that you've been so quiet, I thought you might have been thinking about them, that's all.'

Sarah flicked the dimp out of the window and gave him a tiny grin. 'Think you know me so well, don't you? Well, I *do* think about them, but only now and then. I'm not really bothered – and that's God's honest truth!'

'Well, if that's not bothering you, what is?'

'Nothing. I'm fine.'

'No, you're not. It *is* me, isn't it? You just don't want to say in case you upset me.'

Sighing, Sarah sat back and hugged her pillow to her stomach. This was really difficult, but if she told Harry what was really bothering her, he would be twice as upset as he already was.

For weeks now she had lain awake at night, dreading her birthday, because once it came she would have to leave and there would be no one to protect Harry from Vinnie – or Mark Chambers.

Since *that* night, Chambers's attempts at avoiding her, and his deep blushes whenever their paths crossed, only strengthened her conviction that he was guilty. She believed that he was only keeping his head down until she left, leaving him free to start on someone else. And, being a natural victim, Harry was the obvious candidate.

She had to tell him. It wasn't fair not to.

'Look, there is something, Harry, but, if I tell you, you can't freak out, and you've got to promise you won't say anything.'

Harry nodded quickly. 'Yeah, course.'

Pulling the pillow closer to her mouth, muffling her words, Sarah told him what had happened.

'You're kidding?' he exclaimed when she finished, his eyes wide with disbelief. 'Mr *Chambers*? But he's really nice.'

'He did it!' she hissed, her mouth drawn into a taut line. 'Don't let the nice words and smiles fool you. He was all smiles *that* night, when he was telling me to be quiet 'cos *Dandi* would hear me!'

Harry shook his head. He believed it because Sarah wouldn't lie – not to him, not about something like this. But he didn't *want* to believe it. He genuinely liked Mark Chambers. Trusted him. But Sarah wouldn't lie. She just wouldn't.

'He had the cheek to say that he wasn't going to report me, when I saw him the next day,' she went on venomously. 'I told him to get lost, and I reckon that's the only reason he's kept his hands to himself since. He was scared I was going to grass him.'

'Why didn't you?'

''Cos I knew I'd get the blame. But that's not the point. I'm only telling you so you can keep away from him. And you'd better tell me if he so much as *looks* at you the wrong way after I've gone!'

'Don't, Sarah.' Harry's chin wobbled. 'I can't stand it when you're angry.'

'Oh, come here!' Pulling him to her, she hugged him tightly. 'I'm not angry with you, I'm just worried about you. Vinnie and them are different. A few punches won't kill you. But . . . *that!*'

With his face concealed in her shoulder, Harry squeezed his eyes tight shut, desperately trying to hold back the tears but failing miserably.

'Oh, Harry, don't cry,' Sarah said, feeling the wetness seeping through her nightdress. 'I shouldn't have said anything.'

'It's not that.' He sniffed loudly. 'I'm just . . . I'm just mad 'cos he hurt you.'

'He didn't,' she assured him. 'Honest to God. I was too drunk. I didn't feel a thing.'

'Yeah, but he still shouldn't have done it.' He wiped his nose on his sleeve. 'You've got to tell Dandi.'

'Why?' Pushing him back, Sarah peered at his wretched face. 'What good will it do? She won't believe me.'

'*I* did,' he reminded her. 'And I think she will too. She knows you wouldn't lie about something like this. Anyway, you've *got* to, in case he does it to someone else.'

Sarah closed her eyes and inhaled deeply. Harry was right, but how was she supposed to broach a subject as terrible as this with Dandi?

'Do it before you go,' he went on firmly. 'Promise.'

Exhaling, she looked at him and nodded. 'Okay, but not yet.'

'You've only got a week.'

'Shit, Harry!' She dropped her face into her hands.

'*When*?'

'Tomorrow. That good enough?'

'Just make sure you do, or I'll have to do it for you.'

Sarah didn't sleep a wink after Harry left. She tried, but it was impossible. Tossing and turning her way to daybreak, she reconciled herself to getting it over with.

Making her way downstairs before breakfast, she burst into the office without knocking, startling Dandi who was working her way through the morning mail.

'I need to talk to you. *Now*!'

Smiling, Dandi motioned her into a chair. 'Sure. Go ahead.'

'I was abused last year, and I want you to do something about it.'

Stunned, Dandi gaped at her, open-mouthed. Of all the things that she had imagined could be bothering Sarah, this hadn't occurred to her at all.

'Are you sure?' she asked, immediately regretting it as the blood drained from Sarah's face.

Leaping to her feet, Sarah yelled, 'I should have known you wouldn't believe me!' Furiously kicking her chair out of the way she headed for the door. 'And you wondered why I wouldn't tell you what was wrong when you kept asking, you stupid bitch!'

'Sarah, wait . . . *Please*. This is important.'

Turning back, Sarah folded her arms and stared angrily out of the window, refusing to meet Dandi's gaze.

'I'm sorry,' Dandi said softly. 'Look, sit down and talk to me. I promise I'll listen.'

Taking a deep breath, Sarah righted the chair and sat down. Now that she'd taken the plunge, she had to stay calm – for Harry's sake, if not her own.

'What happened?' Dandi pressed softly. 'From the beginning.'

Several silent seconds passed before Sarah spoke. Then, keeping her voice as level as possible, she said, 'It was on my birthday last year. I had this run-in with Vinnie and had to get out of the house for a—'

'*Vinnie?*' Dandi interrupted, apologizing when Sarah glared at her.

'I went to the old house in the park,' Sarah continued, her voice thick with suppressed anger and shame. 'I needed somewhere to hide where Vinnie wouldn't find me, 'cos he thought I'd grassed him up about something and he was after me.' Pausing, she seemed to drift away with her thoughts.

'Go on,' Dandi urged, the anger evident in her voice despite her efforts to conceal it. It must have been Vinnie. Just wait till she got her hands on him!

'Yeah, well, I ended up falling asleep. It was late when I woke up and I knew I'd be locked out, so I got a bottle of cider to keep me warm.'

'You didn't have to do that. You should have come home. I would have let you in.'

'You didn't even know I was out.' Sarah raised an accusing eyebrow. 'You'd have had a right go at me the next day if you had, but you never said a word.'

Dandi tried to recall what she'd been doing on the night of Sarah's birthday the previous year. It came to her that she'd had to take Manny Dobbs to hospital and had come back with a migraine, leaving Mark to do the night duty.

'You're right,' she admitted. 'I didn't know. But I'm sure Mr Chambers would have let you in if you'd knocked.'

'Oh, he *did*,' Sarah hissed, her eyes full of venomous accusation. 'Don't suppose he told *you*, though?'

'I'm sure he must have.' Dandi frowned. 'I probably just forgot.'

'Yeah, right! He never told you, and you know it. He *said* he wasn't going to. Said I needn't worry 'cos he wasn't going to *report* me!'

'Well, that *is* against the rules. He shouldn't have let you in after lock-up without telling me, but I imagine he was only trying to save you getting into trouble.'

'Saving himself, more like!'

'Look, you're obviously very angry, Sarah, but I don't think blaming us will help. Just tell me what happened so we can work out what to do about it.'

'I *was*.'

Misunderstanding, Dandi said, 'Yes, and I'm sorry for throwing you off track. Now, you were saying you got a bottle of cider . . . What then?'

'I got drunk,' Sarah said, gritting her teeth. 'And I heard my mum talking, telling me that I'm – you know – bad, and that.' She blushed, ashamed to admit that her mother had managed to belittle her without even being there. 'Anyhow, I got really mad at Vinnie then, thinking how it was all his stupid fault that

I was locked out in the first place. And that's when I decided to break in.'

'You broke *in*? Didn't the alarm go off?'

'No. *He*'d switched it off.'

'Who?'

'*Him*!'

'What are you saying?' Dandi asked quietly.

Narrowing her eyes, Sarah said, 'What do you *think* I'm saying?'

'That Mr Chambers let you in.'

'Let me in, took me to bed, and told me to keep quiet so *you* wouldn't hear, then . . .'

'Oh, Sarah,' Dandi croaked. 'Please be careful. If you're saying what I think you're saying, it's a terribly serious accusation . . .'

'Are you calling me a liar?'

'*No*.' Dandi studied her hands. 'I'm just saying you should be careful. Mr Chambers is a well-liked, highly respected member of staff, who—'

'*Abused* me,' Sarah cut in, folding her arms and thrusting her chin forward.

Dropping her face into her hands, Dandi rubbed at her throbbing temples. Looking up after a moment, she said, 'Are you absolutely sure about this?'

'*No*, I'm doing this for a *laugh*!' Sarah replied sarcastically. 'Of *course* I'm sure! He took me to my room, put me in bed, and got on top of me. I said his name and the bastard even had the nerve to say yeah!'

'Well, I don't know what to say. I really don't.'

'You don't have to *say* anything. I just want to know what you're going to *do* about it.'

'I'll follow procedure, of course. But it's not going to be easy. I don't suppose you've any proof?'

'My word not good enough?'

'I'm afraid not.' Dandi sighed. 'How about witnesses?'

'No.'

'What about the clothes you were wearing? I take it you had *something* on?'

'Oh, yeah,' Sarah snapped. 'But they were all over the place when I woke up. That's how I remembered what had happened. I couldn't figure it out at first, and I had to go over everything in my head real careful.'

'So, you don't actually remember it happening at the time?' Dandi asked, seizing upon Sarah's admission of confusion. 'Don't be offended,' she went on carefully, 'but do you think there's a chance it might just have been a dream? You did say you were drunk, and alcohol does funny things to your mind. I mean, you thought you heard your mother talking even though you *knew* it wasn't possible.'

'So, you'd rather think I was too pissed to think straight than admit what a sleaze *he* is!'

'Not at all.' Dandi shook her head emphatically. 'I'm just trying to cover every possibility. Can I ask why you didn't say anything at the time?'

'I knew you wouldn't believe me.'

'If that's really the case, then why now?'

'Because,' said Sarah, leaning forward to stress her point, 'I'll be out of here in a week, and I want to make sure he can't get to anyone else after I've gone.'

'Oh, Sarah, he wouldn't—'

'Excuse me?'

'I didn't mean . . .' Dandi let the rest of the sentence hang because she didn't actually know what she *had* meant. She only knew that she instinctively didn't believe Mark Chambers capable of doing what Sarah had accused him of. But why would the girl say such a thing if there was no truth to it?

'What are you going to do?' Sarah demanded.

Dandi shook her head, releasing a loud breath. 'I'll speak

to Mr Chambers, of course – get his side. After that . . .'
Pausing, she shrugged. 'It'll be for the Board to decide.'

'And that's it?'

'What more do you want me to do?'

'Make sure he gets what he deserves.' Sarah stood up. 'If
he touches anyone else after I've gone, it'll be your fault!'

Nothing could have prepared Mark for what Dandi had to
say when she summoned him to the office.

'Oh my God!' he gasped, horror stealing the vibrancy from
his voice, leaving it little more than a whisper.

Feeling more awkward than she'd ever felt in her life, Dandi
said, 'You know the procedure from here on in, Mark. It's
not going to be pleasant, but I trust I can count on your full
cooperation?'

'Yes . . . yes, of course. Absolutely.'

'I want to assure you that I'll listen without prejudice to
everything you have to say.'

'Thanks.'

'Right, well, let's start with what happened when you locked
up that night. And please, Mark, for your own sake, leave
nothing out.'

Blushing deeply with the shame of having to admit his
misdemeanour in not having informed her of the situation
at the time, Mark told Dandi the absolute truth – right down
to having the glass of Scotch when he really shouldn't have,
given that he was covering for her at the time.

'And you're sure nothing else happened?' Dandi asked
when he'd finished. 'Nothing that Sarah could have misconstrued in any way?'

'No!' he exclaimed, shocked by the very idea. 'I would
never, *ever* behave like that towards a child. I thought you
knew that?'

Dandi clamped her lips together, preventing herself from

giving the assurance that he was expecting. They both knew that denials in cases such as this were as impossible to accept on face value as the accusation itself.

'So, what happens now?' he asked, understanding her predicament.

'You'll be suspended until the Board has conducted its inquiry. What happens from there will depend on the outcome.'

'I suppose I'll have to leave?'

'For now.' Dandi steeled herself against the tears glistening in his eyes. 'Do you have somewhere to go?'

'My mum's, I suppose. I'll sort something out from there.'

'Will you be all right?'

Mark gave a bitter, mirthless laugh. 'I'll have to be, won't I?'

'You can always call if you need to talk,' Dandi said. 'And you've got my mobile number if you don't want to risk someone else picking up this phone.'

'Oh, shit!' he groaned, dropping his face into his hands. 'I hadn't even *thought* about anyone else. I can just imagine what they'll be saying about me when this comes out.'

'Rest assured I'll put a stop to any gossip,' she said, meaning it. 'You have my word that you'll get a fair hearing.'

'Thanks, Dandi.' Mark rose wearily to his feet. 'I'd best get cracking. I'll let you know when I'm ready to set off.'

'Mark,' she called as he went towards the door. 'May I ask a personal question?'

'Fire away.' He shrugged. 'What could be more personal than asking if I'd do something like *that* to a child?'

'Are you gay?'

'Oh, my God!' He wheeled around, an incredulous look on his face. 'What's *that* got to do with anything?'

'It could make a difference to the Board. Think about it.'

'Oh, no!' He shook his head. 'I'm not getting into that with them.'

'They can't judge you on your sexual preferences, and I think it might help prove that you wouldn't be interested in . . .' Trailing off, Dandi shrugged with her hands.

'Girls?' Mark cocked an eyebrow. 'You don't seriously believe that, do you? Come on, Dandi, let's not be naive. They'd assume I was some sort of pervert. Don't you know that us gays are all twisted little kiddie-fiddlers?'

Holding his gaze steadily, Dandi said, 'Does that include the chairman?'

Mark was about to say something else, but stopped himself as her words sank in. '*Him*?'

'Yes, him. Got a problem with that?'

'What? *No*! Of course not . . . I just had no idea.'

'Really?' She raised an eyebrow. 'I've suspected *you* for a long time.'

'How?' He was horrified. 'I mean, I didn't think it was that obvious.'

'Stop panicking,' Dandi said, sitting back in her chair. 'I was never sure. You're very *manly*. Anyway, I don't actually think it's a major issue. I just wanted to reassure you that it won't prejudice your case.'

'Do the Board know?'

'Nobody's said anything.' She gave a casual shrug. 'Not that it's any of their business. I think it would have been a tad hypocritical, don't you?'

Mark shook his head, finding these revelations a little hard to take in.

'Things are never quite as obvious as they seem, are they?' Dandi went on gently.

'Apparently not.'

'But you still don't think it'd be worth a try?'

'No!' He was adamant. 'Honestly, Dandi, this is bad enough

already without giving anyone the ammunition to turn it into a witch-hunt.'

'Fair enough. But don't forget what I said. Anytime you want to talk.'

'Thanks.' He smiled grimly. 'And will you, um, let me know what's happening? I'd rather find out from you than from anyone else.'

'Of course.'

'Thanks.'

Mark ran straight to his room. Locking the door, he threw himself onto the bed and buried his face in the pillow. He couldn't believe this was happening. He had never in his life so much as *looked* at a child in that way – yet here he was, being accused of molesting one! It was a nightmare.

He racked his brain, desperately trying to remember every word he had said to Sarah that night – hoping to find some sort of clue or explanation as to why she might be saying such awful things about him. But try as he might, he couldn't dredge up anything he'd said that could be misconstrued in any way, shape or form.

He had told her she was pretty, but she couldn't possibly have read anything into that. And yes, as she'd said, he *had* told her to do as she was told and lie down . . . But then he'd left – gone straight to his room.

But *his* knowing this didn't count. It was what the Board believed that mattered. And he hoped to God that they would believe *him*. He loved this job with all his heart, and it would tear him apart to lose it over something that he hadn't even done. With any luck, Sarah would come to her senses and tell them why she'd said it in the first place.

A little heartened by this possibility, Mark started packing. There was no point in delaying the inevitable. The best thing he could do was leave as quietly and with as much dignity as possible. Then wait to be cleared – as he surely would be.

Mark tried to sneak out later that morning, but it was impossible to slip away unseen. Some of the kids noticed him carrying his cases out to his car and were upset at the thought of him leaving. He couldn't tell them anything – could barely even bring himself to say goodbye. He was too upset, too close to breaking down.

After the fifth child had gone to her in tears, and she'd caught snatches of rumours being bandied about, Dandi called a meeting with the Board to decide how best to explain Mark's sudden absence. As there was no way of gauging how long the inquiry would take and, therefore, no knowing how long his suspension would be in effect, they decided to say that he had taken indefinite leave to look after a sick relative. If he were cleared – as Dandi truly believed he would be – he'd be offered the option of coming back. If not, he'd be gone already and it wouldn't be a problem. But until a decision was reached, it was essential that the kids didn't get hold of the real reason. If they did there would be no way for Mark to come back – whatever the outcome.

Later that afternoon, Dandi briefed the staff about the situation and reminded them of their duty to keep their mouths firmly shut. She told Sarah the same thing, urging her to do the adult thing and not spread her story around while the inquiry was ongoing. Sarah agreed, and Dandi prayed that she would be mature enough to honour her word.

That evening, when the kids were gathered for dinner, she made the announcement. Standing in the doorway, wringing her hands, she cleared her throat.

'Mr Chambers left us earlier today and a few of you expressed concern, so I want to clear up any confusion. Contrary to the rumours I've heard throughout the day, he has *not* been sacked for stealing, beating someone up, or any other ridiculous thing you may have heard. He has taken leave to care for an elderly aunt who is rather poorly.'

A little girl raised her hand. 'Is he coming back?'

'Maybe,' Dandi replied. 'It will depend how quickly his aunt recovers.'

'He won't,' Vinnie interrupted loudly. 'His aunt will snuff it and he'll be too busy spending her dosh.'

'Yeah,' Ollie joined in. 'That's why he'll be looking after her. She'll be minted, and he'll be creeping round!'

'That's enough!' Dandi snapped, glaring at the boys. 'Now, I've told you why Mr Chambers has had to leave, and I don't want to hear any more rumours. Is that clear?' Nodding curtly at the murmurs of agreement, she went to the office for a much-needed cigarette.

Vinnie and Ollie had annoyed her, and she was glad that Sarah didn't associate with them. If she told them what was really going on, they'd never let it go and Mark would be damned for ever.

Much as she loved Sarah, Dandi suddenly couldn't wait for the girl's birthday. Once Sarah was gone, things would settle down. Until then, they would all be living on a knife-edge.

———◆◆◆———

S arah woke with a feeling of dread. Brilliant sunlight streamed through the gap in the curtain, but she wouldn't have noticed – or cared – if the weather had been as wet and dismal as it had been on her last birthday. She was too scared at the prospect of leaving to appreciate finally reaching the magical age.

Sixteen.

She'd been mentally preparing for this day for years, but now that it had arrived she wasn't nearly as confident as she'd thought she'd be. The events of the preceding year had taken their toll in numerous ways – not least on her attitude, causing her to stubbornly resist sorting out some fundamentally essential things.

'I don't need your help,' she'd said when Dandi had tried to sit her down and discuss housing arrangements, and jobs, and suchlike. 'I don't need *anybody*'s help.'

And she'd meant it – still did, to a degree. But it wouldn't have hurt to take a little advice. What did she know about organizing that kind of stuff? Squat! Well, she'd just have to learn. Necessity was a great teacher. Thank God she had her savings. They would tide her over until she found a job – although it wouldn't last quite as long as it *would* have if Claire Wilson hadn't screwed everything up and put a premature end to her earnings. Selfish cow!

Throwing the quilt aside, she got up and stood in the centre of the room with her hands on her hips, taking a good long look around. The tears scorched the backs of her eyes as she drank everything in, committing it to memory – the only place where she would ever see it again after today.

Everything was so familiar. The dark blue carpet; the faded pink wallpaper; the window overlooking the path and gardens below; the sticker-covered wardrobe; the cup-ring-scarred dressing table; the bed. She had spent more than half her life here. Nine long years of crying, laughing, singing, dancing, fantasizing, scheming . . .

'Pack it in, you stupid bitch!' Sarah scolded herself, swiping at the tears trickling down her cheeks.

There was no point crying. She was on her own from here on in – and that was *good*. Only herself to answer to, no more shit to deal with, no more past to escape. It wasn't a sad ending – it was a happy new beginning.

Vinnie was loitering in the dining-room doorway, waiting for Sarah to come down to breakfast. He, too, had been dreading this day, because once she was gone, there would be no more opportunities to put things right between them. It was today – or forget it. When she came down, he followed her to her table.

Sitting down, Sarah folded her arms and gave him an unfriendly look. 'Yes?'

Shuffling his feet, Vinnie said, 'I didn't get you a card or anything, but I wanted to say happy birthday.'

'That it?'

'No. I, er, wanted to say sorry, as well.' He pushed his hands deep into his pockets as a blush suffused his cheeks.

'What for?' she demanded, enjoying his discomfort.

'Well, I know I've been a bit of a git.'

'No kidding.'

'Yeah, all *right*. But I'm sorry, yeah? And, I'll, er, miss you.'

'You *what*?' Sarah scoffed. 'Don't talk crap! You can't stand me.'

Vinnie's blush deepened. 'Don't take the piss, Sarah. You knew I fancied you from day one. Why d'y' think I got so pissed off when you wouldn't give me the time of day?'

'That right, is it?' She tipped her head to the side, pursing her lips thoughtfully. 'And do you *still* fancy me?'

'Yeah, course. Loads.'

'Well, how do you fancy doing something for me, then?'

'Anything!' Pulling out a chair, Vinnie sat down, an eager look on his face. 'What do you want me to do?'

Smiling with all the warmth of a snake, Sarah leaned forward. 'Leave Harry Shaw alone.'

Vinnie kissed his teeth. 'What is it with you and that little mong?' he demanded, unable to conceal his irritation that she should be concerned about the ugly runt.

'And stop calling him that!' she snapped. 'He's never done anything to you, so why don't you just lay off him? He's got enough shit to deal with without you sticking your oar in. You want to grow up and start acting like the big man you think you are.'

Vinnie narrowed his eyes and pondered how to turn the situation to his advantage.

'Okay, I'll do you a deal,' he said. 'I'll leave him alone, if *you* stop treating *me* like a piece of walking shit.'

'Stop acting like one, then,' she replied coolly.

'Deal!' He grinned. 'Just give me a chance, Sarah, that's all I want.'

Sarah raised a disbelieving eyebrow. Then, motioning over his shoulder with a glance, she said, 'I think your mate's looking for you.'

Vinnie twisted around in his seat. Pete was waving his hands in a *what-you-doing?* gesture. Flipping him a V, Vinnie turned back to Sarah. It had taken him over a year to get her undivided attention. He wasn't about to let Pete put the mockers on it now.

'Is everything all right?' Dandi asked, flicking a disapproving glance at Vinnie as she wheeled the breakfast trolley up to the table. If he was causing trouble on Sarah's last day, he'd have some explaining to do.

'Fine, thanks.' Sarah smiled, glad of the interruption. 'Did you want me?'

'Erm, yes, actually. Could you come to the office when you've finished?'

'I'll come now if you want.'

Waving her to stay put, Dandi said, 'No, I need to finish up here first. And you should have breakfast. You've got a busy day ahead. Toast?'

'Yeah.'

'Vinnie?'

'Same,' he grunted, slouching down in his seat.

'I wish she'd keep her beak out,' he muttered when she'd served them and gone. 'She gets on me nerves. I feel like smashing her face into a wall . . . BAM! BAM! *BAM*!'

'I thought you were gonna try and be reasonable.' Sarah gave Vinnie a disapproving glare.

'I *am*!' he protested. 'So, uh, what you gonna do when you get out, then?'

'What's it to you?'

'I thought *you* was gonna stop treating me like shit. Deals go both ways, you know.'

'And . . . ?' Sarah snatched up a piece of toast.

Scowling, Vinnie glanced slowly, pointedly, around the room. Letting his gaze linger on Harry, he said, 'Bet there's quite a few people here who'll miss you. *When* did you say you were going?'

Sarah knew exactly what he meant: if she didn't entertain him now, Harry would pay when she left.

Gritting her teeth, forcing herself to be civil, she said, 'I didn't, but it'll be in the next hour or so, I should think.'

Vinnie gave a slight nod. 'That's better. Nowt wrong with being friendly, is there? So,' he settled back in his seat, 'have you got a flat and a job sorted yet?'

'No. I'm hoping that's why Dandi wants to see me.'

'You'll be all right,' he said, adding knowingly: 'With all the money you made grafting.'

Sarah almost choked on her toast. 'What you talking about?' she squawked. 'I don't graft!'

Vinnie gave an amused snort. 'Don't lie, I *saw* you. But don't worry, I never said owt – not even to Pete.'

'What do you mean, *saw* me?'

'I followed you,' he admitted, shrugging casually.

'You *what?*'

'Only once, when I first got here. You were being a right bitch and I wanted to see where you kept sneaking off to. I thought you had a fella, or something.'

'And what if I *did?*'

'I'd have smacked him one!'

Sarah was disgusted. 'It'd be nothing to do with you! And where do you get off stalking me?'

'I wasn't!' Vinnie retorted indignantly. 'I had a *right* to find out what you were up to – the way *you* were going on, acting like you were too good for me. I'm not some fuckin' sicko, like you're making out.'

'*Course* not!' she muttered sarcastically.

Vinnie cursed himself for winding her up. He was supposed to be winning her over, not starting a fight.

'So, how come you stopped?' he asked, smiling now, trying to get back on track. 'Grafting, I mean. You must've been making a shit-load. You're good,' he added admiringly. 'I'll give you that.'

Sarah ignored the backhanded compliment. She was too

busy wondering what *else* he'd seen when he *wasn't* stalking her. He knew that she'd been shoplifting, and that she'd stopped. Did he also know about her savings? Was that why he was talking to her now? Distracting her while one of his lackeys raided her stash.

Glancing across to Pete's table, she did a headcount: Pete, Ollie, Rob – they were all there. And Ade and Jimmy were at their own table – obviously still out of favour. But who knew the extent of Vinnie's influence? He could have got anybody to do it for him – one of the girls, even.

'What's up?' He frowned, turning to see what she was looking at.

'Er, Dandi's gone,' she said, standing up, desperate to go and check her room. 'I'd best go and find out what she wanted me for.'

Vinnie realized that his opportunity to say what he'd meant to say was almost gone. 'Just wait a few minutes,' he said. 'I wanted to ask you something.'

'I can't.' Sarah edged her way around the table. 'I've got to get on, or I'll get nothing done.'

'Please,' he urged, grabbing her hand. 'Just two minutes . . . *One*! One minute, an' I swear I'll leave the mong alone for good!'

Sighing, she slid her hand from his grasp and sat back down. 'All right, but hurry up. I've got loads to do.'

Vinnie shifted in his seat, unable for a moment to meet her impatient gaze. 'Um, I, er, wanted to know if we could kick it sometime?' he managed at last. 'When you're set up, and that. We could go for a burger, or something?'

Sarah groaned internally. How was she supposed to get out of this? If she refused outright he'd get annoyed and Harry would cop for it when she was gone. But if she said yes, he'd expect her to come through, and Harry would cop for it when she didn't. And she couldn't, because Vinnie was too much of a snapper.

'Will you?' he asked, taking her hesitance as a positive sign. 'I swear I'll lay off him if you say yeah. Sarah . . . ?'

'I – I can't, Vinnie.' She smiled regretfully. 'Not 'cos I don't like you. I do – honest. But you're – well, you're younger than me.'

'Only a year,' he countered. 'Anyhow, I look older. No one would know.'

'I would.'

'Yeah, but that don't count.' He flapped his hand dismissively.

Sarah drew her head back. So her opinion didn't count, and he thought it was perfectly reasonable to say so. Was there no end to his ignorance?

'Look, I'll think about it.' She stood up. 'But I've got to go now.'

'Promise?' Standing himself, Vinnie looked down at her hopefully. ''Cos I'll keep to my side if you keep to yours.'

But not if I don't, she thought.

'I will, but it might take a while. I'll have a lot to do before I even *think* about going out. You're not gonna get narky and do something stupid if you've got to wait, are you?'

Vinnie gave her a disarmingly handsome smile. 'Look, as long as I know you're not gonna try and blag your way out of it, I'll wait. You get to be good at that in these places.'

Sarah felt a sudden tug of sympathy for him. He wouldn't be here if he hadn't known pain and rejection in his life. Nodding, she said, 'Yeah, I know. I'll see you later.'

'The sooner the better,' he said. Then, holding his hands up at her look of alarm: 'Chill! I can be very patient when I need to be.'

Sarah ran to her bedroom and checked her stash. She was relieved – and more than a little surprised – to find that it hadn't been touched. Making her way back down to the office, she wondered if she hadn't misjudged Vinnie. All right, so he was an aggressive lout who was more than capable of causing a fight in a convent. And he'd made poor Harry's life an absolute misery – although that should stop now, if he were true to his word; which she imagined he would be given how desperately he seemed to want to get into her good books. But surely he wasn't all bad? He *was* good-looking, and he *did* look a lot older than he actually was, which would help if they did go for that burger – not that she'd decided, but she might have no choice if she wanted to ensure Harry's safety.

An idea began to form in Sarah's mind.

Vinnie fancied her, had said he'd lay off Harry if she went out with him. If she played him right, she might actually be able to persuade him to *protect* Harry. It'd be a twist, but if she kept him sweet enough he might just go for it.

But how could she keep him sweet without getting involved with him? He wasn't the type to play platonic. He'd want to go all the way, and she didn't think she could do that – not even for Harry.

No! Vinnie could smile as charmingly as he liked, it wasn't going to get him anywhere. She had more sense than to go weak at the knees over a bad boy like some stupid little tart.

The kind of stupid little tart that Mark Chambers had obviously mistaken her for.

Which reminded her . . . That was probably one of the things Dandi wanted to discuss: the results of the inquiry.

With any luck, there'd be nothing *to* discuss because the Board would have done the right thing and sacked the bastard.

Dandi smiled when Sarah entered the office. But it was not a happy smile and Sarah sensed the things they were about to discuss were not going to be to her liking.

'What did they say?' Sitting down, she folded her arms defensively, preparing for the worst.

Frowning, Dandi scooped together the papers strewn across her desk and stacked them neatly together. Looking up at last, she shook her head.

'I'm sorry, Sarah, you left it too long. I did warn you this would probably happen.'

'Is he coming back?' Sarah demanded icily.

Dandi shifted uncomfortably in her seat. 'I can't discuss that with you, Sarah. It's an official decision. Nothing to do with you.'

'It's *everything* to do with me. It's me he laid his filthy hands on.'

'Sarah, *please* . . . you're making this very difficult.'

'Oh, *sorry*, I didn't realize I was supposed to make it *easy*. Maybe I should've just got up this morning and pissed off without making a fuss?'

'Don't be silly.'

'What, then?' Sarah slammed her hand down on the desk. 'Come on, Dandi. What am I supposed to do? Walk away and forget all about it?'

'No, of course not.'

'So you're admitting I *have* got something to remember, then?'

'I'm not saying that.' Dandi felt as if she were being backed into a corner. Damned if she did – damned if she didn't.

'So you *don't* believe me.' Sneering, Sarah rose to her feet and stalked towards the door. 'Thanks for nothing, Dandi!'

'Sarah, wait. We've still got things to discuss.'

Turning, Sarah shook her head. 'You've said more than enough already. I just want to get out of here and never come back.'

'Well, I'm sorry you feel like that,' Dandi murmured. 'I understand you're angry right now, but—'

'I'm not angry,' Sarah interrupted. 'I'm mad! Really, really mad!'

'Okay . . . but we still have things to sort out. We've got an appointment with the housing project later this morning, and the careers adviser this afternoon.'

'I'm not going anywhere with you. I'll sort myself out.'

'I *have* to go with you. You have to have representation. The best you could hope for if you try to go it alone is a place in a homeless hostel, and even that might take a while.'

'So? I'd rather sleep on the streets than let you help me. And you know me well enough to know that I won't change my mind.'

Sick with regret at having to leave it like this, Dandi opened her drawer and took out an envelope. 'You'll need this, then.'

'What is it?' Sarah eyed it suspiciously. 'If it's *money*, you can stick it. You're not buying *me* off. Or are you trying to set me up for counselling?' she went on bitterly. ''Cos if you are, you can stick that as well. There's nothing wrong with *me*. It's *him* you should be worrying about.'

Dandi shook her head. 'It's details of the appointments – times, names and addresses. If you're determined to go it alone, tell them to ring me for a recommendation. It might help.'

Still Sarah didn't move. Dandi sighed heavily.

'You definitely *will* need your bank account details. Your grant has already been paid in. Your card and PIN number are in here.'

'I don't want it.'

'But it's yours. Everyone gets it when they leave. It's nothing to do with me. It's direct from the government. *Take* it.'

After a stubborn pause, Sarah marched back to the desk. Snatching the envelope she gave the contents a quick scan.

'I'm only trying to help,' Dandi murmured guiltily. 'I do care about you, Sarah – whatever you might think.'

'Just tell me one thing,' Sarah demanded. 'Did they even bother asking *him* about it?'

'Of course they did,' Dandi assured her. 'But look at it from their point of view. You had no witnesses, no actual proof, and you waited a year before saying a word – *a year*, Sarah! And he denied it – *adamantly*, I might add.'

'Like he was gonna admit it.'

'Beside the point. Simply put, it was your word against his. And given that there's absolutely no evidence to support your claim, the Board had no option but to close the matter.'

'Well, that's it, then,' Sarah murmured, the fight draining from her.

Reaching into the drawer again, Dandi took out the small box she had placed there earlier. It was little compensation, she knew, but she refused to allow Sarah's birthday to go by giftless. She slid it across the desk.

'It isn't much, but I want you to have it.' She couldn't bring herself to add 'Happy birthday', for there was nothing happy about this situation.

Sarah eyed it with contempt. 'Is that supposed to make up for betraying me?'

'I'm not *betraying* you. This isn't how I wanted things to turn out, you know? I know I'll never be your mother, but I hoped we'd at least be *friends*.'

'It isn't gonna happen.'

Dandi nodded sadly. She'd have liked to have been able to put things right, but she couldn't give Sarah what she wanted and say that she believed her.

Nor could she tell her that, although the Board had directed that Mark should be reinstated, they had also ordered Dandi to keep an eye on him. They weren't stupid, but neither was Sarah. Armed with the knowledge that they had doubts, she would demand that they should explain why they were putting the kids in danger by letting him stay – and she'd kick up a stink the size of Manchester when, inevitably, they refused. The publicity would be terrible, maybe even resulting in Starlight's closure. And that was something Dandi couldn't even contemplate.

'If it's any consolation,' she said. 'I want you to know that I won't let *anyone* hurt the children in my care. If you think I've failed you, then I can't apologize enough. But nothing is going to happen to anyone else – I *promise* you!'

'Talk is cheap, Dandi.'

'You have my *word*.'

Sarah looked at her for a long, silent moment before saying, 'I know you'll do your best.'

'Yes, I will. Now, will you take this?' Standing, Dandi picked up the box and carried it around the desk.

Reaching for it, Sarah looked into the eyes of the only woman who'd ever even *tried* being a mother to her. Seeing the tears swimming there, she felt the sting behind her own.

'Thanks,' she murmured, blinking rapidly as she gazed down at the box. Carefully removing the wrapping paper she lifted the lid. Inside was a tiny gold crucifix on a long, delicate chain.

'I had the priest bless it,' Dandi told her, blushing and shrugging at the same time. 'I know you're not religious, but . . . well, *I* still subscribe.'

Dipping her face to hide her tears, Sarah said, 'Thanks, Dandi – for *everything*.' Then, turning, she rushed from the room.

Sarah had composed herself by the time Harry crept into her room twenty minutes later. Sitting on the bed, he watched as she packed her rucksack, his face a picture of pure misery, his skinny chest rising and falling.

'Something to say?' she asked, moving him aside to get at a couple of T-shirts.

'I want to come with you,' he blurted out.

'Well, you can't. There's no way they'd let you, so there's no point getting your hopes up.'

'We don't have to tell them. I'll slip out when no one's watching. I wouldn't be any bother. *Please*, Sarah . . . I don't want to stay here without you. I'll get hammered.'

'No, you won't.' Smiling sadly, she ruffled his hair. 'I've had a word with Vinnie and he's promised to lay off you.'

'Yeah, right!' He snorted disbelievingly. 'Why would he do that for you? He can't stand you.'

'*Wrong*.' She rolled her eyes. 'He's just told me he fancies me, actually. And he said he'd leave you alone if I went out with him.'

'*Ugh*!'

'My sentiments exactly, but if it keeps him off your back . . .' She shrugged.

'You won't, though, will you?' Harry was horrified at the prospect. 'It wouldn't stop the others.'

'He's the one I'm most worried about,' Sarah told him. 'If any of the others start, just kick, bite, punch – anything! Just go for it like the little loony I know you can be! Right?'

Harry's face was so pale when he looked up at her, wordlessly pleading with her not to leave him, that she felt a tug at her heart. The poor little sod had nothing going for him, and now she was abandoning him. Sitting down, she took his icy hand in hers.

'Look, I'll tell you what I'll do. As soon as I've got myself sorted, I'll send you my address and some money and you can come and see me. What d'y' say?'

'Really?'

'Really.'

Harry almost smiled. Then his face began to crumple. Putting an arm around his narrow shoulders, Sarah hugged him to her.

'Aw, don't,' she moaned. 'You'll have me at it again if you start.'

'*Please* let me come,' he sobbed. 'I hate it here. No one likes me. Everyone's always taking the mick!'

'Take no notice.' Sarah gritted her teeth. 'Not one of 'em's as good-looking as you're gonna be when you grow up. And that's what's up with them, you know – they're jealous!'

'No, they're not!' He grinned bashfully. 'Who'd want to look like me?'

'*I* think you're cute, and don't you forget it!' Giving him a last squeeze, she stood up. 'Right! Let's get this finished so I can get out of here. Pass us my box.'

Sniffing loudly, blinking back his tears, Harry slid his hand beneath the mattress and brought out the box only *he* had ever been trusted enough to see.

'How about when I'm older?' he asked, passing it across. 'Or how about adopting me? Well, foster, anyhow. You could do that, couldn't you?'

Sighing, Sarah slipped the box into the rucksack. 'Don't talk daft. There's no way they'd let me take you on at my age. You know what they're like round here for *doing the right thing*.'

Giggling at her spot-on impersonation of Dandi, Harry did a not so good one of his own. 'You ain't goin' nowhere, Mongo! *No* one gets out of here alive, so get them trainers scrubbed, and give that toilet a licking so I can have a nice clean crap!'

Recognizing it as Vinnie – despite it sounding more like Fagin – Sarah didn't laugh. Instead, frowning, she said quietly, 'You won't wind him up, will you, Harry? I'll try to keep him dangling till he loses interest, but you're gonna have to do your bit.'

Serious now, Harry nodded. 'I'll try, but you know what he's like. He'll find *something* to do me for if he feels like having a go.'

Sighing, Sarah fastened the clasp on the rucksack. Slipping her jacket on, she hoisted the bag onto her shoulder and looked around. 'Well, that's it.'

Fear flitted across Harry's face like the shadow of an eclipse. 'I don't want you to go!' he cried.

'I've got no choice, kiddo.' Leaning down, she gave him a quick hug. 'I'm a big girl now.'

He stared up at her, his mouth flapping wordlessly, unable to say the words he longed to say: that he loved her, and couldn't bear the thought of a single day going by without seeing her face. He was too scared of the revulsion that he was sure he would see in her eyes.

'I'll miss you, you snotty little slug!' Sarah smiled as she backed towards the door, praying that she wouldn't break down. 'Don't forget to look out for my letter. Soon as I've got somewhere, you'll be first to know. Here, by the way . . .' Reaching into her pocket she pulled out her cigarettes and tossed them onto the bed.

Making a hasty escape, she ran all the way down the stairs and out of the door, only stopping when she reached the gates. Pausing to take one last look back at the house, she headed off down the road.

Harry stayed in Sarah's room long after she had gone – lying on the bed, crying, her pillow clutched to his face so that he could breathe in the sweet scent of her hair.

What was he going to do without her? She was his rock, his salvation – his reason for living and breathing. All he had left was the promise of a letter. And much as he wanted to believe that she would fulfil it, he knew deep in his heart that the contact would soon fizzle out and he'd have nothing but memories.

He tensed when the door slowly opened.

'She's gone, then?' It was Vinnie.

Sitting up, Harry looked at his long-time tormentor nervously, waiting for the scorn at the sorry state of his swollen, red-eyed, shiny-nosed face. It didn't come.

Vinnie was looking around, his gaze lingering on all the empty places where Sarah's belongings had been. He'd known this room so well when she'd been here, had sneaked in on numerous occasions when she'd been out and the coast had been clear. It had given him satisfaction to know that no matter how much she avoided him he could always be near her – touching her things, feeling her presence in her absence. Now she was gone, it would never be the same again.

Harry watched the emotions flitting across Vinnie's face and it gave him a start. Vinnie really felt something for Sarah – he had to or he wouldn't be standing here now, just feet away from Harry but making no move towards him.

'When did she go?' Vinnie asked suddenly, looking at Harry for the first time. 'Did she say anything?'

Harry shook his head, his eyes betraying the fear twisting his guts that Vinnie would take it out on him because she had left without saying goodbye. But Vinnie wasn't even thinking about laying into him. He just wanted to know if he would ever see Sarah again.

'Didn't she say if she was coming back to see Dandi?' he asked, slipping his hands into his pockets, embarrassed to be exposing his heart by begging the kid for information.

'No,' Harry murmured truthfully. Sarah wouldn't come back to see Dandi – he was sure of that. But there was no way he was letting on that she'd promised to write to him. Vinnie would grab the letter for himself if he knew it was coming.

'You sure about that?'

Harry nodded, his whole body tensing.

'All right.' Vinnie's voice was resigned. 'Make sure you tell me if she gets in touch. Later.' He left then, pulling the door quietly to behind him.

Harry exhaled nervously. He was trembling, his heart thudding violently in his chest. Never in his wildest dreams would he have imagined that Vinnie would honour a promise. But Vinnie had spoken to him as if he were a real person, instead of just calling him nasty names or threatening him.

Still, it wouldn't last. Once Vinnie realized that Sarah didn't want anything to do with him, he would be as bad as ever – if not worse.

Reaching for Sarah's pillow, Harry held it tight against his stomach and rocked himself to and fro, praying that he would have the strength to survive when the beatings started up again.

12

---•◆•---

S arah walked into Withington Village, using the twenty minutes that it took to clear her head and plan her next move. She would start as she meant to go on – independently. No one but herself was ever going to take credit for her future successes, and to make sure no one was under any illusions to the contrary she dropped the envelope Dandi had given her into the nearest bin. If they checked with the bank, they'd know that she hadn't touched the account. Just as they would know that she hadn't gone begging for housing, or for help to get a job.

Buying cigarettes, a local paper and a pen, she went to a café and got a pot of tea. Sitting in a secluded corner, she studied the ads. An hour and three cups later, she had circled nineteen – eleven flats to let, and eight job vacancies. Ringing them all from the payphone on the wall beside the toilets, she arranged to see seven flats that day and set up three job interviews for the following week.

Shrugging the rucksack onto her shoulder, Sarah strolled to the bus stop with high hopes. This was going to be so easy.

The first flat wasn't a flat at all. It was just a room in a shared house in a run-down street in the worst part of Longsight. The stench of neglect hit Sarah before she reached the front door, and the woman who answered reeked of it. But, worse, she didn't even flinch when the malnourished-looking baby slung over her shoulder puked down the back of her dress.

Disgusted, Sarah didn't bother going inside. Without a word, she just turned on her heel and stalked away with her head held high. She was desperate – but not *that* desperate!

The next place was a slight improvement. At least it *was* a flat – but that was the only good thing about it. It was on the fifteenth floor of a high-rise on the outskirts of Hulme, and the lift was out of action – its door wedged open by a gang of teenagers. They didn't do anything, but she could feel them watching as she climbed the piss-stinking stairs. Out of sight, she took her knife from the rucksack and held it in her pocket in case they came after her.

The flat was dirty, smelly, and inhabited, the tenant having forgotten to mention that it was a council property he was subletting – illegally – without actually moving out.

Storming back down the stairs, Sarah was glad to find that the gang had gone. Not for herself – for them. The mood she was in right then, she might have done one of them a serious damage if they'd tried anything.

She spent the rest of the afternoon taking long bus journeys to Wythenshawe, Salford and, finally, Stretford, only to find that the rest of the flats were just as unsuitable. The Stretford one was nice and clean, but yet again it was only a room with shared facilities. And the landlady – in residence – had a list of rules and regulations so detailed and rigid that even Dandi would have been proud to put her name to it.

Thoroughly disappointed, her head throbbing, her feet on fire, Sarah went in search of a phone-box to re-call the last number on her list – much as she'd rather not.

The ad had said: 'Property to let, call Mr Gilbert on blah-di-blah.' Mr Gilbert had elaborated a little, telling her that it was a self-contained flat within a shared house. Her hopes had risen at this, but they'd immediately dropped when he'd gone on to say it was in Whalley Range – just a ten-minute walk from Moss Side.

She was just as reluctant to view it now, but her options were severely limited. If it didn't work out, she could always find herself a nice park bench and try again tomorrow.

Calling Mr Gilbert again, Sarah agreed to meet him outside the Megabowl in the White City shopping arcade at five. He would drive her over to see the flat from there.

It was four-thirty when Mark arrived at Starlight. Pulling into his old parking space at the side of the house, he forced himself to wipe the huge smirk off his face before going inside.

Dandi had rung earlier that afternoon to tell him that the coast was clear, and to assure him that the kids knew nothing about Sarah's allegation. But he knew from experience that they wouldn't let on even if they knew the whole story, and he wanted to gauge their reaction for himself. The worst thing he could do was walk in grinning like an idiot when every child in the place knew what he was supposed to have done and hated his guts.

Relieved to find the hallway empty, he went to the office, took a deep breath and tapped on the door.

'Come in,' Dandi called.

Mark almost cried out with delight – her voice was such a warm, welcome sound after a week of his mother's sniping and moaning. Throwing the door open, he rushed inside like an excited little boy.

Smiling broadly, Dandi came around the desk to greet him with a hug. 'It's lovely to have you back.'

'Fantastic to *be* back,' he said, squeezing her tight and lifting her feet right off the floor. 'You don't know how much I've missed the place – and *you*, of course. You wouldn't believe how stressful it's been living with my mum again! That woman could make a saint blaspheme!'

Chuckling as she disentangled herself, Dandi said, 'Sit down. I'll make coffee and we can catch up.'

'Oh, let *me*!' Mark almost ran to get to the kettle before her. 'It'll be great making a brew for someone who appreciates it. My mum says I don't leave teabags in long enough, and I stir coffee the wrong way round. How mad is that? It's too weak, too strong, too dark, too light . . . Honest to God, Dandi, if you hadn't called me, she'd be drinking rat poison tonight!'

'Good job I did then,' she chuckled. 'Can I take it you've decided to move back permanently, then?'

'Hell, yeah!' he yelped. 'I never wanted to leave in the first place.' A shadow flitted across his face. Turning fully around, he leaned back against the ledge. 'Was Sarah all right when you told her I was coming back? Didn't ruin her birthday, did it?'

Smiling grimly, Dandi said, 'It didn't exactly go with a bang, I must admit. But don't blame yourself. She'll get over it.'

Nodding, Mark finished making the coffee in silence. Handing Dandi's to her, he sat down.

'I don't blame myself, you know. Not for that, anyway, because I know I didn't do anything wrong. I just feel so sorry for her. She must have been going through hell, carrying that around in her head day and night. All that time I thought she was annoyed with me for rushing out on her when she was drunk – I wish I'd just confronted her now. At least if I'd known what she was thinking, I might have been able to help her.'

Dandi shook her head. 'Nice thought, but I doubt it would have achieved anything positive.'

Sighing, Mark said, 'I know. But it's all I've been thinking about while I've been gone. I just wanted to tell her that I'd never *dream* of doing something like that. I mean, I've always really liked her. Respected her, even. She's such a lovely-looking girl, but she doesn't flaunt herself. She's got – I don't know – something about her.'

'She has that,' Dandi agreed. 'And I'm sure she'll go far

if she puts her mind to it. We'll just have to wait and see.'

Picking up her cup, she took a sip and sighed blissfully. 'Oh, Lord, I've missed this! Welcome back, Mark.'

Harry didn't know what to do with himself. He'd have stayed curled up on Sarah's bed all day and night if Dandi hadn't kicked him out – gently but firmly telling him to get his backside downstairs for something to eat before he made himself sick. He had sneaked back in just a few minutes ago, only to find the bed stripped and the furniture covered over in preparation for redecorating. Knowing that there was nothing left for him there, he'd gone back to his own room, but Ollie had told him to get lost.

Going down to the TV room, he bumped into Vinnie and Pete. The breath caught in his throat as he waited for a dig, a threat – a shove, at least. But nothing came. Instead, Vinnie gave him the tiniest of nods and pushed Pete up the stairs.

It took a moment for Harry to regain the use of his legs. He was shaking all over. He didn't trust this new laying-off business. At least before, he'd known exactly what was coming and when. Now, he wouldn't be able to relax as he waited for things to revert to normal.

Sitting on the couch, Harry stared at the images flickering across the TV screen. But it was impossible to concentrate. Giving up after a few minutes, he wandered into the hall, intending to ask Dandi if she needed any jobs doing – anything to fill the void. Just as he was about to knock on the office door, however, he heard laughter and muffled voices coming from within and decided against it. He didn't want to disturb her if she had company.

His heart skipped a beat at a creak on the landing above. It was probably Vinnie and Pete coming back to let him know they'd only been playing with his head and were ready to resume the torment. He *could* tell them that the anticipation was worse than the actual act, but he doubted they'd understand.

Dashing outside, he ran head-down around the corner and dived into the dense bushes. Forcing his way through, he sat with his back against the wall and lit one of the cigarettes that Sarah had left him.

He cocked his head when he heard footsteps crunching across the gravel a minute later.

'Just fetching my cases . . .' Mark's voice rang out. 'Won't be a minute!'

Harry felt sick. What was *he* doing here?

Dimping the cigarette, he positioned himself so that he could see the parking lot clearly. Mark was just feet away, his back to Harry as he opened the boot of his car and hefted two suitcases out. Harry was inflamed with rage. He had liked this man once, but the bastard had done something really, *really* bad to Sarah. And now she was gone, and *he* was moving back in. It wasn't right!

Mark's mobile phone trilled. Bringing it out of his pocket, he answered it as he dropped the boot lid down with a heavy clunk.

'Yo? . . . Oh, *hi*, Sean! When did you get back?'

Harry slunk further down as Mark turned and leaned against the car. He was laughing now and Harry wanted to smash his face in. Looking down, he searched the soil beneath his feet for stones. He'd teach the bastard to laugh. See if he still found everything so funny when he had a few rocks raining down on his head!

Spying a sharp point of slate protruding from the earth beneath the bush, Harry dug it out. It was a nice thick piece – too large to waste on a throw. Waiting patiently, he gripped it as if it were a knife – wishing it were, so that he could catch the bastard unawares and slice his dirty dick off!

'Yeah, I know,' Mark was saying now, '*really* good . . . My boss has been brilliant. She's been behind me all the way. I told you about her, didn't I? . . . Yeah! I couldn't believe it myself!' Another laugh. 'Anyway, best go – don't want to look like I'm taking the mick on my first day back. Will I see you later?' Coy now. 'Great! See you at eight, then. Bye-ee.'

Infuriated by the blitheness of Mark's tone when Sarah's world had been completely destroyed, Harry hawked up in his throat and aimed the spit at Mark's grinning face, but it hit the branch in front of his own face instead and slithered down onto his thigh like a foamy yellow bush-worm.

Using the piece of slate to flick it off, Harry waited until Mark had picked up his cases and carried them around to the front door. Then, slipping out of his hiding place, he scuttled across to the metallic-blue Peugeot and, starting at the headlight end of the wing, scratched an enormous gouge into the paintwork, using both hands to drag the slate point along to the rear bumper.

Flinging his tool back into the bush when he'd finished, Harry stepped back to view his handiwork, smiling with justified pride.

One-nil to Sarah! And there would be more to come. Plenty more!

It was almost six before Mr Gilbert pulled up outside the Megabowl. Sarah had been about to give up and leave, and she was short with him when he rolled his window down and asked if she were Miss Mullen.

'Yeah!' she snapped, folding her arms, her nostrils flaring with annoyance. 'And you're late!'

Indicating with a jerk of his head for her to come around to the passenger side, Mr Gilbert said, 'There was a pile-up outside the Arndale. I've been sitting in a massive queue waiting for the police to let me past. Still, I'm here now. Let's get you over to the flat, shall we?'

Climbing in, too tired and footsore to argue, Sarah shivered as the warm air from the vents enveloped her. Sighing, she leaned her head back against the soft leather headrest and closed her eyes.

The drive took ten minutes, and Mr Gilbert spent the entire time telling her how desirable an area Whalley Range had become in recent years, and how lucky she was to get a flat there.

The reality was quite a shock.

It wasn't Whalley Range at all. It was Moss Side. Immediately facing Alexandra Park's east side, to be exact – just *two* minutes from Sarah's former home on the sprawling estate facing the west side.

With a sinking heart, Sarah followed as Mr Gilbert kicked a path through the rubbish-cluttered front yard and mounted the concrete steps leading up to the door of the three-storey Victorian house. Selecting a key from a large bunch, he opened up and stepped aside to let her enter.

The hall was dark and narrow and smelled of damp and – Sarah wrinkled her nose – *dog shit*? An old fridge stood behind the door, its own door hanging off the hinges. Several bicycles leaned against the stained walls – most missing their front wheels, some just their seats. A long-defunct motorbike engine sat atop a spread of oil-stained newspapers. And the fitted carpet might once have been plush, but was now black and shiny from years of feet tramping in dirt.

There were three doors along the passage, two with Yale locks, the third, standing open, that of a kitchen. Sarah shuddered to see that it was as rubbish-packed and filthy as the hall. She was glad she wouldn't have to use that. Mr Gilbert had assured her that her flat was self-contained. If he'd lied about *that* as well, there'd be murder!

'Two down, three up,' he was telling her, waving her to follow as he set off up the stairs. 'Yours is at the top, but you won't mind the stairs. There's one empty in the middle, but we're having a bit of work done on that. All the other tenants are male, by the way.' He smiled back at her over his shoulder. 'You'll be all right if you ever want anything heavy moving, but remember to keep your door locked. Pretty girl like you, you don't want to be giving anyone ideas.'

Sarah didn't say anything. If he was trying to convince her of the merits of living here, he wasn't doing too good a job of it.

The 'self-contained flat' was an attic split into four plaster-board compartments: tiny bedroom and bathroom, miniscule kitchenette, and a shoebox living room – *kiddie's*-size shoes. Each compartment was shrouded in a layer of dust so thick that it looked as if it had been spray-painted grey. And the furniture – what she could see of it – was gross.

'All right, isn't it?' Mr Gilbert enthused, using the edge of the grey net to smudge a hole in the grime coating the window. 'Bit mucky, but you'll soon have it spick and span. Nice and quiet. And you can't *buy* a view like that.'

Sarah had already decided to take it. It was a dump, but it was better than everything else she'd seen. And it was definitely a solo affair – no hidden flatmates, or landladies with rules about what time to be in at night, when to eat, when to use the bathroom . . . And dirty as it was, she was so tired right now that she could happily lie on the dust-coated mattress and sleep for a week.

'I'll take it.' She cut into Mr Gilbert's gushing hard-sell routine.

'Have you ever signed a tenancy agreement before?' he asked, grinning as he took the contract from his pocket.

'No. I've only come out of the – er, I've just left home.'

'Ah, well, don't worry, it's very straightforward. You'll

love it. It's great having no one but yourself to answer to.'
Unfolding the paper as he spoke, he laid it in front of her on
the table and held out a pen.

Signing quickly, Sarah asked when she could move in.

'That's what I like to see,' he said, repocketing the form. 'A
decisive woman. You're a rare creature, my love. It's yours as
of now.'

Taking three keys from the bunch, he handed them to her
and pointed each one out: main door, her door, fire escape.

'That's the only one for the fire escape, incidentally,' he
warned. 'And the other tenants must be granted access in an
emergency, so I'd work out some sort of strategy with them
from the off, if I was you – save them kicking your door
in if the place goes up. Not that it will, of course. We had
an inspection a short while back. I take it you'll be claiming
Housing Benefit?'

Sarah gazed at him blankly. She hadn't even thought about
benefits; didn't know the first thing about making claims. She
didn't even remember Dandi mentioning it.

'Are you working?' Mr Gilbert asked, taking matters into
his own hands in a desire to speed things along.

'Not yet. But I *will* be.'

'Job Seeker's Allowance?'

She shook her head. 'No.'

'I can't see you having any problem. Just go to the Job
Centre in the morning and sign on. They'll help you fill the
forms out. I'll sort the Housing Benefit.'

She gave him a tired smile of gratitude. 'Thanks, but if you
don't mind I'd rather pay. Like I said, I'm going to get a job,
and I want to be straight from the off.'

'No problem.' Mr Gilbert smiled approvingly. 'It's seventy-
five a week.'

'Fine. What do you want now?'

'Just a month for now. I usually take the same as a deposit, but I'm sure I can trust you not to run out on me. You'd be hard pushed to find anything else as nice as this in a hurry.'

Smiling, Sarah reached into her rucksack, opened the box and brought out a wad of money. Counting out three hundred, she gave it to Mr Gilbert who handed her a rent book in return.

'Right, I'll leave you to familiarize yourself with your new home. You've got my number if you need me.'

Showing him out, Sarah locked the door and leaned back against it. Looking around with a frown of disappointment, she released a weary breath. It was a shit pit! But, pit or palace, it was hers.

She set about exploring and soon had a shopping list in mind – mainly cleaning products. She had a list of complaints, too – starting with the fridge, which was warmer than the flat and stank to high heaven. A tentative look in the tiny freezer compartment had revealed a black, shrivelled *something* stuck to the back wall – something very nasty that looked like a petrified human hand!

Taking out some money for the shopping, Sarah looked for somewhere safe to stash the rest. She decided on the filthy cooker's equally filthy grill-pan. If all the other tenants were male, the cooker was the last place they'd look.

Mark stood beside Dandi in the TV room doorway, his arms folded, a frown darkening his good looks. He was annoyed beyond belief about his car. The garage had quoted nine-fifty to repair the gouge and do a respray. Reluctant to lose his no-claims bonus, he would have no choice but to stump up. He had a cat in hell's chance of making the culprit cough up.

He knew for a fact that it was one of the kids because it had definitely happened here. He'd filled up at the garage around the corner before coming back and the petrol cap was on the side that was now damaged. He would have noticed if anything had been wrong.

'That car is Mr Chambers's personal property,' Dandi was saying, her voice cold as she glared at the kids. 'He takes a great deal of care with it, and what for? So that one of you can come along and do this senseless, spiteful, *criminal* thing to it?' Pausing, she placed her hands on her hips and looked slowly around the room. 'I won't rest until I find out who did it, but in the meantime, you will all lose one month's allowance.'

Holding up her hands to forestall the storm of protests, she said, 'I'm sure those of you who are innocent won't begrudge missing out on a few sweets in order to help Mr Chambers cover his repair costs. And the guilty party—' she looked pointedly from Vinnie to Pete to Ollie '—can think themselves lucky not to be standing in front of a magistrate right now!'

'What you looking at me for?' Vinnie demanded indignantly.

'I'm looking at all of you equally,' Dandi replied. 'But feel free to speak out if you know who's responsible. That goes for all of you.' She turned to include the others now. 'If you know who did it, come and tell me and I will reconsider my decision.'

'That's bull!' Ollie objected belligerently. 'He probably done it himself in a rush to cash his aunt's will! He ain't the best driver in the world, is he?'

'Nah, man,' Vinnie agreed, smirking maliciously. 'I've seen him. He's crap. And why should *we* pay for his mistakes when he's got all that money?'

'What are you talking about?' Mark demanded.

Pulling him aside, Dandi whispered, 'I, er, forgot to tell you . . . We had to explain your absence, so we said you'd gone on leave to look after a sick aunt.'

Rolling his eyes, Mark shook his head. 'So now they think I'm loaded?'

'Sorry. It was the best we could think of at the time.'

Mark chewed this over, then nodded. 'Better than them knowing what was really going on. Shame it isn't true, mind. I could do with a nice big inheritance about now.'

Almost smiling, Dandi composed herself and turned back to the kids.

'As a further punishment there'll be no TV tonight, so switch it off, whoever's nearest, and you can all go to your rooms and clean up, do any outstanding homework, read, or whatever. Off you go.'

'Man!' Vinnie grumbled, heading up the stairs. 'The one time it's got nothing to do with me, and I get stuck for it anyhow!'

'It's your face,' Pete quipped. 'You look like a thug.'

'Better that than an arse-bandit like you!' Vinnie retorted, smirking. 'Here, watch this,' he whispered then.

Reaching the top of the stairs, he wheeled on Ollie and grabbed him by the throat, forcing him to jut precariously out over the handrail.

'It was you, wasn't it? You fucked up the man's car and let the rest of us cop for it, *didn't* you?'

Squealing with fright, Ollie clutched at the rail. 'It weren't me!' he spluttered, terror sending his voice into girly pitch. 'Honest, Vin, it weren't! I swear on me ma's life!'

Increasing his grip, Vinnie thrust his face to within kiss-of-death range of Ollie's. 'You hate your ma, you wanker, so why am I gonna believe that?'

'On me dirty mags, then!' Ollie gargled around the crushing constriction in his throat. 'I swear on them I never done it!'

Letting go, Vinnie stepped back. 'Why didn't you just say that in the *first* place? Would have saved you a choking, 'cos I *know* how much you love them magazines.'

Dashing up the last step, Ollie leaned against the solid support of the wall and clutched at his throat.

'Fucking hell, Vin. I thought you was gonna do me in then.'

Throwing a mock punch that whizzed just a fraction of an inch past Ollie's nose, making him screw up his face in anticipation, Vinnie laughed.

'Now why would I do that when you're innocent?'

Ollie laughed, unsure of the seriousness of the threat, but desperate to believe it was a game despite the palpable air of menace emanating from his hero.

'Good 'un, Vin,' he said, his tone creepy and toadying. 'You had me going there, mate!'

Shaking his head, Vinnie hawked up and spat on the carpet. 'Clean that up before Dandi sees it and fines us all!' He slapped Ollie's cheek none too gently. Turning his back, he set off down the corridor, jerking his head for Pete to follow.

Harry came up the stairs just as Ollie pulled the sleeve of his sweatshirt down and began to wipe up Vinnie's mess. For a moment he felt bad for having caused all this trouble, but then Ollie glanced up at him, a look of pure hatred on his face, and the guilt was gone.

'What *you* gawping at?' Ollie snarled. 'Shift your gimpy arse before I make you *lick* it up!'

Keeping his mouth shut, Harry strolled away without looking back. Another revelation. Not only had Vinnie turned on Ollie, he'd obviously warned him to leave Harry alone as well. There was no other explanation for Ollie making a threat without seeing it through. Things were definitely looking up. And while he wasn't stupid enough to believe that his good fortune would last, he intended to enjoy it while it did.

*   *   *

'Did you see the little wuss?' Pete laughed, kicking the bedroom door shut. 'Shit himself, good-style!'

Smirking, Vinnie said, 'It's about time he had a slap-down. Thinks he's some sort of hard man just 'cos he hangs out with us.'

'You gonna give him a kicking?'

'Soon.' Vinnie threw himself onto his bed. 'Might keep him dangling for a bit, though. It's kind of cool having a slave.'

'Tight get!' Pete snorted. Reaching for his cigarettes, he lit one for himself and threw one to Vinnie. Leaning across the gap to give him a light, he said, 'How come you're laying off Mongo?'

Blowing a smoke ring, Vinnie narrowed his eyes. ''Cos.'

''Cos what?'

''Cos of something someone said.'

'Like what?'

'Like none of your business, so shut it!'

'I don't get that, man. Since when has it bothered you what anyone says?'

'I said *shut* it,' Vinnie snapped. 'And hurry up and get the light off.'

Pete did as he was told and stumbled back to bed in the dark. He knew a warning when he heard one. Somebody had obviously got to Vinnie – and it didn't take a genius to work out who. Sarah Mullen.

What Pete couldn't work out was why she had such a hold on Vinnie? She'd treated him lower than dog dirt the whole time he'd been here. Yes, she'd talked to him this morning – let him sit at her table, even. But that didn't mean much when you considered that she'd taken off straight after without so much as a 'See you in hell, sucker'.

Still, whatever had gone down between them, Vinnie must have his reasons for doing what he was doing. And Pete wasn't about to piss him off by questioning him about it.

*   *   *

It was fully dark by the time Sarah finished shopping. Hurrying along the road towards the house, she glanced around her, nervous of the ominous shadows in the park to her left and the rustling noises coming from the hedges and gateways to her right.

Making her way up the path, breathing a sigh of relief that she was safely back home, she had just pulled the keys from her pocket when the door was wrenched open and a pack of savage-looking dogs hurtled out and surrounded her.

Dropping the bags, she stood stock-still as they rammed their drawn-back snouts against her legs, their eyes flashing crazily in the dim light. She was terrified that they would take chunks out of her if she moved, but they were obviously waiting for the go-ahead from the man who followed them out seconds later.

'Back off, you stupid cunts!' he yelled, kicking out at them indiscriminately. 'Back off! *NOW!*' Turning to Sarah when the last dog had scarpered to the safety of the yard, he scowled at her. 'What d'y' want?'

Irritated by his rudeness, Sarah waved her keys at him. 'I live here.'

Narrowing his eyes, the man gave her the once-over, then set off down the steps, whistling his mutts to heel as he headed into the park.

'Nice to meet you, too,' she muttered, retrieving her bags and going inside, slamming the door behind her.

The second door along the hall creaked open and an unkempt head appeared, the sliver of face visible through the strands of rat's-tail hair gaunt and unshaven, the eyes sunken and bruised-looking.

'Who are you? How'd you get in?'

Sarah gritted her teeth. 'I *live* here,' she said. 'Top flat.'

'Oh, right,' the apparition grunted, eyeing her suspiciously.

'Well, you'd best give Dave a knock.' He nodded towards the first door. 'His dogs will have you if you don't warn him.'

'I've already had the pleasure,' she muttered, starting up the stairs.

'Hang about.' Coming out into the passage the gaunt-faced man peered up through the stair-rails. 'You haven't got a spare fag, have you, only I've run out and me giro's been nicked.'

Rolling her eyes, Sarah took out her cigarettes and tossed one down.

'Thanks, love. Don't suppose you could make it two, though, could you? Only me mate's on a comedown and he's feeling a bit rough. Smack,' he explained, rolling his eyes as if he never touched it himself. 'Don't dabble yourself, do you?'

'No!' she snapped, offended that he could think she was a junkie. She threw him another three smokes.

'Sorter,' he grinned, picking them up. 'I'll pay you back when me giro comes. It's John, by the way.'

'Sarah,' she said, wondering why she was bothering. She was hardly going to become *friends* with the slum scum.

'Later.' Waving the cigarettes, John scuttled back into his flat.

'Oh, for God's sake!' Sarah muttered, continuing on up the stairs. 'What the hell am I *doing* here?'

Hours of scrubbing and cleaning later, Sarah finally crawled into bed. She was exhausted, but the instant her head hit the pillow, the dogs started barking down below. And once they got going, they didn't stop. They were at it all night and everything seemed to set them off, from a floorboard creaking to someone coughing or rolling over in bed, to someone daring to walk within a hundred yards of the house, to some distant dog annoying its own neighbours . . .

She finally drifted off at three, her mind full of plots to kill Dave and his hounds.

Vinnie was wide awake. Staring into the darkness as Pete's snores rattled the glass in the window, he wondered what Sarah was doing right now.

Was she lying in bed thinking about him? He'd bet his life she was. How could she not be? There was such a strong pull between them. A magnetic force – pulling them together even as it pushed them apart.

He just had to keep his cool with Mongo – no matter how much he despised the little creep – and not give Sarah any reason to delay the inevitable. She'd better not take too long getting in touch, though. He could out-patience the best of them, but she'd sure as hell better make it worth his while when she did come through!

13

———◆———

Sarah was beginning to feel desperate. She'd been independent for a month now, but nothing was going right. She still didn't have a job, and her housemates were driving her mad – especially the damn dogs with their incessant barking. She had hoped it was her strange presence that was sparking them off, and that they would settle down when they got used to her. But they didn't.

They were an absolute pain, and ciggy-scrounging John was a nuisance best avoided, but Tony, in the flat immediately below hers, was a nightmare. Sarah still hadn't seen him, but she'd sure as hell *heard* him. Every night at ten he would turn on his hi-fi and play heavy-metal music into the small hours. Her floor shook with the thudding bass, and her head throbbed with the screeching guitars, but no matter how many times she hammered on his door to ask him to turn it down, he never answered.

Just as Mr Gilbert never answered his phone. He didn't even come around to collect the weekly rent, sending a huge, menacing-looking man to collect on his behalf. She'd tried passing messages through this goon, but he either didn't deliver them or Mr Gilbert ignored them. Either way, Sarah couldn't reach him to make complaints, and had no choice but to put up with the men down below, the faulty fridge, the sockets that threatened to electrocute her whenever she plugged anything in, the wildly fluctuating water temperatures – scalding one day, freezing the next . . . The list was endless.

And each night was worse than the last, knowing that the days ahead would leave her drained and frustrated as she traipsed from one interview to the next with ever-decreasing hopes of finding steady work.

Jobs, Sarah had discovered, were not easy to find – not decent ones, anyway, when she had no qualifications and nobody to reference her but a worker in a care home. It was amazing how quickly interviewers lost interest when they learned these few facts, and she soon learned the value of truth-juggling.

With her money frittering away, she was seriously contemplating shoplifting again as a means of surviving when she finally got lucky and landed a job as a receptionist in a massage parlour on a dingy back street in Ancoats. It was off cards and she'd be working nights, but she didn't care. The pay was good, and they would send a taxi to pick her up each night and drop her off again in the morning. It was perfect.

As long as they never discovered that she had lied about her age.

The first thing Sarah would do when she had earned enough was find somewhere decent to live and move out of the hell-hole house. Free of the depressing gloom, she would really come into her own and show what she was made of. Then, when she could be really proud of her achievements, she would write to Harry and invite him round for the promised visit.

14

Six months passed before Sarah knew it. She was so busy that she barely had time to think, let alone keep track of the date.

She loved working at Silva's. It was so different from how she'd imagined a massage parlour would be. Much more businesslike and classy.

The reception area was subtly lit, with a curved desk, two black-leather couches, a complimentary coffee machine, and a private side room where the clients could watch a constantly updated range of imported hard-core porn while they waited for the masseuse of their choice.

Six women worked a shift, each of them qualified in legitimate massage techniques and scrupulously clean – certifiably so. Self-employed, they hired the rooms and equipment for a set fee, then set their own rates for whatever 'work' they undertook above and beyond the house menu.

Sarah was in awe of them all. They were so self-assured and sophisticated, with their own flats, expensive cars, and real diamonds. She'd expected junkie prostitutes, but there were no dark roots and greasy ponytails here.

She particularly liked Jenny – the receptionist she'd been hired to assist. At thirty-two, Jenny was a lot older, but she had the vivacity of a teenager and chattered to Sarah as if she'd known her for years. And, dizzy as she made herself out to be, she knew the business back to front and inside out, and wasn't in the least bit precious about sharing her knowledge.

Sarah surprised herself with the ease with which she mastered the computer system. And to think that she'd been told she was a hopeless case at school! It was amazing what a little patience could achieve. Jenny only needed to explain things once for her to grasp it.

The clients were nothing like she had expected. She'd thought there would be an endless stream of perverts and freaks but, apart from the inevitable drunks who managed to gain entry – only to find themselves swiftly ejected at the first hint of trouble by the two huge bouncers who stood guard outside the door – the majority of the men were respectable, well-to-do businessmen. Often married, they came for the assurance of discretion and high-quality service, and they were more than happy to include Sarah and Jenny in their gratitude, leaving some very generous tips.

Jenny had taken Sarah into town after her first night and treated her to a burger-bar breakfast. It became a ritual, one that they both enjoyed as it gave them a chance to gossip about their workmates – particularly the manager, Gaynor, whom they both hated, and the owner, Bernie Silva, whom they both liked.

Bernie was the main reason Sarah enjoyed working there. In his thirties, he was tall, suave, and incredibly good-looking, with slick black hair, perfect teeth, sexy blue eyes, and the softest velvety voice. He always took time to chat to her when he dropped by, complimenting her on her appearance and noticing if she'd done anything to her hair or changed her make-up.

She didn't mention her crush to Jenny. She was really nice, but she had told Sarah everything about the other girls, and Sarah was afraid that she would relay whatever Sarah told her to them and make her look stupid. Which was why she fabricated a normal childhood when Jenny asked about her life. Ashamed of the truth, she explained the absence of her family by saying that her mother had remarried and moved to Wales.

Fortunately, Jenny never delved too deeply. Spending so much time at work, or sleeping in preparation for her next shift, she rarely got the chance to unburden herself and took full advantage of the fact that Sarah was such a good listener. Sarah didn't mind. She found Jenny's life history fascinating, and thought that the tales of her witch-bitch interfering mother and the saga of her own never-ending search for Mr Right were hilarious.

The only dark cloud on Sarah's bright new horizon was guilt that she still hadn't written to Harry. And then there was Vinnie. Since she hadn't been in touch to fulfil her side of their bargain, would he have started picking on Harry again?

It was fear of this that finally forced her to make the time to write.

Harry had never given up hope. Each morning, he would get up early and wait for the post, sometimes amusing himself by damaging Chambers's car, sometimes just kicking gravel. Taking the envelopes from the postman, he would rifle through them, then deliver them to the office and get on with the day as best he could when he invariably didn't find one for him.

When it finally came, he almost didn't believe it was his name he was reading. Stuffing it under his sweater, he ran inside and tossed the rest of the mail onto Dandi's desk. Then he raced upstairs to his bedroom, sidestepping Ollie who was on his way to the bathroom.

Dear Harry,

Babe, I'm so sorry for taking this long to write. I hope you're not too pissed off to read it.

Well, I got my flat – like you couldn't guess from the

address! It's a dump, but it's okay for now. Give me a bit
more time and we'll make plans for you to come round. Not
yet, though, because I'm working nearly all the time.

Yeah! I got a job, and it's ace. I'm a receptionist at a
massage parlour in town. I work with a woman called
Jenny – she's really nice. We book men in for massages
and that – but don't you dare tell anyone, or they'll think
I'm a prozzy, or something!

Everyone's great at work, but you should see the boss. He's
well fit! His name's Bernie, and he's got black hair like mine,
real sexy eyes, and the most gorgeous smile you've ever seen
in your life. Anyway, I'll tell you more when I see you.

Well, that's it for now. Use the tenner I've put in and get
some stamps to write back. Save some for coming to see me,
'cos I'm missing you like mad.

Loads of love,
Sarah
xxx
PS – If Vinnie's picking on you again, just tell him I'll
get in touch with him soon.

The tears were streaming down Harry's cheeks when he
reached the end. She *did* still care! She hadn't forgotten him.
He should have known she wouldn't.

But he had been right about her getting a new life. She was
having loads of fun, and he was jealous. Not of what she'd
achieved – of the people she was hanging out with. Jenny, her
new friend, and this Bernie man – Harry hated him already.

Wiping his eyes, he forced the resentment away. He should
be happy that Sarah had a place to live, and a good job. It
could have been a lot worse. She could have been sleeping
rough, or anything.

Memorizing the address, he rolled the letter up and stashed
it inside one of the pairs of socks at the back of his drawer.

No one would find it there, and he'd be able to take it out whenever he was alone and reread it.

Hearing footsteps outside, he slammed the drawer shut and sat on the bed with an innocent look on his face. Seconds later, Dandi came in.

'Come to the office, Harry,' she said, her face unsmiling. 'There's something I need to discuss with you.'

Following her down the stairs, Harry was apprehensive. Someone must have seen him taking the letter. Dandi probably thought he'd stolen it.

Mark Chambers was in the office. Harry's eyes narrowed when he saw him and his mouth drew into a tight line.

Waving Harry inside, Dandi told him to sit down. Standing over him then, arms folded, she said, 'I've heard some rather disturbing news about you, Harry, but I thought I'd give you a chance to explain yourself before making a judgement.'

Harry folded his own arms. It had to be the letter.

'Well?' Dandi said. 'I'm waiting.'

'It was mine,' he muttered.

'What was?' She frowned, not at all sure what he was talking about.

'The letter. It's got my name on it, so it's mine. I didn't have to tell you if I didn't want to.'

'I don't know anything about a letter. I was talking about Mr Chambers's car.'

Harry's head jerked back defiantly. 'What about his stupid car?'

'I saw you,' Mark said quietly. 'This morning.'

Harry didn't reply. He just stared straight ahead, his mouth drawn so tight that it looked like the knot in the neck of a balloon.

Gazing at the livid little face, Mark felt a tug of regret for having had to report him. But he'd seen him with his own eyes, and if he didn't say anything they would never get to the bottom of what was making the boy behave so oddly.

'Did you hear Mr Chambers?' Dandi said when Harry didn't answer. 'He said he *saw* you, Harry – slashing his tyre.'

Impossibly, Harry's lips tightened even more, but still he refused to answer.

Pulling a chair up beside him, Dandi sat down and tried a different tack. 'Look, you were seen, so there's no point denying it. But Mr Chambers and I have talked it over, and we don't believe this is something you would do.'

Snorting softly, Harry turned his head slightly so that he could no longer see her concerned face out of the corner of his eye. Were they stupid, or something? How could it *not* be him if he'd been seen?

'We think somebody is making you do these things,' Mark joined in. 'You're far too intelligent to do something like this without reason. Is there anything you'd like to tell us?'

No reply.

Dandi decided that the direct approach might be best. She and Mark had discussed the situation fully and had both come to the same conclusion. It was worth a shot.

'Is Vinnie putting pressure on you?' she asked. 'Has he been making you damage the car?'

'We'd understand if that's what it is,' Mark added. 'And I wouldn't blame you – you do know that, don't you? I know you're not a bad boy, and I'd be quite prepared to let the matter drop if you'd only tell us the truth.'

Harry's heart was hammering in his chest. He felt sick. Trapped. If they accused Vinnie of putting him up to this, Vinnie would know who had made them lose their allowances – whose fault it was that Dandi had extended the curfew and put the blocks on late-night TV on Saturdays. And once he knew, the tenuous ceasefire would be over. Harry would be dead!

'It was nothing to do with Vinnie,' he muttered, his voice so low that Dandi and Mark had to lean closer to hear him. 'It was me – all of it. Nobody told me to do it, and nobody knows anything about it.'

Mark's brow creased with disbelief. 'But why? Don't you realize how much it's been costing me to repair it? Don't you feel at all bad about what you've done?'

'No!' Harry turned to look at him, his eyes shooting sparks of pure hatred. 'I don't feel bad about *any* of it, because I *hate* you, and if I knew how to cut brakes, I'd do that, too!'

'Harry!' Dandi was stunned. She had never witnessed such vehemence from a child before. And from Harry Shaw, of all people. 'What on Earth's got into you? There's no reason for this sort of nastiness. It's absolutely intolerable! Have you nothing to say for yourself?'

Mark reached out and touched her arm. He wasn't convinced that this was as simple as Harry was making out. In fact, they should have expected this kind of reaction. Of course Harry wasn't going to admit Vinnie's part in this – he'd probably been warned what would happen if he did. He'd be a very strange child indeed if he weren't petrified. Thugs like Vinnie made a religion out of terrorizing the Harrys of the world.

'I want you to know,' he told Harry, 'that I don't believe this is your doing, and I won't hold it against you. We've always got along pretty well, and I'm sure you didn't mean what you just said. But, while I understand your reluctance to tell us the truth – and I do understand, believe me – I just want to know that you won't do it again. This will go no further, but it has to stop – *now*.'

Harry glared at him. Sarah had been right about him. He *was* all smiles when it suited him – all nicey-nicey words and understanding. But why, when he now knew that it was Harry who had been wrecking his car? Why wasn't he annoyed about it like Dandi? That was the natural reaction, so why was Chambers being so reasonable? Because he felt guilty! He knew exactly why Harry had done it, and he was trying to butter him up by letting him off the hook.

'Are we agreed?' Dandi asked. 'It stops now, and nothing more will be said about it.'

Harry shrugged, staring straight ahead again. They could think what they liked. He'd stop when he was good and ready. In fact, it might actually be more fun to put them off the scent – leave the car alone and start on something else. He'd have to think about it.

'Okay,' Dandi sighed. 'You can go, Harry. Breakfast will be ready by now.'

Getting up, Harry strolled to the door. Just as he got there, Dandi called, 'By the way, what was that about a letter?'

Tensing, he cursed himself for having mentioned it.

'Nothing,' he said. 'Just something from a friend.'

'Which friend?'

'Sarah,' he muttered grudgingly.

Dandi and Mark exchanged a surprised glance as the pieces simultaneously fell into place for them both. Neither had realized that Sarah and Harry had been friends – never mind close enough to *write* to each other. No wonder Harry had been behaving so badly. Sarah must have told him about the imaginary attack.

'Come back,' Dandi said wearily. 'I think we need to talk.'

Letting out an exasperated breath, Harry came back to his seat and slumped down, folding his arms against the denials he knew would come.

'Look,' Dandi began quietly, 'I think we all know what's going on here. Has Sarah been talking to you about something she thinks happened to her?'

Harry gave a contemptuous snort.

'This is really important.' Mark's eyes were dark with

sincerity as he peered into Harry's stubborn face. 'You need to know the truth – not for my sake, for yours. This is obviously distressing you a great deal if it's causing you to do the things you've been doing. You *do* know what we're talking about, don't you?'

'Yeah,' Harry spat. 'It's about *you* hurting Sarah and getting away with it!'

Choosing his words carefully, Mark said, 'Do you really believe that, Harry? Can you honestly say you think I'd do something bad to anyone?'

'I *know* you did.' Harry gritted his teeth. 'Sarah told me, and *she*'s not a liar.'

'We're not saying that she is,' Dandi said, holding up her hand when Harry turned to her with an incredulous look on his face. 'Let me finish . . . We're not saying she's lying, but she *is* wrong. Something probably did happen to her and, for whatever reason, she thought it was Mr Chambers who'd done it.'

'But I didn't,' Mark insisted. 'Believe me, Harry. I never laid a finger on her.'

'Liar!' Harry hissed. 'She *told* me.'

'I love Sarah dearly,' Dandi told him gently. 'She's a very special girl who I've known for a very long time. But, while I agree that she wouldn't *lie* about something like this, I do think she made a mistake. She'd been drinking that night, you see,' she went on, careful not to sound too condemnatory, 'and the alcohol twisted everything up in her mind. Now, I know this because we had a long talk and there were certain things she said that made no sense. She's going to feel terrible when she remembers what really happened. How much worse will she feel when she finds out what you've been doing? It'll just add to the guilt. Do you understand what I'm saying?'

Harry didn't answer. He couldn't. It sounded too reasonable – too *possible*. But he wouldn't betray Sarah by admitting that – he just wouldn't!

'I think you know in your heart that Dandi is right,' Mark said now. 'Neither of us blames Sarah. We care about her and feel sorry that things worked out the way they did. But she's got to come to terms with things in her own way, however long that takes. All *we* can do is wait, and be ready to talk if she ever wants to.'

'Can I go now?' Harry was perilously close to tears.

'Do you understand what we've said?' Dandi asked. 'And can we trust you to give Sarah the time she needs to sort this out, without making things worse by spreading rumours that will ultimately hurt her?'

Swiping at his runny nose, Harry leaped to his feet. 'He's already done that!' He pointed an accusing finger at Mark. '*He*'s the bad one, not her!' He ran to the door then, sobbing loudly as he yanked it open.

'Harry, come back,' Dandi called, going after him as he ran out into the hall. 'We need to sort this out.'

'Leave me alone,' he screamed back over his shoulder. '*He* should have gone and she should have stayed! I *hate* him, and so does Sarah! Just leave me alone or I'll tell everyone what he did!'

'Harry!'

'Let him go,' Mark said, closing the door as Harry raced up the stairs. 'Give him a bit of time to calm down. He's a smart kid. He won't do anything stupid.'

When all was quiet, Vinnie stepped out from the shadow of the grandfather clock standing against the wall beside the dining room.

Peering up the stairs, he squinted thoughtfully, wondering who the 'he' was that Harry had been shouting about. The 'he' who should have gone while Sarah stayed. Had she remembered what had happened and told Harry? If so, Harry had obviously just told Dandi, which meant that the police would be here before too long, and Vinnie would have to make himself scarce.

Glancing around to make sure that no one was watching, he darted across the hall and raced up to Harry's room.

Harry was on his bed, his knees drawn up to his chest, his eyes red from crying.

'Who were you talking about down in the office just now?' Vinnie demanded, his voice low and urgent as he closed the door.

'N-no one,' Harry stuttered, fear making him stumble over the words. 'They were asking me if S-Sarah had been in touch, but I said no.'

'Don't lie to me!' Reaching down, Vinnie grabbed Harry's hair. 'I want to know who you were talking about, and if you don't tell me I'll rip your fucking head off!'

Squealing as Vinnie gave a vicious tug, Harry said, 'It was nothing, Vinnie, honest! I was just shooting my mouth off!'

'About Sarah – yeah, I heard. Now tell me the rest. Were you talking about me?'

'No!' Harry screwed his face up as he felt his scalp separating from his skull.

'*WHO*, THEN?'

'Mr Chambers!' Harry blurted out. 'I was talking about Mr Chambers!'

'You sure about that?'

'Yeah!'

Peering into Harry's eyes, Vinnie instinctively believed him. Letting go of his hair, he said, 'So, what was it about?'

Harry gulped loudly, rubbing at his sore head. He hadn't meant to say anything, but now that he had, maybe it was for the best. Who better to give Chambers what he deserved than Vinnie?

'If I tell you, you've got to promise not to say anything to anyone else.'

Slapping Harry's legs out of the way, Vinnie sat down. 'If it's to do with Sarah, I won't say nothing. I just want to know what's going on. And you'll tell me, if you know what's good for you, 'cos you're not the only one who likes her.'

Harry couldn't dispute that. He'd seen how upset Vinnie had been when she'd left.

'All right,' he said. 'But she made me swear not to tell anyone, so you can't tell Pete or any of that lot.'

'Yeah, yeah!' Vinnie nodded, impatient to hear the rest.

Taking a deep breath, Harry told him everything.

Vinnie didn't say a word. Staring at the floor, he digested the information and turned it over in his mind. Sarah not only believed that Mark Chambers had shagged her that night, she had reported him to Dandi, too. That was why Chambers had gone AWOL just before Sarah had left. And that was why Harry had been systematically damaging Chambers's car since Chambers had come back.

Vinnie couldn't even get angry about the resulting loss of privileges, or the fact that he'd been inevitably blamed for every scratch and dent. Now the fuckers knew that Harry had been doing it, and why, they'd have to drop the punishments – and watch their backs in case Harry blabbed. It was all too perfect for words.

Vinnie needed to think now – to decide how best to turn it to his advantage. He also needed to find Sarah, and it seemed logical that she had kept in touch with the kid, otherwise why would he go to such lengths for her?

'Where is she?' he asked.

'I don't know.' Harry shrugged, the fear returning to his eyes.

Vinnie didn't believe him. But, while it would have been easy to knock the truth out of him, he thought Sarah would appreciate it more if he *eased* it from him instead.

'Look, I know you think you're protecting Sarah but I can

do that better than you. Think about it . . . They're not just gonna sit back and wait for her to drop Chambers in it now you've let them know she's blabbing, are they? They'll go looking for her to shut her up.'

'They wouldn't hurt her,' Harry murmured guiltily. 'Dandi says she's special.'

'She is,' Vinnie agreed slyly. '*We* know that, but they're just saying it to cover their backs.' Pulling his head back, he gave Harry a matey smile. 'Who knows her best, eh? Him who did that shit to her, and that fat-arsed slag that's protecting him, or us? Why d'y' think she brought him back the minute she got rid of Sarah? Don't tell me they're trying to help her, 'cos I'm telling you now that they'll be looking to shut her up. Is that what you want?'

'No!'

'So, help me make sure they can't get to her. Tell me where she is so I can warn her.'

Harry didn't like the way things were going. Vinnie probably *did* want to help her, but would she *want* his help?

'I haven't got all day,' Vinnie was saying now, his voice tight with irritation. 'Give me her address.'

It wasn't a request – it was an order. Backed into a corner, Harry blurted out the first address that came to mind – that of a couple who'd fostered him a couple of years earlier. Vinnie would get really mad when he found out, but Harry would jump off that bridge when he came to it. At least by then he'd have had a chance to warn Sarah. If she did want Vinnie's help, he'd just say that he'd made a mistake and take the other boy to her.

Watching nervously as Vinnie scribbled the address onto the back of his hand, Harry winced when Vinnie reached the hand towards him. But Vinnie just nudged his chin and smiled before leaving.

Alone, Harry made plans. As soon as it was dark, he would

sneak out and warn Sarah what was going on. He just hoped that she didn't get mad at him for stirring things up.

In his own room, Vinnie was making plans of his own. He would sneak out after dark and visit Sarah – put her in the picture and let her know that he was there for her; that he fully intended to take proper care of her as soon as he was officially free of this place.

The important thing was to stay low. If Dandi noticed that Vinnie was missing, she'd have the police after him in a flash. And that was the last thing he needed when he was so close to getting out with a clean record. Sarah wouldn't want the hassle of a 'wanted' boyfriend. If he was to stand a chance with her, he had to play it straight until he was in the clear.

Straight, and heroic. Sorting Chambers would be Vinnie's big gesture. She would be for ever in his debt once he'd punished the bastard for taking advantage of her like that.

Harry sat alone at dinner, his face so pale and troubled that he didn't have to try too hard to convince Dandi that he felt ill.

Feeling partly responsible for stressing him out in the confrontation that morning, she sent him to bed with a cup of cocoa. She would talk to him in the morning, she said – try to clear things up, and help him deal with the whole Sarah misunderstanding.

Harry drank the cocoa. It was cold outside and he would need something warm in his belly. Pulling two jumpers and two pairs of trousers on, he slipped into his winter coat and wrapped his scarf around his neck. Arranging the pillow beneath his quilt to look as if he were sleeping should anyone decide to check on him, he turned off the light and slipped out.

Staying close to the wall, he crept down the back stairs. The kitchen door was ajar and he could hear the clatter of knives and forks going down as dinner came to an end. Peering through the gap, he saw the housekeeper bringing a stack of plates to the sink. When she went back for another lot, he ran through the kitchen and slipped out of the back door, closing it quietly behind him.

Pulling his hood up, he made a head-down dash across the garden, out of the gates and all the way to the bus stop at the end of Wilmslow Road.

Five minutes later, Harry was on the bus headed for Moss Side, praying with all his heart that Sarah would be in when he got there.

15

Sarah got out of the taxi and slammed the door. She begrudged the five-pound fare, but she had spent far too long in town and had little time left to get ready for work. She really needed to get a bath and wash her hair – just in case Bernie decided to pop in.

She was soon to discover that looking less than perfect was the least of her worries.

Rushing inside with her bags, she ignored John when he came out of his door. She avoided him whenever possible these days. He'd had all the free cigarettes he was going to get.

'Sarah,' he called as she started up the stairs. 'Just a minute.'

Something in his voice made her turn around.

'You've got a visitor.' He gestured back towards his flat. 'You were out when he got here, so I took him in. He's been waiting ages.'

'Who?' she asked, frowning.

Holding up a finger, John turned and shouted back into his flat, 'Yo, kid! Come here.'

Sarah almost fell back down the stairs when Harry appeared. Dropping her bags, she ran to him and hugged him tight. Pushing him back after a moment, she gazed at him with concern. 'What are you doing here? What's happened? Are you okay?'

'He's fine, aren't you, Harry?' Grinning fondly, John

reached out to ruffle his hair. 'He was sitting on the steps when I come back. Freezing he was, but he's all right now. I give him a brew and a bit of toast.'

'Thanks,' Sarah murmured gratefully.

'No problem.' John shrugged. 'He's a good lad. We had a nice chat, didn't we, Harry?'

'Yeah.' Harry nodded, grinning. 'He was telling me about the mad dogs.'

'Well, thanks again,' Sarah said. 'I really appreciate it.'

'Any time,' John said. Then, 'I, er don't suppose you've got a couple of ciggies?'

Taking four from her pack, she handed them to him. Then she turned and picked up her bags, saying to Harry, 'Come on, you. Let's get you upstairs and find out what you're up to.'

Harry followed her up to the flat, a broad grin splitting his face.

Letting him in, Sarah dropped her bags and went to run her bath. Coming back, she made tea and sat him down to quiz him.

'So, what's going on?' Lighting a cigarette, she peered at Harry closely. 'And don't say nothing, 'cos this is way too late for a visit. You're gonna get in a pile of trouble for coming out at this time.'

'Don't care,' he muttered, taking the smoke from her fingers and puffing on it. 'Told you I didn't want to stay there without you.'

'You haven't run away?' she groaned. 'Please tell me you haven't?'

'I didn't mean to.' He passed the smoke back. 'But I'm here now, so why don't I just stay? I won't get in the way, or nothing. John was gonna let me kip on his couch if you didn't come back. I can just sleep on yours instead.'

Sighing heavily, Sarah said, 'No, you can't. We've had

this out already, remember. You're too young. There'll be ructions when they find out you're here.'

'But they won't find out,' Harry argued. 'I didn't tell anyone I was coming – not even Vinnie.'

'Vinnie? Oh, no! That's why you've run away, isn't it? He's started on you again, and it's my fault.'

'No, it's not like that. He's been dead good since you went. Honest. He really likes you. He – he just wanted to know where you were so that he could look out for you.'

'What you talking about? Why do I need looking out for?'

Blushing, Harry looked at the cup in his hands and told her what he'd been doing since she left, and what had happened earlier that day.

'You've been wrecking his *car*?' Sarah gasped. 'How could you be so stupid? They could send you to Borstal for that.'

'I don't care,' he muttered unhappily. 'I hate it without you. And I hate *him* most! You should see him, Sarah. Laughing and joking like he's done nothing wrong, and all the kids falling for it. Vinnie's the only one who knows the truth, and he hates him as much as we do.'

'You've told Vinnie? What d'y' do that for, you pillock? He's the last person I wanted to know. He'll *love* that.'

'No, you're wrong. He's really mad about it, I could tell. He wants to protect you.'

'From what? I'm out of there. I never have to see the bastard again.'

'They know you told me,' Harry admitted, blushing again. 'And Vinnie reckons they'll come after you to shut you up. I'm sorry, Sarah, but they were winding me up, going on about how you'd remember what really happened one day and feel terrible about it. And that I'd make it worse, 'cos you'd feel guilty about me smashing up his shitty car as well.'

'And what did *you* say?'

'That I'd tell everyone if they didn't get off my back.'

'Oh, great.' Sarah sighed. 'Well, you know what's going to happen now, don't you? It's *you* they'll be after shutting up. They'll be watching you like a flipping hawk.'

'They didn't do too good a job of it tonight.'

'They'll check your room, you idiot. They've probably got the police out already.'

'They won't know I'm not there yet. I said I was ill and went to bed. Dandi said she'd see me in the morning.'

'Yeah, well, even if you get away with it tonight, I reckon you're on your way out. They're covering for him and you're threatening to blow it. They'll want rid.'

'I don't care!' Harry was defiant. 'I hate them.'

'You're a brat.' Sarah laughed, amused despite the potential seriousness of the situation. 'Honest to God, Harry, you're a brat. What am I gonna do with you?'

'You're letting me stay, then?' He looked up, his face glowing with hope.

'I didn't say that. Anyway, what did you tell Vinnie? 'Cos if you gave him my address he'll lead that lot right to my door.'

Grinning sheepishly, Harry said, 'I gave him a false address.'

'What are you *like*, you crazy little sod! Vinnie will kick off good style when he finds out.'

'He'll have to find us first.'

'*Us?*' She snorted. 'Listen to the little fugitive.' Sighing again, Sarah slapped her hands down on her knees and stood up. 'Right, well, I'm going for a bath. You'd better have a good think while I'm gone, and come up with a sensible solution.'

Giving him a mock-stern look, she went to turn the taps off. Coming back a moment later to change out of her clothes, she found Harry standing in the middle of the room with his hands on his hips and a disapproving frown on his face.

'What are you doing?'

'Figuring out where to start cleaning. It's a tip in here!'

Laughing, she pushed past him and went into the bedroom, calling back over her shoulder, 'If you're trying to persuade me to let you stay by making yourself handy, forget it. You can stay tonight, and that's it. First thing tomorrow, you're going back.'

'Really?' he yelped, running to the bedroom door. Blushing when he saw that she was about to undress, he turned his back. 'Can I really stay?'

'Yes, really. You can have my bed while I'm at work. But I meant what I said – you're going back tomorrow.' Leaning forward, she pushed the door shut.

'Whatever you say,' Harry called through, thinking *Yeah, right!* 'Where's your polish?'

'Kitchen drawer. And you can do the dishes while you're at it. I haven't got round to them in a while, either.'

Twenty minutes later, bathed and dressed, Sarah was sitting cross-legged on the floor, curling her hair. Harry was lying on the couch watching, a rapt expression on his face. Catching sight of him in the mirror that she had propped against the table leg, she said, 'What you staring at?'

'Nothing.' He blushed. 'I, er – do you want a brew?'

'Not enough time.' Unwinding the tongs carefully, Sarah inspected the last ringlet. 'Look at that. Perfect!'

'It's nice,' Harry said, his tone darkened by a sudden pang of jealousy. 'Do you always get dressed up for work?'

'Kind of,' she admitted, grinning bashfully as she pinned some of the curls up. 'I like to look good in case my boss comes in. I told you about him, didn't I?'

'Mmm.'

'Oh, he's gorgeous, Harry. You should see him. He's got these blue eyes that go all crinkly when he smiles.'

'Must be old if he's got wrinkly eyes.'

'I said crinkly, not wringkly. And he's not old. He's only about thirty something.'

'*Really?*'

'You got a problem, snot-rag?'

'No. You've already told me all this in your letter.'

'Didn't go on too much, did I?'

'Kind of.'

'Sorry, babe. But he's gorgeous. Wait till you see him.'

Harry smiled to himself. It was pissing him off that Sarah was gushing over this Bernie, but she was talking as if Harry would be around for a while, and that had to be a good sign. Maybe she was changing her mind about sending him back? He hoped so.

The taxi horn blared down below. Looking at her watch, Sarah frowned. It was early, but never mind. She was ready. Slipping her jacket on, she did a twirl in the middle of the floor.

'How do I look?'

'Nice,' Harry murmured, feeling the tears welling up in his eyes. She didn't look like the Sarah he knew. She looked like a proper woman.

'I do, don't I?' Sarah agreed, stepping back to view herself in the mirror. The dark green dress accentuated her curves and strengthened the luminous green of her eyes. Her lips were glossy and full, and her hair was clipped into place with tiny, sparkly clips, some ringlets loose around her face and some snaking down her back. She looked good, and that made her *feel* good. Leaning down, she kissed Harry's cheek.

'Right, I'm off. Don't forget what I said about keeping the door locked, and make sure your feet don't stink up my sheets. See you in the morning.'

Looking up at the window when she climbed into the taxi a minute later, she saw Harry silhouetted there and felt a twinge of remorse for leaving him on his own. He looked so tiny and vulnerable. But he'd be safe enough. And he could always go to John if anything happened.

For some reason, he had really taken to John, and he had pretty good instincts. But she'd keep her eye on them, nevertheless – make sure that John didn't corrupt him. Harry wasn't stupid, but there was no telling what he'd agree to if his new friend put the pressure on.

Settling back, Sarah cleared her mind and concentrated on what Coxy, her regular driver, was saying as he filled her in on the latest exploits of the girls from Cheetham Hill – his all-time favourite subject.

Ollie went to his room and turned the light on, sneering when he saw Harry huddled beneath his quilt.

Snatching up his dumb-bells, he glared at the lump as he began his nightly exercises, wishing things were back to normal so he could get his exercise from a good old kicking session instead. But Vinnie had put the mockers on that particular activity. Fuck knew why, but Ollie wasn't going to risk getting his own head kicked in for going against him. At the same time, there was no way he was going to bed at *this* time. No way he was going to let his developing muscles turn to mush just because mong-boy wasn't well and wanted the light off!

Dandi popped her head around the door just after he got started. Glancing pointedly at Harry, she put her fingers to her lips before withdrawing. Rolling his eyes, Ollie dropped to the floor and started his push-ups instead.

He couldn't wait till Vinnie got his head sorted. It was just a good job the little git didn't snore! That *would* have pissed him off, having to listen to a racket like that while he was trying to concentrate on his body.

Coxy turned off the Princess Parkway, heading towards

Hulme instead of into town. Leaning forward, Sarah tapped him on the shoulder.

'Er, where are we going?'

'Oh, sorry, didn't I say?' He grinned sheepishly in the rear-view. 'I've just got to nip to my sister's for a minute. I'll be dead quick. I've just got to drop something off. Don't mind, do you?'

'Suppose not.' Sitting back, she looked out of the window. It was a bit of a cheek, doing his errands on Bernie's time, but it was all right, she supposed – as long as he didn't take too long. If he made her late and she got into trouble, she'd kill him.

She shivered when they turned into the Crescents. She hadn't been here since she was a kid and her mother used to bring her along on a score. The huge concrete blocks joined together by steel-railinged walkways had always terrified her. They were so dark and menacing, and the people who lived there looked shady and dangerous.

Pulling into the pitch-dark parking bay between the Iron Duke pub and the back of John Nash Crescent, Coxy killed the engine and opened his door, telling her that he'd be back in a minute.

'Hang about,' she yelped, wrestling with her door. 'I'm not stopping here on my own. I could get mugged, or anything!'

Sighing, Coxy ran a hand through his hair. May wouldn't like it if he took Sarah to her flat, but he couldn't leave her sitting here if she didn't want to. And he'd never forgive himself if anything happened to her.

'All right,' he said. 'But don't say I didn't warn you, 'cos it isn't nice. Our May's a sloppy bitch, and her kids are a load of little bleeders.'

'I don't care,' Sarah said, sticking close to his side as they made their way up to the third floor.

★   ★   ★

May tutted when her brother came into the living room with a tart. What was he playing at? He knew she didn't like strangers in her gaff. He'd best not have told the bitch what he was here for, that was all!

Plucking a cigarette from an open pack on the table, she lit it and squinted up at Sarah through a thick haze of smoke. She looked like one of the hookers her brother ferried about. The lecherous swine was probably after a freebie.

'Before you go getting your knickers in a twist,' Coxy said. 'Sarah's a friend. And she's all right, so stop giving her the evil eye . . . Unless you'd rather I got off? I could always come back when you're in a better mood.'

Grudgingly, May nodded hello. She supposed she could put up with the tart for a couple of minutes if kicking her out meant delaying things.

Sarah smiled nervously, then jumped when something tugged on the back of her dress.

'Get out of it, Leroy!' May leaned forward and swiped at her son, smacking his cheek. 'Keep your hands to yourself, you messy little get! Sorry about that, love,' she said to Sarah then. 'He ain't messed you up, has he?'

Twisting to look down at herself, Sarah saw that she had escaped lightly. The now-crying child had melted chocolate all over its face, but he'd managed not to share it with her. She shook her head, guilty for having got him into trouble.

Rolling his eyes in shame, Coxy told May to get her arse in gear. He had better things to do than stand here all night.

Sarah stayed by the door when they disappeared into the kitchen, nervously eyeing the children who were watching her from various positions around the room. They were like extras in a Gothic horror film: filthy – and none too pleasant on the nose.

'Who're you?' one of the girls demanded, her voice containing the same hardness as her mother's. A battler in the making.

'Sarah. Who are you?'

'Tara,' the girl said, sniffing repeatedly as she looked Sarah up and down.

'Got a cold?'

'Piss off!'

'Charming,' Sarah muttered.

'*Maaaam*!' Tara yelled, shoving one of her little brothers roughly away as he hurled himself at her in defence of the pretty lady. 'This bitch just told me to fuck off!'

Sarah opened her mouth to protest, but there was no need because Tara immediately lost interest when the doorbell rang. Launching herself across the room, she shoved past Sarah and went to answer the door.

'Took your bleeding time, didn't you?' A loud female voice rang through the hall. 'It's freezing out there.'

The voice sounded vaguely familiar, but Sarah couldn't put her finger on where she'd heard it before. Seconds later, she gasped out loud when Claire Wilson walked into the room.

'Claire! What are *you* doing here?'

Claire gave her a suspicious glare, then grinned as recognition sank in, revealing a gap where one of her front teeth had been knocked out. 'Sarah Mullen. Well, well!'

'D'y' know her?' Tara stood between them with her arms folded. 'Where from? What's she doing here?'

'Piss off, you,' Claire barked. 'Don't bother talking to me when you kept me in the cold. Make yourself useful for a change and get the keckle on.'

'Do it yourself,' Tara muttered, retreating to a chair in the corner. 'I ain't your slave.'

'Where's your mam?' Claire asked, throwing herself down onto the couch.

'Wiv Uncle Gaz in the kitchen,' one of the boys told her.

'Nice one,' Claire said, taking a cigarette from the pack on the table.

'They're me mam's,' the boy complained. 'She'll punch your lights out for nickin' one.'

'An' I'll punch yours out if you don't shut your grassing gob,' Claire said, sitting back heavily.

Looking down at her, Sarah realized that Claire was pregnant – again. Standing, with her baggy jumper concealing her belly, she looked as stick-thin, dirty and unhealthy as May and her brood. But when she was sitting, you could see that her stomach was definitely swollen.

'So, what have you been up to?' Claire looked Sarah up and down with undisguised envy. 'You look good, I'll give you that. The grafting must be paying.'

Sarah frowned. Had *everyone* known about that? 'I don't do that any more,' she said.

Smirking disbelievingly, Claire flicked her ash onto her knee and rubbed it in. 'Still at Starshite?'

Perching gingerly on the arm of the couch, Sarah shook her head. 'I left a while back. But never mind me, what happened to you? No one heard a word after you took off.'

'Was they worried?'

'Yeah! Dandi was going off her nut. She saw on the news about the police finding a baby in a bin bag and she *well* thought it was yours. She felt dead guilty for ages.'

'Good!' Claire snarled, her face darkening. 'I wouldn't have lost it if she hadn't tried to send me away.'

Sarah stared back at her open-mouthed. It hadn't crossed her mind that it might have actually been Claire's baby.

'God, Claire, that's awful,' she said. 'What happened?'

Before Claire had a chance to answer, May came out of the

kitchen. Seeing them chatting, she narrowed her eyes. 'You two know each other, or summat?'

'I asked 'em that,' Tara said snidely. 'But Claire told me to fuck off.'

'Why you still here, then?' May snapped, jerking a thumb towards the door. 'Go on – do one, the lot of you!'

'Mam and Claire's havin' a fix,' little Leroy piped up – screaming when he received a sharp kick in the back from Tara.

'Ready?' Coxy asked, anxious to get Sarah out before she heard too much.

'Er, yeah, sure.' She stood up. 'Nice seeing you again, Claire. Hope everything goes all right with this one.' She nodded at the other girl's stomach.

Shrugging, Claire said, 'Yeah, whatever. See you later.'

'Sorry about that,' Coxy apologized as they went back to the car. 'I take it you knew her?'

'Claire?' Sarah murmured, deep in thought. 'Yeah. I've not seen her for ages, though. I thought she was dead, to tell the truth.'

'She goes the right way about it,' he muttered, opening the car door for her. 'Sorry, I know I shouldn't say that seeing as you know her, but she's pure trouble, her. Our May should kick her skanky arse back where it came from, but she's too soft.'

In the dark at the back of the car, Sarah raised an eyebrow. From what she'd seen, May Cox was anything but soft. And she was just as skanky as Claire – if not more so. Her house was a mess, and her kids had foul mouths.

She contemplated giving Dandi a ring to let her know that Claire was all right, but decided against it. It would only stir up trouble – and Claire looked more than capable of doing that all by herself. Anyway, Sarah had enough shit of her own to deal with – like sorting Harry out.

'You're looking nice tonight,' Coxy interrupted her thoughts. 'Got something special planned?'

Smiling as she remembered why she'd made such an effort, Sarah said, 'No, nothing special. Bernie likes us to look decent, that's all.'

Glancing at her in the rear-view, Coxy smiled when he saw the sparkle in her eyes. So, she was into the boss, was she? Well, he couldn't say he was surprised. A lot of the girls held a candle for Bernie Silva. He had money and a flash motor – a regular gold-digger's dream. Not that he would have classed Sarah as one of them. From what he'd seen of her so far, she was a nice girl. A little naive, maybe, but nice, all the same.

Far too nice for the likes of Claire. He wondered what the story was there, but he didn't ask. It was none of his business. He was just surprised that Sarah knew the scummy bitch.

And the same went for his sister. It gave him ulcers thinking about the dregs *she* mixed with. In fact, that was the reason he'd taken to scoring gear for her in the first place – to keep her away from the Billy Normans and Makka Caines of the world. If she insisted on sticking needles into her veins, at least she wouldn't have to touch the poisonous shite that Billy put out.

If he'd known that his sister cut what he gave her and sold it on, using the money to keep herself supplied with Billy's cheaper shit, he'd have killed her with his bare hands.

'Here you are.' Coxy pulled up outside Silva's with minutes to spare. 'Sorry for dragging you into all that. Hope I haven't put a downer on your night.'

'Not at all,' Sarah told him, smiling as she climbed out. 'At least I know Claire's alive. It makes you wonder when someone just disappears like that. Anyway, thanks. I'll see you tomorrow.'

16

Pete was sound asleep by nine – just as Vinnie had planned. Pete couldn't stay awake for more than five minutes in the dark and once asleep nothing roused him. All Vinnie had to do to guarantee a few hours' peace was get into bed and insist on having the light off. It never failed.

And tonight, it was especially important to have his room-mate out of commission. If he was going to see Sarah, the last thing he needed was Pete tagging along. Alone, he'd be out and back in again before anyone realized.

Fully clothed beneath the covers, Vinnie waited for Dandi to complete her rounds. At nine-fifteen she paused outside their room for a few seconds, then continued on her way, reassured by Pete's heavy snoring.

Getting up when he heard her footsteps receding along the landing, Vinnie crept to the window and eased it up. Dandi always looked in on the girls first. She would go downstairs to lock up when she'd finished checking the boys, which meant that he had approximately five minutes before she activated the alarm. If he didn't make it out before that, he was stuck.

Holding a cassette case between his teeth, he cocked his leg over the sill and felt around with his foot for the drainpipe to the left of his window. Manoeuvring his body out, he wedged the window open with the case and climbed down the pipe. Then, staying well out of range of the security light, he darted across to the fence and hauled himself over and out.

Running the two miles into Moss Side, Vinnie had to stop

for a breather when he reached the run-down estate. The house he wanted, according to Harry, was in the middle of a row of six parallel to the imposing side wall of Java-Java – the old cinema-turned-club-turned-local exhibition centre.

It was dark down there, the dim street lamp bent from years of joyriders using it as a brake. Narrowing his eyes, he peered all around before venturing in. He knew these estates. The residents prided themselves on turning them into no-go areas, viewing strangers and the police with equal hostility. You had to keep your wits about you in places like this – or suffer the consequences.

A man was squatting beside the burned-out shell of a car, removing salvageable bits. He whipped his head around at the sound of glass crunching underfoot. Seeing Vinnie, he eyed him with suspicion. Nodding to show he wasn't about to interfere, Vinnie walked on.

Finding the house he wanted, he glanced around to make sure he wasn't being watched, then stepped over the low back wall and ducked into the shadows of a doorless garden shed.

There were several full, rancid-smelling bin bags spilling out of it, and more piled beside the gate. A mangled pram frame lay upended on the scrubby patch of grass, and a pair of child-size roller skates sat on the back step beside a heap of empty, unwashed milk bottles. On the washing line, a small jumper hanging by a single peg flapped listlessly in the breeze.

Vinnie wasn't impressed. If Sarah was here, then she obviously wasn't alone. But had she moved in with some man to play mummy to his kid, or was she lodging with a family? Either way, he would have to suss the situation out before he made any sort of move. The last thing he needed was some jealous boyfriend or irate landlord bringing the pigs down on his head.

He had the don't-give-a-shit attitude down to a fine art

when it came to fronting for the kids at the home, but he rarely stepped out of line when it really counted. He didn't want to go to a lock-down facility. He wasn't completely stupid. There was far more to be gained by being seen to toe the official line – freedom, for example. And you didn't have to be a wuss to stay out of trouble, you just had to keep your head down and not get caught.

He had managed so far. He just hoped he didn't blow it now.

Creeping stealthily towards the house, Vinnie squatted low and inched his way along the wall until he was directly beneath the window. Holding on to the ledge with his fingertips, he raised his head until his eyes were level with the gap at the bottom of the curtains.

The room was bare but for bits of rubbish scattered about the floor. There wasn't so much as a *stick* of furniture.

Getting up, he went to the next window and, using his hands to shield his eyes, peered in through a hanging scrap of net curtain. This was the kitchen, but, apart from a sink unit that was half-ripped from its holdings, it too was bare.

The house was empty, and obviously had been for some time. Harry Shaw had lied.

Starlight was in darkness when Vinnie got back. Climbing the fence, he ran commando-style across the lawn, zigzagging all the way to avoid the security light.

Shinning easily up the drainpipe, he cursed under his breath when he found the window shut. The cassette case was gone. Either Pete had removed it, or it had dropped. Whatever – he was stuck. Raising the window would trigger the alarm. But so what? He'd be safely in bed by the time the staff got moving.

Digging his fingers in beneath the window, Vinnie slid it up

– and was already dragging himself in when the alarm went off. Within seconds, lights were going on all over the house as Mark ran downstairs to check for burglars, and Dandi and Gloria began checking on the kids.

Vinnie was in bed snoring when the door opened and the light came on.

'Whazzup?' he mumbled, squinting at Dandi as if she had woken him.

'Go back to sleep,' she whispered, flicking the light off again. 'The alarm's been triggered, that's all. Nothing to worry about. We'll sort it out.'

Smiling to himself as Dandi pulled the door shut, Vinnie reached for Pete's cigarettes. It was too easy.

'Dandi!' Gloria called in a loud whisper from Ollie and Harry's bedroom doorway down the corridor. 'You'd best take a look at this.'

'What's wrong?' Dandi rushed to her.

Stepping aside, Gloria pointed to Harry's bed. 'I'd bet my life that's a pillow.'

Roused by their voices, Ollie said, 'What's going on? Why's the alarm going off? Is there a fire?'

Ignoring him, Dandi marched across the room and snatched Harry's quilt back. As Gloria had suspected, there was nothing beneath but a pillow.

'Oh, no,' she murmured, her heart sinking into her stomach. 'What's he done?'

'What's the matter?' Sitting up now, Ollie rubbed at his eyes.

Turning to him, Dandi said, 'Did you see him leave?'

'Harry?' Ollie sounded as surprised as he actually was. 'I thought he was asleep.'

Dandi looked at Gloria. Gloria shrugged. 'I thought he was ill.'

'So did I,' Dandi murmured. 'He must have sneaked out after we locked up.'

'He couldn't have,' Ollie said. 'I only went to sleep a bit ago and he never moved.'

'Want me to call the police?' Gloria asked.

'No, I'll do it,' Dandi said, leaving the room. 'But let's finish checking the house first. Something triggered the alarm. My bet is he was hiding somewhere, waiting till he thought everyone was asleep. He's probably still around.'

After a fruitless search of the house and gardens, she gave up and phoned the police.

In the office, fifteen minutes later, Tony West smiled as he accepted a steaming cup of tea from Dandi. It was just what he needed after four freezing hours in the squad car – having the knackers bored off him by his new partner, Bill Vine.

Vine was a pussyfooting fool. Too respectful for his own good, always trying to find the virtue in people that West wouldn't piss on if they combusted under his nose. But now that Kay Porter had succumbed to the temptation of promotion to CID in Crewe, he was stuck with him.

He hadn't thought much of Kay to start with, but she'd proved herself more than capable and, once they'd got each other's measure, they'd made a fair old team – in more ways than one. West didn't blame her for moving on, but he missed her, and Vine was no substitute. Still, time would tell, he supposed. He'd give it six months. If they hadn't come to some sort of understanding in that time, they never would.

Sipping his brew now, he listened as Vine went through the routine questions.

'How old is Harry?'

'Just turned eleven,' Dandi told him.

'Red hair, approximately four-ten, and skinny?'

'That's right. I have his school picture, if you'd like to see it. It's very recent. Just two weeks old, in fact.'

Taking a small photograph from Harry's file, she handed it across. Vine looked at it, taking in the mournful emptiness of the eyes. This was not a happy child.

'Can we take this?'

'Yes, of course.'

Vine handed the photo to West. Looking at it, West immediately felt sorry for the kid, wondering what kind of hell it must be to go through life with a face like that.

'You say he was in a spot of bother this morning?' Vine went on.

Clasping her hands together, Dandi murmured, 'Yes. We had to ask him about a series of mishaps that have been occurring.'

West suppressed a desire to snort out loud. She didn't half waffle on. But did she always speak like this, or was she putting on the airs for their benefit?

'Mishaps?' Vine smiled questioningly. 'Could you elaborate?'

Dandi flicked a glance at Mark. He gave a slight shrug. Neither of them had wanted to turn Harry's recent behaviour into a criminal matter, but the police needed to know what was going on in order to find him as quickly as possible.

'He's been damaging Mr Chambers's car,' she said.

'That's you, is it?' Vine turned to Mark.

'Yes.'

'And he's been damaging your car? In what way, precisely?'

'Several nasty gouges in the paintwork,' Mark said, marking the points off on his finger. 'The windscreen was cracked once, had words scratched into it another time. The radio was ripped out twice and left beside the car, smashed to pieces. Wing mirrors ripped off, causing damage to the holding plates. Exhaust blocked with a potato.'

'And this boy did all that?'

'Mmmm. We weren't sure at first, but I actually saw him slashing a tyre this morning, and when we confronted him he admitted being responsible for the other damage.'

'What punishment did he receive?'

'Well, none, actually. We said we wouldn't take it any further if he promised to stop.'

'And did he?'

'Not exactly, no. He, er, said that if he knew how to cut the brakes, he'd do that, too.'

West perked up. A twisted care-home kid on the rampage. This was more like it!

'Did he say *why* he'd done it?' he cut in. 'I imagine he must have been pretty upset to say something like that?'

Dandi's knuckles whitened. It wasn't lost on West. He peered at her expectantly.

'There was a situation some time ago,' she explained reluctantly. 'Certain allegations were made against Mr Chambers by an ex-resident. Unfortunately, we didn't know that Harry knew about it until this morning. If we had, we'd have taken steps to counsel him.'

'So it's revenge,' West mused. 'He's paying your Mr Chambers back for whatever he did.'

'I didn't *do* anything,' Mark interjected huffily. 'It was all a terrible mistake, and the inquiry exonerated me.'

'Absolutely,' added Dandi, giving Mark a loyal smile.

'Could I ask the nature of the complaint?' Vine asked politely.

'Is this really relevant?' Dandi was reluctant to get into the details. 'Mr Chambers was officially cleared.'

'By us?' West asked.

'No.' Dandi gazed down at her tangled fingers. 'It was never a criminal matter. The board of directors dealt with it internally.'

'And I take it the complainant wasn't too happy with the outcome?'

'You could say that.'

'I'm sorry to delve into areas you're clearly uncomfortable with,' Vine said. 'But it could help give us a clearer understanding of Harry's state of mind. This matter appears to have affected him quite badly.'

'A girl accused me of assault,' Mark said, fed up with all the beating around the bush.

'Assault?' West pounced. 'What are we talking here? Verbal, physical?'

'Sexual,' Mark admitted, sighing wearily. 'It absolutely wasn't true, but she was convinced otherwise.'

'And it never came to us?' West peered at the care workers disbelievingly. 'I'd say that was a matter for criminal investigation.'

'The girl had been drinking excessively on the night in question,' Dandi explained. 'And she left it a year before reporting it. There was no evidence, no witnesses, and, to be honest, she wasn't entirely sure what she actually remembered as opposed to what she had imagined.'

'In your opinion?'

Dandi's nostrils flared with irritation. 'In the Board's opinion.'

'I'd like to speak to this girl.' West took his notepad from his pocket and flipped it open. 'What's her name and address?'

'Sarah Mullen. But I'm afraid I can't tell you where she lives. We've had no contact with her since she left.'

West frowned deeply as he rolled the name over in his mind. Sarah Mullen . . . It couldn't be the same one, could it? But it must be. Starlight! He'd thought the name was stupid when he'd heard that was where the girl had been taken.

'This Sarah,' he said. 'She come to you when she was little?'

'Yes, she was seven.'

'Stabbed her mother?'

'Yes. But I don't see what this has got to do with anything.'

'I removed her from the house, that's all.'

'Do you think that's where Harry might have gone?' Vine asked. 'To see this Sarah?'

'I really couldn't say,' Dandi murmured. 'We didn't even know they were friends until this morning.'

'What happened this morning?'

'He received a letter from her, and told us about it thinking we already knew.'

'Did you see it?' West asked. 'Maybe you'd remember the address?'

'I'm afraid it didn't occur to me to ask to see it.'

'Maybe we should take a look around his room,' Vine suggested, standing up. 'He probably took it with him, but it's worth a try.'

Going up ahead of the others, Mark told Ollie to go in with Vinnie and Pete so that the police could search the room. Ollie started to object, but Mark shot him down with a look.

'Just hurry up. I'll tell them to give you a minute to get dressed.'

Leaping from the bed, Ollie retrieved his stash of dope from the wardrobe and his cigarettes, skins and roaches from the bedside drawer. Hiding them in his quilt, he carried it out right under the noses of the uniforms.

★   ★   ★

'What's going on?' Vinnie asked when Ollie came into the room.

'Mongo's done one,' Ollie told him, laying his bedding down on the floor. 'Shit, man, that was close! I nearly got busted. I only just managed to get all my shit together. D'y' think they'd notice if I skinned up?'

'Behave, you mad bastard!' Pete was awake now, and not in the best of moods. 'They're only next door! What they doing, anyhow?'

'Searching his shit.'

'What for?'

'Dunno.' Ollie shrugged, lighting a straight instead. 'They're probably trying to suss where he's gone. But he ain't got any friends, so he's probably face down in some canal by now.'

Vinnie narrowed his eyes. He knew exactly where Harry Shaw had gone. The lying little turd had gone to Sarah. He would rip his ugly, scheming little head off when he got hold of him!

'Which side is Harry's?' West asked, looking at the identical chests of drawers and wardrobes.

'The tidy side.' Dandi waved her hand.

'Thanks.' Smiling, Vine motioned her and Mark out. 'We'll let you know if we find anything.' Closing the door after them, he turned to West, asking quietly, 'What do you make of it?'

'Something's not right,' West said, his own voice low.

Vine's eyebrows twitched in silent agreement. There did seem to be something fishy going on. An allegation of rape should never have been suppressed by officials connected to the home where the alleged attacker worked.

Squatting down, he pulled open the bottom dresser drawer and poked through the neatly folded trousers stacked inside.

Shaking his head at the backwards way Vine worked –
whoever started at the bottom and worked their way up?
– West opened the wardrobe and raised an eyebrow at the
unnaturally neat line of shirts on the hangers. Finding nothing
among them, he reached up to swipe his hand across the top.
It was clear.

Dusting his hands on his trousers, he moved to the
bed, lifting the mattress and leaning it against the wall.
That was when he saw the slit in the material of the
bed base.

Slipping his arm inside, West groped blindly with his
fingers, grimacing at the dust balls and bits of squishy stuff
he didn't even want to guess at. He was about to withdraw
when he felt something hard and flat. Drawing it out, he blew
the dust off it. It was a five-year diary. Two photographs fell
out when he opened it. Picking them up, he whistled through
his teeth.

'What is it?' Vine asked, leaving what he was doing to
come and have a look.

'Sarah Mullen.' West showed him the first photo. 'All
grown up, and twice as nice. She was seven last time I
saw her, but you could tell she was going to be pretty
even then.'

'She's lovely,' Vine agreed. 'Striking eyes.'

'Aren't they? I wonder how old she is there.'

'Fourteen or fifteen, I'd say. What's the other one?'

'Don't know.' West looked at the pretty, somewhat sulky-
looking woman. 'Mother?'

'Doesn't look much like the boy. What's the book?'

'Diary.' West flipped through the pages. Stopping midway,
he read a bit, then said, 'Here, listen to this. "Dreamed about
her again. She was on a swing, laughing, but she couldn't hear
me or see me. I really, really miss her and just want to see her.
I've got to get out of here!"' Pausing, he looked at Vine, one

eyebrow raised. 'Sounds like he's been planning a breakout for some time.'

'Sounds bloody unhappy,' Vine commented. 'Let's have a look.'

Speed-scanning several pages, he saw that it was all pretty much the same. Harry hated being in the home without Sarah, and particularly despised Mark Chambers. He also mentioned being bullied, and the anguish it had caused him. Wishing the bullies and Mark Chambers dead was a recurrent theme throughout.

It saddened him that an eleven-year-old boy should have suffered so much. In the supposedly safe environment of a children's home, he should have been learning to get over the traumatic circumstances surrounding his placement here, not having to deal with fresh abuse.

'Find anything?' Dandi popped her head around the door.

Surreptitiously pocketing the diary, Vine shook his head. 'Just these.' He showed her the photographs. 'Do you know who they are?'

'This is Sarah.' Dandi smiled fondly. 'It's one of her school pictures. Year ten, I think. I don't know who the other one is, but I've a feeling it's probably Harry's mother. He adored her.'

'Dead?'

'I wouldn't know,' Dandi admitted. 'There's been no contact from her. Harry was taken away on an absolute protection order. No visits – supervised or otherwise.'

'Would you have her name, or a contact address?'

'There are a few details in his file. Would you like me to look it up?'

'If you would. We're almost finished. We'll be down in a minute.'

Going through the last drawer when she had gone, Vine was about to conclude the search when he detected something slightly different about one of the pairs of socks at the back of the drawer. It could have been just the roughness of over-washed towelling, but he pulled them out to check.

'Bingo!' He grinned, extracting the letter and unrolling it. 'Flat five, 226 Demesne Road.'

'Gone back to her roots,' West commented, taking the letter and scanning it. 'This is directly across the park from where her mum lived. Funny how blood will out, isn't it? You can take the kid out of the shit, and all that.'

'Bit harsh,' Vine said, sure that a child as good-looking as Sarah Mullen, with such an extraordinarily direct gaze, couldn't be a hopeless case.

'Maybe,' West conceded, hoping that Vine was right. It would be a tragic waste if she had rushed headlong back into the life he had rescued her from. 'Let's go check her out before we jump to conclusions, eh?'

When they got back to the office, Dandi gave them Harry's mother's last known address, and Sarah's bank account details.

'We opened it the week before she left,' Dandi said. 'I imagine she'll have updated her details – with them, if not us. It might help.'

Climbing into the car, West grinned as they set off, amused by the underhanded behaviour of his normally by-the-book-or-die partner. Vine had not only pocketed the lad's diary, he hadn't mentioned to Dandi that they had found Sarah's letter, either.

Vine shrugged when he questioned him about it.

'Under the circumstances, I thought it might be better to speak to the girl without them knowing where she was. And as for the diary, I've a feeling that the lad's going to find it hard enough when he's brought back without everyone knowing what he really thinks of them.'

'Should have just put it back,' West said, heading towards Moss Side. 'He'll think they've got it anyway when he realizes it's missing.'

'Maybe. Better him thinking that, though, than them searching after we've gone and really finding it.'

West tipped his head in agreement. Maybe Vine wasn't as thick as he made out, after all.

17

Dave recognized the rapping as a copper knock. Peeping through the curtain, he saw the uniforms on the doorstep and kissed his teeth. Whatever they were after, at least it wasn't a raid or his door would have been booted onto his bed by now.

Kicking a path through the overexcited dogs, he went into the hall and yelled 'Five-O!' into the air before opening the front door.

'Someone need warning, did they?' West hawked up and spat into the yard.

Unimpressed, Dave said, 'What d'y' want?'

'Girl from flat five,' Vine told him. 'Don't suppose you'd know if she's in?'

'Nope.'

'Go and look for ourselves, shall we?' West pushed past into the hall. 'Upstairs, is it?'

'Suss it out,' Dave muttered, going back into his flat and slamming the door.

'Charming.' Vine shook his head as he followed West up the stairs.

There was no answer from flat five, but West knocked several times, just in case. It was late, after all. She might be sleeping. He gave up after a few minutes. There was no light beneath the door, and it was silent within – although it was difficult to tell with the music blaring up from the floor below.

Going down a flight, he hammered on the door of number four where the offending racket was coming from. Getting no answer, he cupped his hands to his mouth and yelled, 'POLICE! OPEN UP!' The volume dropped several degrees immediately and seconds later the door creaked open an inch.

'Yeah?' Tony peered out at them.

Taking in the too-wide eyes and the tongue flicking lizard-like in and out of the mouth, West sussed he was looking at a full-blown speedfreak.

'Keep that down.' He nodded through the door. 'It's a contravention of the Human Rights Act, playing garbage like that at this time of night.'

'Someone complained?' Tony gabbled. 'They should've come and said something to me before calling you out. I'm not a complete cunt, you know.'

'No one's complained,' Vine said.

'Yet!' added West.

'We're looking for one of your neighbours,' Vine went on. 'Girl from number five. Do you know where she might be?'

'Don't know her. Never saw her. Done something wrong, has she?'

'You wouldn't know if she's had a young lad round here today? Red hair. Small.'

'Don't know. No idea. That it?'

West said, 'Yeah, thanks for your—' the door was already shut '—help,' he finished.

Number three didn't answer. Going back down to the ground floor, West rapped on John's door.

'Yeah?' John came out into the hall, pulling the door shut behind him. 'What's up?'

West sussed him as a junkie even though he could barely see his eyes through the hair hanging over his face. It was clear to see in the stooped stance, plain to hear in the slow drawl.

'Girl in flat five,' he said. 'Know where she is tonight?'

'She not in?'

'We didn't get any answer. Have you seen her today?'

'Nah, man.' John shook his head slowly. 'She's probably asleep.'

Or nodding out, like you! West thought, wondering if Sarah had succumbed to the influences she was living close to. Very likely, statistically speaking, but he hoped not. He hoped the spark of something extra that he'd seen in her as a child had sustained her and was lifting her above it all.

'Would you know if she's had a young boy with her today?' Vine asked. 'Red hair. Small. Eleven years old?'

John folded his arms and pursed his lips, frowning thoughtfully. 'Nah. I haven't seen no one like that.'

'You sure?'

'Yeah.'

'Have you seen the girl today?'

'Don't think so.'

'If you had,' said West, 'would you say that she looked different from usual? Like she had something on her mind, say?'

John didn't fall for it. He was stoned, but not half as much as he was making out. 'Nah, man, I'd say she looked her usual too-good-to-talk-to-the-likes-of-me self. But I haven't seen her, straight up. She could be working, or something.'

'Don't suppose you'd know where?'

'Nah.'

'Regular little drug den,' Vine mused when they left the house. 'Should we set up a bust?'

'No point,' West said, wondering what planet Vine was from. 'They'll be registered addicts. That's their usual get-out.'

'Where to now?' Vine asked, following West back to the car.

'Her letter said she was working at a massage parlour in town, so we're going to check some out. You ever been to one?'

'Never.'

'You, my friend,' West drawled, 'have not lived. Stick with me, kid. I'm gonna introduce you to the darker side of life.'

'They didn't know I was here, did they?' Harry was wide-eyed with panic, his complexion sicklier than usual as he paced the floor in John's dimly lit mess of a flat.

'Chill,' John said, sitting down in front of the fire to finish rolling the spliff he'd been making when the police knocked. 'They had no clue.'

'You don't think that man with the dogs said anything?' Harry went on, concerned because Dave had seen him coming down the stairs an hour earlier.

'Him!' John snorted. 'He wouldn't tell 'em the *time*.'

Sitting down heavily on the couch, Harry chewed his fingernails. Sarah was going to kill him. He'd really blown it this time. And he'd blown going back to Starlight as well. They'd send him into a secure unit for this. Running away was major, especially on top of all the stuff he'd done to Chambers's car.

Taking a couple of deep drags on the smoke, John held it out. 'Here, have a toke. It'll sort your head out. The last thing you wanna be doing is freaking out. It'll only make you fuck up, and you need to keep a cool head for shit like this. Work out what they're gonna do before they do it.'

'Who?' Harry squinted up through the smoke.

'Hawaii.' John took the spliff back. 'They'll come back, but when they do, you just come down here. Sarah show you the fire escape?'

'No.' Harry shook his head.

'Well, it's in her flat, comes right down the side of the house. All you have to do when they turn up is nip down and bang on my window. You can hide in here till they've gone.'

'Yeah?' Harry felt a giggle creeping into his throat.

'Yeah.' John grinned, his face widening before Harry's eyes, his eyes growing smaller and redder. 'Can't let them get a grip of you, can we, mate?'

Sarah was arranging an appointment with a new client over the phone when the intercom buzzed at three-thirty a.m.

Coming back to the desk with two cups of coffee, Jenny pressed the button. 'Yeah?'

'Police. We'd like to speak to the manager, please.'

'There's no one from management available right now.' Jenny waved for Sarah to radio the bouncers to alert them that something might be about to kick off. 'Could you tell me the nature of your call?'

'It's a missing-person inquiry, but I'm not prepared to go into it out here. Could you open the door, please?'

'One moment.'

'What is it?' Sarah asked. 'What do they want?'

'No idea. Something about a missing person.'

Sarah felt sick. They were looking for Harry, she just knew it.

Pulling her head back, Jenny squinted at her, suspicious of her sickly expression. 'This got something to do with you?'

'I don't know,' Sarah murmured. 'I think so.'

'Bloody hell, you dozy cow!' Jenny tutted. 'Well, whatever's going on, they're coming in. What do you want to do?'

'Can you tell them I'm not here? . . . *Please?*'

'Okay, but don't think I'm making a habit of it. And I want to hear every single detail as soon as they've gone, 'cos you've obviously been holding out on me, lady! Right, go to the whip room. There's no one in there. But you'd best hide in case they decide to check the place out.

'Dozy cow!' she said again, pressing the button to release the door to the massage mile – the corridor only those who had paid were allowed to enter. 'Gaynor would scalp you if she was here. You'd better hope she doesn't find out.'

West's eyebrows crept up as he gazed around Silva's reception area. It was by far the classiest of the parlours they had visited tonight, most of which had been the usual cheap, thrown-together fronts for the real business at hand. There was real money invested in this place, and it showed. The bouncers looked pro, and the receptionist was a bit of all right, too – pretty, polite and with a nice figure.

'You say you're looking for someone?' Jenny twirled a pen between her fingers as she stood in front of them.

'That's right,' Vine confirmed. 'A sixteen-year-old girl called Sarah Mullen. We have information that she's working in one of the parlours. Do you have anyone of that name?'

'Sarah Mullen.' Jenny repeated the name thoughtfully. 'No, I don't think so.'

'Are you sure? She'd have only started in the last few months. Maybe she works a different shift?'

'I'd know her if she was here. I organize the rota. Have you tried Lulu's on Peter Street? They're always taking new staff.'

'Been there.' West leaned an elbow on the counter. 'They sent us to Honey's, Honey's sent us to Topaz, and Topaz sent us here. And they all said the same thing.' He smiled with his eyes.

Holding his gaze, Jenny's lips twitched. He was coming on to her, she could smell it. Horny toad! Not bad-looking for a copper, though. Sexy eyes, nice smile, lovely thick hair. Bit podgy, but she'd soon ride the excess pounds off him.

'Sorry.' She deliberately lowered her voice to a more sexy register. 'I can't help you.'

Vine had taken Sarah's photograph from his pocket. He held it out.

'She could be using a different name. You might recognize her from this.'

Jenny peered at the picture for a moment, then shook her head. 'Sorry. Very pretty, though.' She flicked a slow glance at West. 'Looks sweet.'

'Mmmm, well, thanks for your time,' Vine said, aware of the sparks passing between Jenny and West. 'Sorry to disturb you. We'll see ourselves out.'

'No problem.' Smiling, Jenny walked them to the door. Holding West's gaze again as he went out into the corridor, she said, 'Any time.'

'Thanks, Mrs . . . ?' He looked at her questioningly.

'*Ms*,' she corrected him flirtatiously. 'But *you* can call me Jenny. Bye-ee.'

It didn't register until they were outside. Turning back halfway to the car, Vine said, 'Did she say her name was Jenny?'

'Yeah, why?'

'That was the name of Sarah's friend, wasn't it?' Taking the letter from his pocket, Vine held it beneath the light from the street lamp. 'Yeah, look.'

Snatching the letter, West read it for himself and slapped the paper with irritation. 'Damn.'

'Bit of a coincidence if it's not the same one,' Vine said. 'And Sarah said her boss's name was Bernie, and this is one of Bernie Silva's premises. You think she was lying back there?'

'Hell, no! I think she's a straight-up Catholic girl with morals!' West snapped, annoyed for having let Jenny's charms distract him. 'Come on, Einstein. Let's go see if we can't persuade her to confess.'

They pressed the buzzer a number of times to no avail. They weren't getting back in there tonight, no way, no how. And a warrant was totally out of the question because no one in their right mind was going to give them the authority to search the place on the strength of such a weak suspicion. They could hang about waiting for someone to enter or leave but that meant staying close enough to get to the door before it shut – they would be too visible. The men who frequented these places bolted at the sight of a uniform. And waiting in the car was just as bad. No man in his right mind was going to approach the place with a squad car in plain view.

The car radio crackled to life behind them, the operator putting out a call for assistance for officers attending a gang fight outside one of the city centre's gangster-frequented casinos. Letting out an exasperated sigh, West jerked his head and strode towards the car.

'Come on. We're only five minutes away. We'll make inquiries about this place when we're done – find out what time the staff change shift. See if we can't catch her coming out in the morning.'

Jenny was not amused. In fact, she was blazing. Sarah was well out of order. She knew they were in the adult industry and Bernie would lose his licence if the police found a minor on the premises.

Telling the bouncers not to open the front door under any circumstances, Jenny went to confront Sarah and find out what the hell she thought she was playing at.

'Right, you!' She threw the door open, startling Sarah who was hiding behind a rack of assorted whips and lashes. 'What's going on? And don't give me any bull, 'cos I think you've done enough lying already. Start by telling me how come you never mentioned that you're only sixteen?'

'I'm not! I'm eighteen – honest.'

'I said no bull! Don't push me, girl. You're in the right place if you're asking for a beating!'

'All right, it's true,' Sarah admitted, gazing shamefacedly down at the floor. 'You're not going to tell Bernie, are you?'

'Are you *crazy*? Do you know what would happen if they caught you here? They'd close us down like that!' Jenny clicked her fingers sharply.

'But I'm good,' Sarah argued. 'And I don't look my age. Nobody's ever said anything, have they?'

'Only the goddamned *police*!'

'Yeah, but they've gone now.'

'Oh, you reckon, do you? So how come they've just been ringing the flaming buzzer off the wall trying to get back in?'

'Please, Jenny . . . Don't tell Bernie. I really need this job.'

Sighing heavily, Jenny closed her eyes and chewed her lip. Much as she liked Sarah, her loyalty had to lie with Bernie and the girls. Not to mention herself.

'Go home,' she said at last, folding her arms to steel herself against Sarah's forlorn expression. 'The police have got you down as a missing person, and they'll be back. What you on the run for, anyway? What have you done?'

'It's not me. They're after someone else.'

'They've just *told* me they're looking for you. Shit, girl, they had your photo. Stop lying.'

'I'm not! I swear it's not me.'

'*Who*, then?' Jenny was losing patience now. 'Your twin sister, who just happens to have the same name?'

'It's my friend Harry,' Sarah told her quietly. 'He's from the home I was in.'

Jenny pulled a disbelieving face. 'You were never in a home. You told me how you grew up, remember? With your mum and sister in Stretford. Your mum got married and moved to Wales. You think I'm stupid, or something?'

'It wasn't true,' Sarah admitted. 'My mum put me away when I was seven. I only came out a few months back. I met Harry last year. He's only eleven, and he's had a really rotten time. He ran away last night and turned up at my flat.'

'You stupid idiot. No wonder the police are after you.'

'What was I supposed to do? Kick him out?'

'Well, *yeah*! Rather that than the shit you're in now. You've practically lost your job, and you're sure as hell gonna cop it from the police. If I was you, I'd get my butt home and send him packing.'

'But he's in trouble.'

'All the more reason to get rid. Let the home sort him out. You don't need to get involved.'

'Jenny, you don't know what's going on,' Sarah sighed. 'It's because of me that he's in a mess. He's been taking revenge for . . .' Pausing, she looked at her hands, then murmured, 'Something that happened to me.'

'No shit?' Jenny peered at her concernedly. 'What?'

'This man at the home kind of did something to me.'

'*Kind* of?'

'All right,' Sarah looked up now, her eyes ablaze with shame. 'He got in bed with me when I was drunk! Satisfied?'

'And you let him?'

'I didn't even *know*!'

'Oh, Christ,' Jenny murmured, sitting down heavily. 'That's awful. Did he – you know?'

Thoroughly ashamed, Sarah nodded.

'But you didn't know anything about it?'

'No.'

'That's rape!' Jenny exclaimed. 'Didn't you do anything about it?'

'Yeah, I reported him.' Sarah swiped at a tear trickling down her cheek. 'But he got away with it.'

'And this Harry, what's he been doing?'

'Wrecking the guy's car. He's been at it for months, but he got caught this morning.'

'And he ran away to tell you about it?'

'No, he wanted to warn me that the man knew I'd been talking. He thinks he's going to come after me to shut me up.'

Worried now, Jenny said, 'Do you think he will?'

'Who knows?' Sarah shrugged.

Jenny mulled over what she had just learned. She felt truly sorry for Sarah, but whichever way she looked at it, she had to get her out of here. The police had obviously smelled a rat, and if they had tracked Sarah down to Silva's, they probably had her address by now, too. Sarah needed to go home and get the boy out of her flat before she got arrested for kidnapping him. And then she needed to get herself out of harm's way in case the man came looking for her.

'What about Bernie?' Sarah asked when Jenny told her what she thought. 'Are you going to tell him?'

'Get the police off your back and I'll think about it,' Jenny said. 'Go and get your stuff together. I'll get the lads to check the cops have gone. Is there anywhere you can go and stay until you know you're safe?'

'No. I'll just have to keep my head down.'

'I'd have a real good think if I were you,' Jenny said grimly. 'Believe me, if the police can find you this fast, anyone can. I'd let you come to mine,' she said then, smiling regretfully. 'But I've got the witch-bitch staying.'

'Don't worry about it.' Standing, Sarah walked resignedly to the door.

Following her back to the reception area, glad that it was a slow night and there were no clients hanging about, Jenny arranged for a cab to take Sarah home.

Five minutes later, one of the bouncers popped his head

around the door to tell them that it was here, and that the coast was clear.

'Don't mess about,' Jenny warned as she walked Sarah to the door and gave her a hug. 'I'll say you went home ill for now, but you'd best ring me in a couple of days and let me know the score. If you're not sorted by then . . .' She shrugged.

The flat was in complete darkness when Sarah let herself in. It was almost four-fifteen, so she wasn't overly concerned. Harry was probably asleep.

She panicked when she saw that the bed was empty, the quilt exactly as she had left it. The police must have found him. They *had* wanted her, then – to arrest her. What was she going to do?

First off, she had to find out exactly what had happened.

Harry was asleep on the couch, a smelly tweed overcoat covering him. John put his fingers to his lips as he led Sarah in.

'He's only been out an hour or so.' He waved her to take a seat. 'He was in a right state, thinking you're gonna kick off at him for bringing the pigs round. I told him you wouldn't get mad, but he was proper freaking out. You want a tea, or something? You're not looking so hot yourself.'

'Yeah, thanks.' She nodded, sitting on the edge of the couch by Harry's feet. 'So what happened? Did they come in here?'

'Nah, I went out to them. It was lucky Harry had come down for a chat. He'd have crapped himself if he'd been up at yours on his jack. They were knocking for ages.'

'What did they say?' She gazed at Harry's sleeping face. He looked exhausted, his eyes sunk deep into their sockets.

'Just wanted to know if I'd seen you, did I know where

you worked – shit like that. I said no, and they pissed off.'

'Did they speak to anyone else?'

Nodding, John poured boiled water into the cups and gave them a quick stir. 'Tony,' he told her, handing a cup across. 'They told him to keep his shit down. Hear how quiet it is?'

'I hadn't even noticed.' Sarah cast a glance at the ceiling. 'I must be getting used to it.'

'You're lucky you're not right under him,' John muttered, sitting down to roll up. 'I don't just get the shite music, I get him walking about all night. Squeak, squeak, squeak on the fucking floorboards. He drives Dave's dogs mental. Haven't you heard 'em kicking off?'

'I thought they just did that anyway.'

'Well, yeah, but he *really* winds them up.'

'Did the cops see Dave?'

'He let 'em in. But don't worry, he didn't say anything.'

'Does he know about Harry?' Sarah's eyes widened with alarm.

'Yeah. He saw him coming down to mine. But he won't say owt. None of us is exactly squeaky, in case you hadn't noticed.

'So, what you gonna do about this situation youse have got yourself in?' John asked then. 'Harry filled me in a bit. Sounds tricky.'

Sarah frowned, wondering exactly how much Harry had confided to his new friend. He'd better not have told him the whys and wherefores. It was bad enough John knowing the police were after her without him knowing her personal history as well.

'I'll have to talk to him,' she said, shaking her head when John offered the spliff to her. 'Persuade him to go back before we get into any more trouble.'

'You know he don't want to go back, don't you?' John

peered up at her through his hair. 'But he don't want to get you in lumber, either. He thinks the world of you.'

'Me, too,' she sighed. 'That's why I have to get him back before it gets any worse.'

'I don't think it *could* get any worse for him. All he wants is to be with you. Isn't there any way?'

'No. And after this, I doubt they'll let us see each other again.'

'You could always take off,' John suggested. 'Go somewhere no one knows you, say you're brother and sister, or something.'

'We don't look anything like each other.'

'Cousins, then.

'It wouldn't work.'

'S'pose not. So what *are* you gonna do?'

'What *can* I do?' She looked at him with an expression of helplessness.

Shrugging, John picked up his cup and took a noisy sip. This wasn't his problem. He was willing to let the kid hide out here, but more than that – forget it!

West and Vine had a busy few hours. After dealing with the fight, they were called to assist with an overturned petrol tanker on the Mancunian Way.

It was coming up for seven when they headed back to the station. En route, West decided to pass by Sarah's house one last time on the off chance. It was a lucky decision.

Sarah and Harry came out of the gate at the exact moment West and Vine turned along the road. Deep in discussion about what Harry would say when he got back to Starlight, they headed for the bus stop at the opposite end. Neither saw the car or heard it easing up alongside them. The first they knew about it was when the doors flew open and the policemen leaped out.

'Sarah Mullen?' West gripped her arm.

'Get off her,' Harry squealed, fighting to get free of Vine. 'Leave her alone! She hasn't done anything! She was out! I've been in the backyard all night! Tell them, Sarah, tell them!'

'This true?' Vine asked her.

Sarah gazed at Harry for a long moment, then nodded. 'Yeah. I just came home and found him here. I was taking him back to the home. That's where we were going just now – to get the bus.'

West and Vine exchanged a weary glance. It sounded feasible enough, and they knew that no one had been in her flat when they had called during the night.

'All right,' West said. 'We'll give you the benefit of the doubt. But we still want to talk to you, Sarah, so don't do a runner. It's *really* important.'

Sarah frowned at the stress he'd placed on his last words. She supposed that meant she was in trouble for working at Silva's.

'You're letting her go, aren't you?' Harry asked, his face so pale that Sarah wanted to cry. Even West and Vine felt sorry for him.

'Yes, we're letting her go,' West told him, placing a reassuring hand on his shoulder. 'But you're coming with us, son. Say goodbye, but make it quick.' He nodded to Vine to let Harry go.

Running to Sarah, Harry threw his arms around her and held on for dear life, sure he would never see her again.

'Be good,' she whispered into his ear. 'And write to me as soon as you can.'

Sobs racking his thin frame, he said, 'I – I love you Sarah.'

'Love you too. Now, get!' Squeezing him tight, she pushed him at West and ran into the house without looking back.

West shook his head sadly as he watched her go. He felt

as if a huge, heavy stone was tied around his heart weighing it down. She had turned out so beautiful. And she genuinely cared for the ugly little fella here. It was no wonder that Jenny had covered for her. She was obviously worth putting yourself out for.

Turning, he motioned Harry into the car.

All the kids saw the police bringing Harry through the front door. Most had no clue what was going on and watched open-mouthed as Dandi hurried the two cops and the boy into the office.

Uninterested, Ollie and Pete went straight into the dining room to get their breakfast, but Vinnie hung back until the hall was deserted. Strolling casually to the office, he stepped into the recess beside the door and listened to the conversation going on inside.

Making his way to the dining room minutes later, he picked at the toast Pete had got for him, answering 'Loo' when Pete asked where he'd been.

They didn't need to know that he had just found out where Sarah lived – direct from the pig's mouth.

Sarah waited until nine that night before ringing Silva's. When Jenny answered, she gabbled out the story of Harry's return to the home, and her own let-off, then asked if Jenny had made her mind up about reporting her to Bernie.

Jenny took a long time to answer, and when she did, Sarah's heart sank.

'I'm really sorry, but it's out of my hands. One of those coppers spoke to Bernie this morning. Do-good sod reckoned he was doing you both a favour. Bernie called me at home and had a right go at me. He knows everything, Sarah – your age, and that you came straight from care and lied about working before . . . everything.'

'Should I talk to him?' Sarah was desperate to find a solution. 'Tell him my side? You've got his mobile number, haven't you?'

'Yeah, but I can't give it to you.' Jenny sighed miserably. 'He's fuming. I'd stay well clear if I were you. I've already copped it for not telling him as soon as it happened. I said you'd gone home sick before the coppers came and I didn't know it was you they were looking for, but I forgot to tell the bouncers to say the same thing. I'm sorry, Sarah, but Bernie says you're out. He's going to send your pay in tomorrow's post.'

Going home with her tail between her legs, Sarah cried herself dry. She was devastated. Silva's had become a huge part of her life, and she'd been good at the job – really good. Six months down the drain, and now she was back to square one. It just wasn't fair.

But she couldn't blame Harry. He'd thought he was doing the right thing. Pity he'd lied to Vinnie in the process. There was no telling what Vinnie would do to him now. She'd have to get in touch with Vinnie to get him back on side and ensure Harry's safety. But she couldn't risk contacting anyone at Starlight just yet – not with Chambers on the warpath.

18

Finding a new job was hard. Knowing that she both enjoyed the work and was good at it, Sarah tried all the massage parlours in town, but it seemed that everywhere she went, the mention of her name brought a negative response and the vacancy would suddenly have been filled already.

When it finally dawned on her that she had been blacklisted, she tried other jobs, but these were just as fruitless. Either the pay was terrible and the hours too long, or they wanted experience she didn't have – and, the way things were going, would likely never get.

After a few weeks, with her money all but gone and no food in her cupboards, Sarah had no option but to go back to shoplifting. But even this didn't work out. She had lost her nerve. Before, she had been doing it to save towards a precious goal. Now she was doing it to survive, and the desperation made her feel conspicuous, as if she had a flashing light above her head, saying: 'Watch me, I'm a thief.'

Sweating and shaking whenever she neared the more expensive stuff, she resorted to snatching easy targets instead. But the easy stuff was the cheap stuff, and no one wanted to pay for it. Not even grubby old Mr Gerber.

Giving Sarah just a tenner for five bottles of perfume that she'd spent all day getting, he suggested that she might like to consider a different line of work. Blue movies. He had a friend in the business who was looking for a pretty girl like her. She'd only have to do a few hours, and she'd have a whole two hundred pounds to herself.

Thanking him for the offer, she said she'd rather die than go down that road. Leaving his shop, she vowed she would never go near the place again – unless it was in the middle of the night with a can of petrol and a box of matches in her hand.

It was the most miserable time of Sarah's life.

Harry hadn't replied to the three letters she'd written since he'd been taken back, leaving her to wonder if he had been shipped out as a result of his run-in with Chambers. And she still hadn't been able to bring herself to contact Vinnie. In any case, there hardly seemed any point if Harry wasn't there.

The police had called round a number of times, but Sarah had ignored them and they'd finally given up.

She was a month behind with her rent, and Mr Gilbert had sent his goon round with a warning. She had until the following Monday to bring it up to date, or she was out.

She spent the weekend packing her possessions into carrier bags. She was determined to take it all with her when she left. All she needed on top of everything else was for Mr Gilbert to seize the little she owned before she'd had a chance to come back for it.

Late on the Sunday night, with the bags stacked neatly beside the door, Sarah sat down and smoked her last cigarette.

She needed help, but who could she turn to?

Dandi? No way!

Harry? She had no clue if he was still at Starlight, and even if he was there was nothing he could do for her.

Vinnie? She didn't *think* so!

John, Dave and Tony? Bollocks to that!

Jenny . . .

Why not? They *had* been friends. Jenny wouldn't see her out on the street. Even if she had to sleep on her floor, it would be something until she was back on her feet.

Running to the payphone, she tapped in Silva's number. A recorded message said that it was unobtainable. Sure she must have misdialled, she tried again – and got the same message. Thinking they must have changed the number, she decided to go and see Jenny face to face.

Walking all the way to Ancoats, Sarah was mortified to find that Silva's had closed down. A night-security guard having a smoke outside a neighbouring business told her that they had relocated a couple of weeks earlier, but he didn't know where to.

Defeated, she wandered aimlessly into the city centre and slumped down on a bench. Tears streaming down her cheeks, she stared off into the distance and pondered how she had let her life crumble to nothing. All her dreams, her hopes, her aspirations – gone in the space of a year. She didn't have a soul to call a friend, and she had no clue how to track down the one woman who might be able to help her. She was truly alone – as hopeless a case as all the losers she had known. Her mother . . . The abusive men . . . Claire Wilson . . .

Claire!

Claire was a friend of Coxy's sister, May. And Coxy would know where Jenny was. All she had to do was remember which flat May lived in and get his number, and she might still have a chance.

It was almost one in the morning when Sarah reached the Crescents. Hurrying past the open garages where the sinister shadows danced in the dark corners, she was more nervous than she had ever been in her life. Her pulse was hammering in her ears, her whole body tense with dread.

Miraculously, she found the flat straight away. She recognized the scruffy girl who answered the door. It was Tara – May's obnoxious daughter.

And Tara recognized *her*.

'Mam . . .' she yelled back over her shoulder. 'It's that tart Uncle Gaz brought round that time. Want me to tell her to piss off?'

Fortunately, May Cox was more annoyed with her daughter at that particular moment than with her brother's friend for taking it upon herself to call round uninvited.

'How many times have I told you about opening that door when you don't know who's knocking?' she yelled, storming into the hall and walloping Tara around the back of the head. 'I swear I'm gonna swing for you one of these days, you brainless little cow! Get to bed!'

Turning to Sarah then, shaking her head with exasperation, she said, 'Don't ever have kids. They do your bleedin' head in! Well, don't just stand there letting all the heat out. Come in if you're coming.'

Following May into the living room, Sarah was relieved to find it free of children.

Flopping onto the couch, May waved her to take a seat. 'So, what's up?' she asked, lighting a cigarette and peering at Sarah with open suspicion.

'I just wanted to ask if you've got a number for your brother,' Sarah told her. 'I'm sorry it's so late, but I'm a bit stuck.'

'How so? He got you in trouble, or something? 'Cos if he has, I'm telling you now there's no point trying to get owt off him. He's married with two little 'uns to feed. And much as I can't stand his wife, I'd rip your face off before I'd let you muck his family about. We straight on that?'

Sarah stared at her open-mouthed. Where the hell had *that* come from? Did she look the sort of girl who'd mess about with an older, married man?

'What you gawping at?' May said. 'You got nothing to say for yourself?'

'I didn't want to see him for anything like that,' Sarah managed. 'I'm looking for a friend from work, but they've closed down and I can't find out where they're gone. I thought Coxy might know, that's all.'

May narrowed her eyes some more, making her look even harder and more threatening than she already did. Leaning forward, she said, 'You sure about that? You'd best not be trying to blag me, 'cos you'll be sorry if you mess with me.'

'No, it's nothing like that!' Sarah was beginning to bristle. 'I'm just looking for my friend.'

May sat back. The girl sounded sincere, but she still wasn't getting Gary's number until May knew what the rush was. If he was involved in some sort of shit and he found out that May had dropped him in it, he'd stop the deliveries – *and* kick the crap out of her.

'Who's this friend you're so desperate to find?' She expelled a huge plume of smoke in Sarah's direction.

Sarah inhaled deeply, hoping for a second-hand nicotine hit. If she weren't so proud, she'd have asked for a cigarette but May's attitude had put her back up. There was no way she was begging favours from the bitch.

Standing up, she said, 'Look, just forget it. I'll find her some other way. Sorry for disturbing you, I just thought with us both knowing Claire you might want to help. I won't bother you again.'

'Oi!' May called as Sarah went towards the door. 'I've got a right to find out what you're up to with me own brother.

Just 'cos he brought you round once don't mean you can be trusted. You might be trying to make a mug of him, for all I know. And I ain't gonna sit back and let *no* one do that, you got me?'

Sarah felt a lump rise in her throat. Gulping it back noisily, she turned around with tears stinging her eyes.

'Do you really think I'd have walked all the way here in the middle of the night just to mess you about? I've got no job, no money, no family, nothing! All I wanted was to find the one friend I've got, to see if she'd let me stay when my landlord kicks me out, and the only way I'm gonna do that is if I find Coxy. But if you don't want to help me, fine! Just don't sit there going on with yourself like you're something special, 'cos you're not!'

'Watch it!' May warned. 'You're in my house, don't forget!'

'Stick your fucking house up your arse!' Turning, Sarah marched out, slamming the door behind her.

Outside, with the cold night air stinging her cheeks and nowhere to go, she followed the landing all the way to the end of the block. Standing in the shadows, she leaned on the railings and looked down on the black sea of grass down below, wondering if it would swallow her up if she dived into it.

Claire found her there a short time later.

'Sarah?' she called, approaching her cautiously, concerned that she may be contemplating throwing herself over. She'd seen that before, and it wasn't a pretty sight. 'May says you've been to hers, kicking off. You all right, or what?'

Turning, Sarah looked at her tearfully and shook her head.

Claire patted her on the shoulder. It was an awkward attempt at comfort – the true mark of the long-term care-home kid.

Hugging herself, Sarah closed her eyes and breathed deeply to calm herself. It wasn't fair to break down. Claire had enough problems of her own.

'She said you was going on about losing your flat, and having no money, and that.' Claire stuck her hands into her pockets, as if to restrain them from further intimacy. 'So, I was thinking, I've got a place down there.' She jerked her head backwards. 'It's only a squat, but I don't mind if you want to fetch your stuff round for a bit.'

'Thanks,' Sarah sniffed. 'I might take you up on that. I was worried what I was going to do with it. It'll be safe, won't it? I mean, I wouldn't want to lose anything else.'

'I didn't just mean your stuff,' Claire said. 'I meant you, an' all. Till you get sorted, like.'

'Really?' Sarah couldn't believe what she was hearing. 'Are you sure?'

'Yeah, whatever.' Claire shrugged. 'It's no skin off mine, is it? It's mostly empty, anyhow. It won't make no difference.'

Sarah didn't need asking twice. The sheer relief of knowing she would have a roof over her head convinced her to accept.

'Great! I'll go and fetch my stuff tonight – if you don't mind?'

'Whenever. Come on, I'll show you round. Be warned, though, I'm not exactly tidy.'

'Don't worry about it.' Sarah grinned. 'You should see the state of *my* place. I've really let things slide.'

'That's depression, that,' Claire stated knowingly. 'You'll have to sign on at my doctor's. He's great. You just tell him you're a junkie, and he gives you Temazies and Valium, and all sorts.'

'I don't want anything like that.'

'*You* don't have to take 'em, you can give 'em to me – for your keep, like. Just go see him in the morning and lay it on a bit thick – cry, and that. I'll come with you, show you how to do it. I'm due a Methadone script, anyhow.'

Sarah shrugged. Why not? It was a cheap price to pay.

19

―――◆―――

Vinnie was on a total high. It was his birthday tomorrow. He was nearly free. And he'd managed to achieve it without going into remand. He was just counting the hours now, waiting for the moment when he could turn up on Sarah's doorstep.

He was more than ready. His things were packed, his grant was in the bank account that Dandi had opened for him, and he had an assured place in an after-care housing project in Hulme. It wasn't as nice as the one Pete had been sent to a few weeks earlier, but it would do. And it was only a ten-minute run from Sarah's place in Moss Side.

Life was sweet. And it was soon to be even sweeter. He couldn't wait.

There was just one last thing he had to take care of before he walked out of these doors for the last time. Well, two, actually. Harry Shaw and Mark Chambers.

Since the police had brought him back, the mong had been impossible to get at. Dandi's little lapdog Chambers was always pussyfooting round the stupid little prick, like he was some sort of fragile baby that needed twenty-four-seven seeing-to.

Well, they'd both get a seeing-to before Vinnie left. Mongo, for lying to his face. Chambers, for being a cunt – and a woofter cunt, at that. He'd found out a lot about that man recently.

It was amazing what people kept in their bedrooms.

Chambers was an idiot for thinking that a poxy Yale lock would secure his deep, dark secrets. Vinnie had slid a metal ruler past the latch and it had sprung open first time, and no one had been any the wiser. After rifling the man's possessions and reading his personal letters, he knew all about Chambers's bum-chum boyfriend *Sean*. All about the parties they'd been going to, and the drugs they'd been experimenting with. And once he knew, a plan began to grow in his mind.

It was so easy it was absurd. And first thing tomorrow he'd be gone, and no one would ever be able to point the finger at him.

Tonight was the night when Vinnie would exact his revenge, under cover of the grudge match of the season: Man City versus Man United. Everyone in the house would be watching. Everyone but Chambers, who had – rather considerately, Vinnie thought – chosen this particular day to take his weekend leave.

Everyone had been buzzing for days. Even the girls had caught the bug – although from the amount of giggling going on, they were obviously more interested in watching the players than the ball. The TV room was filling up already, the kids securing their seats, while Dandi and Gloria prepared the mid-match snacks in the kitchen.

Bagging one of the huge floor-cushions, Vinnie dragged it up beside the door at the back of the room, getting into position nice and early.

Mark hummed softly as he got ready. He'd arranged to meet Sean and a few of the lads in town. They were going to watch the match on a giant open-air screen in Albert Square, then he and Sean were going somewhere 'special'. He didn't know where, but Sean had said to bring a weekend case along, and he was praying that his gorgeous boyfriend had decided to use his all-expenses bonus holiday to take him for a dirty weekend in Paris – one of the perks of being a trolley-dolly for a major airline. He could really use a bit of Sean-style pampering after the stresses of the last few weeks.

Mark felt truly happy for the first time in ages. Harry hadn't touched his car since he'd been back, and the police seemed to have decided not to pursue the Sarah thing. He knew he shouldn't have been so worried about it, but he couldn't help it. Many an innocent man had been condemned on the strength of a false allegation. Still, the police hadn't troubled him since bringing Harry home. And after three weeks, he was optimistic that it was done and dusted.

Ready at last, he splashed on some cologne and stepped back to look in the mirror. He looked great. Slipping his jacket on, he checked that he had his passport, picked up his case and headed out.

Pausing outside Harry's room, he put the case down and eased the door open. Harry was huddled beneath his quilt – no doubt crying again. Tiptoeing across the room, Mark reached out and gently touched his shoulder.

'You awake, Harry?'

No reply.

'Okay, well, I'll see you when I get back. And I, er, know it probably doesn't mean much right now, but I really hope we get back on track one day, 'cos I really hate us not being friends. See you later, kiddo.'

Leaving quietly, Mark picked up the case and made his way downstairs. Passing by the TV room, he thought about popping in to say goodbye, but decided against it. He was already late, and they knew he was going, so he didn't need to announce it and delay himself further.

Throwing his case onto the back seat of the car, he set off without a backward glance. Goodbye Starlight, hello gay Paree!

*   *   *

With minutes to spare, Dandi wheeled the snack trolley in and plonked herself on the fattest armchair facing the screen.

'If everyone's got a seat, let's have the light off,' she said, already dipping into a bowl of crisps.

'Oh, just look at those buns,' Gloria groaned, sprawling on her stomach on the floor with a bowl of nuts she had no intention of sharing. Propping her chin on her hands, she ogled Brian Robson as he led his side onto the pitch. 'Hurry up and settle down, you lot, that's my future husband you're watching!' Flapping a hand back over her shoulder at the chorus of groans, she said, 'Don't hate me 'cos I'm gorgeous! You're all invited to the wedding.'

Settling back on his cushion, Vinnie ignored the girly nonsense and waited for an opportunity so that he could slip away.

City won the toss and took control of the situation for the first torturous few minutes, making several determined attempts to score and thwarting United's efforts to commence the thrashing that the majority of Manchester's population was anticipating.

Ten minutes in, Ryan Giggs redressed the balance. Taking advantage of a bungled City pass, the youngster surged down the left wing, skipped a crafty slide tackle and powered to the by-line, crossing deftly to Clayton Blackmore who was waiting outside the eighteen-yard box. Volleying a thunderous shot into the roof of the net, Blackmore leaped into the air with a jubilant yell, along with sixty-odd thousand ecstatic United supporters – and twenty-odd Starlight residents and staff.

Harry heard the cheering down below and pulled the pillow over his ears. How could they carry on as normal when he was dying of heartache?

He had thought it would cheer him up to see Sarah again,

but it hadn't. It had made everything a million times worse. He wanted to be with her more than ever. It wouldn't have been so painful if she'd written to him, but he hadn't heard a word from her. She had obviously decided that it was easier to get him out of her life.

The staff had been trying to cheer him up, but he knew what they were up to. They were just trying to poison him against her, always talking about her 'mistake' and trying to get him to say he believed them not her. But he wouldn't. He'd never betray her like that. Never!

Mark Chambers was good, he had to give him that. He was really piling it on, and if Harry weren't so smart, he might have believed the man was innocent by now.

Hoped they'd get back on track one day, did he? Well, Harry knew what kind of track he'd like to get Chambers on: a high-speed train track!

Lost in his thoughts, he didn't hear the door opening and being eased shut again. Didn't know that he was no longer alone until the heavy body fell on top of him, pinning him to the bed, forcing the breath from his lungs and his face into the pillow.

He bucked impotently as rough, wool-gloved fingers prised his lips apart and pushed something bitter-tasting into his mouth. He tried to push it out with his tongue but there was nowhere for it to go and it slid down his throat, making him gag even more than he already was as the hands tore at his pyjama bottoms.

Harry screamed, first with terror when he realized what was happening, then with absolute, all-consuming agony. The sound filled his head and reverberated through his soul, but it didn't get past the pillow. And all the while, an all-too familiar voice hissed venomous confessions down his ear.

Letting himself into Chambers's room, Vinnie stashed the

gloves at the back of the wardrobe and slid the last of the three tablets he had bought under the mattress. Getting out of there when his work was done, he slipped down the back stairs and in through the back door of the TV room unnoticed.

The final score was a resounding five-one to United. City had rallied towards the end, managing to net a fluky one, but United had stomped them into the pitch. There would be riots tonight. There always were when the reds and blues met up, but more so when they met at the blues' Maine Road stadium. Too many angry Mancunians and over-zealous police crammed into the claustrophobic maze of Moss Side streets made for an atmosphere guaranteed to ignite at the slightest provocation.

Ollie tried to slink from the room to prevent a closer-to-home riot, but Vinnie beat him to the door.

'Going somewhere?' he demanded. 'We had a bet, remember? You said your sad-sack team was gonna win, but they got battered just like I told you. Where's me twenty?'

'I was just going to get it, man.' Ollie grinned. 'It's in me room.'

Stepping aside, Vinnie said, 'Off you go, then. And don't take all night about it.'

Ollie cursed under his breath as he ran upstairs to his room. He wished he'd never opened his mouth about the stupid match. And he should have stayed out of the way tonight. If he'd just laid low, Vinnie would have been gone in the morning and the debt would have been trashed.

Snapping the light on, irritation turned to anger when he saw Harry huddled beneath his quilt. The little shit was always in his pit since the pigs had nabbed his arse and dragged him back, snivelling and whingeing over that snotty bint, Sarah. It made Ollie sick – almost as sick as having to hand over twenty quid to Vinnie.

'Think you're too good to watch the match with the rest of us?' he demanded, prodding the boy in the back as he crossed the room to fetch his money.

Getting not so much as a moan or a sniff in response, he narrowed his eyes and slammed the drawer. Still nothing.

'Oi, Mongo,' he snarled, going to the bed now and punching Harry in the back. 'I'm talking to you! Don't ignore me, 'cos you ain't gonna have Vinnie to protect you after tomorrow, remember?'

Riled by the continued ignorance, he reached down and snatched at the tufty orange hair sticking out above the quilt edge.

'Oi, you little arse bandit, I said—'

Dropping the hair as if it had burned him, Ollie backed away, a look of horror on his face.

'Oh, shit!' he gasped, stumbling backwards to the door and fumbling with the handle. '*DANDIIII* . . .'

20

———◆◆◆———

Harry was barely alive. Reviving him as best they could, the paramedics whisked him away to the MRI. There the full extent of his condition became apparent and the police were alerted.

He had been subjected to a violent sexual assault, prior to – or during – an attempted suffocation. A condom had been used, causing him to go into anaphylactic shock, and the as yet unidentified substance he had ingested was causing him severe breathing difficulties and prolonged unconsciousness.

Harry was not in a good way, and no one expected him to survive the night.

West and Vine reached Starlight before the detectives who would ultimately take over the case. They would take the preliminary statements and check out any likely suspects, but they would not interfere with the crime scene. That was for Forensics, when they eventually arrived.

'I don't believe it!' Dandi gasped when they told her what they knew. 'Who would do such a terrible thing? I would have heard something. I would have known.'

'I'd choose your words carefully if I were you,' West sniped, dropping heavily into a seat. 'Wouldn't want to incriminate yourself.'

Flicking his partner a disapproving glance, Vine said, 'I'll make tea, shall I?'

Dandi nodded, her whole body shaking as she sat down and lit a cigarette.

West watched her with narrowed eyes as Vine bustled about with the kettle like a concerned relative – or like a good little female PC. Dandi was either really shocked, or a fuck of a good actress, he decided.

Rape was bad enough for a girl, but it seemed so much worse for a boy. West knew it was a terrible thing either way, but he could maintain a level of detachment when the victim was female, whereas male rape seemed so much more *personal*. His body revolted against the idea, making him feel murderous and frustrated at the same time.

'Let's go through it from the beginning,' West said when they were all seated with cups of tea in their hands. 'As far as you were aware, Ms Matthews, everyone was in the TV room watching the match tonight?'

'Yes . . . I – I didn't realize Harry had decided to stay in his room. I would have checked on him if I'd known. But he's – he's been really quiet since you brought him back. He can be there one minute, gone the next. We keep finding him in bed, crying.'

'This business with Mr Chambers.' Vine rested his cup on his crossed legs. 'The reason Harry ran away in the first place. Was it resolved?'

'Well, Harry stopped sabotaging his property, if that's what you mean.'

'And their personal differences?'

'They didn't really have any. Everything that happened was a result of Sarah's accusation. But I've told you this already. I don't really think it's got anything to do with what happened tonight. In fact, it couldn't have, because Mark – Mr Chambers – isn't even here.'

'Ah, yes,' West butted in. 'The convenient weekend leave?'

'Yes, that's right,' Dandi said, disapproving of his use of

the word 'convenient'. It implied far too much ungrounded suspicion for her liking.

'Starting this evening, ending Monday?'

'Yes.'

'So when exactly did he leave?'

'I'm not sure of the exact time, but he was gone when . . . when we discovered Harry. He must have left while we were preparing for the match.'

'How do you know it wasn't during?'

'He was *not* here,' Dandi insisted, her chin jerking up. 'He had to meet his friends at a certain time. He told me his plans days ago.'

'He could have altered his timetable,' West said coldly, disliking Dandi for her dogged loyalty to a man who had already been accused of abusing a former resident.

'How can you be so sure that he left before the attack took place?' Vine asked calmly.

'I just know he wouldn't do something like this,' Dandi answered tightly. 'I'm sure he'll tell you the same when you speak to him. He's a decent man. Decent, honest and, in my opinion, absolutely trustworthy.'

'Anyone spoken to him since this happened?'

'No. I tried but his mobile's switched off.'

West and Vine exchanged a glance.

'Who are these friends he was meeting?' West asked. 'Where were they planning to go, and are you expecting him back tonight? He lives here, doesn't he?'

'Yes,' Dandi replied curtly. 'But he's under no obligation to sleep here if he's on leave. His friend, Sean, is the only one I know by name. They were going to Albert Square to watch the match. And I, um, don't think he'll be back tonight because I think he and Sean might have plans to go away.'

'This Sean a *special* friend, is he?'

The question was loaded and Dandi knew it. But, loath as

she was to discuss Mark's private life with this animal, she had little option.

'They're a couple,' she admitted reluctantly. 'Have been for some time.' Legitimizing it. 'Committed. Absolutely monogamous.'

'Into drugs, is he?' West went on mercilessly. 'Not uncommon on that scene.'

'Not that I'm aware of.' Dandi's nostrils were flaring now. Not only was the man obviously homophobic, he was sarcastic and insensitive too.

She turned her attention to Vine. 'Has anyone said what's likely to happen? I mean, do . . . do they think Harry will . . .'

'Die?' West supplied cruelly, wanting to shatter her smug *This has got nothing to do with me or mine* bubble. 'Hard to say, given the time it took anyone to rescue the poor little—'

'Tony!' Vine cut him off. Standing, he put his cup on the desk. 'We'd like to take a look around Mr Chambers's room, if you don't mind?'

'Why?' Dandi frowned. 'I've already told you he wasn't here. We'd have heard him leave.'

'But you didn't, did you?' West raised an eyebrow. 'Didn't hear him leave. Didn't hear him drive away. Not before, during *or* after the match, even though you *know* he left at *some* point. And, quite by coincidence, you have no clue where he's gone and can't reach him.'

'Let's take a look around before we jump to conclusions, shall we?' Vine suggested.

'What are you looking for?' Dandi hovered in Mark's bedroom doorway minutes later, twisting the key in her hands and watching nervously as West and Vine poked around in the drawers. 'This is all just personal stuff.'

'We'll let you know if we find anything,' West told her

tersely. 'Anyone else but you and Mr Chambers have access to this room?'

'No.' She shook her head. 'Staff rooms are strictly private. The staff hold their own keys, and the duplicates are locked in the safe at all times. I never use them – only in case of emergencies. Why do you ask?'

'To ascertain that whatever we find in here can only belong to Mr Chambers,' West told her, smiling nastily as he added, 'Or yourself, of course.'

Looking up from the drawer he was rifling, Vine gave Dandi a reassuring smile. 'Don't worry, Ms Matthews. We'll try not to make a mess.'

A couple of minutes later, West gave a jubilant yell – somewhat muffled by the mattress he was holding up against his mouth. Motioning for Vine to come over, he said, 'Grab this a sec, Bob.'

'What is it?' Dandi moved into the room.

'Would you mind staying back there by the door,' Vine told her, taking hold of the mattress.

Pulling on a pair of latex gloves and taking a small evidence bag from his pocket, West leaned down and picked something up. Dropping it into the bag and sealing it in, he showed it to Vine.

'What is it?' Dandi said again.

West gave her a nasty half-smile as he held the bag up in front of her. 'Seems I was right about your Mr Chambers and drugs. If this is what we think it is, he's nailed.'

Dandi watched helplessly as Vine radioed in their findings to the station and West continued searching. She didn't like this change of pace one little bit. Things were going too quickly – and too smoothly in the police's favour – for her liking. They could have planted that tablet, for all she knew. She hadn't seen West pick it up; he'd been neatly hidden by the mattress and his partner's body. They were probably in it

together. They certainly *wanted* Mark to be guilty, especially
after the Sarah thing.

She wished that she hadn't agreed to let them into his room
now. She should have just said that she didn't have a spare
key. But she hadn't wanted to make them suspicious. She
hadn't wanted them to think there was something to hide,
and she'd genuinely expected them to draw a blank. What
a bloody mess.

'Oh, dear, oh, dear,' West piped up, reaching into the waste
bin and pulling something out.

'What now?' Dandi was almost in tears.

Bagging his find, West said, 'A condom, Ms Matthews.
Now, surely even *you* must agree that's an unusual thing to
have lying around in a place like this?'

'That should be switched off,' the stewardess scolded Sean
playfully, arching an eyebrow at the mobile phone he was
trying to conceal beneath his lap blanket. 'You *know* that,
naughty.'

'Just texting my mum.' Sean grinned back at her. 'She likes
to keep track of my adventures. Nearly done.'

'Well, hurry up. And if the captain sees you, I didn't know.'
Smiling, she moved away with her little trolley.

'I gather you know *her*, as well?' Mark sniped huffily, jealous
of all the attention Sean had been getting from the moment
they had set foot in the airport. He was obviously a lot more
popular than he'd made out.

'I know *everyone*, honey,' Sean replied, reaching across to
give Mark's thigh a squeeze beneath the blanket. 'Doesn't
mean I've shagged them all, though, so stop with the green-
eye nonsense, and enjoy!'

Smiling as he adjusted his jeans to accommodate his hard-
on, Mark rested his head back. It was only a short flight, but
he wanted to catch a bit of shut-eye before landing. Paris never

slept – according to Sean. They would be dropping their gear off at the hotel then going straight out to do a tour of the mega-depraved nightspots Sean had either already visited on his travels or had heard about from his mile-high comrades.

'I got my joeys,' Sean whispered into his ear seconds later, having finished his texting and dutifully switched off his mobile. 'White chocolate and wild strawberry. They smell *divine!*'

'Wait till you get a load of mine,' Mark whispered back. 'I found these really weird vodka-and-mint-liquor ones. I tried one on last night, and it kind of burns and chills at the same time.'

'Funky!' Sean teased. 'Hope you didn't get too carried away?'

'Shut up!' Blushing, Mark glanced nervously around.

'Chill, babe,' Sean whispered. 'No one's got a clue what we're talking about. Pass me your drink.'

Mark smiled as he handed over his glass. Sean had a voracious appetite. Drink, drugs, food, sex. Nothing was ever quite enough. But while Sean was a taker, Mark was a giver, so it evened itself out. Mark would give his all and more to be with Sean. He was everything Mark had ever wanted in a man. Gorgeous, with immaculately cut sun-bleached hair, expertly plucked eyebrows and long, curly black eyelashes, he had a gym-fit body, and a lovely hard—

'Nearly there.' Sean was peering out of the tiny window into the pitch-dark sky. 'Fancy dropping an E before we land?'

'No way!' Mark gasped. 'I'll only end up acting weird and getting strip-searched.'

'You should be so lucky!' Sean snorted. 'You're with me, remember – we'll sail through. I'm having one, anyway. They're supposed to be brilliant, and I want to be up, up, up when we touch down. Sure you won't change your mind?

It'll be a mind-blowing taxi ride . . .' He waggled his eyebrows suggestively.

'Oh, go on, then.' Grinning, Mark held out his hand. Why not? He'd never have dared to be so adventurous on his own, but he'd been thoroughly corrupted since he and Sean had got together. Still, it was all good, clean fun. And it didn't interfere with his professional life in the slightest – he made absolutely sure of that.

21

D andi called Vinnie to the office after breakfast the
following morning. She gave him his bank card and
a five-pound note, explaining that the latter was taxi fare
because, under the circumstances, she wouldn't be able to
drive him to the housing project as planned.

'I hope you don't mind, but the police will be coming to
see me again soon, and then I've got to get over to the
hospital.'

'Don't worry about it,' Vinnie told her, pocketing the
money. 'What's going on, anyway?'

'I can't discuss it,' Dandi said. Then, forcing a more
cheerful tone, 'Anyway, the taxi will be here in half an hour.
Have you got everything ready?'

'Yep.'

'Anything you want to ask?'

'No.'

'Well, I guess that's it, then.' Standing, she extended her
hand across the desk. 'Goodbye, and good luck.'

'Thanks.' Standing up, Vinnie took her hand.

Holding him there, Dandi peered into his eyes. 'I won't
pretend it's always been a pleasure, but I *will* miss you –
believe it or not. Watching you struggle your way up to
where you are today will give us a far better understanding
of the next Vinnie who struts through our doors.' Giving his
hand a final squeeze, she let go and came around the desk to
show him out. 'I want you to know that I'm very proud of the

efforts you've made to better yourself. You're a good-looking young man with a very bright future ahead of you. Just make sure that you take care of yourself.'

'Yes, *Miss*.' Embarrassed to feel a sudden softness towards her, Vinnie thought it best to get moving before he made a real tit of himself. 'See you,' he said, racing out before she took it into her head to hug him, or something.

Closing the door behind him, Dandi smoked a cigarette then pulled her coat on and set off to visit Harry in the intensive care unit at Withington Hospital.

Reaching the project at just gone ten, Vinnie introduced himself to the pretty receptionist and asked for the keys to his room. Under normal circumstances he would have indulged in a little flirting, but he had more pressing things on his mind right now.

He tapped his fingers agitatedly on the chest-high desk as the young woman wandered into the back office. He was in a mega-hurry to dump his gear and get out. The project manager had different ideas. Strolling out, he clapped a friendly arm around Vinnie's shoulder.

'Glad you could join us, Vinnie. I'm Keith Lomax, the manager, and your personal port of call for help and advice. Let me show you your room, then we'll grab a cuppa and have a chat. I've drawn up your schedule for the first week, so we'll go over that – see what suits, what needs adjusting.'

Propelling Vinnie along a series of corridors and up in a lift to the second floor, he unlocked a door and stepped back to let Vinnie enter. Following him inside, he conducted a lightning tour of the bedroom-cum-sitting room, the tiny bathroom and the even smaller kitchenette.

'Now, the rules,' he said when they had finished. 'Make brews and heat food up, but do *not* attempt to cook. Smoke, yes. Drink, no. No visitors in the room, but you may bring a maximum of two into the day room for one hour per week – by prior arrangement. Taking it all in so far?'

'Yeah.'

'Good. Now, your property is *your* responsibility, so the onus is on you to keep your door locked, but anything valuable may be left in the safe. Keys are collected at the front desk when you come in, and left there when you go out – no exceptions. And, lastly, be back by ten, or stay out. First time, I'll hear you out. Second, you're gone. Any questions?'

'No.' Vinnie shook his head and folded his arms, willing the man to shut up so that he could get out of there.

'Okay,' Keith said, smiling as he opened the door. 'Shall we get that coffee?'

'Er, I can't just now.' Vinnie glanced at his watch. 'I've got something to do.'

'Important?'

Nosy bastard! Vinnie thought. 'Yeah, pretty much,' he said.

Putting his fisted hands on his hips, Keith thought about it for a moment then nodded. 'Okay, but make sure you're back by three because the careers adviser is coming to sign you on. We'll have that chat later, yeah?'

Vinnie fought his irritation as he made his way to Sarah's address. It seemed as though the housing project was going to be even more restrictive than Starlight. Still, if everything went according to plan, he wouldn't have to put up with it for too long. He'd move in with Sarah as soon as he could and fuck the world and its rules.

No one answered when he knocked. Squatting down, he raised the letter-box flap and peered into the dim hallway, wrinkling his nose at the sour, dirty smell that wafted out. No one seemed to be home.

Wandering into the park across the road, Vinnie kept an eye on the house as he strolled around the fishing lake, kicking stones into the water to deter the fierce-looking swans from venturing too close.

After circling the lake twice, he sat on a bench beside a scruffy old man and scrounged a couple of roll-ups – in return for listening to the old dude prattle on about his kidney stones, his snuffed-it wife, and the war.

Leaping to his feet when he spotted someone going up Sarah's path some time later, he flipped a goodbye to the man and raced across the road. Reaching the door just as it was closing, he thrust out a hand and pushed it back, calling, 'Hang about!'

Yanking the door open, letting the dogs loose, Dave said, 'Yo! What d'y' think you're playing at, man? You'll get your fuckin' head blown off barging into people's gaffs like that!'

Eyeing the snarling dogs, Vinnie said, 'Sorry, mate. I'm looking for someone.'

'Oh, yeah?'

'Yeah. Girl called Sarah.'

'She ain't here no more.' Calling the dogs in, Dave began to close the door.

Despite the risk of having the dogs set on him properly this time, Vinnie once again pushed it back.

'Man, you're really pissing me off now!' Dave glared at him. 'I said she ain't here. You deaf, or something?'

'You sure about that?' Vinnie glared back. ''Cos if you're trying to blag me, I'll rip your fuckin' head off – dogs or no dogs!'

'Don't threaten me, you little dickhead.' Coming outside, Dave shoved Vinnie so hard he almost fell down the steps. 'She fucked off a few weeks back, and if I was you, I'd do the same!'

Before Vinnie could retaliate, Tony the speedfreak ran up the path and joined Dave at the door.

'What's going on?' He looked at Vinnie with bulging-eyed suspicion.

'He's after her that used to live up top,' Dave told him. 'I've told him she done one, but he thinks I'm blagging.'

'Well, he's not,' Tony said. 'She took off a while back.'

'Where to?'

'No idea.'

'Bull!' Vinnie snorted.

'What do you think these are, gob-shite?' Tony reached for a stack of letters sitting on the meter cupboard just inside the front door and shoved them under Vinnie's nose, showing that they were addressed to Sarah. 'If she was here, she'd have 'em, wouldn't she? Now do one, and don't come round here causing trouble again, 'less you want to take us both on?'

His eyes narrowed to angry slits, Vinnie looked at each of the men in turn. They were pretty old, but they looked handy – especially the dog man, who looked like a bit of a psycho. He had no doubt he'd wipe either of them separately, but together they might cause too much aggro.

'See you around,' he said, backing down the steps. Pausing at the gate, he cocked a two-finger gun at their heads then strolled away.

Sarah had gone. What was he supposed to do now? If he'd been smarter, he'd have got in touch when he first found out she was there. But he'd wanted to surprise her, and now it was too late.

Stupid, really stupid.

But not as stupid as her former housemates. They would pay for talking to him like that.

Dandi sat on the chair beside the crisply sheeted hospital bed and a range of emotions rolled over her as she gazed at Harry's colourless face. Pity, regret, sadness, anger. Guilt. Sarah had warned her. Why hadn't she listened?

But, no, that wasn't entirely true. She *had* listened – she just hadn't believed. And this was the result. This child, whose whole life had been dogged by rejection and torment, clinging to life against the odds, his future bleaker now than it had ever been.

Holding his cold little hand as the hours ticked away, Dandi battled with her thoughts. The evidence was overwhelming, but even now she didn't want to believe that Mark was guilty of this heinous crime. She prayed that Harry would wake up and tell them what had really happened, so sure was she that he would clear Mark Chambers.

22

West and Vine accompanied the two detectives handling the Shaw case to Manchester Airport on the Monday morning. Surrounding Mark Chambers and Sean Jacobs as they strolled through the arrivals gate, they took them into a side room and searched them.

Jacobs had nothing more incriminating than a stack of cellophane-wrapped hard-core porn magazines in his suitcase. Confiscating these – for the hell of it – they sent him on his way.

Chambers, however, wasn't nearly so lucky. He had a clear-plastic bank bag containing two Ecstasy tablets in the hip pocket of his jeans. And in his wallet there were a couple of unusually 'flavoured' condoms of the same sort as the one that West had found in his waste bin.

Reading him his rights, they strip-searched him – as invasively as possible – then bagged his clothes and made him put on full nonce-whites before cuffing him and leading him out to the waiting van.

A ferocious blush suffused the stark whiteness of Mark's face as several hundred pairs of eyes watched his progress through the airport. Avoiding the curious stares, he fixed his gaze on the puffy white slip-ons covering his feet, fully aware that he looked like some sort of mass murderer. He'd never been so humiliated in his life.

And he wasn't at all sure what he was being charged with. He'd been so shocked to be grabbed like that he'd hardly taken in a word they'd said. Except rape – he'd heard that, all right. And all he could connect it to was Sarah's false allegation, and the way the two PCs had reacted when he'd had to tell them about it. They'd said they were going to talk to her. Had she decided to bring charges against him after all?

Harry came round later that night, but he didn't clear Mark because he couldn't remember a thing about the assault. In fact, he couldn't remember much of anything after being picked up by the police outside Sarah's house that time he'd run away.

The psychologist spent hours with him over the following days, talking to him and assessing his mental condition. She concluded that he was unfit to give evidence at Mark Chambers's trial. In her report she stated that it was a common phenomenon for the victim of such a traumatic event to suppress all knowledge of it, and as there was no way of forcing recall all they could hope was that he would one day recover his memory and give them the information he had locked away.

In the meantime, the psychologist recommended that Harry should be moved to a new location. He obviously couldn't return to Starlight, and she felt it would be beneficial to send him out of Manchester, to enable him to start afresh.

Dandi wouldn't have raised an objection even if she could have. Racked with guilt for having failed Harry so miserably, she packed up his belongings and handed them over to his new social worker, asking only that the woman please keep her informed about the boy's progress.

Three months later, the case finally came to court.

Mark was brought from the holding cell that he had occupied throughout his time on remand. Handcuffed and flanked by two stony-faced guards, he took his seat behind the glass screen and peered nervously out at the people crammed into the public seating area and gallery above.

His heart sank when he saw that Sean wasn't among them. In his letters, Sean had assured him that he believed in him and wouldn't turn his back. Mark was disappointed that he had decided not to come, but he wasn't entirely surprised. He didn't know if *he* could have faced it had the tables been turned. Still, at least Dandi was here to support him – even if she seemed to be having a little difficulty meeting his eye.

The atmosphere was heavy as the trial got under way, but it was to grow darker still as the evidence was outlined in much fuller detail than the media had previously been able to release. Everyone knew that the accused was supposed to have assaulted a child, but they had no clue what the word 'assault' really meant until the prosecution team got going – in as strong and unrelenting a way as possible, in order to convince the jury of Chambers's guilt.

It took little more than four hours.

Despite Harry having no recall of the night in question – and the previous allegation made against Mark by Sarah not being allowed to be mentioned – the jury decided that the evidence of the items found in Chambers's room, his subsequent weekend disappearance, and the fact that he had been found with illegal drugs both on his person and in his blood when he was arrested was compelling enough to convict.

Satisfied that it was a fair and reasonable conclusion, the judge delivered a sentence of eleven years.

Mark was stunned. He truly hadn't expected to be found guilty. Searching for Dandi among the baying crowd, he felt as if a knife had been plunged into his heart when he saw her staring coldly back at him.

Shaking her head, Dandi rose to her feet. She hadn't wanted to believe it, but after hearing it laid out as starkly

23

Claire was a nightmare to live with – far dirtier than Sarah remembered her being at Starlight, and twice as nasty. And her friends – if that's what you could call the group of codependent dregs she lived among – were even worse.

May Cox was vile. And Billy and Makka were two of the foulest creeps she had ever met, who thought nothing of fixing up in front of whoever was around at the time – May's kids included. They were all filthy, and they smelled rancid. Their flats were disgusting, and not one of them seemed to own a toothbrush.

Much as Sarah detested the others, she particularly disliked Claire. But she was finding it almost impossible to get away from her. Every time she said she was going to find a place of her own, Claire would develop sudden problems with her pregnancy and beg her to stay, saying she was terrified that she would lose the baby if she was left alone – just like she'd lost all the others. Sarah felt like pointing out that she hadn't cared about *any* of the others, but she didn't want to risk being the cause if Claire *did* miscarry. Still, her patience was wearing very, very thin.

It finally snapped the day she went to May's house to remind Claire that they were supposed to be collecting their prescriptions and would be too late for the chemist if she didn't get a move on.

Tara answered the door wearing the necklace that Dandi had given Sarah for her birthday – the necklace that had gone missing not long after she'd moved in with Claire.

'Where did you get that?' she demanded.

'*Maam*!' Tara yelled, running into the living room. 'Sarah's after me cross!'

Following her in, Sarah pointed an accusing finger at her. 'That's mine!'

'No, it ain't,' May said, standing between them, a threatening scowl on her face. 'And don't you be coming round here shouting at my kids, you stuck-up bitch!'

'It's my necklace,' Sarah stood her ground. 'I got it for my birthday and it went missing a few weeks ago. I want it back.'

'Oi!' May prodded Sarah's chest with a rigid finger. 'You'd best not be accusing my kid of nicking it, or I'll break your fuckin' neck for you! I *bought* that cross for her.'

'Bullshit!' Sarah hissed. 'It's mine.'

'Well, it's not no more. I bought it fair and square. It's Tara's now.'

'Bought it off who?' Sarah demanded. '*Claire*?'

'Don't blame me,' Claire said. 'It ain't my fuckin' fault if you can't remember where you put things!'

'What's going on?' Makka asked, coming in through the front door that Sarah had left open.

'This cheeky bitch is accusin' us of nicking her fuckin' necklace,' May told him. 'Just 'cos our Tara's got one like it!'

'The one I give you?' Makka said, frowning.

'Yeah. She reckons it's hers.'

'Well, it ain't.' Makka turned on Sarah. 'I give her that years ago.'

'Thought you said you bought it?' Sarah glared at May.

'No, I never, you lying bitch!'

Glaring at the three of them, Sarah turned and marched out. There was no point arguing with them. She wasn't going to get anywhere. They professed to hate each other, but they would lie and fight to back each other up.

'Sarah!' Claire yelled after her from the doorway. 'Where you going?'

'To get my stuff,' Sarah shouted back.

'But, you can't . . . You've got to get your prescription. They won't give it me.'

'Tough!'

Throwing everything she had into a bin liner, Sarah walked out of Claire's squat without a backward glance. With her head held high, she marched down the communal stairs and across the road to the next Crescent with just one thought in mind – to find an empty place on a block where Claire didn't have mates.

Ten minutes later, she had found one. She knew the ropes now. The council would give her the tenancy rather than go through the hassle of taking her to court to evict her. And now that she knew how to claim benefits, she would be fully legit by this time tomorrow.

Free of Claire and her vile mates.

All she needed to do was buy a new lock and break in. That was the tricky bit, but she was sure she could manage it. She just hoped that the hardware shop was still open.

Pete Owens was visiting his Nan at the old people's home in Hulme. The bus stopped right outside, so he could usually get in and out without being seen. But this day, she wanted him to go to the chemist's to pick up her prescription and he couldn't refuse.

It was already growing dark, but he pulled his hood up anyway and hurried down the road, dreading bumping into Vinnie and being forced to make arrangements to meet up. He rarely saw him these days, and he was relieved, if truth be told. He had changed a lot since leaving Starlight, and knew he wouldn't have tried half the things he had done if he'd had Vinnie sneering over his shoulder. College, for example.

Pete's project manager had got him onto a computer course, and he was doing really well. His tutors had said he was a dead cert for a distinction if he carried on the way he was going, and he had every intention of fulfilling their prophecy. He'd already decided to sign on for the second year. Then, when he had passed his finals, he would net himself a good job at some high-tech company and work his way up, earning enough to get himself a flash car and a really good pad by the time he was twenty. He had it all mapped out in his mind, and he really believed it was within his grasp – as long as he stayed away from the undesirables.

Hurrying down the road with his gaze fixed firmly to the pavement now, Pete didn't see the girl coming the other way and was shocked when he bumped into her, knocking the bin bag she was carrying out of her hands. He was already apologizing when he realized who it was.

Sarah recognized him immediately, and her heart sank.

They looked at each other for long, agonizing seconds. Finally Sarah said, 'How are you?'

'Fine,' Pete said, glad that she'd broken the silence because now they could get the hellos over with and go about their business. 'You?'

'So-so.' Bending down, she scooped up the things that had fallen from the bag. 'I'm moving,' she explained, seeing his gaze flick to it.

'Oh, right. You don't live round here, then?'

'Yeah, but not from choice. I've been staying at Claire Wilson's.'

'*Claire*? I thought she was dead, or something.'

'Might as well be.'

'What happened to her?' Pete was intrigued despite himself. 'Did she ever have that baby?'

'She lost that one,' Sarah said with a hint of disapproval. 'She's had another since that, but they took it off her. And she's expecting again now.' Straightening up, she rolled her eyes. 'That's one of the reasons I'm moving out. I've had enough of her moaning and puking.'

'Rather you than me.' Pete grimaced. 'Anyhow, look, I'd best get off. I'm, er, trying to avoid Vinnie, to be honest.'

Blanching at the mention of Vinnie's name, Sarah glanced around nervously. 'He's not round here, is he?'

'Yeah, in the project.' Pete motioned back the way she'd come with a nod. 'Next to the barracks up Bonsall Street. Didn't you know?'

'No. I haven't seen him since I left Starlight.'

Pete peered at her questioningly. 'Don't think I'm being nosy, but what was it with you two? I mean, I know he's supposed to be good-looking and that, but I didn't think you'd be interested.'

'I wasn't!' Sarah snorted. 'That was the problem. *He* was, but it wasn't happening. Not after what he did to Harry, anyway.' Frowning now, she said, 'Why *did* you do all that shit to him? He was really sweet, you know.'

Blushing, Pete shoved his hands deep into his pockets and looked down at his feet. This was another of the reasons he'd been glad to cut off ties with Vinnie. Since moving to the Stretford project and being helped by the mentors there, he'd got involved in some of the special activities that they organized for younger kids, and there were lots who were just like Harry Shaw – disabled, dispossessed, and just plain disowned. He had learned a lot, and was more than a little ashamed of the way that he'd behaved in the past. But how could he explain this to Sarah without sounding insincere?

'I'm really sorry about all that,' he managed. 'I'd never do it these days.'

Watching him, his eyes downcast, his cheeks ablaze with shame, Sarah believed that he meant it.

'I'm sure Harry would be glad to hear that,' she said. 'What happened to him, by the way? I didn't hear from him after he was taken back that time. Was he all right?'

Looking up, Pete frowned. 'Didn't you hear?'

'What?' Her voice was thick with dread. 'He's not dead? . . . Please don't tell me he's dead.'

'No.' Pete shook his head, his face grim. 'But I bet he wished he was that night. He was attacked.'

'Oh, my God!' Sarah's hand flew to her mouth. 'What happened?'

'It was a bit after I left, so I'm not positive, but they reckon he was drugged and . . . you know.' He shrugged. 'Anyhow, he never went back. They took him somewhere else from the hospital. And Chambers was nicked straight after.'

'*Chambers!*' Sarah exclaimed angrily. 'I fucking *knew* he'd get to Harry! I warned Dandi, the stupid bitch! God!'

'He got eleven years.'

'Good! What about Harry? Was he all right?'

'Yeah. They reckon he didn't remember anything – with getting spiked, and that.'

'Well, that's good, I suppose,' Sarah murmured, exhaling loudly to relieve the tension. 'Where did they send him?'

Shrugging, Pete folded his arms. 'Somewhere in London, I think. Dandi said that some couple were adopting him.'

'I should get in touch. Do you still speak to Dandi?'

'Not much.' Pete blushed again, embarrassed to admit that he was one of the 'uncool' ones who had stayed in touch. 'Now and then – just to let her know how college is going, and that.'

'You're in college?'

'Yeah, computers. What about you? Are you working, or anything?'

'No. I was, but I need to sort my own place out before I can get something else.'

'You want to try college,' Pete suggested. 'You get a grant, and you'll end up with qualifications.'

'Nah.' Sarah shook her head. 'I don't think me and the teachers would get on too well. I've had enough of rules. I just want to get into my flat and sort myself out.'

'Have you locked yourself out?'

'I haven't got *in* yet.' Sarah grinned sheepishly. 'I was just going to buy a lock. They're not hard to change, are they?'

'Nah, it's a doddle. It's only a barrel and a couple of screws. I'll do it for you, if you want?'

'Yeah? That'd be great. Thanks.'

''S all right.' Pete shrugged bashfully. 'Not right now, though, 'cos I'm supposed to be fetching something for me Nan.'

'Your Nan?'

'Yeah, she lives in there.' Pete thumbed towards the windows of the home to their left. 'I don't see her that much, but she gets me doing all sorts. Anyhow, this lock,' he changed the subject. 'An hour do you?'

'Yeah, that's great. I'll wait in the launderette. Just come and get me when you're ready.'

'Okay. See you in a bit, then.'

'Yeah, see you.'

An hour later, Sarah took Pete to the flat that she had chosen. It was separated from the rest of the landing by the stairwell – which was precisely why she liked it. It was unnerving to live on the main run, where someone was always walking past day and night. In the corner like this, there was no reason for anyone to be outside your door unless they were calling there specifically.

'You sure you want this one?' Pete glanced nervously about.

'You're not gonna change your mind when I start ripping the lock out? Only I don't want to get arrested for breaking and entering.'

'I'm sure.' Sarah took the new lock from her pocket. 'You sure you can do it?'

'Aw, come on!' Drawing his head back, Pete mock-frowned as he pulled his Nan's claw hammer from his pocket. 'It might be rocket science to a bird, but it's a piece of piss to a bloke.'

Minutes later, they were inside. Putting the hammer down, Pete took out a screwdriver and set about changing the barrel.

'How old is your Nan?' Sarah asked, shivering in the cold, emptiness of the flat.

'Seventy-eight. Why?'

'Just wondering how come she's got tools.'

'They were my grandad's. She only kept them so I could fix stuff for her.'

'Don't they have wardens for that?'

'Yeah, but she likes to see me sweat. There you go.' Stepping back, Pete handed her the keys.

Slipping one into the lock, Sarah turned it and grinned. 'Thanks. You don't know how good it feels to know I won't have to spend one more night with that bitch.'

'No problem.' Lighting a cigarette, Pete offered one to her. Taking it, she leaned towards him to get a light, leaving a faint trail of perfume behind. It stirred something in his gut. 'What's Claire doing these days, anyway?' he asked. 'Apart from getting knocked up.'

Sarah sat down against the wall. 'Being a junkie. She'll be having a proper shit-fit today, 'cos I didn't pick my script up for her.'

'Eh?' Pete sat facing her. 'You've been getting prescriptions for her?'

'Yeah. I had to tell her doctor I was a junkie so he'd give me all the usual shit, and I give it to her instead of rent.'

'He believed *you* were a junkie?' Pete was incredulous. 'You don't look anything like one.'

'It don't matter what you look like.' Sarah exhaled noisily. 'He isn't exactly legal. He kind of trades the drugs for shags. Claire set it up so she does mine, but that's her business.'

They were quiet for a moment, their cigarettes glowing in the dark.

'You know all that stuff Vinnie said that day,' Pete said after a moment. 'About your mum and a cat. Was it true?'

'Mmmm.'

'And that day when you caught us with Harry – would you really have stabbed Vinnie?'

Sighing, Sarah said, 'Yeah, probably. I was in a bit of a mess back then, and he was being such a prick that I could have easily taken it out on him if he'd pushed me.'

'Lucky he didn't, then,' Pete said. 'I reckon that's when he started getting into you again, you know. He always had this funny look in his eye when he saw you after that.'

'Tell me about it,' Sarah chuckled. 'It freaked me out. I didn't even know he *liked* me, never mind fancied me.'

'What did you tell him that day you left?'

'That I'd think about chilling with him if he laid off Harry.'

'Ah . . . no wonder he made us pack it in, then.'

'Did he?' Sarah asked, peering hard across the dark expanse to gauge whether Pete was telling the truth.

'Yeah. It did my skull in at the time, 'cos one minute he's getting us to kick Harry's head, then the next he's threatening to kick *ours* in if we so much as *look* at the kid wrong. It was weird, man.'

'What about after Harry was brought back after he ran away? Did he start on him again after that?'

'Not that I know of.'

Sarah was glad. At least Harry had enjoyed *some* respite.

Pete illuminated his watch, making his face glow a strange shade of green. Seeing it was almost nine-thirty, he pushed himself to his feet.

'I'd best get going or I'll miss my bus. They're pretty laid-back at the project, but I've still got to be in by ten.'

Sarah felt a sinking sensation in her stomach. She'd never have thought it possible, but she'd enjoyed talking to Pete and was almost reluctant to see him go. Apart from which, she had to admit to more than a passing fancy. He was much better-looking than she remembered, with his glossy black hair, his smoky grey eyes and his even, white teeth. She was surprised that she'd never noticed how cute he was. But then, she hadn't bothered looking at *any* of the lads at Starlight.

Getting up, she said, 'Thanks for helping me out, I really appreciate it. You'll have to come round for a brew sometime – when you're visiting your Nan, or whatever. Do you think you'll remember where it is?'

'I reckon so.' Pete gave her a shy grin. 'Will you be all right on your own?'

'Yeah, I'll be fine.' Sarah opened the door. 'See you then.'

'Yeah, see you.'

Pete visited Sarah the following week.

Three months later, he moved in.

PART THREE

2003

24

Vinnie got out of the shower and strolled naked into the bedroom to get ready for the party he wasn't looking forward to.

At twenty-five, he was a big man – six-three, and a muscular fourteen stones. And he was exceptionally handsome, with strong, even features, thick, dark-blond hair, and killer blue eyes.

Women loved him, couldn't get enough of his bad-boy charms and satin-smooth tongue. And he loved them right back – in a woo-'em-and-screw-'em kind of way. But he hadn't met one yet that was worthy of more.

What a world it was: drugs, money, fast women, and faster cars. Every young man's dream. And it was all his, thanks to Glen Noble – the biggest semi-legit gangster in Manchester: his boss, his friend – and the man whose latest woman Vinnie had met and conquered months before Glen ever laid eyes on her.

Carina was a stripper when Vinnie met her, and he'd fancied her from the off – in a purely lustful sense. Tall and slim, with platinum-blonde hair, nice tits, and come-fuck-me brown eyes, she held his interest for all of two months before the inevitable boredom set in and he stopped returning her calls.

That, Vinnie had thought, was the end of that. So he hadn't been overjoyed to come back from a fortnight's holiday some months later to find that Glen had met Carina and shacked up with her in his absence.

It was a tricky situation because Glen was a dangerous man to cross. If he found out that he was living with one of Vinnie's ex-shags – and that neither Vinnie nor Carina had seen fit to mention it before he'd got involved – he'd be murderous. Illogical, given that Vinnie hadn't been around to warn him at the time, but Glen didn't think like that. In their world, where loyalty and respect were everything, letting the boss man unwittingly slip one to your sloppy seconds was a cardinal sin.

As soon as Vinnie saw Carina that day, he warned her with a look not to acknowledge him, and she was smart enough to catch on. But later, when they got a moment alone, she made it more than obvious that she was still interested, even going so far as to say that she would finish with Glen if that was the only thing stopping Vinnie from hooking up with her again. Vinnie told her she was crazy, spelling out exactly what would happen to them *both* if she dared let Glen know the score. Fortunately, she took the warning to heart. But it didn't stop her trying to get it on with Vinnie whenever she got the chance, and he had to stay on his toes to avoid being caught out.

Carina was the reason that Vinnie was dreading the party tonight. It was at Glen's house, and she was bound to be wearing as little as possible. There was no telling how indiscreet she'd be once she got started on the fizz, and he didn't want to be in the country if she chose tonight to spill the beans.

He couldn't get out of going because only mutilation or death was reason enough to snub Glen Noble, so Vinnie had decided to try and put an end to the mess in the only way he knew how. He was going to get off with the first available woman he laid eyes on and rub her firmly in Carina's sexy little face.

It was a gamble, but it had to be done. Carina would either grass him up to Glen out of spite, or accept that they were done and lick her wounds in private until she got over it. Vinnie was banking on the latter option. Carina was persistent, but she was also proud – and greedy. She liked the lifestyle that being Glen's woman afforded her: the money, the clothes, the fancy house and car. Once she'd weighed up how much she had to lose against the nothing that she had to gain by chasing Vinnie, he was sure that sense would prevail.

Fastening the top button of his black silk shirt, Vinnie slipped his silver-grey suit jacket on and stepped back to admire himself in the mirror. He looked great and the frown that had been creasing his brow all day immediately smoothed out.

Turning onto Glen's drive fifteen minutes later, Vinnie drove into the parking bay to the left of the pillared double-front doors and found a space behind the several cars already parked there. He was glad he wasn't the first to arrive – there was nothing cool about that, and he had a reputation to uphold.

The house was ablaze with light, and the DJ whom Glen had hired was testing his equipment to the limit inside. Vinnie could feel the vibration of the bass thrumming up through his feet. It excited him. Maybe it wouldn't be too bad after all.

Climbing out of the jeep he turned at the sound of a car, and waved when he saw Glen's sleek BMW coming through the gates. Joe Fielding was driving, Al Goldman sitting beside him and dwarfing the spacious passenger seat. Glen's oldest mates, they were the longest-serving members of the Noble firm – and two of the most dangerous. Between them, they had sorted more would-be gangsters than the Krays had probably ever met.

Vinnie shook his head when he saw the joke-shop Santa standing on the dash, its coat whipping open every few seconds to reveal a huge, illuminated red knob.

'Someone's in the party mood,' he said, opening the driver's side door to let Joe out.

'Can't help it.' Joe grinned like the big kid he always was at Christmas. 'Ever since I seen me mother fucking the cunt when I was a nipper, I've had a thing about his cock.'

'Sad bastard,' Vinnie chuckled, shaking his hand.

'He wants to grow up,' Al grunted, coming around to join them. 'Nearly got pulled 'cos of that.'

'Aw, put a sock in it, for fuck's sake,' Joe moaned. 'It's supposed to be a laugh.'

Carina came out onto the step in the tiniest slip of a sparkling silver dress that plunged far below her cleavage and barely reached the tops of her endless legs. Vinnie's heart sank. She looked stunning – and she obviously knew it. She'd be on full bitch-heat, and impossible to ignore.

'Jeezus,' Joe hissed under his breath as they made their way towards her. 'I wouldn't let her out like that if I was Glen.'

'Put your tongue away,' Al growled.

'I ain't lusting,' Joe grumbled. 'I'm just saying she's a bit fresh, that's all.'

'Merry Christmas,' she said, kissing each of them as they entered.

'And you,' Joe said, shouting over the music.

Closing the door, Carina twirled around to flash a major diamond and ruby ring at them.

'Look what I got for Christmas. Glen hid it on the tree and it took *ages* to find! Isn't it gorgeous?'

'Lovely,' Joe agreed, flicking a glance at the others. It had to have cost a small fortune. Glen was getting in a bit deep with this one.

Al smiled, but the expression didn't reach his eyes. Carina didn't deserve a strand of tinsel, in his opinion.

'What do *you* think, Vinnie?' She thrust her hand under his nose.

'Nice,' he muttered, barely glancing at it. She was trying to make him jealous but it wasn't going to work.

'Doing well for yourself, ain't you, girl?' Joe commented slyly, hanging his overcoat up.

'What's that supposed to mean?' She turned on him, her expression darkening. He might be one of Glen's best mates, but if he was taking the piss . . .

'Just that you've done yourself proud, love,' he replied smoothly. 'Never seen Glen treat a bird so good. He must think you're a bit special.'

'That's right, Joe, he does!' She gave a small, tight smile. 'And don't you forget it.'

'Who's here?' Vinnie said, strolling down the hall to avoid getting involved in the brewing argument. It was no secret that Joe, Al and the rest of the guys resented Carina for wrapping Glen's balls up so tight. And judging by the stink of alcohol coming off her, it wouldn't take too many of Joe's sly digs to send her into a loose-lipped rage.

Catching up in time to have to squeeze past Vinnie in the living-room doorway, Carina whispered, 'Just about everyone, but I was only waiting for you, sexy.'

Jerking away from her as Al and Joe came up behind, Vinnie went after a passing tray of wine. Snatching a glass, he slipped a hand into his pocket and wandered into the heart of the crowded room. It was mostly women in here, and there were quite a few unfamiliar faces – girls invited by wives and girlfriends as fodder for Glen's unattached men. Catching the eye of an attractive blonde, he raised his glass and smiled at her.

A sharp nudge in his ribs almost made him spill the drink.

'What was that for?' he demanded, turning to find Carina glaring up at him.

'Stop eyeing up the bitches,' she hissed, her eyes blazing. 'It isn't exactly *polite*, under the circumstances.'

'Behave,' he hissed back from one corner of a fake smile. 'And lay off the juice if you're gonna start any nonsense.'

'Thanks for the concern,' she drawled. 'But if I wanted someone to monitor my alcohol intake, I'd have brought my dad!'

'Just go and see to your guests,' Vinnie muttered, still trying to appear unfazed in case anyone was watching.

'I can't.' Carina smiled exaggeratedly at a passing couple. 'You're too gorgeous to leave on your own. I don't want anyone getting their little claws into you.'

The doorbell rang just then and as lady of the house she was forced to go and answer it. 'Stay there,' she ordered in a whisper. 'I haven't finished with you yet.'

Exhaling wearily as Carina sashayed from the room, Vinnie made his escape and went into the dining room where most of the men were standing around the mile-long table chatting and laughing, the smoke from their assorted cigarettes, cigars and spliffs blanketing the room.

This was the inner core of Glen's business empire – the tried and trusted members, of which Joe was the oldest and Vinnie the youngest. There were many more in the sub-crews but this was the 'family', and it still gave him a kick to be on the inside.

'Yo, Vinnie, why you on the piss-water when we've got the hard stuff?' Freddie Peters shouted. A huge bruiser of a man with a long black beard that made him look like Rasputin, he was waving a bottle of Walkers in the air. 'Feed the fucking fish with that shite and give us your glass, man. It's Christmas!'

Downing the wine, Vinnie handed the glass across and greeted everyone with handshakes and nods. He had worked his nuts off to gain the respect of these men, but he was under no illusions about just how fast they would take him down if he stepped out of line.

'Where's Glen?' he asked, looking around for the boss.

'Sorting something,' Al told him cagily.

Vinnie didn't press for details. Al was a paranoid fuck, who viewed curiosity as a sign of double-dealing. If he wanted you to know something, he'd tell you. If he didn't, you kept it zipped.

'Vinnie!' Pam Noble bellowed from the midst of the men. 'Get your arse over here, you handsome bastard, and give us a snog!'

Grinning when he saw Glen's mother sitting at the head of the table, Vinnie went to her and hugged her. Of all the women in the world, this was the only one he respected. An ex-hooker, she had worked her backside off to set Glen on the right track. Long since retired, she lived the life of Riley, flitting between Glen's house and the bungalow he had bought her with his first 'wage'. She was the true queen of the Noble clan, and Glen worshipped her, as did the rest of the family – not least Vinnie. She had treated him like one of her own from the start – giving Glen a roasting once in the early days for giving him a well-deserved slap. Vinnie had never forgotten her sticking her neck out for him – nor the lesson Glen had been teaching him at the time.

'Sit down,' she ordered now. 'I want to get a proper look at you.' Peering at him hard through a ton of cracked black eyeliner and silver shadow, she pursed her wrinkled, scarlet-painted lips. 'You been eating right?'

'Course.' He patted his rock-hard stomach. 'You know I like my food.'

'I know you like *mine*. So why didn't you turn up for that lasagne the other week? You begged me to make it, then never showed your face.'

'Oh, shit! I forgot.'

'Don't worry.' Reaching beneath the table, Pam squeezed

Vinnie's thigh. 'I've been keeping it warm in the oven. You can come round for it later.'

'Do us a favour! It'll have a dick and two bollocks by now!'

'Watch your gob, you. It's called a cock and balls where I come from! Haven't I learnt you nowt?'

'More than you'll ever know.' Vinnie grinned, shaking his head. Pam was outrageous. Seventy years old, with the mouth of a twenty-year-old docker whore.

'You'll be here tomorrow, won't you?' she asked, taking a noisy slurp of whisky.

'Yeah.' He reached for the drink that Freddie had poured him. 'But I'm not looking forward to it if you're not cooking.'

Drawing her head back, Pam gave him a wry smile. 'Who says I'm not? You don't seriously think I'm trusting that tart to make my Glen's Christmas dinner, do you? She might rule the bedroom, but that kitchen's mine!'

'Nice one.' Grinning broadly, Vinnie raised his glass. 'Here's to you wearing the crown for another seventy years.'

'And I'd stick around that long out of sheer spite, if I could,' she said, leaning towards him, 'just to wipe the smirk off madam's mush.

'Subject of madams,' she went on, sitting back. 'What happened to that stuck-up bit I saw you with at The Honeypot the other week. You giving it one, or what?'

'That's all I *ever* give 'em,' he quipped. 'And that's more than most of them deserve. What were you doing at a place like that anyhow, you dirty stop-out?'

'We're talking about you, not me,' Pam scolded. 'I know your brain's in your boxers and you think you've got to shag everything that moves, but don't you think it's time you got yourself a steady?'

'What for?'

'The cleaning and ironing.'

'I can do that myself.'

'Yeah, but why wag your own tail when you can get a dog?'

'I might like wagging it.'

'I said wagging, not wanking.'

'Pamela Noble!' Drawing his head back, Vinnie gave her a mock-shocked look. 'Don't be rude.'

'Aw, piss off,' she cackled, slapping him playfully. 'You know what I'm talking about. It ain't decent, a man doing housework. Take her over there.' She nodded towards Carina who was busy flashing her new ring in the living room. 'She mightn't be me first choice for Glen – nor even me last, truth be told. But she keeps the house nice, you've got to give her that. And she's obviously doing something right upstairs, the grin he's got on his face these days. So, how about it?'

'How about what?' Vinnie narrowed his eyes. 'You propositioning me?'

'In your dreams!' Pam snorted. Rising to her feet then, she put her fists on her ample hips and yelled, 'At last! What took you?'

Turning, Vinnie saw that Glen and Carl Howard had arrived. Greeting everyone, Glen edged around the table to hug his mother.

'Been looking after her?' He slapped Vinnie on the back.

'Course he has,' Pam said, reaching up to pull her son's face level so she could kiss him. 'He's a good lad, him – which is more than can be said for you. What you playing at, leaving me on me tod with all these randy blokes?'

'Behave, mother.' Glen pushed her gently back down into her seat. '*They*'ve got more to worry about than you.'

'Hear how he talks to me?' she complained, loving every second of it. 'You lot talk to your mothers like that, do you?'

'No, but we don't socialize with ours.' Joe leaned down

to plant a kiss on her wrinkled cheek. 'See how special we treat you.'

Patting his hand, she said, 'If you're trying to get in me knickers, forget it – you're way too old.'

Laughing with the others, Joe said, 'She slays me, she really fuckin' does.'

'Someone should,' Pam muttered, shooting him a sly wink. 'Put you out of your misery.'

'A-*hem*!'

Turning at the obvious interruption, they saw Carina posing in the doorway.

'There she is.' Glen held his arms out. 'Come here, you sexy bitch.'

Folding her arms, she pouted sulkily. 'Thought you'd forgotten me.'

'As if!' Taking a long, thin package from his pocket, Glen held it behind his back and swaggered towards her. 'Been a good girl, have you?'

Smiling coyly now at the scent of another gift, Carina said, 'I'm *always* good, babe. You know that.'

Vinnie glanced at Pam and had to force himself not to laugh as she mimed poking a finger down her throat. Turning back when he heard Carina squeal with delight, he watched as she tore the paper from the box.

'Oh my God!' she cried, taking out a glittering bracelet. 'It matches my ring! Look, everyone! Isn't it gorgeous?'

'Not as gorgeous as you, babe.' Picking her up, Glen gave her a deep kiss, then plonked her back on her feet and slapped her backside, propelling her into the middle of a group of dancing women. 'Oi, Dread,' he yelled at the DJ. 'Turn the music up. It's supposed to be a bleedin' party!'

Going back to the table as the volume rocketed, Glen helped Pam to her feet and told her to go and keep her eye on the guests while he had a chat with the guys. Ushering her out with a bottle of whisky clutched in her hand, he closed the sliding doors and took his place at the table. Lighting a cigar, he waved the others to sit. The grin was gone now, a dark scowl in its place.

Taking a seat at the far end, Vinnie lit a cigarette and leaned both elbows on the table, his expression attentive.

There was a deadly silence around the table when Glen explained why he and Carl were late. They had been checking out a tip-off that Jimmy Rogers – head of the Stockport rock-production house – was in the process of selling them out to a London firm. Dex Lewis, the head of the firm, was plotting a takeover and was reportedly planning on sending a crew up in a couple of weeks to do hits on all the houses, using information bought from Jimmy as to when the coast would be clear.

'Bastard!' Freddie muttered, cracking his heavily scarred knuckles. 'Where is he? I'll kill the little shit!'

'Too late,' Carl told him quietly, folding his arms and rocking back on his seat. 'He's floating down the Medlock with his dick in his gob as we speak.'

'Anyone else in on it?' Joe demanded.

All stares swivelled back to Glen.

'No.' He frowned darkly. 'I made Jimmy tell me everything before I sorted him. He was on his own.'

'Hand-biting little fuck,' Freddie snarled, shaking his head in disgust. 'What was his excuse?'

'He reckoned Lewis had threatened to gut his missus.' Glen's voice was cold. 'But it don't matter who said what – there's no reason good enough for shafting me and the next one who tries will get the same.'

'What if he was lying?' Joe said angrily. 'We can't let our lads pull a fast one. They've got to be dealt with.'

'We can't just take them all out,' Glen told him. 'Anyway,

no one but us lot knows we've whacked Jimmy yet, and that's the way it stays 'cos I don't want Lewis alerted.'

'He ain't thick enough to think we're gonna lay out the red carpet and hand him everything on a fucking plate,' Al said. 'He'll be on the alert already.'

'Mmm,' Freddie agreed, nodding sagely. 'And he ain't small-time. It'll be a bloodbath.'

'His, not ours,' Glen snapped, glaring at the big man. 'You going arse-up or something, Fred? 'Cos if you are, you'd best open your trap while it's still got a tongue in it.'

Freddie held his gaze for a long, silent moment, then said, 'You know me better than that, Glen. I'm just saying he ain't easy.'

'Well, thanks for that,' Glen drawled sarcastically. 'I can always count on you to keep up with current affairs, can't I?' He slammed his fist down hard on the table. 'I *know* his fucking rep! What d'y' think I do all day – walk about with me head up me arse? I know how he operates, just like I know how many men he's got, what they carry, *and* what they can get their hands on in a hurry. Me and Carl are going over there tomorrow to have a quiet word – see if we can't persuade him to stay on his own turf.'

'And if he won't?' Joe asked, voicing what the others were thinking.

'He will,' Glen stated confidently. 'If he don't want a war.'

'If he's already putting feelers out, he probably thinks he can take us. That's what he'll be waiting for.'

'I'm sure he'll realize he's out of his league once me and Carl have had a word.'

'What you gonna say?'

'Never mind the ins and outs. Just take my word this'll be sorted by the time we get back.'

'We'll all go,' Joe said, looking to the others for support.

'No!' Glen's voice was sharp. 'I need you lot to stay here and keep things running smooth. We know most of the lads are safe, but we don't give 'em an inch till we know who's involved in this. I want you breathing down their necks till one of the cunts cracks.'

There was a murmur of agreement.

'Right.' He reached for a bottle of Scotch. 'Let's have a run-through – make sure everyone knows what they're supposed to be doing.'

Frowning as the guys discussed their various responsibilities, Vinnie waited to be given a job. As the youngest, he didn't have a crew of his own. Glen seemed to like having him around as a kind of personal assistant. But if Glen was going to London, what was he supposed to do?

'What about me, G?' he asked after a while. 'You want me to drive you there? I could stick around in case you need back-up.'

'Nah.' Glen shook his head. 'You're babysitting.'

'Eh?'

'Carina and me mother.'

'Aw, come on,' Vinnie protested. 'I want to do something useful, man. What about Jimmy's crew? They'll need a boss now he's out of the picture.'

'They're sorted,' Glen told him curtly. 'And so are you, so button it. And think on,' he pointed a warning finger. 'You mightn't think this is important, but her and me mother mean more to me than *any* crack house, so you'd best not fuck it up. If I come back and find out one of Lewis's men got so much as a *foot* near either one of them, I'll kill you. Got that?'

'Got it,' Vinnie muttered, folding his arms.

Glen stared at him for a moment longer, then nodded.

Snapping out of his mood as fast as it had come over him, he raised his glass. 'Now we're sorted, we'd best make the most of the time we've got left. Happy Christmas, you bunch of tarts!'

Vinnie tried to get into the spirit of things as the night wore on, but it was impossible. He was still sulking, and Carina made it worse by following him around, touching him up and whispering what she'd do to him when she got him on his own.

Slipping out into the back garden when she wasn't looking, he slumped down on the bench and closed his eyes to think in peace. Babysitting! It was a pure fucking humiliation and Glen was taking the piss. Vinnie wanted to be in on the *real* action, not looking after a couple of birds. He'd be a laughing stock when the sub-crews found out.

Sensing a presence, he looked up and saw the woman he'd raised his glass to earlier smiling down at him.

'Hi, there,' she purred. 'I saw you slipping out. I thought you'd gone home or something.'

'No, I'm still here,' he muttered, taking a slug of whisky and staring out across the dark expanse of grass.

'Am I disturbing you? I'm sorry . . . I just thought . . .'

Vinnie sighed wearily. He felt like telling her to piss off, but he still had the plan to get Carina off his back to carry out, and she was obviously willing. Blonde, pretty, decent tits, slim. She had to be worth a shag.

'I just needed a breather,' he said, smiling now, turning on the charm. 'Missed me, did you?'

'Don't flatter yourself.' She laughed softly. 'I only came out for a bit of peace.'

'Bit of a piece of what?'

'Don't you mean *who*?' Sliding onto the bench, she took the glass from his hand and sipped his drink. 'It needs ice.'

Handing it back, her gaze fell to his crotch. 'Lots of ice to cool it down.'

Vinnie gave her a slow smile. 'Don't worry about me, babe. I like it hot.'

'I bet you do,' she murmured flirtatiously. 'So, what were you so deep in thought about?'

'You,' he lied, giving the answer she was expecting – and getting the expected response in return.

'Oh? I didn't think you'd noticed me.'

Vinnie gave a silent groan. It was all too easy and he didn't know if he could be bothered.

Pulling himself together when Carina's laughter floated out through the partially open door, he slid his arm across the back of the bench.

'Course I noticed you,' he drawled, laying it on thick. 'I've been thinking about you all night, as it happens.'

'Really?' She was more than a little flattered that this gorgeous man seemed to want her as much as she wanted him. 'And *what* were you thinking?'

'Oh, you know.' He held her gaze, his eyes glinting wickedly in the moonlight filtering through the clouds. 'Wondering what colour knickers you're wearing and how long it's going to take to get them off.' He was perversely pleased to see the blush suffusing her cheeks. Served her right for coming on so strong to a strange man.

'Whoa!' She held up a hand, her smile faltering. 'What's the rush?'

'What's the *wait*? *You* followed *me*, remember.'

'Yeah, to get to know you a little better.'

'And how much better can you know someone than in bed, naked?' he reasoned, flipping her a wink.

Bored of the foreplay now, Vinnie downed his drink and tossed his glass onto the lawn. 'I'm out of here. Coming?'

She looked at him uncertainly, a little afraid now. She

couldn't make him out. One minute he was nice, the next abrupt and cold. She wanted him, but did he want her, or was he just after an easy lay?

Pulling his sleeve back, Vinnie glanced impatiently at his watch.

'Okay,' she said, standing up. 'But it'll have to be your place. My, er, husband might object if I take you to mine.'

Vinnie gave a sly smile. She was married. Perfect. No post-fuck whining for affection, or demands for future contact. Going to the patio door, he slid it back and waved her through.

'It's Lucy, by the way,' she said, touching his arm as she stepped inside. 'My name.'

Vinnie felt a surge of irritation. He hadn't asked for details, and she was seriously on the verge of fucking her chances by trying to make this personal. He wasn't exactly in the mood as it was, and if she didn't quit yakking he'd never get it up.

He was just contemplating sacking the whole thing off when he heard Carina laughing again. Looking at her draped all over Glen in the living room, sucking up to him over the jewellery when not long before she'd been giving Vinnie shit just for *smiling* at this woman, he scowled.

'Tell you what,' he said to Lucy, an idea of a way to have a real dig at Carina occurring to him. 'How do you fancy going to a club first?'

Lucy immediately perked up. If he wanted to spend time with her outside the bed she might actually get a conversation out of him – and who knew where that might lead? Linking her arm through his, she smiled up at him.

'That's a great idea. Hope you like dancing 'cos I'm in the mood to get *down*!'

'Hold that thought.' Vinnie gave her a lopsided grin, making her wet with a flash of his perfect teeth. Disentangling himself, he shooed her towards the door.

*   *   *

'Someone's been a good boy,' Glen yelled as Vinnie approached to tell them he was leaving. 'Santa delivered yours early, eh, Vin?'

'Yeah, he's brought you a right cracker!' Joe joined in. 'Hope your *sack*'s big enough!'

'Hope *he*'s big enough in the sack, more like!' said Freddie. 'Sure you don't need a hand, young 'un? Few pointers to stop her leading you a-*sleigh*!'

'Aw, shut your gobs,' Pam scolded. 'Vinnie knows what he's doing, don't you, love?'

'I think I can manage.'

'Got clean sheets, and that?'

'Sheets are fine, but we're not going straight to mine.' Vinnie flicked a sly glance at Carina. 'I'm taking her to Foxies.'

'Go on then, my son!' Glen roared, reaching across to shake his hand. 'Show her how the professionals do it so she knows how you like it, eh?'

'Something like that.' Vinnie grinned, glad to see that Carina wasn't laughing now. 'Anyhow, best not keep her waiting. See you tomorrow.'

'Two o'clock. And it's a big bird, so don't wear yourself out on that one!' Glen called after him. 'Lucky little bastard,' he said then. 'Don't know how he does it, but he always pulls the lookers, don't he?'

'If you like that sort of thing,' Carina snarled under her breath.

'He does that,' Joe said, rolling his eyes in mock despair. 'I was eyeing that one up for meself.'

'Piss off!' Glen snorted. 'What's a bird like that gonna do back at your mother's?'

'Get her kit off and moan and groan till morning,' Pam said, reaching out to pinch his cheek. 'Same as all the tarts you used to bring back to mine did! The good old days, eh, son?'

'Don't know about that,' Glen said, oblivious to the furious scowl on Carina's face. 'I had me fair share of barkers.'

'You did that,' Pam agreed. 'But that's the booze for you. Just like your father for that, you was – God damn his miserable soul. In with the gut-rot – out with the meat and two.'

Laughing, Glen put his arm around Carina's rigid shoulders and gave her a squeeze. Gazing down at her when she stiffened, he said, 'What's up with you? You've gone a bit quiet. Feeling iffy, or something?'

Forcing herself to smile, Carina said, 'Yeah, I'm getting a headache. I think I'd best go to bed. I've got a lot to do tomorrow.'

'Me mother will sort all that in the morning,' Glen told her, leaning down to nuzzle her neck. 'And you can't be going to sleep just yet.' Picking up her hand, he angled it so that the diamonds caught the light. 'You've still got to thank me for this little lot, remember.'

Carina gritted her teeth. She didn't know if she could face going ten rounds with him tonight. Glen was rampant at the best of times, but tonight, full of champagne and cocaine, he'd be insatiable – and rougher than he realized, relentlessly grinding her into the mattress as he strove to reach the orgasm they both knew wouldn't come. If she were walking tomorrow, it'd be a miracle.

'I'll see you upstairs,' she muttered, getting up and pushing her way out of the room.

'Where's she going?' Pam asked snippily. 'Katie would never walk out halfway through a party.'

'No, 'cos she was always too busy seeing to everyone else to think about warming the bed up for me,' Glen told her. 'And stop going on about my bloody ex-wife in front of Carina. You know it upsets her.'

'I was only saying.'

'Yeah, well, don't. We're getting divorced, end of!' Giving his mother a stern look, Glen had to laugh when she stuck her tongue out. 'Right!' He clapped his hands. 'Who wants another line before I kick you all out and go for me dessert?'

Carina raged against the world as she undressed.

Why Glen had to have his mother around all the time, she did not know. But he adored Pam for some unfathomable reason, and Carina knew better than to complain – *yet*. Still, the old bitch couldn't live for ever. And the day she did the decent thing and snuffed it, Carina would dance all over her rotten grave!

And the same went for Pam's precious daughter-in-law, Katie – Glen's whore of an ex-wife. She might think she had a right to his money because she had his brat of a son under her belt, but she was another one who was going to get a rude awakening before too long. As soon as those divorce papers came through there would be no more demanding that he pay this bill and that. She wouldn't get a single penny more than the brat's maintenance.

Ditto Glen's freeloading mates. The party was coming to an end for them, too – and not just the noisy affair going on down below, the whole shebang. They would pay their own way when Carina got her say, support their own habits on their more than generous wages. She was sick to death of them taking the piss while Glen footed all the bills.

As for Vinnie Walker . . . Damn him to hell and back for taking that skinny bitch to Foxies! That was *their* place. How *dare* he defile it by taking some worthless little slag there! The bitch had better not even *think* about showing her face round here again. And just wait till Glen went away. Vinnie was going to pay dearly for betraying Carina tonight! The cunt wasn't getting away with spitting in her

25

It was still dark when Sarah woke up. For a moment she was disorientated by the clean smell of the room. No sweaty feet, stale smoke, or sour booze-breath. Then she had a flashback of Pete crawling into bed at three a.m., plastered and expecting a legover he had a hope in hell of getting, and remembered that she had slept in their daughter's narrow single bed.

Looking at Kimmy curled up beside her now, her impossibly long eyelashes resting against her flushed cheeks and her rosebud lips softly fluttering around the barely audible snores coming from her sweet-smelling mouth, Sarah smiled. This child was the flame of her heart – the reason she still bothered to get up in the mornings.

Easing herself out of bed, she tiptoed from the room. Flipping on the living-room light she looked at the small heap of packages littering the floor beneath the tinselled tree and gritted her teeth. The pram wasn't there. The one thing Kimmy had actually *asked* for, and Pete had forgotten to bring it back. He was such a prick sometimes! She'd have to drive round to Hannah's and pick it up now – and try to get it wrapped before Kimmy woke up.

Going to her own bedroom, Sarah switched on the lamp and took her clothes from the wardrobe – avoiding looking at Pete for fear that she might slap his stupid face.

Dressing, with a scowl etched deeply into her brow, she caught sight of herself in the mirror and groaned. She was only twenty-six, but she looked and felt more like forty-six. Her hair was lank, her skin dull, and her eyes were sunken and lifeless. If anyone had warned her that marriage would do *this* to her she'd have run a thousand miles.

Nine years they had been together and what, apart from Kimmy, had they achieved? Nothing! Oh, sure, they had an okay flat – if you overlooked the fact that it was council and furnished with second-hand bargains. And they had a car – albeit a ten-year-old Orion. But it hardly matched up to the plans they had made once upon a long time ago. Pete's brilliant career, the terrific wage, the apartment on the Quays. Where had it all gone wrong?

In Pete's head, Sarah thought bitterly. Yes, he was working – and she had to give him credit for struggling on in a job that he hated – but he'd long ago given up on the idea of promotion, and he had the strange idea that whatever was left over from his wages after the bills were paid was *his* to spend on things that brought *him* pleasure. Getting pissed with his mates, for example – leaving her to get on with everything else: washing, cleaning, cooking . . . Kimmy.

That was another thing that galled her – his belief that being a good father meant spending as little time as possible with his child. But she'd given up trying to force him to understand the value of creating and nurturing the bond that she herself shared with Kimmy. So what if he had no clue what she liked to eat or what her favourite cartoons were? It was *him* who was losing out.

Still, for all the complaints, Sarah knew that she wasn't as badly off as some. At least she always had food in the cupboard – unlike most of the women round here who trained their kids to hide behind the couch at a knock on the door and were constantly on the scrounge. And, unlike their men, Pete had never laid a hand on her. If all she had to worry about was being taken for granted, she wasn't doing too badly.

Hannah said, 'Steve's done that already, love, being his usual wanker self. You know where they were last night, don't you?'

'Yeah,' Sarah muttered. 'The bloody pub on a lock-in – *again*.'

Glancing back at the living-room door, Hannah said, 'No, they weren't.'

'Oh?' Sarah frowned. 'You know something I don't?'

'Only that they spent about half an hour in total at the pub,' Hannah said, so quietly that Sarah had to strain to hear. 'After that, they went on a club crawl. You'll never guess where they ended up.'

'Where?'

'Foxies.'

'The lap-dancing place?'

'Mmm-*hmm*.' Hannah nodded, pursing her lips for added emphasis. 'I wouldn't have found out, only Steve had the receipts in his pocket and I found them. You know how much it costs to get in there?' she went on, tipping Brasso onto her cloth and passing the tin to Sarah. 'Twenty-five quid apiece! He's lucky I didn't rip his gonzos off and hang them off the tree in foil this morning!'

Sarah didn't laugh as she might have under different circumstances – she just set about the polishing with vigour, her nostrils flaring to split-apart width.

'Can you believe the cheek of them?' Hannah grumbled on, her generous chins and tits wobbling in unison as she rubbed at the pram frame. 'Handing our money to some skinny-arsed bitches for a flash of split! I flew for Steve this morning, I can tell you. Said if he thought I was ever gonna trust him again after this he had another think coming.'

Sarah didn't interrupt as Hannah prattled on: she was too busy digesting the information and allowing it to solidify in her heart. How *dare* Pete go to a place like that, then try to

Lacing her trainers, she took the keys from Pete
and let herself quietly out of the flat.

Pulling up outside her friend's house a few minutes late
smiled when she saw the lights blazing inside. At least *so*
knew how to kick Christmas morning off in style. If she
Hannah, the house would be a mess of ripped paper, bi
toys and melted chocolate by now, and Hannah herself w
be relaxing at the kitchen table with a fag and a steaming
of tea in her hand.

Hannah answered the door and shivered exaggeratedly
the chill air. Wrapping her dressing gown tighter aroun
herself she waved Sarah in.

'Come for the pram?' she asked, closing the door quickly.
'I told your Pete to take it last night, but he said he was
too tired.'

'Too idle, more like,' Sarah muttered. 'Is it ready?'

'Not exactly.' Hannah nodded towards the pram standing
in the far corner. 'I was going to give it a going-over the
other day but Pete said to leave it. Reckoned he was going
to respray it.'

'Christ!' Sarah hissed. It was a mess, the seat stained with
two years' worth of glop that Hannah's youngest had spille
on it, the silver framework in need of major surgery to repa
the pits and scrapes. 'How am I supposed to give it to h
like that?'

'Stop panicking.' Hannah opened the sink cupboard
pulled out a small tub of cleaning equipment. 'It won't
long to put right.'

'You sure you've got the time?' Sarah asked, catchin
cloth Hannah threw to her. 'I don't want to ruin *you*
as well.'

Pulling a face as she gave her own cloth a shar
to free it of any bugs that might have been nestin

get into her knickers when he came home. Just wait till she got her hands on the lying, cheating toe-rag!

Sitting back on her heels after a while, her face sweaty from her exertions, Hannah looked at Sarah and frowned. 'You all right?'

'Fine, thanks.' Sarah forced a tight smile, determined not to let Hannah see how pissed-off she was. She'd be the laughing stock of the estate before the day was through. 'I think this is just about done. Have you got something to give the seat a wipe?'

'Just a sec.' Puffing unhealthily, Hannah got up and wad-dled to the sink. Throwing the sponge to Sarah, she sat at the table and lit a cigarette. 'You paying for it, by the way?' she said. 'I'm not hassling, but I could really do with it if you've got it.'

Sarah looked back over her shoulder. 'Pete said he paid you a couple of weeks back.'

Hannah shook her head. 'He kept saying he'd fetch it round, but he never did. I'm not being funny, love, but I did tell him I had another buyer lined up if he couldn't manage it.'

'I don't believe this!' Sarah was furious. 'He swore blind he gave it to you. Honest to God, Hannah, he stood there and told me how he'd given it to you in your hand, and you'd said not to mention it to Steve 'cos he'd only take it off you and piss it up the wall.'

'Never happened.' Hannah shrugged. Sympathetic as she was, she couldn't help but think that Sarah was partly to blame. If she'd climb off her pedestal and stop kidding herself that she was too good to be treated like that by *her* man, she might wise up and do what the rest of the women round here did – get a step ahead of him and beat him at his own game.

'Look, I'm sorry you didn't know,' Hannah said. 'But I can't let it go if someone doesn't pay me. You can give us half now and owe us the rest if you're stuck, but I'm really desperate.'

'No, it's all right.' Taking her purse from her pocket, Sarah took out her last twenty-pound note and handed it over. 'I only needed cigs, but I'm sure I can manage a day without.'

'Oh, well, I can help you out there.' Grinning now, Hannah got up and went to the wall cupboard. 'I've still got a few of them cartons Steve nicked off that truck.' Reaching up to the top shelf, she pushed a pile of plastic bags aside and groped for the cartons. Pulling one out, she tossed it to Sarah.

'I only need a pack,' Sarah said, offering the rest back.

'Behave!' Hannah pushed them into her hand. 'It's Christmas. You'd do the same for me.'

Thanking her, Sarah got up and put her coat on.

'Come round for a drink later,' Hannah said, showing her out. 'No doubt them two will be off on the piss again so I don't see why we shouldn't have a bit of fun an' all.'

Making it back in time to wrap the pram – albeit roughly, and in two different colours of paper – Sarah crept into Kimmy's room and gave her a gentle shake to wake her.

'Santa Christmas!' Kimmy yelped, bursting to immediate life. Racing into the living room, with her black ringlets flying out behind her, she launched herself at the presents, tearing the paper off each one and showing it to Sarah before moving on to the next.

'Look, mammy, look!' she squealed when she got to the pram.

Sarah's eyes filled with tears as Kimmy threw her arms around her mother's neck. Life might be the absolute pits at times, but she wouldn't have traded moments like these for all the money in the world.

Pete surfaced at just gone eleven. Groaning at the pain in his temples, he pushed the quilt aside and dropped his feet to the floor. Cradling his aching head in his hands, he groaned some more as memories of the night before flooded his mind.

He should *never* have agreed to go to that club. Only sad blokes with ugly wives, blokes like Steve and Clive, pulled stupid stunts like that. Sarah was going to kill him when she found out – and she would, she always did. The best thing he could do was come clean before someone let it slip – and pray that she'd believe him when he said he would never do it again.

Wandering into the living room with a sheepish look on his face, he crossed to Sarah, who was sitting on the couch, and kissed the top of her head. 'Happy Christmas, babe. Sorry about last night.'

'Don't worry about it,' she said, her gaze glued to Kimmy who was busy giving every soft toy she possessed rides in the new pram. 'She's happy, that's all that counts.'

'You went and got it, then?'

'Yeah – and before you ask, I paid for it as well.'

'Eh?' Pete drew his head back questioningly. 'I gave Hannah the money weeks ago.'

'Don't lie,' Sarah said wearily. 'I know you didn't, so let's just drop it.'

'But—'

'*Pete!*' she snapped, looking at him now. 'Don't push it, eh? I'm *not* in the mood.' Getting up, she went into the kitchen and filled the kettle.

Following her, Pete leaned against the door frame and chewed his lip as he watched her take a cup from the cupboard and spoon coffee into it. Her back was so rigid that he didn't need to see her face to know she was furious. It was coming off her in waves.

'Why are you staring at me?' Sarah asked irritably. 'Haven't you got anything better to do – like play with your daughter? You didn't even say Happy Christmas to her.'

Pete decided to come clean while the atmosphere was already strained. She'd be mad but she wouldn't kick off and ruin Christmas for Kimmy. She'd save the real roasting for later when Kimmy went to bed, but he had a plan to avoid that. He would suddenly 'remember' the best news and, with any luck, she'd be so made up that she'd forget all about being angry.

'I've got something to tell you,' he said now, closing the door. 'About last night . . . I, er, wasn't in the pub the whole time like I said.'

'Oh, *really*?'

'No, I, er, went with Steve and Clive to this club. Don't get mad, babe, 'cos I was really, really pissed, and I swear I didn't see a thing, but it was sort of a . . . strip club.'

'Oh, yeah?' Turning around, Sarah folded her arms. 'Now, *there*'s a surprise.'

Blushing, Pete looked at his feet. 'You already knew, didn't you?'

'Oh, yeah, I knew, all right. Hannah couldn't *wait* to tell me. But you figured that out, didn't you? That's why you decided to come clean, isn't it?'

'No!'

'Bullshit! You've been caught out and you're trying to blag your way out of it. So what did you do, Pete? Get your kicks watching the tarts strutting their stuff, then come home to me for the finale? Charge too much for the actual shag, did they?'

'It wasn't like that,' he protested helplessly. 'I swear to God, Sarah. Look, I know I'm a fuck-up, but I didn't do anything. I was going to tell you when I got back, but I didn't know what to say when you started kicking off.'

'I was kicking off because you went out on Christmas bloody Eve and left me and the baby on our own,' she snapped. 'I thought we were supposed to be a family.'

'We are.' He moved towards her with a hangdog look in his eye. 'You're all I've ever wanted, Sarah – you and Kimmy.'

'Don't!' She held her hands up to stop him touching her. 'I've got a really bad headache. I just want a coffee and a bit of quiet.'

Backing off, Pete said, 'Can I do anything?'

'Yeah.' She turned back to the sink. 'Go and play with your daughter.'

The atmosphere was chilly for a while, but Sarah gradually thawed as the day wore on and by the time they ate dinner she had decided to forgive and forget. Pete was making such an effort to please her, and she had to admit he looked more like his handsome old self when he took a shower and slapped on some of the aftershave that she had given him. Best of all, though, was the way he was playing with Kimmy, helping her to do one of the pictures in her new magic paint book and letting her waffle on about how much her dolly liked her new pram.

Sarah was smiling as she cleared the table, glad that things were back to normal. Nothing was ever as bad as it seemed, and wrong as he'd been for going to that club at least Pete had told her the truth in the end – which was more than could be said for Steve.

When she'd finished putting the kitchen to rights, she bathed Kimmy and put her to bed in her new Barbie pyjamas. Worn out, Sarah wandered back into the living room to put her feet up and have a proper drink.

Pete soon put paid to that idea.

'Oh, by the way,' he said as soon as she walked through the door. 'I forgot to tell you . . . I saw Vinnie last night.'

Stopping in her tracks, she stared at him. 'Vinnie Walker?'

'Yeah! Mad, isn't it? I haven't seen him since just before we got together, but I recognized him straight away. He was in that club with a woman. Proper tart, by the look of her, but you know Vinnie. I couldn't believe it.'

Sarah's jaw clenched. So, he remembered enough about the club to know that he had seen Vinnie and a woman in there. What else had he seen and conveniently forgotten – or *done*, for that matter?

'I invited him round for a drink later,' Pete went on. 'Don't mind, do you?'

'Yes, I *mind*!' she said, astonished that he should even *consider* bringing Vinnie back into their lives. 'What do you think you're playing at?'

Pete was genuinely surprised by her response. It had been years since she'd seen Vinnie. Surely she didn't still hate him for the things he'd done as a kid.

'He's not like he was,' he tried to reassure her. 'You should have seen him, Sarah. He's well minted.'

'I wouldn't care if he was gold-bloody-plated!' she snarled. 'I don't want him here. He's trouble.'

'So was I,' Pete reminded her quietly. 'But I changed, didn't I?'

Muttering 'Huh!' Sarah went into the kitchen and snatched a cigarette from the pack on the ledge. Sucking on it furiously, she threw Pete a dirty look when he popped his head around the door.

'You're not mad, are you?' He smiled nervously. 'I didn't think you'd mind, or I wouldn't have asked him.'

'Well, I do, so you can just ring him and *un*-ask him.'

'I can't. I didn't get his number.'

'*Forget*, did you?' she sniped. 'Like you *forgot* to tell me you'd been to that club when you first got in, and *forgot* to pick up your daughter's present?'

'Oh, don't start that again,' Pete moaned. 'I was pissed out of my head. What do you want me to say? I've screwed up again. Okay – I have. I'm sorry.'

'Yeah, you are.' Exhaling a thick stream of smoke, Sarah turned to look out of the window. After a moment, she said, 'So, what did you tell him?'

'That we're married with a kid. And that you'd be made up to see him.'

'Oh, *yeah*, I'm ecstatic.'

Sighing, Pete lowered his head. 'I'll wait for him outside and tell him you don't want him to come in.'

'You will not!' she retorted angrily. 'You're not making me out to be some sort of bitch.'

'Well, I won't answer the door, then. We'll pretend we're out.'

'Don't be so stupid. What if Kimmy starts crying?'

'What do you want me to do?' Pete sounded as helpless as he felt. 'Tell him *I* don't want him here when it was me who asked him round?'

Sarah was silent for a moment, then, tutting, she said, 'You'll have to let him in. But don't go making him comfortable. Give him one drink, then tell him we're going out.'

'Thanks, babe,' Pete said, the relief clear in his voice. Then, tentatively, as if testing the water, he said, 'Don't get pissed off again, but will you do me a favour?'

'What?'

'Will you put that red dress on and tart yourself up a bit?'

'You *what*?' she squawked, turning to glare at him now.

'I just want him to see you at your best,' he explained. 'Let him – you know – see what he missed.'

Sarah was furious. It was bad enough that he'd invited Vinnie round in the first place, and now he wanted her to dress up for him. It was pathetic.

'Will you?' His eyes were pleading with her. 'Please?'

'Why's it so important what Vinnie thinks?' she demanded.

Pete shrugged miserably. 'I just don't want him to think he's better than me.'

'Because he's *minted*?'

'Well, yeah. You should have seen the suit on him, Sarah. It probably cost more than I make in a year.'

'So?'

'You wouldn't understand.'

Pete took a cigarette from the pack and Sarah was surprised to see that his hands were shaking when he lit it. Vinnie had really got to him.

'All right.' She relented. 'I'll dress up, if it makes you happy.'

'Really?' Looking up, he grinned. 'Thanks, babe.'

'Don't be smiling,' Sarah warned him, stubbing her smoke out aggressively. 'I'm *not* impressed!'

26

A chorus of catcalls greeted Vinnie when he arrived at Glen's house and strolled into the smoky living room.

'Eh up! Here comes the shagmaster general!'

'Yo, Vin, did you leave it begging for more?'

'Hope you give it one for me!'

Even Pam took time out of the kitchen to come and give him a good-on-you! punch on the arm.

Only Carina refused to participate in the banter. Tight-lipped, she laid the dining-room table, her stiletto heels punishing the polished wood floor as she banged the cutlery down.

'Chill out, babe,' Glen said when he came through to fetch another bottle of wine from the cooler. 'Me mother's got everything under control. Leave that and come for a drink.'

'Later.' She shooed him out of the way. 'I know she's perfect, but even *she* can't do everything on her own!'

Glen frowned, wondering if Carina was taking a pop at his mother. Then he decided that she was probably just edgy. It was her first big function as woman of the house and she was bound to be feeling the pressure of living up to his mother's standards. If he were honest, his mother wasn't exactly helping to put her at ease. He wasn't stupid, he knew they hadn't got to grips with each other yet. But, as the most important women in his life, he was banking on them doing the female bonding shit when he was out of the way. With any luck, they'd be best mates by the time he got back. Getting what he'd come for, he left her to it.

Alone again, Carina placed her hands flat on the table and exhaled shakily. She had to stop this before she dropped herself right in it. Glen was still a bit pissed off with her cutting his mega-shag short last night. If she carried on biting his head off he was likely to get suspicious and demand to know what was wrong. And what was she supposed to say? . . . That she was mad at Vinnie for fucking off with that slag last night? Oh, yeah, she could see that going down a bomb!

Pam came through from the kitchen, struggling to keep the enormous turkey from sliding off the plate she was carrying. Seeing Carina standing there like that, she frowned.

'What's up with you? Got a hangover, or something?'

'Yeah, something like that.' Straightening up, Carina forced herself to smile. 'Don't worry. I'll take something for it when I've finished the table.'

'I wasn't worried,' Pam muttered, plonking the turkey down. 'You polished them knives and forks yet?'

'Yes.'

'Good, 'cos I don't want my Glen getting ill off of 'em. What about the glasses?'

'*Yes!*'

Picking one up, Pam held it up to the light and peered at it. Sucking her teeth softly when she saw that it was spotless she put it down and went to get the vegetables.

Sticking her fingers up at the swinging door Carina carried on with what she was doing.

'That wasn't very nice,' Vinnie said quietly, coming in to get a couple of glasses for some late arrivals.

'Piss off!' she hissed, shooting him a murderous look.

Leaning close as he passed by her, he whispered, 'My, but we're narky today. Something upset us, has it?'

'Do *not* mess with me,' she warned in a low voice.

'Or what?' he persisted. 'Gonna tell sugar daddy on me? Tell him to give me a little slap for winding Queen Carina up?'

Before Carina had a chance to deliver any kind of retort, the kitchen door swished open and Pam came in carrying a platter of roast potatoes.

'She ain't half winding herself up over this dinner, Pam,' Vinnie said, taking the platter and laying it down on the table. 'You want to show her how it's done – put her out of her misery.'

'I don't need any help, thank you!' Carina snapped. 'I'd be *fine* if everyone would just let me get on with it!'

Rolling his eyes exaggeratedly, Vinnie got the glasses and left the room with a spring in his step. His plan seemed to have worked. Carina was mad as hell with him for shagging the lovely Lucy. He wondered what she would say if she knew what had *really* happened: that he had shoved the poor cow into a cab outside Foxies, then gone home alone – his head too full of Sarah to be bothered even going through the motions.

It had been a turn-up seeing Pete after all this time. What a *loser* he'd turned out to be, in his snide DKNY tracksuit, pissed out of his head with some seriously tacky mates in tow. Vinnie almost hadn't bothered talking to him – probably wouldn't have if Pete hadn't mentioned Sarah straight off. He'd found it hard to believe that Sarah Mullen would take up with Pete when she had never shown the slightest interest in him at Starlight, but Vinnie would know all the ins and outs by tonight. And maybe, just maybe, he'd be free of Sarah's ghost once and for all. If she'd turned out anything like Pete, he doubted he'd feel anything but pity for her.

Dinner was a riotous affair with the men cracking increasingly filthy jokes – to the chagrin of their women; Carina flinging malicious eye-daggers left, right and centre; Pam taking every opportunity to mention what a belting daughter-in-law Katie had been; and Vinnie trying desperately not to think about what was coming later, because it gave him butterflies just thinking about seeing Sarah again.

When they had finished eating and the women had cleared the plates away, Glen called a final meeting before he and Carl set off for London.

'You all know what I want so I don't expect any unnecessary calls,' he warned. 'Emergencies, yeah – advice on how to tie your fucking shoelaces, no! Right . . . what you on, Joe?'

'Didsbury and Whalley houses, and Stocky pubs.'

'Freddie?'

'Longsight streeters, Longsight and Levenshulme pubs.'

'Al?'

'Everything.'

'Nelson?'

'Moss Side and Hulme.'

'Vinnie?'

'Guarding the women,' Vinnie muttered, refusing to tag himself as a babysitter.

Grinning, Glen said, 'Good lad. Did you bring a case, by the way? I didn't see you bring one in.'

'A case of what?'

'Cham-fuckin'-pagne!' Glen laughed. '*Clothes*, you dickhead!'

'What do I need clothes for?'

'Planning to wear that shite every day while you're stopping here, are you?' Glen nodded at Vinnie's suit.

'Stopping here?' Vinnie repeated. 'How come?'

'How else d'y' think you're gonna look after them?' Glen was beginning to bristle now. 'You think we're playing games here or something, Vin?'

'No, but—'

'But nowt! This ain't a joke, man. It could get seriously

moody, and if it does I want to know that no fucker's gonna take an easy pop at them two. I thought we had this sorted last night.'

'We did,' Vinnie assured him. 'I wasn't thinking, that's all. I'll go and grab some stuff in a bit.'

'"In a bit" ain't good enough,' Glen told him. 'I want you back here before me and Carl set off. You've got an hour. Shift it.'

Driving at speed to his flat, Vinnie grabbed a few clothes and stuffed them into an overnight case. Zipping it up, he checked his windows, set the alarm and went out. Flinging the case onto the back seat, he set off with a squeal of rubber.

He was fuming. No way had Glen said anything about Vinnie having to move in with Carina and Pam while Glen was away. Vinnie would have told him right where to stick it if he had.

Yeah, right!

Checking the dash-clock he saw that he still had forty minutes. It wasn't long for the most important reunion of his life, but it was better than nothing.

Pete had been looking out of the window for the better part of an hour when the jeep pulled up behind his car and Vinnie stepped out.

'He's here,' he yelled excitedly. 'Sarah . . . Did you hear me?'

'All right, you don't have to shout!'

Staring at her as she came through from the bedroom, Pete felt something lurch in his chest. He'd forgotten how fantastic Sarah looked when she made the effort – how stunning her figure was when she wore a dress instead of the baggy tracksuits she lived in these days; how strikingly beautiful her face was when she wore make-up, and how lustrous her hair was, brushed to a gleam and loose of its usual ponytail.

'This good enough?' she asked tetchily.

'God, yeah!' he spluttered. 'You look gorgeous – just like when we got married.'

'And the rest of the time I'm . . . *what*?' she challenged, folding her arms. 'The dog you completely take for granted?'

'I don't,' Pete protested. 'And I've never called you a dog.'

Waving dismissively towards the door when the knock came, Sarah said, 'You'd best let your friend in before he changes his mind and goes back to his *minted* life.'

Peering at her across the great divide that their small living room had suddenly become, Pete said, 'You're not gonna be funny with him, are you?'

'Oh, *no*.' She gave a tight smile. 'I'll be the perfect hostess.'

Murmuring 'Thanks', he went to answer the door.

Taking a cigarette from the pack Sarah lit it and sat down on the couch. Glancing around the room she gave a sigh of disappointment. It was tidy but it was obvious that they were not doing well, and she was ashamed that the one person she had always felt superior to was about to witness how crap her life had turned out.

Maintaining as impassive an expression as possible when Pete led Vinnie in a moment later, she felt something twist in her gut. He was a lot taller and broader than she had imagined he would be, and far more self-assured. He looked every bit as well off as Pete had said, but there was no way she had expected him to be so handsome. He'd always been a good-looking lad, but now he was an absolutely gorgeous man, and she had to force herself not to let her admiration show on her face. He had been nothing but a common thug when she had known him and it wasn't fair that he was doing so well for himself.

'Look who's here,' Pete announced, as if Vinnie's arrival were a complete surprise. 'You remember Vinnie, don't you?'

Flicking Pete an irritated glance, Sarah said, 'Of course I remember him.' Then, forcing herself to smile, she said, 'How are you, Vinnie?'

'Fine, thanks,' Vinnie murmured, taking her appearance in with a surreptitious all-over glance. He'd had some stunning women in his time, but Sarah still had the *something* that none of them had possessed: the ability to make his heart beat so hard that it felt as if it were struggling to burst from his chest. 'You?' he asked.

'Oh, you know.' She shrugged. 'Can I get you a drink?'

Drawing back the edge of his sleeve, Vinnie glanced at his watch. If it had just been Pete, he wouldn't have bothered turning up at all. But he'd been curious to see Sarah, and now that he had, he wasn't sure he could bear to tear himself away so soon. He would just have to tell Glen that something had come up.

'Okay.' He nodded. 'But it'll have to be quick. I was only coming to tell you I couldn't make it, to be honest.'

'You don't have to stay,' she sniped, folding her arms. 'I'm sure you've got far more important things to do than sit around here talking about the *good* old days.'

Unnerved by the edge in her voice, Vinnie said, 'No, it's fine. I wanted to come. But . . . well, something came up at the last minute that I can't get out of. I'd love a drink – if *you* don't mind?'

'Course she doesn't!' Pete assured him blithely. 'Make yourself at home. I've got some nice brandy in the kitchen.'

'Where from?' Sarah demanded, immediately clamping her mouth shut to prevent herself adding 'What with?' The last thing she wanted was to make out like they were skint – true though it was.

'I nipped out while you were getting ready,' Pete told her.

'Won't be a minute.' Grinning happily, he dashed into the kitchen.

'All right if I sit here?' Vinnie asked, waving towards the other end of the couch.

'Whatever,' Sarah muttered.

Sitting down, he glanced around the room as Sarah smoked on in silence. 'Nice place,' he said after a moment. 'How long you been here?'

'It's a dump,' she replied coolly. 'And we've been here since Kimmy was born.'

'Kimmy . . . ?'

Sarah narrowed her eyes. He obviously didn't have a clue what she was talking about.

'My daughter,' she said. 'Didn't Pete tell you?'

'I don't think so.' He shrugged. 'So . . . you've got a daughter?'

'Yeah.'

'Right.' Another awkward silence. 'Er, she not here?'

'She's in bed.' Despite her determination to cold-shoulder him, Sarah's tone softened of its own accord.

Vinnie saw the hint of a sparkle in her eye as she told him about her daughter and the new pram. It was the first hint of joy he had witnessed since arriving. The kid obviously meant the world to her.

'Tell me about her,' he said, hoping to score bonus points by showing interest.

'Well, she's three,' Sarah began. 'And she's into everything at the moment . . .'

She immediately clammed up when Pete came back with the brandy and three glasses. Pouring the drinks, he handed them out and sat down.

'So, what have you been up to, Vin?' he asked. 'I know you said you were working, but I can't remember if you said what as.'

Sitting casually forward with his elbows on his knees, Vinnie gave a slight shrug. 'All sorts,' he answered evasively. 'Mainly driving, and a bit of bodyguarding, and that. But never mind me, what's this about you having a kid?'

Blushing as Sarah turned and stared at him accusingly, Pete said, 'Kimmy? . . . Didn't I tell you about her? I thought I had. Yeah, she's our little 'un, isn't she, Sarah?' Beaming now, the proud father.

'I'd love to meet her.' Vinnie was looking at Sarah again. 'Maybe I could come back sometime when she's awake?'

'If you want,' Sarah murmured, wondering why she was encouraging him when he was the last person she wanted in their lives.

'That'd be great,' Pete chipped in enthusiastically. 'You'll love her, mate. She looks just like her mum.'

'I'm sure she's gorgeous.' Forcing himself to stop staring, Vinnie downed his drink and stood up. 'Look, I've really got to go. Thanks for that.' He handed the empty glass to Pete. 'I'll bring something next time.'

'Nice one!' Pete grinned. 'Did I give you the number?'

'No. You want to give it to me now?'

'I'll write it down.' Getting up, Sarah went to the kitchen for a pen and paper – shooting Pete a poisonous glare as she passed.

Showing Vinnie out, Pete said, 'Thanks for coming, mate. It was really good to see you again.'

'Yeah, you too.' Smiling, Vinnie shook Pete's hand. 'See you soon.'

Climbing into the jeep, Vinnie exhaled loudly. That had been far worse than he'd expected. Sarah was even more gorgeous than he remembered, and he was jealous as fuck that she was married to Pete. Married, for God's sake – with a kid! It wasn't right.

Still, he had the number now. There was plenty of time to do what had to be done.

Taking his mobile from his pocket, he flipped it open as he did a neat u-turn in the middle of the road.

'Yo, Glen. I'm on my way back. No, no problem. I just had a flat, but it's sorted now. I'll be there in ten.'

Pete watched from the window as Vinnie rapidly disappeared from view. 'God, I thought his gear was good,' he murmured enviously, 'but did you see his wheels? Come and have a look, Sarah. Quick, he's nearly gone.'

'I'll see it next time,' she said, snatching up the glasses and carrying them into the kitchen.

'What did you think?' he shouted after her. 'Can't you tell he's loaded? Did you see his watch? It must've cost a bomb, that.'

'Jealous?'

'Nah.' Coming into the kitchen, Pete wrapped his arms around Sarah and planted several kisses on the smooth skin of her neck. 'He might have dosh and a flash car but I've got you. If anyone's jealous it's him. He couldn't take his eyes off you.'

Smiling slyly, Sarah prised his hands away and began to dry the glasses. So Vinnie was still into her, was he? Good! Maybe the realization that other men still found her attractive would give Pete the kick up the backside he needed to get his act together and stop seeing her as just a wife and a mother.

'Thanks for that,' Pete said. 'I know you can't stand him, so thanks for being so cool about him coming round.' Kissing her cheek then, he said, 'I'm just gonna nip round Steve's for a bit – if that's all right?'

'Why wouldn't it be?' Turning around, she looked him straight in the eye. 'It's not like you're going to do anything stupid like try and sneak off to a strip club again, is it?'

Blushing furiously, he shook his head. 'No way! You can trust me, babe. I'll never do that again. I swear it.'

Believing him, Sarah relaxed. 'All right, I'll see you later. But don't wake me up if you come back late. I'm already knackered.'

As Vinnie loaded the cases into the boot of the BMW Glen strolled around the jeep, inspecting the tyres.

'Thought you said you had a flat?' he said accusingly. 'These don't look no different to me. Which is the spare?'

'None,' Vinnie admitted. 'I didn't have to change it. I was right by the garage when it went down so I got them to take a look at it. They reckoned someone must have had the cap away and let the air out while I was getting my stuff together. They just pumped it back up.'

'Took long enough, didn't it?'

'Yeah, but you know what it's like. They had to put it on the machine, check it had no punctures.'

'And did it?'

'No, it's fine.' Vinnie was frowning now. 'What's up, Glen? Don't you believe me, or something?'

Peering at him through narrowed eyes, Glen said, 'I don't know, Vin. All I know is I give you an hour and you took the piss. If me and Carl miss the train you're gonna know about it.'

'You won't,' Vinnie assured him confidently. 'Joe will get you there in time.'

'Best had,' Glen warned. 'Anyhow, remember what I said.' He changed the subject. 'Don't leave them two alone for any reason. Do full security checks before you lock up, and don't let no fucker in. I don't care who they say they are or what they want, no one gets in except Al and Joe. Got that?'

'Yeah, no problem,' Vinnie agreed, wishing Glen would stop going on with himself and go.

'We right?' Carl asked, coming out of the house with a thick package of turkey sandwiches in his hand – courtesy of Pam.

Glen checked his watch and tutted when he saw that they had just fifteen minutes to get to the station. Pointing a warning finger at Vinnie, he wrenched the front passenger door open and hopped in, yelling at Joe and Carl to get a move on.

Vinnie waited until they had turned out of the drive before going inside.

'Can I get you anything, love?' Pam came into the hall with a tea towel in her hands. 'A butty or a brew?'

Vinnie frowned when he saw how drained she looked. She was usually vibrant and lively, but right now she looked as if she had the weight of the world on her shoulders. She must have been more worried about Glen than she'd been letting on.

'A brew would be great.' Going towards her, he put an arm around her shoulders. 'But how's about I make it while you have a sit-down?'

'Oh, no, I'm fine.' She patted his hand. 'You know me, Vinnie. I like having things to do.'

'Yeah, but you've been running round after everyone all day so let *me*,' he insisted. 'And don't argue, 'cos I ain't listening.' Walking her into the dining room, Vinnie pulled out a chair and sat her down.

Carina stalked in seconds after he had gone into the kitchen.

'Where's Vinnie?' she demanded.

'In there,' Pam nodded towards the door. 'Making me a brew. Give him a shout if you want one.'

'I just want a word,' Carina said, shaking out the coat she was holding.

'Going somewhere?'

'Yes. But don't worry, I won't be long.'

'Glen don't want you going out on your own. That's why Vinnie's here, isn't it?'

'*You* might need looking after,' Carina replied huffily, 'but *I* don't. I've got things to do, and I'm not putting my entire life on hold just because Glen's chosen to take a bloody trip.'

'Aw, do what you want.' Pam flapped her hand dismissively. 'I've got a stonking headache, and I ain't gonna let you make it worse by arguing with you.'

'Well, hurray for that!' Carina smiled tightly. 'Maybe we *will* get along, after all.'

Pam made a huffing noise, but didn't bother saying anything. Carina going out was probably the best thing she could imagine right now. She felt rough as hell and relished the thought of a bit of peace and quiet.

'What's going on?' Vinnie asked, coming back in time to see Carina pulling the coat on.

'I'm going out,' she told him coldly. 'And don't tell me I'm not supposed to because, as I've already told Pam, I *have* got a life of my own!'

'Oi!' he barked, giving Pam her coffee and following Carina into the hall. 'What d'y' think you're playing at?'

'I'm going *out*,' she snapped, shrugging his hand off as he reached for her arm.

'Oh no, you're not.' Stepping in front of the door, Vinnie folded his arms.

'Get out of my way,' she demanded. 'You've got no right to hold me prisoner!'

'I'm just following orders,' he told her firmly. 'And if it's any consolation, I don't want to be here any more than you.'

'That's blatantly obvious.' Carina glared at him hatefully. 'I bet it was *your* idea to move that old bitch in, wasn't it? How d'y' think it makes me feel having her *spying* on me?'

'Grow up!' he snorted. 'You don't reckon she wants to be under the same roof as *you*, do you?'

'Yes! I think she bloody loves the idea of lording it over me in me own house!'

'Well, I'll tell you for nothing, she doesn't!' Vinnie hissed. 'Who'd want to see your sour face morning, noon and night? You've never had a nice word to say to the poor cow.'

'It's more than mutual, isn't it? You think I like listening to her going on about her precious fucking daughter-in-law? Let's not pretend she's made an effort with me and I'm the big, bad bitch who's thrown it all back in her face. I really *tried*.'

'Bollocks!' Vinnie sneered. 'You never gave her a chance. She might have a gob on her, but she's sorted if you don't rub her up the wrong way.'

'I don't give a toss what *you* think of her.' Carina pulled her gloves on. 'All I wanted was a bit of time with you – on our own. But obviously you couldn't care less, so don't bother telling me what I can or can't do. Move!'

Before Vinnie could argue, there was a loud crash in the dining room. Pushing Carina out of the way, he ran down the hall. Pam was lying on the dining-room floor with shards of shattered china all around her, coffee spreading out across the polished wood like diluted blood. Rushing to her, Vinnie kneeled down and patted her cheeks.

'Pam! What happened? . . . *Pam!*'

Getting no response, he yelled back over his shoulder for Carina to come and help. Hearing the muted roar of her car starting up followed by the crunch of gravel under tyres, he hissed 'Shit!' under his breath. Getting up, he ran to the phone and called for an ambulance.

Vinnie paced the A&E waiting-room floor for an age before

a nurse came to tell him that they were keeping Pam in the observation ward overnight. She had suffered a minor stroke and would need to be monitored, but she was conscious now if he wanted to see her for a few minutes.

Going into the cubicle, Vinnie saw that Pam's eyes were closed. Approaching the bed cautiously, he gazed upon the face he knew so well and felt a jolt of real sadness. He had never seen her without her trademark make-up before. She looked ancient, her skin paler and far more wrinkled than he'd expected, her almost transparent eyelids laced with an intricate fretwork of fine blue veins. For the first time ever, it occurred to him exactly how long she had inhabited this body – and how close she was to reaching its use-by date.

Knowing instinctively that Pam would rather die than be seen without her slap, Vinnie turned to leave.

'Oi!' she croaked weakly. 'Where you sloping off to?'

'I thought you were asleep.' Going back, he drew the visitor's chair up close.

'Well, I'm not, so you can stop for a bit, can't you?'

'I'm only allowed a few minutes, so don't go getting me into trouble.'

Turning her head towards him, Pam reached for his hand and gave it a weak squeeze. 'Gave you a scare, didn't I, love?'

'Too right!' Vinnie joked to cover his emotions. 'You know your Glen's going to blame me for wrecking his floor, don't you? Couldn't you have drunk the coffee before you dashed it all over the shop?'

'Send him to me if he says owt,' she murmured, her words slurring as the left side of her mouth began to twist. 'Me head don't half feel bad, Vin. Ask them nurses to give me summat, will y'?'

'Yeah, all right, but you just wait there.' Getting up, Vinnie frowned with concern as he backed towards the curtain.

'Don't let me catch you up dancing when I get back, or there'll be trouble!'

Dashing from the cubicle, he ran to the nurses' station to get help.

'Doctor is sending your mother for a scan,' the ward sister told Vinnie, bustling him aside as a team of nurses and technicians surrounded Pam's bed. 'She'll be going to the ICU from there, but I'm afraid you won't be able to go with her. Leave your number at the desk – we'll contact you as soon as we know what's happening.'

'What's wrong with her?' Vinnie glanced nervously over the sister's shoulder. 'I thought she was all right. The nurse said it was just a little stroke.'

Leading him away from the cubicle with practised firmness, the sister explained that Pam had suffered a second, more serious stroke. It had affected the speech centre of her brain and probably caused scarring to other areas, but they wouldn't know the full extent of the damage until they had done the scan.

Leaving his details with the receptionist, Vinnie wandered outside. He felt helpless, and more than a little guilty. Glen had trusted him to take care of his women, and what had he done? Lost one, and nearly killed the other.

It was almost eight now and completely dark. Standing to the side of the doors, he lit a cigarette and leaned his head back on the cool glass to think about how to break the news to Glen.

The peace was immediately shattered by the siren-blaring arrival of an emergency ambulance. As if materializing from thin air, several nursing staff raced out of a door that Vinnie hadn't noticed. Their movements looked eerie in the strobing blue light as they whisked the drip-attached stretcher case out onto the tarmac and rushed it in through their invisible door, leaving a gruesome trail of blood behind.

Grimacing, Vinnie finished his smoke and took his mobile from his pocket. Time to get things in order before he ended up like the poor sucker on the stretcher.

Carina sounded decidedly cagey when she answered, raising his suspicions about her whereabouts.

'Look, I don't give a shit what you're doing,' he said. 'I just thought you'd best know I'm about to ring Glen to—'

'Why?' She cut him short. 'Are you trying to drop me in it, or something?'

'No, I'm letting him know his mother's in the MRI.'

'Why? What's happened?'

'Like you didn't hear the crash.'

'Yeah, she dropped her cup. So what? Did the silly bitch scald herself, or something?'

'No, she had a stroke,' Vinnie said, anger making his voice surprisingly even. 'And another after we got here, so they're keeping her in.'

'Oh, my God,' Carina gasped. 'Is she all right?'

'No, she ain't. That's why I'm ringing Glen. I thought I'd warn you first, though, 'cos he's gonna ring you soon as he puts the phone down, and there's no way you're dropping me in it if he finds out you did a runner. I'll say you've switched your mobile off 'cos you're in the hospital, so you'd best do it and get your arse home. I'll get a cab. Pick me up at the corner so we're together if Al and Joe have got there first. Ten minutes – and don't even *think* about fucking me about.'

Cutting the call dead, he rang Glen and explained what had happened.

'I'm just waiting for her,' he said when Glen inevitably asked for Carina. 'She's having a word with the nurse. No, there's no need to come back. There's nothing you can do. She's in safe hands, and me and Carina will come straight back if anything changes.'

Running to the taxi office when he ended the call, Vinnie jumped into the back of a car that was just returning to base. Directing the driver to Glen's house, he promised him an extra tenner if he put his foot down.

Climbing into Carina's car ten minutes later, he filled her in on Pam's condition as they drove up to the house.

Al was waiting on the steps.

'Glen told me to come and get the low-down,' he said. 'Joe'll be back in a bit, so make it quick.'

'Anyone want a drink?' Carina asked, hanging her coat in the hall and sloping into the living room without looking Al in the eye.

'Scotch.' Al followed her. 'You all right? You look a bit peaky.'

'It's the shock.' Vinnie covered for her. 'We didn't know what was going on. One minute we're having a brew, the next Pam's keeling over.'

'She was fine earlier,' Al murmured, sighing deeply. 'A stroke, eh? Wonder what brought that on?'

'She wasn't fine.' Vinnie took the drinks from Carina and handed one to Al. 'But you know Pam – she wasn't going to say anything that'd stop Glen getting on. She said she had a headache so I made her a brew. I was just going to give her a painkiller and send her for a kip when she collapsed.'

'Easy to forget she's getting on, isn't it?' Al mused, twirling the drink thoughtfully. 'Glen was proper worried. Wanted me to go to the MRI and sit with her.'

'No point. They've taken her to intensive care and they won't let you in. They said they'd ring if anything changed.'

'Let me know as soon as.' Downing the drink at the sound of a car, Al peered out through a slit in the blinds. 'It's Joe. You'd best come and lock the gates after us, Vin. We'll do a quick scan first, make sure no one's hiding out in the grounds.'

Frowning, Vinnie followed him outside. 'What's going on, Al? Glen don't usually lock the gates.'

'This could get heavy if Glen don't sort it,' Al warned him cagily. 'Lewis is a beast. First thing he goes for is women and kids, but you won't see him coming 'cos he sends his crews out to make sure he's got a clear runway. If he gets in and finds her on her tod,' he motioned towards the house with a nod, 'he'll fuck her up. We understanding each other?'

'Yeah.'

'Good. Now give us one of the gate keys off the ring. We'll do checks when we're passing.'

Vinnie wondered how much of the story he wasn't being told as he helped Al and Joe search for intruders. The precautions seemed a bit over the top for what he *had* been told, and he wasn't sure he liked being planted here like a spare plank waiting for the axeman.

'Don't start,' Carina snapped when Vinnie strode back into the living room. Lurching off the couch, she crossed to the fireplace and grabbed the bottle of Scotch.

'How much have you had?' Vinnie asked when she sloshed a large measure into her glass.

'Four.' She waved the glass at him. 'And this makes five. Five *big* ones!'

'Well, that's your last.' He snatched the bottle. 'Enjoy it.'

'Piss off!' Tilting her head back, Carina narrowed her eyes drunkenly. 'You can't tell *me* what to do. This is *my* house now. I don't even have to let you stay if I don't want. I can just *kick* you out.'

'Like to see you try,' Vinnie snorted, pouring what was left of the bottle into a glass and sitting down. Crossing his legs, he watched Carina weave her way back to her seat.

'So, what you been up to?' he asked. 'Found another mug to screw behind Glen's back, have you?'

Pointing an unsteady finger at him, she smiled knowingly. 'You're jealous, aren't you, Vinnie-winnie? You think I've got a new man and it's pissing you off.'

Vinnie chuckled softly. 'You really should lay off the loopy juice. It's addling your brain.'

'Aw, get stuffed,' Carina sneered, leaning forward, her breasts spilling over the top of her Lycra vest. 'You can't fool me! I know you hate Glen for taking me away from you. What d'y' think he'd say if he knew what you've been up to behind his back, you naughty boy?'

'You're talking shit,' Vinnie retorted, angered by her mention of Glen. 'Yeah, he'd take a pop at me if he knew I'd been there first, but it's nothing to what he'd do to you.'

'He loves me,' she muttered, slumping back.

'For now, maybe, but if he finds out what you're really like he'll get rid of you like *that*!' Vinnie clicked his fingers sharply. 'Don't kid yourself, darlin',' he went on cruelly. 'There's only two women Glen's ever loved – his mother and his wife.'

'*I*'m his wife.'

'I don't see no ring on your finger.'

'What d'y' call this?' She waved her new ring at him.

Sighing, he shook his head. 'Look, pack it in. I didn't want a stupid argument about who loves who, I just want to know where you took off to today.'

'None of your business,' Carina told him sullenly. 'It's family stuff.'

'Didn't know you had any.'

'Everyone's got *someone*. Even you.'

Vinnie didn't say anything. He never spoke about his family. What was there to say? That his mother had battered him senseless as a child for daring to look like his runaway father, then got rid of him when he was big enough to fight back, forcing him to grow up the hard way? Nah. That was no one else's business. And if he'd learned one thing, it was that when you started letting people know your secrets they inevitably aimed the poisoned arrows of your confidences right back at you.

'My mother's a bitch,' Carina was saying now, more to herself than Vinnie. 'A greedy, selfish *bitch*. And she's got the nerve to lay guilt trips on me because I've moved on and she's exactly where she's always been – on her fat, lazy arse, sticking booze down her neck.'

Vinnie was intrigued. Carina had never mentioned her mother in the whole time he'd known her. If he'd actually thought about it he'd have sworn she came from a privileged background. She was the spoilt kind – the sort who'd had everything handed to her on a plate all her life and still expected everything for nothing: the contents of her latest man's wallet, for example.

Swinging her gaze up from the depths she was sinking into, Carina saw Vinnie looking at her and made a conscious effort to drag herself back to the present.

'Why did you go off me, Vinnie?' she asked.

'I was never *on* you,' he replied, his rough edge mellowing with each mouthful of whisky – but not enough to make him forget that he was supposed to be avoiding exactly this. 'We fucked, it was fun – end of.'

'It was more than that.' She was becoming tearful now. 'You know it was. There's always been something between us.'

'Don't talk crap. It was never real.'

'Yeah, it was. You were jealous when I got with Glen, admit it.'

'To be honest,' Vinnie said coolly, standing up, 'I didn't give a shit.'

Following him unsteadily as he went into the dining room,

Carina said, 'You're a liar. I know you want me, you just don't want to tread on Glen's toes.'

'You're not wrong there,' he agreed. 'But I still don't want you.'

Pulling a bottle of vodka out of the cupboard, he twisted the cap off with his teeth. Pouring some into his glass, he offered the bottle to Carina.

'Thought you said I'd had my last?' She gazed up at him coyly.

'Of the Scotch, yeah.' He sloshed some into her glass. 'But I'm hoping this'll shut you up.'

'Don't like hearing the truth, do you?'

'And what would that be?' Bored now, Vinnie downed his drink and refilled his glass.

'That you *do* like me.'

'Never said I didn't. I just don't *feel* anything.'

'No one asked you to.'

'So what's your point?'

'I thought we both just wanted a bit of fun?'

'Unfortunately,' Vinnie said condescendingly, 'your idea of fun involves being possessive and careless, and that don't interest me.'

'What if I promise not to get heavy?' Stepping right up to him now, Carina held his gaze for a moment. Then she sank slowly to her knees.

Thinking she was going for the kill, Vinnie reached down and pulled her back up.

'Forget it! It ain't happening.'

'Don't panic,' she giggled, showing him her empty hands. 'I was only putting my glass down. Makes everything so much easier, don't you think?' Taking the bottle and glass from him, she put them down too. 'Why don't you just relax, Vinnie?' Smiling sexily, she looped her arms around his neck.

Closing his eyes wearily, Vinnie reached up to pull her clasped hands apart, but as soon as his hands connected with her flesh he had a vision of Sarah and got an instant hard-on. It wasn't lost on Carina.

Thrusting her hips against him, she trailed her tongue up his neck and circled the tip of his ear lobe.

'See,' she whispered. 'I knew you wanted me. Come on, babe. We've got the whole house to ourselves, we can do whatever we want and no one would ever know. I need you . . . Glen could never do me like you do.'

Before he could stop himself, Vinnie had lifted Carina off her feet and laid her on the table. Eyes closed, he pushed her skirt up around her waist and tore her panties down. Thrusting himself into her, he rode her hard, seeing with every stroke Sarah's face, Sarah's breasts, Sarah's everything . . .

'Come upstairs,' Carina whispered when he collapsed onto her minutes later.

Vinnie went stone cold at the sound of her voice. What the fuck was he playing at? Not only had he fallen right into her trap, he'd done it right in front of the uncurtained patio doors when Al had told him they could drop by at any time to check that everything was all right. If Al and Joe had seen them at it, they'd dip Vinnie in concrete and drop him off the side of a cliff without a second thought. Pulling himself from Carina without a word, he zipped himself up and walked away.

'Vinnie!' she called after him, propping herself up on her elbows. 'Where the hell are you going?'

'Away from you,' he called back. 'That won't happen again, so just leave me the fuck alone.'

'Yes, it will!' she yelled as he strode from the room and up the stairs. 'Yes, it will, Vinnie! *You* know it and *I* know it, so there's no use pretending! Did you hear me, you bastard . . . ?

27

In the kitchen the following morning, the atmosphere was strained. Sober now, neither Vinnie nor Carina wanted to be the first to speak for fear of causing an argument that would likely get out of hand.

Vinnie was furious – with Carina for getting her own way, and with himself for letting his dick rule his head, putting him into an even more precarious position with Glen.

Carina was upset – ashamed and humiliated. She had thrown herself at Vinnie, risking everything for a meaningless fling – meaningless for him, anyway. To her, it was something she had craved for months – the resumption of their affair, the beginning of the next chapter. She'd been so sure that he felt the same way. How could she have got it so wrong?

'We're going to the hospital,' Vinnie said, breaking the silence at last as he washed his plate. 'Hurry up and get ready.'

Carina dreaded the prospect of being stuck beside him in the close confines of the car, but she knew it would cause trouble if Glen found out she'd stayed home when she could have been visiting his mother. Anyway, Vinnie was unlikely to let her stay, knowing that Glen would drag him over the coals for leaving her alone. Leaving her plate on the table, she went to get dressed.

Vinnie hoped her quietness signalled an end to the games. He had thought she might turn nasty and threaten to grass him up, but she seemed to have come to terms with things.

Still, he would have to tread very carefully to avoid pushing her into revenge territory.

Carina pulled a black trouser suit from the wardrobe. She didn't feel colourful today. She felt dark and depressed and the suit reflected the mood. It also seemed appropriate for visiting Pam, who – she hoped – might be nearing death's door. It would score points with Glen if he saw that she had dressed respectfully for his precious mother. And right now, she had a feeling that she needed all the points she could get.

If Glen found out she had slept with Vinnie while he was away he was sure to sling her out, and who would take care of her then? Not Vinnie, that was for sure. She'd be back to stripping for peanuts, sharing rooms with the other girls and getting her gear ripped off left right and centre. Or worse – living with her *mother* again. She'd rather die than go back to that.

During the silent ride to the hospital, it occurred to them both that they might not yet be out of danger. *They* might have agreed to keep their mouths shut about their past, and neither was in a position to mention the latest fall from grace. But what about Pam? If she told Glen that they had been arguing in a less than innocent way when she collapsed, and that Carina had taken off without a second thought, there was no telling what he would do.

They were visibly nervous as they followed the charge nurse to Pam's room, but their fears were soon allayed by the realization that Glen's mother didn't actually remember anything about the day before.

Propped up against the pillows, in the midst of what looked like an adventure playground of tubes, wires and probes, Pam was just as pale and weak as she had been the previous night. But she seemed a little chirpier, despite the appalling downward pull of the left side of her face.

Leaning down, Vinnie kissed her good cheek. 'You all right, darlin'?'

'Yeah.' She gave him a hideous grimace of a grin. 'You?'

'Fine.' He pulled up a chair and took hold of her hand. 'It isn't me stuck in here, is it? Anyway, what have they said? You gonna be out clubbing it tonight, or what?'

'Piss-taker,' she slurred, chuckling. Looking at Carina then, she said, 'Sit down, love. You look pale. Y'all right?'

Humbled that Pam was being so considerate, especially in view of how poorly she obviously was, Carina nodded and made her way to the other side of the bed. Sitting stiffly on the edge of a chair, she waited for the accusations to come. She was more than a little relieved when they didn't.

'What happened?' Pam asked, her words difficult to understand. 'Can't remember a thing. Glen went out, I got a headache. That's it.'

'Don't you remember falling off your chair?' Vinnie asked gently. Pam shook her head. He flicked a quick glance at Carina to see if she understood the implications of this. Carina gazed back at him wide-eyed, hoping against hope that she was reading this right.

'Well, we were having a brew,' Vinnie lied. 'You, me and Carina. And you said you weren't feeling too good so Carina went to get you a painkiller, but she couldn't find any so I went to help her, and that's when we heard the crash and came running back to find you on the floor. We called an ambulance and I went with you while Carina followed in the car. That's about it. Don't you remember any of it?'

Shaking her head, Pam said, 'No, nothing. But thanks, love.' Turning her head to include Carina, she said, 'Thanks.'

Reaching out to pat her free hand awkwardly, Carina said, 'It's all right. Any time.'

They stayed for another half-hour, chatting about nothing

in particular until a nurse glared at them through the window and pointedly tapped her watch.

'We've got to go,' Vinnie said, getting up. 'We're getting the evil eye off your keeper.' Leaning down to kiss Pam goodbye as Carina rushed to the door, he said, 'See you tomorrow, babe. Be good and I might smuggle you a couple of fags.'

Walking along the corridor towards the exit, Vinnie thanked Carina.

'I know she isn't my mother but she means a lot to me, and Glen will be chuffed when she tells him you came to see her.'

'I know,' Carina murmured, blinking back the tears that were stinging her eyes. She had never, even when they had been an item, seen the tenderness in Vinnie's eyes that she had witnessed when he had looked at Pam just now, and it hurt that he should care so much for that foul-mouthed old trout when he felt so little for her.

'You know what this means, don't you?' Vinnie was saying.

'Yeah. We're off the hook.'

Stopping mid-stride, Vinnie reached for her arm and turned her around. 'It means we've had a lucky escape, so this messing about has got to stop. Understood?'

Carina peered into his eyes for a moment, then dropped her gaze and nodded.

Satisfied that she meant it, he said, 'Good. Now let's just get back to the house and try and get things back to normal for when Al and Joe come round, eh?'

'Yeah, okay,' she agreed. 'But . . . there's just one thing.'

'What?' He narrowed his eyes.

'I've got to go out now and then, and you can't come with me.' Her eyes were dark and serious as she looked at him now. 'I know you don't believe me, but I've not been seeing anyone.

It's my mother. She's not too well and there's no one else to look after her. If I don't go, she won't eat. You won't try and stop me, will you?'

'I thought you hated your mother,' Vinnie said, reminding her of her complaints of the previous night.

'Doesn't mean I can just turn my back on her when she needs me.'

'So why lie about it?'

Carina looked down at the floor. 'I don't want Glen to know about her or he'll expect me to take him round and introduce him to her. Come on, Vinnie, you must have someone in your past you don't want anyone to know about?'

Sighing heavily, Vinnie ran a hand through his hair. He could refuse to let her go, but it would probably put them right back where they started – and that was the last thing either of them needed. And what harm could it do, as long as she kept her visits to an absolute minimum? It would give him a break.

'Okay,' he said. 'You can go, but only after Al and Joe have been round, and you don't stay out more than an hour. Agreed?'

'Agreed.' Carina smiled shyly, her pupils expanding as she gazed up at him. 'Thanks for understanding.'

Getting a hard-on, Vinnie gave an irritated jerk of his head and set off walking again. It pissed him off that no matter how determined he was, he couldn't control his dick. Carina was an attractive woman at the best of times, but vulnerable, like this, she was sexy as hell.

The rest of the week passed without incident, and Carina and Vinnie quickly settled into a routine. They would visit Pam after breakfast, then return to the house and do their own thing for a couple of hours. After dinner, they would wait for Al and Joe to turn up, give them the latest news on Pam's progress and assure them that nothing had happened on the intruder front. Then, when they were alone, Carina would nip out to see her mother.

None of that was a problem. It was what happened when Carina got back home that was.

If they hadn't been stuck in the house with nothing to do but drink and watch TV all night, Vinnie would have had no trouble keeping his distance. But drinking made him horny, and Carina always smelled so good and dressed so sexily. He'd look at her lying on the couch, her legs so lean and smooth, her breasts swelling each time she took a breath, her tongue so pink when she laughed, and he would remember how good those breasts felt in his hands, how sweet that tongue tasted, how those legs felt when she wrapped them around his neck and drew him in deep . . .

He resisted for several days, but being under house arrest with all the booze he could drink and no means of seeing the girl who was plaguing his thoughts, it wasn't long before temptation got the better of him.

Reasoning that they had already broken the rules so it couldn't do any harm if they were careful, and that it was Glen's own fault for putting him in such an impossible position anyway, Vinnie reached for Carina's hand as she passed him en route to the kitchen.

She struggled to get free as he pulled her onto his lap. She had tried so hard to accept that he didn't want her and she didn't think it was fair of him to play games with her heart. Apart from which, she was sure he was testing her and was afraid that if she responded favourably he would get mad with her.

Grinning wickedly as she struggled, Vinnie ran his hand up her leg and eased his fingers beneath the hem of her skirt.

'You know you want me,' he told her huskily. 'Don't play hard to get, it doesn't suit you.'

'I'm not!' Carina protested, slapping at his hand. 'You really hurt me, Vinnie, and I'm not letting you do that to me again. I'm not some doll you can play with whenever you feel like it!'

Teasing her neck with his tongue, Vinnie felt the thrill pass through her body.

'Yes, you are,' he murmured, cupping her breast now and running his thumb around her rigid nipple. 'You're my own little Barbie doll, and I can touch you and taste you and play with you any time I want.'

'What about Al and Joe?' she gasped, trying hard to resist the desire that was weakening her resolve by the second.

'We'll go upstairs,' he said, pushing her hand onto his erection. 'Tell me you don't want it, and I'll let you go.'

Groaning, Carina gave up the fight and fell against him. Seizing his hair, she pulled his mouth onto hers and kissed him hard.

Lifting her, Vinnie carried her up to his bedroom.

'Just promise you won't turn on me again tomorrow,' she begged as he tore off her clothes and stepped out of his jeans.

'I won't,' he said, forcing her legs apart, 'as long as you don't get clingy, because *this*,' he thrust into her, 'is just fucking – nothing more, nothing less. Tell me what it is?'

'Just fucking,' she moaned, digging her nails into his back. 'Nothing . . . *mooore* . . .'

28

<hr>

Pam was discharged from hospital on the Wednesday of the second week. She was very weak, and still had no memory of Christmas Day from Glen's leaving to waking up in hospital. But her speech was improving, and the doctors were optimistic about her chances of a reasonable – if not full – recovery.

Settling her into her room, Vinnie and Carina spent the rest of the day fetching and carrying for her. It wasn't long before the usual tensions began to surface between the women.

Having had him all to herself, Carina resented having to share Vinnie. She was jealous of his affection for Pam, couldn't bear to see him fussing around her. She tried not to show her displeasure, but it seemed that the harder she tried to be nice, the more Pam criticized her. When Pam turned her nose up at the meal that Carina had spent two hours cooking, she finally blew up.

'Right, that's it!' she snapped, snatching the barely touched tea tray away. 'I'm not doing another thing for you, Pam. You're an ungrateful bitch! I know you can't look after yourself any more, but if you think I'm gonna be your personal maid, you've got another think coming. As soon as Glen comes back, you're going into a home!'

They both knew that Glen would never allow his mother to go into a home, but it had given Carina satisfaction to say it. And it had given Pam pause for thought. It was true that she would need looking after, but there was no way she was moving in here with Madam. Nor was she giving up her beautiful bungalow and moving into a residential care home. She'd go to her own home and have Glen hire a carer, and that would be the end of it. Her mind was made up. And her Glen knew her well enough not to bother arguing once she'd made her mind up.

Glen and Carl arrived home later that day in celebratory mood.

Calling the family together for an impromptu party, Glen sent Vinnie and Freddie out for food and booze while he got a shower and spent some time with his mother.

When everyone had arrived, he gathered them around the dining-room table. Sweeping the mats aside, he pulled a large plastic bag of powder from his pocket and spilled a healthy heap out onto the gleaming wood. Spreading it around, he licked his fingers and grinned at the men.

'Help yourself, guys. Pure fucking snow, that is, courtesy of Dex Lewis.'

'You what?' Joe laughed. 'He give you all that?'

'With a little persuasion.' Winking, Glen waved his hands, motioning the men to get stuck in. 'And there's plenty more where that came from. Our late friend had a fair old stash, I can tell you.'

'Late?' Freddie quizzed.

'Too right,' Carl affirmed. 'We give him a chance to back off, but he decided to try and tangle with us. What can you do?'

'Shame, really,' Glen mused. 'I should have let the little prick live. I'll never know where he got his shit from now, and it's Grade A, you've got to give him that. Still, at least we won't get no more Smoke clowns nobbing about with us now he's sorted. Word'll spread. No one messes with the Nobles and walks away.'

Taking Vinnie aside when everyone was busy burying their noses, Glen handed him a thick wad of money.

'It's a bonus, for looking after my mother. I don't even want to think what would have happened if you and Carina hadn't been here for her.'

'I don't need paying for that,' Vinnie told him, hoping he didn't sound as guilty as he felt. 'I think the world of her.'

'Yeah, well, I won't forget it.' Glen slapped him heartily on the back. 'How was Carina?'

'Bit quiet.' Vinnie shrugged. 'Missing you, most likely.'

'I'll make up for that now I'm back,' Glen said, grinning lewdly. 'The pros in the Smoke ain't a patch on her, but it was either that or slip Carl one when he wasn't looking, and I don't think he'd have been too pleased. Anyhow, thanks for looking out for her, and I don't want to see your ugly mush for a week.'

'Eh?' Vinnie eyed him nervously.

'I'm giving you a week off.' Glen laughed. 'Jeez, man, don't look too enthusiastic or I might change my mind. Go on – piss off.'

Vinnie broke the speed limit getting home, but he wouldn't have cared if he'd been pulled over and given ten tickets. He was just so glad to be free. There was only so much you could take of being stuck in someone else's house – servicing someone else's woman.

He was relieved to be off duty on that particular score. Carina was sexy and gorgeous and more than willing to try anything, but that wasn't enough to keep Vinnie's interest. It never had been, which was why he'd stopped seeing her in the first place. And second time around didn't make for a sweeter reunion, it just brought the tedium on faster. A few more days and he would have been too bored to get it up – which would have got her back up and put him back to square one. At least this way they had parted on relatively good terms, and now that Carina understood where he was coming from, she wouldn't make the mistake of trying to get more from him again.

Unpacking his case, Vinnie turned his stereo up loud and climbed into the shower. Whistling along to the music, he luxuriated in the scalding spray and made plans for the rest of the week.

First thing he'd do would be to contact Pete and Sarah and set up another visit. Then he would go out on the town and find himself some fresh pussy to get his blood pumping again.

Sarah had been in a bad mood for days and Pete was walking on eggshells trying not to antagonize her. It was his own fault, he knew, but no matter what he did, no matter how much he apologized, she didn't want to know.

It had started a couple of days after Christmas when the bills began to arrive. Usually he grabbed the post first thing on his way to work and Sarah only saw what he wanted her to see. But the holiday drinking and smoking had made him forgetful, and she had got her hands on everything.

The electric company were demanding two hundred, the gas three-twenty, the water board had gone a step further and were threatening to send the bailiffs round, and the bank had put a dead stop on him withdrawing a penny until he had paid off his three-hundred-pound overdraft.

Sarah was livid. How had things got this bad, she wanted to know, when Pete had told her he was paying everything by direct debit? He tried to bluff his way out of it by insisting that he *had* paid and that the bank must have screwed up, but when she put her coat on and threatened to go and play hell with them, he'd had to come clean and admit that he had been withdrawing more than he'd paid in, in order to cover his gambling debts.

Gambling. Pete didn't know how he'd let it take over his life, but it had wormed its way in like a sweet-talking whore and had completely fucked him over. He'd been so sure that he would net the big one any day now, convinced himself that he would return all the money he had withdrawn – with interest. But there was always another dead-cert horse – another sure-fire set of Lotto numbers – another casino that was just dying to line his pockets . . .

He wished Sarah would just beat the shit out of him and get it over with, but she punished him by withdrawing from him instead – absolutely, in every way. It was torture.

Unable to cope with the disdainful look in her eyes, and the cold edge to her voice, Pete began to spend more time out of the house – which inevitably angered her even more. It was a lose-lose situation, and he was on the point of giving up when Vinnie rang.

'What's the matter?' Vinnie asked, picking up from Pete's voice that something was amiss.

Pete poured out the whole sorry saga.

'I don't know what to do, man. She hardly talks to me, and she won't let me near her. She sleeps with Kimmy every night, and she's stopped washing my clothes and cooking, and that. I know she's got every right to be mad, but what am I supposed to do? My wages are crap. There's hardly enough to buy food and fags, never mind pay bills.'

'How much do you owe out?' Vinnie asked when Pete finally stopped whining.

'Too much to think about,' Pete admitted. 'If it wasn't for me mates subbing me a few pints and spliffs of a night, I'd seriously think about topping myself.'

'All right, look,' Vinnie said, seizing the opportunity to put Pete into his debt and make it easier to keep in touch with Sarah. 'I'm gonna bung you a few quid to get it sorted.'

'You don't have to,' Pete murmured, trying not to sound too hopeful.

'Don't argue,' Vinnie told him flatly. 'We've known each other too long, and I know what it's like being skint. Remember all them smokes you used to give me? Yeah, well, consider this payback. A grand do you?'

'A grand? No way, man! I can't take that much. I'll never be able to pay you back.'

'Did I ask you to?'

'No, but . . .'

'But nowt. I'll bring it round in a bit.'

'I've, er, arranged to go out,' Pete said, glancing at his watch. 'I'm supposed to be there in five.'

'Is Sarah in?'

'Yeah, but I'd rather you didn't say anything to her about this. She's really mad at me already.'

'Don't worry.' Vinnie sounded confident. 'You can't exactly hide it from her, can you? She'll only get more suspicious if you suddenly get the money to pay off your bills and don't tell her where it's from.'

'You think she'd go for it if you told her?'

'Course. You know me, mate – I can make anyone believe anything.'

'I remember,' Pete snorted, his spirits lifting by the second. Sarah was bound to stop ball-aching once they were back on their feet. 'Tell you what, why don't you call round tonight? You could have a chat to her – see if you can't persuade her to stop treating me like a dog.'

'I'll try.' Vinnie chuckled softly. 'But it won't be easy.'

'Nah, she'll listen to you. She knows you know me better than anyone. If you tell her that I'm really sorry and I'm absolutely crazy about her, she'll know it's true.'

'I'll do my best. Let me have a think about it and I'll come round in about half an hour. I'll say I turned up on the off chance. It'll be easier if she doesn't know we planned it.'

'Thanks, mate,' Pete murmured gratefully. 'You don't know what this means to me.'

'I've just had a thought,' Vinnie said. 'I might have a way to help you out. Say no if you're not interested, but how do you fancy doing a job with me?'

'What kind of job?'

'Nothing major, but it'll give you a fair few quid. Interested?'

'Too right!' Pete exclaimed greedily. 'When?'

'Might take a couple of days. Let me sort things out my end and I'll get back to you. But not a word to Sarah or anyone else, or it's no go.'

Putting the phone down, Vinnie shook his head. Pete was a tosser if he thought that Vinnie was helping him out for *his* sake. Whatever trace of respect or friendship Vinnie might have harboured for him was well and truly shattered when Pete accepted the offer of money so easily. Any man with a scrap of dignity would have put up a better resistance than Pete's pathetically transparent attempt. No wonder Sarah was treating him badly. The guy was a disgrace.

But it would all be sorted soon enough. The plan that had literally just come to him as they spoke could be the perfect opportunity to kill two birds with one very heavy stone.

Sarah was rinsing Kimmy's hair in the bath when she heard knocking at the front door.

'Just a minute,' she yelled. 'I'm coming!'

Lifting Kimmy from the tub, she wrapped a huge towel around her and gently rubbed the soap from her face as she carried her up the hall. Whoever was knocking went into a fresh burst just as she got there.

'For God's sake!' Sarah snapped, wrenching the door open. 'I said I was com—'

Stopping mid-rant, she looked at Vinnie and felt a blush creep up her neck. He looked as gorgeous as he had the last time she had seen him. And Sarah looked just as dowdy as she normally did when she wasn't making the effort she had made that particular day.

'Vinnie.' She found her voice at last. 'I wasn't expecting you. You said you'd ring.'

'Sorry. I was passing and thought I'd call. I can come back later if you're busy.' He nodded towards Kimmy, who was staring up at him wide-eyed.

'No, it's fine.' Sighing, Sarah stepped back. 'You might as well come in now you're here. You'll have to excuse the mess, though. I haven't cleared up after madam yet.'

'This is Kimmy, I take it?' Vinnie followed them through to the living room. 'She's beautiful.'

Sarah couldn't prevent the proud smile.

'Have a seat.' She waved him to the couch. 'I won't be long. I'm just getting her ready for bed.'

'Does she have to go right now?' He smiled at Kimmy who was playing peek-a-boo with him now, giggling as she hid her face in Sarah's shoulder. 'I wanted to spend a bit of time with her – if you don't mind?'

Sarah relaxed a little. It was obvious that he was making an effort – and Kimmy certainly seemed to have taken to him.

'Okay. I'll bring her back when she's got her jammys on. But not for long. She's murder if she doesn't get a good sleep.'

Settling back when they had gone, Vinnie lit a cigarette and looked around the room. It was drab, but Sarah had obviously made an effort to make it cosy and keep it clean. It angered him to think of her living like this. She deserved better, and if – *when* – she was his woman, she'd *get* better.

He smiled when they came back a few minutes later. 'All dry?'

Kimmy hid behind her mother's legs, peeking shyly out at him.

'Come out of there,' Sarah chided, sitting down and swinging the child up onto her lap. 'This is Daddy's friend Vinnie. Say hello.'

Murmuring 'Hello' in a tiny voice, Kimmy peered up at Vinnie through impossibly long lashes as Sarah brushed her hair.

'She really does look like you,' Vinnie said. 'Bet you're glad about that. She could have ended up looking like Pete.'

'She's got his nose,' Sarah muttered, frowning. She was pissed off with Pete, but he was her husband – for better or worse – and she wasn't about to be disloyal.

'She's got your eyes,' Vinnie commented quietly. 'They're incredible.'

Feeling a little uncomfortable, Sarah finished Kimmy's hair and stood up. Hefting her daughter onto her hip, she said, 'Say goodnight.'

'Night night,' Kimmy whispered, hiding again.

'Night.' Vinnie waved as Sarah carried her from the room.

Coming back a few minutes later, Sarah reached for a cigarette. 'Looks like you've got a fan. She says you're *funny*.'

'Nice to know I still have that effect on the girls,' Vinnie quipped, sparking his lighter before she had a chance to reach for her own. Inhaling her scent as she leaned towards him, he felt a little light-headed. He wanted her so badly, but he knew her too well to leap straight in. He would have to be extremely careful how he went about things, or she would kick him out without a backward glance.

'Where's Pete?' he asked as she sat down.

'Out.' Sarah flicked her ash sharply. 'He probably won't be back before two. He'll be sorry he missed you.'

'Don't worry about it.' Vinnie glanced at his watch. 'I'm not staying long. I just wanted to give him something – but I can leave it with you, if that's all right?'

'Yeah, whatever.'

Taking an envelope from his pocket, Vinnie handed it across. Feeling the bulky wad, Sarah knew instinctively that it was money and her suspicions were roused. Why was Vinnie giving Pete money? What had they been doing that Pete had conveniently forgotten to mention to her?

'What's this for?' she asked, frowning.

'It's just something I owe him,' Vinnie lied.

'Bullshit!' She thrust the envelope back at him. 'He's never had that much money in his life. How could he have lent it to you?'

'It's from a bet,' Vinnie told her, knowing from what Pete had told him that the mention of gambling would piss her off, but banking on her believing it because of the mess Pete had got them into.

'That figures,' she snorted disapprovingly, reluctant to say anything more. It was no one's business but theirs that Pete had a gambling problem.

'Well, are you going to take it?'

Sarah shook her head stubbornly. 'No. I don't want anything to do with it. It's dirty money.'

'It isn't stolen. Honest, Sarah, it's just winnings from the dogs.'

'Oh, really?' She gave him a disbelieving look. 'He told me he goes for the horses, not the dogs.'

'Yeah, *now* he does,' Vinnie said, kicking himself mentally. 'But it was always dogs when we were kids.'

Sarah's disbelief increased. 'So you're trying to tell me this bet was made when you were a kid?'

'Yeah. That's how come it's so much now – the interest, and that.'

'Nice try,' she scoffed. 'But you couldn't have won it. They wouldn't have let you put the bet on.'

Vinnie smiled. 'Ah, but that's where you're wrong. Come on, Sarah. You know I've always looked older than I am.'

Sarah couldn't argue with that.

'It's only a grand,' he persisted. 'Please, Sarah . . . I'm sick of having it hanging round my neck. How d'y' think it makes me feel knowing I owe one of my oldest mates? I just want it done with.'

'All right,' she conceded, taking the envelope and putting it on the ledge behind her head. 'But I'm still not happy. Something's not right about this. I reckon you're covering for Pete, but I don't suppose you're gonna tell me, are you?'

'Nothing to tell.' He shrugged with his hands.

Shaking her head, Sarah said, 'Thought not. Anyway, can I get you a coffee, or anything?' She didn't really want to detain him, but it was the least she could do now that he'd provided a plug – however temporary – for the great yawning abyss that Pete had created in their finances.

'I'd love one,' Vinnie said, exhaling with relief.

That was the tricky part over. Now he just had to work on getting her to like him. With any other woman that would have been the easy bit, but he and Sarah had history, and he would have to tread carefully to ensure the right response.

'So, what did you think when Pete said I was coming round the other week?' he asked when she carried the cups through.

'I went mad,' Sarah told him straight out.

'Really?' Vinnie drew his head back. 'Why?'

'Why so shocked?' Drawing her feet up beneath her on the chair, she peered at him with a hint of amusement. 'We were never exactly friends.'

'Yeah, but that was years ago. I've grown up since then. I've changed.'

'I can see that,' she agreed. 'I was quite surprised, actually. You're . . .' Pausing, she considered her words carefully. 'Nicer, I suppose – less edgy. You always felt like you were on the make, but you look more laid-back now.'

Nodding, as if giving her words serious consideration, Vinnie said, 'I suppose I am. I never thought of it like that, but you're right. I feel better about myself, like I don't have to put on a show or kick off to get what I want.'

'About time,' she teased, realizing that he wasn't as difficult to talk to now that she was actually making the effort. 'So, what have you been doing with yourself? Pete said you were in the project in Hulme.'

'Yeah, for about six months.' Vinnie smiled wryly. 'We didn't see eye to eye, so they kicked me out. Anyway, what about you? Last I heard you were living in Moss Side. I called round there once, you know.'

'Oh?' She gave him a questioning look. 'How come?'

'I wanted to tell you about your mate. I didn't know if you still spoke to any of them at Starlight, with you not coming back after you left, and that. But I thought you'd want to know what happened to him.'

Sarah gripped her cup hard. It still hurt to think about Harry. Still racked her with guilt that she had not only been unable to prevent his suffering but had never laid eyes on him again after letting the police take him back that time. If she'd only tried harder to stay in touch it might never have happened, but, as per usual, she'd been too wrapped up in her own problems.

'Thanks,' she murmured. Then, 'Sorry I didn't keep in touch, but everything went a bit haywire after I left. Anyway, when did you go round to mine?'

'The day I got out,' Vinnie told her. 'Some junkie blokes said you'd already left.'

Sarah's expression darkened even further at the mention of her former housemates. 'They're all dead now, you know,' she said.

'Serious?' Vinnie gazed at her disbelievingly.

'Yeah. It was in the paper a few months after I left. The house burned down in the middle of the night. The police reckoned it was arson, but they never got anyone for it.'

Vinnie shook his head. 'That's terrible, but it doesn't really surprise me. You make all sorts of enemies when you mess about with drugs, don't you?'

'Suppose so,' she murmured, sinking into a gloomy silence at the mention of drugs and enemies. Harry and Chambers.

'You all right?' Vinnie asked.

Looking up, Sarah was surprised to see concern in his eyes. It reminded her of what Harry had once said about Vinnie really caring for her.

'Yeah.' She nodded. 'I was just thinking about Harry. I'm glad that bastard was sent down for what he did. I'd have killed him if I'd got my hands on him.'

'I bet you would as well.' Vinnie chuckled softly. 'I've had a taste of your temper. Remember pulling that knife on me?'

Smiling now, Sarah said, 'Yeah, I remember. Guess I've grown up a lot since then as well, but I was really mad at you.'

'Don't blame you.' He shrugged. 'I was a real bastard back then. I've thought about it a lot since, and I'd never do anything like that now. It's like you get these mad rages when you're in care, and everyone cops for it except them who put you there in the first place.'

Listening to the sincerity in Vinnie's voice, Sarah remembered that Pete had said practically the same thing when they had met up again. She'd given *him* a chance to prove he'd changed, and that had paid off – for the most part. Maybe it was time to let go of the negative feelings she harboured against Vinnie.

Sensing the shift in her mood, Vinnie decided to get out while the going was good. Glancing at his watch, he stood up.

'I'd best get going. Thanks for the coffee. Tell Pete I'll be in touch, and, I'll, er, see you soon.'

Showing him out, Sarah smiled when he thanked her for letting him meet Kimmy.

'She liked you. And that's an honour, let me tell you. You'll be Uncle Vinnie before too long, if you're not careful.'

'I'd like that,' he told her softly. 'Coming from our background, our mates are the only family we've got. Take care.'

'And you.'

Closing the door, Sarah leaned her back against it for a moment, thinking about what he had said. It was true, he *was* part of the family, and Pete would be made up that she had finally allowed him in.

Pete Owens. Her husband. The father of her beautiful child. The man who screwed up everything he touched, but was completely without malice.

Maybe it was the relief of knowing that thanks to Vinnie they now had the money to pay off their debts, but it suddenly occurred to her that whatever problems she and Pete were having, she should be helping him sort it out, not blaming him as she had been doing. He was good at

29

Vinnie became a regular visitor over the next few weeks, and Pete never failed to ask about the 'job' when he showed him out. Telling him to be patient, and reiterating that he mustn't breathe a word to Sarah or it was off, Vinnie assured him that he was still working on it. Finally, almost two months later, he put Pete out of his misery. Calling him on his mobile to be sure that he rather than Sarah answered, he gave him the good news.

'When?' Pete asked in a whisper, going out into the hall.

'Midnight tonight,' Vinnie told him. 'Can you get out without making Sarah suspicious?'

'Yeah. Where should I meet you?'

'You know where they used to have the Sunday market down the side of the Quays?'

'Yeah.'

'Well, just before that – down the back of the old railway sidings. Turn left on the tracks and keep going till you see me.'

'*On* the tracks?'

'Yeah, but don't worry about it, they ain't been used for years.'

'Oh, right. Do I need to wear anything special?'

'Just something dark, and keep your lights off. You haven't said anything to Sarah, have you?'

'No way, man.'

'Good. Don't even tell her it was me on the phone.

The less she knows, the less she'll be involved if it comes on top.'

'I won't! You can trust me. I wouldn't do anything to hurt Sarah. Things have been a lot better since you had a word with her. I wouldn't want to muck it up again.'

'Yeah, well, sort yourself an alibi so you've got a legit reason for getting out.'

'Will do. See you later.'

Cutting the call, Pete made one of his own before going back into the flat.

'What are you grinning at?' Sarah asked, amused by his excited expression.

'Nothing.' Pulling her into his arms, he hugged her hard. 'Have I told you lately how much I love you?'

Peering up at him narrow-eyed, Sarah laughed. 'Only every day. I don't know what's got into you lately, but I'm not knocking it. It's better than seeing you moping about all over the place. Who was that on the phone, by the way?'

'Oh, just Clive.' It was semi-truthful. The second call had been to Clive. 'He wants me to go round his for a bit. Needs help putting some shelves up, or something. I said yeah, but I won't if you don't want me to.'

'No, you go and do your good deed,' she said, pushing him away. 'I remember how much Tina moaned last time he tried a bit of DIY. What was it he buggered up that time? The bunk beds?'

'Yeah, and they're still not right.' Pete laughed. 'He was telling me the other day that their Michael falls on the floor every time he rolls over. The kid's got bruises all up his side.'

'Better have a look at them while you're at it, then.'

'The bruises?'

'No, the bunk beds, you pillock!'

'If you don't mind?' Pete said, gazing at her innocently. 'It might take a while.'

'I don't mind.' She smiled. 'Just don't—'

'Wake you up if I'm late.' He finished for her, grinning sheepishly. 'Yeah, I know.'

Pete turned onto the industrial estate approach road at ten to twelve that night. Conscious of the three cans of super-strong lager that Clive had given him in return for helping put right all his botch jobs, he drove slowly, keeping one eye out for police and the other for the turning that Vinnie had told him to take.

It was pitch dark between the tall windowless buildings lining the old dock road, and with no street lights to guide him it was a good ten minutes before he spotted the faint fretwork of train tracks criss-crossing the tarmac up ahead.

Easing left, Pete felt every dip and hole beneath his tyres as he straddled the tracks and steered the car even deeper into darkness. With his headlights off he could barely even see the silhouettes of the freight-storage building to his left and the overgrown bushes to his right. He felt as if he was entering a tunnel, and it unnerved him.

His forehead was almost touching the windscreen when he spotted the flash of headlights up ahead. Exhaling shakily, he realized he had been holding his breath and wondered if this was such a good idea after all. It wasn't exactly his style, sneaking about in the middle of the night, playing with the big boys.

'Thought you weren't coming,' Vinnie called out from his window in a harsh whisper. 'Leave your wheels there and come in here.'

'No way was I backing out,' Pete said, feeling the apprehension turn to excitement as he clambered into the jeep beside Vinnie. Rubbing his hands together in the warm blast of air coming from the vents, he looked over the plush interior with approval. 'Man, this is *flash*. How much did it set you back?'

'Enough,' Vinnie murmured, reaching through the gap for the bottle he'd put on the back seat. 'You never know,' he went on, grinning in the dark as he twisted the cap off and handed it to Pete, 'if this comes off like expected tonight, you might be able to get yourself some better wheels.'

'Yeah?' Pete grinned back. 'Sarah will be well chuffed to see the back of that shit-heap of mine.' Taking a mouthful of the drink, he spluttered as it burned its way down his throat. 'Shit, man! What's *this*?'

'Ninety per cent Jamaican gut-rot,' Vinnie told him. 'Illegal smuggle job. Good, eh?'

'You can say that again!' Pete took another slug. 'Christ, I can feel it already. You not having any?'

'Nah.' Vinnie shook his head. 'I had some earlier. You get tanked up while you can. We could be in for a long wait.'

'What we waiting for?' Pete took another long drink.

'The nod,' Vinnie replied evasively. Pulling a spliff from his pocket, he handed it across. 'Here, take a toke on that and see what you think. It's *pure* Sensi.'

Taking it, Pete lit up and took several puffs. A creeping stone started in his toes and quickly spread up his legs.

'Head-fuck paradise,' he said, grinning broadly. 'This is the *business*!'

'Plenty more where that came from,' Vinnie told him, peering out of the window into the darkness. 'Have another drink, man. You'll never get it finished at that rate. You're drinking like a pussy. What's up with you?'

Laughing, Pete took the challenge and necked as much as he could take.

'Got'ny tunes?' His words had begun to slur and his head was rolling drunkenly on his shoulders.

Slotting a mini-disc into the system, Vinnie pressed a switch, flooding the car with groove-heavy Seal.

'Aw, fuck, this is *wicked*, man!' Resting his head back, Pete took another long pull on the smoke and sang along tunelessly: 'Music takes you round 'n round 'n round 'n *roooound* . . . Hold on . . .' Sighing, he said, 'This is smooth shit, man. *Smooooth* . . . shiiiit . . .'

Catching the bottle and the heroin-laced spliff as they fell, Vinnie reached across and turned Pete's face towards him. Pete's mouth was slack, and his eyes had rolled to the tops of their sockets. Vinnie slapped his cheek with a leather-gloved hand. 'Pete?'

Getting no response, he dimped the spliff, recapped the bottle and slipped them into his pocket. Climbing out, he went around to Pete's door and wrenched it open. Catching him as he fell, he pulled him out onto the ground and, peering all around in the darkness, dragged him across the tracks to the Orion.

Manhandling Pete into the driver's seat, Vinnie gave him another slap to make sure he was really out for the count, then took the bottle from his pocket. Uncapping it, he placed it in one of Pete's hands and put the cap and the spliff into the other.

Running back to the jeep, he checked the dash-clock. He had fifteen minutes left to finish the job and get out of there. Cursing Pete under his breath for taking so damn long to conk out, he threw the jeep into gear and raced out of the sidings and onto the road.

Forcing himself to maintain a respectable speed, Vinnie drove the two hundred yards to the unmanned – un-cameraed – car park used by the shift workers from the cereal-packing factory some way further down. Parking up, he took the long-handled sweeping brush out of the boot and ran back to the sidings.

Sweeping backwards and forwards over the places where his wheels had touched, he ran back to the jeep with just minutes to spare. Pausing to listen before climbing in, he smiled when he heard the faint rumbles of the approaching freight train making its last reverse trip of the night into the sidings.

Bang on time.

More fool Pete for believing that the trains had stopped running. He should have checked. Vinnie would have if the situation had been reversed.

Easing the jeep out, he set off in the opposite direction.

He didn't need to stick around to see what happened next. He'd hear about it soon enough.

30

<hr>

Sarah was woken by banging on the front door. Forcing her eyes open, she gazed blearily at the clock on the bedside table. It was just after two.

Dragging herself upright, she pushed the quilt aside and reached for her dressing gown. Stumbling from the room, she stubbed her toe on a pair of work shoes that Pete had left beside the door and cursed him under her breath.

'If you've lost your bloody keys again,' she was saying as she answered the door, 'I'll kill y—' She stopped speaking abruptly when she saw the two uniformed policewomen standing there.

'Mrs Owens?' one asked.

'Yes.' Fully awake now, Sarah looked questioningly from one to the other.

'I'm PC Tannis, and this is PC Rushden. Can we come in for a minute?'

'Why? What's wrong?'

'We'd rather discuss it inside,' PC Rushden said firmly, already stepping forward.

Sighing, Sarah stood aside to let them in. Closing the door, she waved them through to the living room and switched the light on.

'Would you like to sit down?' PC Tannis said a little awkwardly.

Sarah looked at her guardedly. She was standing too close, and she looked all set to get sympathetic. Something was very wrong.

'What's happened?' Sarah demanded, standing her ground, pulling her robe belt tighter around her waist.

The officers exchanged a glance, then PC Rushden said, 'We've reason to believe your husband was involved in an accident tonight.'

Slumping down onto the couch now, Sarah stared up at them disbelievingly. 'Pete? . . . But how? He's not hurt himself with one of Clive's tools, has he?'

'There was an RTA,' PC Tannis told her gently.

Sarah gazed back at her blankly.

'A road accident,' PC Rushden explained. 'Do you own a white Ford Orion?'

'Y-yes, but . . .'

'We're sorry to have to inform you that a vehicle of that description registered to this address was involved in a major collision with a train a couple of hours ago.'

'No way!' Sarah gasped. 'A *train*? It can't be Pete. He's only at a friend's house round the corner. He'd be nowhere near a train. Someone must have pinched the car. I'll ring him . . .'

Another glance between the PCs.

'Mrs Owens,' PC Tannis said kindly, 'the driver of the vehicle was found to be carrying documentation relating to your husband. I'm afraid we're going to have to ask you to come and do an official ID.'

'What do you mean?' Sarah's voice sounded strange to her own ears – far away, and slurred, as if her tongue had swollen to twice its normal size. 'He's not . . . ?'

'I'm afraid so.' PC Rushden sat beside Sarah now and touched her arm. 'Is there somebody we could contact for you? A family member, maybe?'

'There's no f-family,' Sarah stammered. 'Just me and Pete, and K-Kimmy.'

'Kimmy?'

'My daughter. She – she's in b-bed.' Sarah pointed at the wall. Bringing the hand to her mouth, she stared helplessly at the PC as the tears spilled over and splashed off her knuckles onto her knees. 'I'm sorry. I just can't . . . I just don't believe it. It can't be Pete.'

'I'm going to make you a cup of sweet tea,' PC Tannis said decisively. 'If you could think of somebody to come over and sit with your daughter for an hour in the meantime . . . ?'

'Hannah,' Sarah murmured, swiping at the tears. 'I'll ring her. Should – should I get dressed?'

'That's probably a good idea,' PC Rushden said. 'Give me your friend's number. I'll call her while you're getting ready, get her to come over.'

'Thank you,' Sarah mumbled numbly.

She dressed in a daze, as if she were a bystander watching her body going through the motions. Stumbling out into the hall when she heard Hannah arriving ten minutes later, she fell into her arms with a sob.

'It's all right, pet.' Hannah patted her back soothingly. 'Now don't you worry. We'll get through this. I'm here for you – me *and* Steve.'

'If you could just stay with the child for a while?' PC Tannis said, gently prising Sarah from Hannah's arms. 'We'll bring Sarah back when she's done.'

'Course.' Hannah nodded. 'Go on, Sarah. You go with them. And don't worry about Kimmy. She'll be fine. I'm stopping over tonight. I've already sorted it with Steve.'

'Thanks,' Sarah mumbled, allowing herself to be led away between the policewomen.

It was the worst night of Sarah's entire life.

Having to look at her husband's smashed body lying cold and helpless on the slab was bad enough. But having to hear details of the horrendous accident – how the train had reversed into his car, shunting it into the buffers, crushing it *and* Pete beyond repair – that was terrible.

'How could this happen?' Sarah asked over and over. 'Didn't the driver see him? And what was his car doing on the tracks in the first place?'

All they could tell her was that Pete appeared to have driven there deliberately, and that he had not only consumed a significant quantity of almost pure alcohol but it appeared that he had also taken heroin just prior to the accident.

Was she aware that he was a heroin user? they asked. How long had he had a habit? Was he depressed? Had he displayed any suicidal tendencies?

'No, no, *no*,' Sarah cried, refusing to believe what they were saying, challenging their cynical glances with steadfast denials. 'I would have known. It isn't true. Pete never touched smack in his life! He was dead against it.'

She was still shaking her head when the two PCs drove her home some time later.

'I know what you're thinking,' she said, when they had escorted her back to the flat. 'But I know Pete didn't take that stuff. Someone must have spiked him. Ask Clive. That's where he was all night. Clive must know something.'

Hannah agreed.

'I know Pete well,' she said, holding her friend's hand. 'He hated that shit. Spliff, yeah – everyone does weed now and then. But smack? No way! He never touched it. And there's enough doing it round here to know the difference. Pete was *not* a smack-head.'

The inquest was held a week later. The verdict was suicide.

In summing up, the coroner said that he was satisfied that Pete had driven his car onto the tracks with the express intention of placing himself in a position that would lead to an unavoidable collision with a train.

He went on to say that, given the family's financial problems, and Sarah's admission that her husband's gambling addiction had recently caused a rift between them, he was in no doubt that Pete had suffered a severe – if temporary – depression. This had caused him to make the out-of-character decision to use heroin as a means of anaesthetizing himself in order to carry out his plans without fear of losing his nerve.

Leaving the court, Sarah sobbed as she climbed into the cab beside Hannah.

'See that judge,' Hannah complained loudly. 'He wants stringing up, I swear to God. Did you hear all that shite he came out with? He shouldn't be allowed to get away with it! I'd sue, if I was you.'

Regaining her composure, Sarah wiped her eyes and told her friend to leave it. 'He was right,' she said. 'And there's no point denying it.'

'But we all know Pete never touched smack,' Hannah protested.

'Well, he did that time,' Sarah told her firmly. 'It's a *fact*. He had heroin in his system, and there were no needles involved so he couldn't have been spiked. I've just got to face it. He did it on purpose, and he didn't give a *shit* what happened to me and Kimmy.'

The tears came again at the thought of her daughter. What was Kimmy going to do without her daddy? How was the little girl supposed to live with the knowledge that he had abandoned her so cruelly and absolutely?

The anger came then.

The bastard! The weak, cowardly bastard! How could he do this to them?

Sarah had been beating herself up since that night, convinced that she should have known what Pete was going through, that she should have been able to save him. But

it wasn't her fault. It was *his*. He'd taken the easy way out –
again. Just like he always had. From letting Vinnie take over
his gang at Starlight, to moving into her flat and *allowing* her
to make all the mundane decisions. He wasn't just the nice,
easygoing guy he'd made himself out to be, he was a bone-idle
passenger – jumping on board and letting everyone else do the
pedalling. Abdicating responsibility so he wouldn't be blamed
when the going got rough. Right down to driving his car into
the path of a train, forcing the poor train-driver to do his dirty
work for him, and filling himself with booze and smack so that
he didn't have to feel the pain.

'Thanks, Pete,' Sarah muttered, glaring at the roof of the
cab. 'Thanks a fucking bunch!'

31

———◆———

Vinnie waited a couple of days after the newspaper report appeared before going to see Sarah. Staying away had been agony when he had wanted nothing more than to run to her side and comfort her, but, to avoid the light of suspicion falling upon him, he'd had to wait until it was old news.

'I've just heard,' he said when she opened the door. 'It's terrible. I don't know what to say. Are you all right?'

'I'm fine,' Sarah assured him, holding her head high. In fact, she was anything *but*. Her emotions were see-sawing wildly: anger one day, pain the next. Today, she was missing Pete like crazy, and blaming herself – yet again – for not realizing that he'd been so depressed.

'I was away on a business trip,' Vinnie told her, feeling it necessary to explain why he hadn't come sooner. 'Why didn't you call me?'

'I didn't have your number.' Her chin wobbled as the ever-ready tears flooded her eyes. 'It was stored in . . . in Pete's m-mobile.'

'I'm so sorry.' Stepping inside as the tears streamed down her cheeks, Vinnie took her in his arms and held her to him. 'So, so sorry.'

Sarah allowed him to hold her for a while then pulled free. She was embarrassed to be seen like this, at her most pathetic. And also more than a little perturbed by the feelings that Vinnie managed to stir in her. Even now, when intimacy with another man should be the furthest thing from her mind, her body was reacting to the nearness of him, the smell of his aftershave, the sound of his voice.

'Can I get you a coffee?' she asked, waving him into the living room. 'I was just about to make one.'

'Let me do it,' he said, leading her gently to the couch. 'You just sit down and relax. You must be wiped out. Where's the baby?' he asked then, looking around. 'Is she in bed?'

Sarah's tears began again at the mention of her daughter.

'Hey!' Sitting down, Vinnie put an arm around her. 'What's wrong? She's all right, isn't she?'

'She's at Hannah's,' Sarah sobbed, burying her face in his shirt. 'I wanted to keep her with me but people were saying things about Pete – that he was a junkie, and he didn't love her. She's only little, but she knew what they meant. Hannah took her for a couple of days.'

'Do you want her back?'

'*Yeees . . .*'

'Right, well, calm down.' Vinnie lifted her face and peered into her eyes. 'You'll be no use to her like this, will you? Now, I'll make you a coffee and run you a bath, and when you're feeling a bit better we'll go and pick her up. Okay?'

Resting against his broad shoulder, Sarah nodded. She felt safe for the first time since it had happened – as if someone had stepped in and taken control of the mess that her life had become.

Hannah distrusted Vinnie on sight. He was way too good-looking, and he thought far too highly of himself. She considered herself an excellent judge of character, and this man wasn't right.

'Are you sure you're ready?' she asked when Sarah said

she'd come to take Kimmy home. 'She can stay with us as long as you need. There's no rush. Why don't you leave her till morning?'

'No, I'll take her now,' Sarah insisted, smiling shakily. 'I'm fine, honest.'

'Well, if you're sure.' Hannah eyed Vinnie with suspicion. She'd have betted that this was his idea. And was he the reason for Sarah's sudden composure? Was there something going on here that she didn't know about?

'This is Vinnie,' Sarah told her, picking up on Hannah's curiosity. 'He's one of my and Pete's oldest friends. He's only just heard, and he's going to look after us for a bit – get us through the funeral, and that.'

'Oh, right,' Hannah murmured, a little put out that this handsome stranger had usurped her position as chief supporter. 'Well, if you're sure?'

'I am,' Sarah assured her. Then, understanding the unspoken disquiet of her friend, she said, 'You'll still come with me though, won't you? I still need you there.'

'Course I will.' Hannah smiled. 'I wouldn't desert you at a time like this. I'll just fetch Kimmy. She's playing with our Danni upstairs. Won't be a minute.'

'Can I get youse a drink?' Steve asked, awkward in his wife's absence. He didn't know how to deal with Sarah's grief, and the man was making him nervous. 'A beer, or a brew, or something?'

'Not for me.' Vinnie shook his head. He didn't want to stay any longer than absolutely necessary.

'Nor me,' Sarah agreed. 'I'm really tired. I just want to get home and get things back to normal.'

'Here she is,' Hannah said, opening the door and ushering Kimmy in.

'Mammy!' Kimmy yelped, flinging herself at Sarah as if she hadn't seen her in a year. 'Mammy, mammy!'

'Hello, baby,' Sarah cried, kissing her tiny face. 'Have you missed me?'

'Wanna go home now. Wanna see Daddy.'

'I know you do, sweetheart, I know you do.'

'Might be best if we get moving,' Vinnie suggested. 'Get her into her own bed.'

Twisting her head at the sound of his voice, Kimmy peered up at him with heartbreaking eyes.

'She's tired out,' he said, reaching out to touch her silky hair. 'Poor little thing.'

'You look after them,' Hannah told him, walking them to the door. 'She's got my number if she needs me. Just give me a ring – any time, yeah?'

'I will,' Vinnie assured her. 'Thanks for being there for her.'

'She's my friend,' she reminded him pointedly. 'Her *and* Pete.'

'Mine too.' He smiled, refusing to let her see the irritation building in his gut at her interference.

Back at the flat, Vinnie cleaned up while Sarah put Kimmy to bed. He was sitting on the couch when she came back. Flopping down beside him, she rested her head back and released an exhausted breath. Lighting a couple of cigarettes, Vinnie passed one to her.

'I'm glad you came round,' she told him, smiling gratefully. 'I thought I was cracking up, but I feel loads better now. Thanks.'

'My pleasure.' Reaching out, he took her hand in his. 'That's what friends are for. Anything I can do, you only have to ask.'

'I think you've done enough already,' she said, looking around the dust-free room with a smile of embarrassment.

'Nothing's too much for you,' he murmured, wanting with all his heart to kiss her, carry her to bed, and . . .

Pete's bed.

Pulling himself together, reminding himself that he had to play this to the letter, Vinnie eased his hand from hers.

'Look, I'd best get moving. I didn't realize it was so late. You must be shattered. I'll come back in the morning and check you're okay – if that's all right?'

Sarah sat up straighter. She didn't want him to leave – didn't want to be alone with her thoughts.

'You don't have to go,' she said, blushing furiously. 'I doubt I'll get to sleep. I'll be too busy listening out for Kimmy. She'll be feeling a bit weird back here, with all this going on.'

Vinnie frowned and glanced at his watch. 'I don't know. I really should be getting back. I'd love to stay, it's just . . .' Pausing, he shrugged. 'Someone's coming round to mine.'

'Oh, God, I'm sorry,' Sarah spluttered as she suddenly understood what he was trying to say: that he had a date, and she was delaying him. 'I didn't realize. Look, go. I'll be fine.'

'You sure?'

'Absolutely. Go on . . . I'll see you in the morning.'

At his own flat a little later, Vinnie poured himself a drink and carried it to the couch. Switching the stereo on with the remote, he closed his eyes and let the strains of vintage Boyz II Men wash over him.

The words were poignant, perfectly apt for his and Sarah's situation. They *had* come to the end of the road – the old road. And he couldn't let her go because she did belong to him, and he to her. He had always known it. It had just taken longer to achieve than he'd imagined it would.

Vinnie'd had plenty of time to think in the years since leaving Starlight, and he regretted the way he'd handled things in the early days. He should never have done what he had to her. He should have waited, instead of taking what she wasn't ready to give.

Okay, so he'd been wrong about that, but he'd been too young to know better back then. Now things were back on track, he had only to wait for the right time.

32

Sarah made it through the cremation. She even managed to hold it together back at the flat afterwards, smiling as she handed out the sandwiches and booze to her friends and neighbours, enduring their anecdotes and memories with good grace. Pete, it seemed, had suddenly become everybody's best friend.

She'd been glad to get them out of the flat that night, wasn't sure she could have carried on being so good-natured when she found their behaviour so hypocritical. These were the same people who had been indulging in some pretty slanderous gossiping in the days leading up to the funeral – and who quickly resumed it straight after.

Sarah no longer cared what they said, as long as they had the decency not to say it to Kimmy. Pete might not have been the best husband or father in the world, but his daughter didn't need to know that. And if it was the last thing she did, Sarah vowed that Kimmy would grow up with only good memories of her daddy.

Which was why she was concerned when she realized that Kimmy was becoming so attached to Vinnie.

It was four months since the funeral and Vinnie had called round almost every day, to check that they were all right and to see if they needed anything. He always made a fuss of Kimmy, and he was so sweet and gentle with her that Sarah began to worry that Kimmy was transferring her desire for a daddy onto him. It was Vinnie that the little girl talked about now – Vinnie that she looked out of the window for. He didn't seem to have noticed, but Sarah was afraid that when he did he would run a mile, leaving Kimmy to suffer yet another desertion by a man she loved.

Thinking it would be better if he took off sooner rather than later, she sat him down and told him her concerns.

'I'm flattered,' Vinnie said when she had finished. 'She's a lovely kid, and any man would be proud to be her father. I'm perfectly happy to be a stand-in, if that's what she needs.'

'Are you sure?' Sarah frowned, afraid that he didn't realize the depths of the responsibility that he was offering to take on.

'Absolutely positive.' Reaching out, he gently stroked a stray hair from her face. 'I'd take care of you *both*, if you'd let me.'

Sarah didn't pull away. Instead, she held his gentle gaze, her own eyes wide with apprehension. This was something she had dreamed of, but had fought against because it seemed so ridiculous. Vinnie was Pete's friend. *Her* friend. She loved him for everything he had done for her since Pete had died, but beyond that . . .

Anyway, even if she admitted that she herself was becoming too attached to Vinnie, it wasn't just about her and what she wanted, was it? She had no clue if he felt the same way about her. He'd made no secret of the fact that he had a girlfriend. He'd never mentioned any names, but when he made his excuses to leave it was invariably because he was expecting 'someone' at his flat, or he was meeting 'someone' in town, at a club, a restaurant, or whatever. Did she really want to get involved with him if he already had a woman? And was he even offering that?

'Take your time,' he was saying now, his voice low and husky. 'I'm not going anywhere. Just let me know when you're ready.'

'I think I might be.' The words slipped out of their own accord and Sarah covered her burning face with her hands, cursing her mouth for betraying her. It was only four months. Vinnie would think she was cheap and indecent. But, God, she wanted him. She wanted to be held and loved, craved the intimacy that only a couple can truly share.

Vinnie gently pulled her hands aside. He had been waiting for this from the moment he'd laid eyes on her again on Christmas Day. It was the outcome of a carefully manoeuvred plan, and he was going to seize it with both hands.

Taking Sarah gently in his arms he carried her into the bedroom and laid her on the bed. Easing himself down beside her, he drew her to him, stroking her hair, taking it slowly. Feeling a dampness seeping through his shirt, he tilted her face up and kissed a path from her eyes to her lips.

'Don't cry, Sarah. I'll never let anyone hurt you. I've always loved you.'

Kissing her properly now, tasting the salt of her tears and the sweetness of her tongue, he ran his hands down her body, thrilled by her response as she rose to meet his touch.

Undressing her slowly, Vinnie looked down at Sarah's naked body and groaned. She was so beautiful, so perfect. Her breasts large and satin-soft, her skin as smooth and tanned as cocoa butter, her waist slender.

Dropping delicate kisses onto her flesh, he circled his tongue around each nipple then trailed a path down, savouring the taste and smell of her.

Pulling his head up when she could stand no more, Sarah gazed deep into his eyes and drew him onto her.

Forcing himself to hold back, Vinnie hovered above her.

'Are you sure you want to do this?' he asked, his voice husky with desire.

'Yes,' she moaned, pulling him down. 'Absolutely positive.'

33

<hr/>

Everyone noticed the change in Vinnie. He'd always been vain, but now his self-interest soared to new heights. His clothes and his hair always had to be immaculate, and he developed a passion for body sprays and aftershave – much to the amusement of Glen and the others.

Taking it all in his stride, Vinnie adamantly refused to admit what they had already guessed – that he had a serious woman tucked away. Sarah was his secret, and he wasn't ready – or willing – to share her. He wanted to protect her from this side of his life. Didn't want her exposed to the crudity of the guys. And he especially didn't want her anywhere near Carina.

Carina would swallow him having another woman as long as she still got the occasional legover, but he wasn't fool enough to think Sarah would stick around if *she* found out. And how was he supposed to explain that, much as he loved and desired her, he wasn't the kind of man to fight his natural urges? If it was there, he was going to take it. It was just the way he was. It didn't reflect on Sarah in any way shape or form, but Vinnie knew instinctively that she wouldn't get it. No, as far as Sarah and this side of his life were concerned, the further apart he kept them the better.

Carina was no fool. She knew that Vinnie was messing around with some tart, but with no proof she couldn't accuse him outright of anything. She and Vinnie were still doing their thing, but not anywhere near as often as she'd have liked. It wasn't easy to snatch opportunities at the best of times, with Glen calling Vinnie out to do this, that and the other, but these days Vinnie rarely stuck around for long enough at the end of work to snatch much more than the odd kiss and grope. It ate her up to think of him loving another woman, but she knew better than to let it show. It would destroy their truce, and that was the last thing Carina wanted when deep in her heart she still harboured the dream that, one day, when they were both free, Vinnie would see that she was the only one for him.

Pam was the last to hear the rumour.

Bed-bound now, having failed to make a full recovery, she had insisted on moving back to her beloved bungalow. Glen wasn't happy about it, but he'd had to admit that it wouldn't work having her at his place. It was no secret that Carina and his mother couldn't stand the sight of each other, so he'd finally let his mother go home – on condition that she have round-the-clock nursing care. And Pam readily agreed – anything being better than putting up with Carina twenty-four-seven. She now had a daytime carer who gave her a bath and made her lunch, then a private nurse who came at nine and stayed overnight. And Glen and the guys took it in turns to look in on her during the unmanned hours.

It was Joe who told her about Vinnie, laughing as he described the kid's sudden passion for aftershave and telling her how the guys had ribbed him that he was turning into a tart, asking if he was doing punters on the side.

'Shady little shit!' Pam laughed, pleased as punch. 'Just wait till I see him. I'll tan his arse for holding out on me.'

She had another three days' wait before she got a chance to quiz Vinnie. His day for calling in was Wednesday, and she was more than ready to pounce when it finally arrived.

'Park your arse, you,' she ordered when he walked through the door. Gripping his hand when he obliged, she peered deep into his eyes for a moment then slapped a hand down on the quilt, declaring jubilantly, 'I knew it! You *have* got a woman. And don't give me that guff you've been feeding our Glen and them, 'cos you can't fool me. I've got the vision.'

'You've certainly got the imagination,' Vinnie chuckled.

'Oi!' Pam scolded, slapping him on the arm. 'Since when have you and me lied to each other? I thought you was one of me own, but if you're just gonna sit here and tell me bare-faced lies you can bugger off!' Pursing her lips, she folded her arms and huffily turned her face from him.

'All right, you win.' He sighed exaggeratedly. 'Yes, I have got a woman, but I don't want anyone to know, so I'd appreciate it if you'd keep your big trap zipped for once.'

Peering round at him, Pam narrowed her eyes. 'That special, is she?'

'Yes, she is.'

'Told you it'd happen one day,' she gloated. 'How long has it been going on?'

'About four months, but we've know each other for years.'

'Tell me about her,' Pam demanded. 'And don't leave nothing out.'

As Vinnie began to describe Sarah, Pam listened in silence, nodding every now and then. The girl sounded lovely – just what he needed. Beautiful and straightforward, with no airs, and no baggage but a little fatherless girl whom Vinnie claimed to adore.

'Bring her round,' she said when he'd finished. 'I want to meet her.'

'You sure?' He asked.

'Since when did I invite strangers round to me house if I didn't want to?' Pam snapped. 'Bring her. Tonight.'

*　　*　　*

Sarah got into a flap when Vinnie told her that he was taking her to meet someone special that night, and that he wanted her to dress up real pretty for the occasion.

'But who is she?' Sarah asked. 'And why does she want to meet me?'

'She's my boss's mother,' he told her, 'and she thinks she's mine as well.' Grinning wickedly, he said, 'I expect she's going to give you the third degree. Find out if you're good enough for me.'

He laughed when she looked horrified.

'I'm only joking, babe. She just wants to meet you because she knows how serious I am about you. You'll come, won't you?'

'All right,' Sarah agreed. 'But I'm warning you now, if she turns her nose up at me I'm out of there!'

'She won't,' he assured her, pulling her into his arms and kissing her. 'No one could turn their nose up at you, princess.'

Sarah frowned. 'What about Kimmy? Should I bring her, or ask Hannah to have her for a bit?'

'Whatever you think best,' Vinnie said, a flicker of irritation crossing his face at the mention of Hannah. 'But Pam'll be cool if you want to bring her with us. She won't mind.'

Pursing her lips, Sarah thought about it then shook her head. 'No, I think I'll leave her out of it for now. She's still a bit iffy with strangers – she might get upset. Maybe next time, when I've got to know your friends.'

Kissing her again, Vinnie let her go and checked his watch. 'Best give *her* a ring then.' He didn't even like saying Fat Slag Hannah's name. 'Only make it quick, 'cos I don't want to be too late. Pam's tough, but she still needs her sleep.'

Pulling up outside the bungalow an hour later, Vinnie looked at Sarah's pale face and laughed. 'Stop panicking. It'll be fine.'

'I'm not,' she protested. 'I'm just . . . hungry.'

Shaking his head, Vinnie said, 'Feeble excuse. Couldn't you come up with something better than that?' Still smiling, he climbed out of the jeep and smoothed his trousers down.

Frowning, Sarah unclipped her seat belt. This was going to be terrifying. She hadn't met a single one of Vinnie's friends so far, and now she was about to be introduced to the most frightening one of all – the queen of the clan.

Cocking his head as he watched her climb out, Vinnie gave a sexy half-smile. Waiting until she came around to his side, he pulled her to him and pressed her up against the driver's side door.

'Feel that?' he whispered, pushing his hardness against her. 'That's because you look so beautiful. Just wait till I get you home.'

'Get off,' she scolded, pushing him away. 'You'll crease my dress.'

Walking up the path beside him, Sarah smiled at the tingling sensation still crawling over her thighs. With him beside her, she could face anything. Even this.

'It's only me,' Vinnie called, opening the front door. 'You decent?'

'No, I'm butt naked with a daffodil up me arse,' Pam called back. 'What do *you* think, you dozy sod? Stop shouting and get your arse in here before you let all the heat out. And I hope you've brought the lass with you, or you can piss right off out again. I don't want me neighbours talking if they see you coming in on your tod. They'll think I'm back in business, or something.'

'See what I mean?' Vinnie whispered as he ushered Sarah along the passage towards the bedroom. 'Mad.'

'She certainly sounds . . . *different*,' she whispered back.

'She's that, all right,' he agreed, smiling fondly. 'But that's her. No front, no surprises. If she likes you, she'll tell you. If she don't, she'll tell you that, an' all.'

'I hope she does,' Sarah murmured.

'She will.' Giving her a reassuring smile, Vinnie pushed the bedroom door open. Gripping tight to his hand, Sarah followed him in.

Pam was propped up in bed facing the door and Sarah was shocked to see how old she looked. Vinnie had told her Pam's age, but the voice had sounded so vibrant that she had stupidly expected someone far younger-looking.

'So, this is her, is it?' Pam looked Sarah up and down. 'Well, she's every bit as gorgeous as you said. I can see why she's got your bollocks in a tizzy.

'Don't mind me, darlin',' she said when Sarah immediately blushed. 'I'm only teasing. Come and sit down, let me get a proper look at you.'

Sarah was nervous when Vinnie dropped her hand and propelled her forward. But she was positively petrified when he said he was going to put the kettle on – to give them a chance to get to know each other.

Going to the bed, she sat down on the chair pulled up beside it and smiled nervously as Pam peered at her face for a full minute.

Breaking the awkward silence at last, Pam said, 'He's proper gone on you, you know?'

Embarrassed by the other woman's directness, Sarah just nodded.

'You're not gonna hurt him, are you?' Pam went on. 'I may be old and knackered, but I could still kick your arse if I felt like it.' Smiling now, she reached for Sarah's hand. 'Only joking, pet. I can see you like him, and I'm glad. He's like one of me own, that lad, and he deserves the best. Anyhow, tell me about yourself. Vinnie says you're a widow?'

'Er, yes.' Sarah squirmed in her seat, uncomfortable that her laundry had been so freely aired with someone she had never laid eyes on before.

Tutting sympathetically, Pam shook her head. 'That's a terrible thing to happen at your age. And you've got a kiddie?'

'Yeah – Kimmy.'

'That'll help, you know,' Pam said wisely. 'It takes your mind off things when you've a little one to think about. So, when did you meet Vinnie?'

'Oh, years ago. He was—'

'You two all right?' Vinnie interrupted, coming back into the room with three steaming cups in his hands. 'Not scratching each others' eyes out?'

'Behave,' Pam snorted, tipping Sarah a wink. 'We're getting on like a house on fire, ain't we, Sarah love?'

Smiling, Sarah nodded.

'I knew you would.' Vinnie grinned happily. 'How could you not when you both love me.'

'Have you heard him?' Pam scoffed. 'Vain as a cat on heat. Makes a lovely brew, though, you've got to give him that. I hope you can cook, though, Sarah? He might be a stud in the boudoir, but he's crap in the kitchen. And I should know. He's burned me a few rounds of toast since I've been laid up!'

'Didn't hear you complaining at the time,' Vinnie protested.

'What, and starve to death?' she squawked. 'I'd rather your burnt offering's than Carina's slop, any day!'

'Carina?' Sarah gave Vinnie a questioning look.

'My Glen's girlfriend,' Pam told her. 'Her and Vinnie were looking after me when I had me stroke. Only for a day, mind, 'cos Glen sorted me out as soon as he come back. Here, Vin,' she said then, grinning. 'Remember that time he broke his foot and Katie got that nurse in?'

'God, yeah.' He laughed. 'He thought he'd be getting some fit bird, but Katie got a man instead.'

Taking the opportunity to excuse herself while they were reminiscing, Sarah went to the bathroom to comb her hair and touch up her lipstick. Seeing how close Vinnie and Pam were, it was suddenly very important that Pam should like her.

'What's the verdict?' Vinnie asked when Sarah had gone.

'Lovely,' Pam declared. 'But I reckon she's still a bit delicate about her hubby, so don't go getting heavy and screw it up.'

'I've got no intention of messing this up,' he said, meaning it. 'I've waited too long.'

'She's obviously worth it,' Pam remarked. Then, looking thoughtful, she added, 'She don't half look familiar, though. I've been thinking since she walked in that I know her from somewhere, but I can't put me finger on it.'

Coming back just then, Sarah saw them looking at her and blushed. 'What?' she asked, checking that her skirt wasn't tucked into her knickers, or something equally embarrassing.

'We were talking *about* you, not *to* you,' Pam quipped. 'Anyhow, come here a minute, love. I want to have another look at you.'

Doing as she was told, Sarah sat down and endured another close scrutiny of her face. It made her feel most odd and she couldn't bring herself to look into the old woman's piercing eyes.

'That's it!' Pam declared suddenly. 'I *knew* I'd seen them eyes before. Only one man on Earth could have passed on eyes like that. You're Alan Bell's kid, aren't you?'

Sarah's mouth flapped open but nothing came out. She had

no idea what to say. She didn't know her father – had never been told his name.

Seeing her look of confusion, Pam drew her head back. 'Don't tell me she never told you?'

'Who?' Vinnie asked. 'What are you talking about?'

'Her mam,' Pam told him, still gazing at Sarah. 'You *are* Maggie Mullen's lass, aren't you?'

Eyes widening, Sarah nodded mutely.

'Thought so!' Pam slapped her hand down on the quilt, overturning the ashtray, scattering dimps and ash every which way. 'How is the old cow?'

'No idea,' Sarah said when she found her voice at last. 'I haven't seen her for years. She put me in care when I was seven.'

Picking up on the stark bitterness behind her words, Pam said, 'Ah, I see. Put you through the wringer, did she?'

'Something like that,' Sarah muttered, reluctant to talk about it.

'Was she always bad, or was it just when she was needing a fix?' Pam persisted.

'More when she was withdrawing,' Sarah admitted, wondering how Pam knew so much. 'But it was pretty crap in general.'

'Men?' Pam asked, cutting right to the heart of it.

Flicking a nervous glance at Vinnie, Sarah gave the slightest of nods.

'Nuff said,' Pam murmured, letting it drop. Maggie Mullen had always been a self-serving old tart. It didn't surprise her one bit that the bitch had put her kids forward as bait when her own appeal had shrivelled up and died along with her veins. 'So, she shoved you in a home, did she? Well, I never. And you haven't seen her since you got out? Didn't you want to?'

'I thought about it, but I wouldn't know where to start,'

Sarah admitted quietly. 'She'd moved last time I went round to the old house.'

Pam gazed at her for a long silent moment, considering whether to tell her that she knew where Maggie was. She decided to go for it.

'I know her address.'

'You know where she lives?' Sarah gasped.

Pam nodded. 'I never saw her for years after her and your dad split. I was more his mate, you see, and you always sided with your own. Anyhow, she moved straight after and we lost touch, but I bumped into her a couple of years back, down the market, and she give me her new address. Never went round, 'cos I never reckoned that much to her if I'm honest, but I should still have it somewhere if you want me to root it out?'

Stunned, Sarah looked at Vinnie. Shrugging, he said. 'It's up to you. Do you *want* to see her?'

'I don't know,' she mumbled, finding it all a little hard to take in.

'Take your time.' Pam patted her hand kindly. 'You can always take the address, but you don't have to use it if you don't want to, do you?'

'What about my dad?' Sarah asked in a tiny voice, the word 'dad' feeling foreign on her tongue because she had never had cause to use it in relation to herself. 'Did he know about me?'

'Course he did.' Pam was smiling now. 'You were the spit of him and he was proud as anything. I should have clicked straight off that you was his. He was *such* a good-looking man when he was young, with them eyes and all that lovely black hair. Proper Irish dapper, he was, lovely soft voice.' Sighing, she peered at the ceiling for a moment, lost in her memories. 'Your mam wasn't too bad herself,' she said sniffily, coming back to Earth. 'But she bollocksed herself up good-style when she started on the gear. Al moved out not long after, and that's when she did the moonlight. He never saw you after that, didn't know where she'd took you or nothing.'

'Where is he now?' Sarah asked, barely breathing now at the prospect of maybe meeting the man who'd shared his looks with her.

'Southern cemetery, last I heard.' Pam sighed regretfully. 'Died of cancer about ten years back, poor love. A shame and a half, that was. Anyhow, about that address . . . You reckon you might want it?'

'Yeah.' Sarah nodded decisively. 'No harm in taking it, I suppose. Like you said, I don't have to use it if I don't want to.'

Pointing to the wardrobe, Pam said, 'Fetch us the brown leather bag out of there, Vin. It should be at the bottom under the shoes.'

Rooting through the mess of papers and old make-up stuffed inside the handbag when Vinnie handed it to her, Pam found the address and handed it to Sarah.

Gazing at her mother's childlike handwriting, Sarah felt peculiar, as if the years had been stripped away and she was a child again, making her way to the shops with a list in her hand.

10 Bennies . . . Bog roll . . . Pint of sterry . . . tin foil . . .

'And don't be taking all day about it . . . You know what you'll get if you make me miss my score . . .'

'You all right?' Vinnie asked, concerned by her sickly expression.

Snapping back to the here and now, Sarah nodded. 'I – I think I'm getting a headache.'

'Take her home,' Pam told him quietly. 'It's a lot to take in, this.

'Sorry if I upset you, love,' she said to Sarah then. 'But I think it's better knowing who you are than walking about wondering for the rest of your life. You know where I am if you ever want to ask me owt.'

Struggling to hold back the tears, Sarah thanked her.

'Come on,' Vinnie said, putting a protective arm around her. 'Let's get you home.'

Sarah didn't sleep that night. Alone – having persuaded Vinnie to sleep at his own flat for a change – she stared up at her bedroom ceiling and thought about everything that she had learned.

Alan Bell. Her father. She was supposed to be the spit of him, but she hadn't even known his name. It didn't seem right.

It *wasn't* right.

Her mother had had no right to keep her from him. And how dare she give Sarah away to strangers when she could have sent her to her own father. Sarah would *never* do something that terrible to Kimmy. Pete could have beaten her black and blue every day of their marriage and she *still* wouldn't have taken his child away from him.

But maybe she wasn't being fair. Her mother had had a serious drug problem. She probably hadn't known any better than to up sticks and run when the going got tough. That was exactly what she had done straight after putting Sarah into care. Maybe it was her way of dealing with guilt?

Sarah battled these conflicting emotions all night long, finally reaching a decision as the sun crawled into view outside the window.

She *would* go and see her mother, but she would go alone. There was no way she was letting Vinnie witness her humiliation if she was rejected again. And she wouldn't expose Kimmy to a potential cold-shouldering, either.

Getting up, Sarah made breakfast, then rang Vinnie and

told him her plans. Assuring him that she would be fine, and promising to tell him everything when she saw him later, she said goodbye. Then she rang Hannah to beg her to babysit – again.

34

The house was a scruffy end-of-terrace in the back streets of Rusholme. Less than two miles from Sarah's flat, it might as well have been on the moon for all the similarities between the areas. In Hulme, people were constantly on the move, ducking and diving, wheeling and dealing – and generally making as much noise as possible. Here, with no people milling about and no cars zooming by, it felt stagnant – as if all the residents had died but nobody had bothered telling them.

Unable to see through the grossly overgrown hedge shrouding the fence and broken gate, Sarah had to force her way through to the muddy litter-strewn garden to check it was the right number on the peeling brown-painted door. It was.

Any doubt that she was in the right place was dispelled when she spotted the Maggie Mullen trademark in the window immediately above the door: the grotesque statue of Christ with His arms outstretched, His crown of thorns and His bloodstained cheeks. The cause of many a childhood nightmare for Sarah, it was Maggie's pride and joy. She might move from house to house and man to man, leaving abandoned possessions and children in her wake, but that hideous statue was the one thing she *never* forgot to pack.

Sarah closed her eyes and forced the bitter memories away. The past was done. The future was an open book. She wasn't a helpless child any more, she was a fully grown woman with a child of her own and a dead husband under her belt.

Taking a deep breath, she knocked. Then she stepped back, her stare riveted to the door, the blood pounding through her ears like a hammer-drill.

Several seconds passed before a young woman answered. 'Yeah?' she said, her voice decidedly unfriendly.

Sarah couldn't speak. Surely this wasn't her sister. She was a pretty, blonde, full-grown woman, with a shapely figure and long, slender legs. Karen was a plain, mousy-brown, five-year-old child.

'What do you want?' the woman asked impatiently. When Sarah still didn't answer, she tutted and went to close the door.

'Wait!' Sarah managed. 'Please . . . I just . . . Are you Karen?'

The woman's eyes narrowed to slits as she stared at Sarah. Then realization sank in and they widened.

'*Sarah*?'

'Yes!' Sarah nodded, her eyes filling with tears.

'Oh my God!' Karen gasped, throwing her hands up to her mouth. 'I don't believe it!' Staggering off the step, her own eyes swimming with tears now, she threw her arms around the sister she had thought she had lost for ever.

Breaking away after a minute, Sarah pulled a tissue from her pocket. Tearing it in half, she was laughing as she handed a piece to Karen.

'Here, wipe your nose. You look like you did last time I saw you – snotty!'

'I do not!' Karen protested, laughing as she wiped. 'Oh my God, Sarah.' She shook her head slowly from side to side. 'I never thought I'd see you again.'

'Me neither.' Sarah made an effort to pull herself together. 'But I'm here now, so are you gonna let me in, or what?'

Frowning, Karen bit her lip and glanced back nervously over her shoulder.

Sarah's heart sank.

'What's wrong? Am I not allowed in?'

'It's not that. It's just . . . well, we were right in the middle of an argument when you knocked, and she might take it out on you.'

'Ah, who cares?' Shrugging, Sarah gave a sad smile. 'It wouldn't be any great shock, would it? She didn't exactly hold back when we were kids. I doubt there's anything she could say that I haven't already heard.'

'All right,' Karen said, stepping back into the house. 'But don't say I didn't warn you. She's worse than ever these days.'

Grossly obese, Maggie Mullen rarely ventured off the couch these days. The telly was her world now. That, and the booze her mate Rob bought her when he cashed her disability book.

Sprawled there now, with a dirty grey quilt covering her lap, a cigarette in one hand and the remote for the TV in the other, she grumbled when Karen opened the door.

'Bloody hurry up, will you? I'm freezing my tits off here. You trying to give me pneumonia or something?'

Rolling her eyes at Sarah, Karen said, 'Shut up moaning, mam. You've got a visitor.'

'Who?' Maggie grunted, struggling to turn her head on its pedestal of fat-rolls. 'Rob?'

'No, it's not bloody Rob. You think I'd have let him in if it was?'

'It's me,' Sarah said, stepping into view. Whatever reaction she'd expected, she didn't get it. Her mother looked at her as if she'd never seen her before in her life.

'Who are you, when you're at home?' Maggie demanded. 'You from the social, or something?'

'In a way,' Sarah said curtly, returning the glare.

'Well, you can piss off out of it, then, can't you?' Maggie thumbed towards the door. 'You ain't got no business coming round here on the sneak. I'm disabled, me – long-term!'

'She isn't from the social,' Karen said, coming to stand beside Sarah now. 'Don't you recognize your own daughter?'

Maggie's eyes disappeared into her cheeks as she squinted up at the two of them, then hardened to two stony little pebbles.

'Don't know what you're talking about.'

'Don't come the innocent. You know exactly what I mean. Our Sarah – *my* sister.'

'You ain't got no sister.'

'Oh, behave yourself!' Karen was losing patience now. 'She's your flesh and blood. Stop being such a fucking bitch.'

'Don't you talk to me like that!'

'Or *what*?' Karen snorted incredulously. 'What you gonna do, mam? Lay into me, when you can't even move off the fucking couch? Give it up, you gobby bitch, or I'll piss off right now – and I *won't* come back!'

'Piss off, then! See if I care.'

'You never *did*.'

'You ungrateful little cow! I sacrificed everything for you.'

'No, mother.' Karen leaned forward aggressively. 'You *took* – and you're *still* taking. And what do you give back? Nothing! You just moan and gripe about every goddamned thing I do for you.'

'Shut your friggin' mouth!'

'*Make* me!'

Maggie looked as if she were about to explode. Watching her, Sarah felt a surge of pity. Maggie was helpless, and she knew it. It must be killing her to know that she couldn't batter her daughter like she would have done in the good old days if they'd dared to disagree with her.

'You've always put yourself first,' Karen went on venomously, 'and sod what it did to the rest of us. You're just selfish. Always have been, always will be.'

'That's you, more like,' Maggie retorted. 'You *and* her.'

'Oh, so you *do* remember her?'

'Yeah, I remember her,' Maggie snarled. 'And I don't see why you're so pally with her all of a sudden. It was *your* bleeding cat she murdered.'

'It was *hers*, actually,' Karen corrected her angrily. 'Don't you remember? I do. I've thought about it often enough over the years. That's right, mother, *hers*. And guess what? . . . *She* didn't kill it – *you* did!'

'I did *not*!' Maggie spluttered indignantly.

'Yeah you did, 'cos it wasn't *dead* till you put your big fucking feet on it.'

'She cut its throat.' Maggie pointed at Sarah accusingly.

'No, mother.' Karen shook her head. 'Want me to remind you what really happened?'

'Shut up!' Scarlet-faced, Maggie fumbled a fresh cigarette from the packet on her lap. 'You're pissing me off now.'

'Funny how the truth always does that to you,' Karen sniped. 'I remember when I first came clean. You could have put everything right then, couldn't you? But oh, no – not Maggie Know-it-all! You couldn't back down and admit you'd been spreading a pack of lies about your own daughter, could you? So you belted me and told me I was imagining things instead.'

In the momentary lull, Sarah stared at her sister openmouthed.

Turning to her, Karen said, 'I'm sorry, Sarah. I was only twelve when I admitted it. I wouldn't give you the cat and we started fighting and I fell on the glass.'

'*She* was holding it when I come out,' Maggie cut in. 'You can cover for her if you want, but I know the truth.'

'She had hold of the glass because she'd just pulled it out of the cat's fucking neck – as you well know.'

'She knew?' Sarah felt numb.

'Yeah.' Karen nodded guiltily. 'But she didn't want to admit she was wrong.'

'I wasn't wrong about her going for *me*, though, was I?' Maggie said, flicking Sarah a cutting glance.

'No,' Karen conceded. 'But I'll tell you something, mam – if I was her, I'd have done the same thing, the beating you were giving her.'

Slumping down like a deflated balloon, Maggie stared at the TV screen.

Shaking her head, Karen straightened up. 'That's right, mam. Switch off like you always do when you can't get your own way. That's why Lol pissed off, and God knows *he* had the patience of a saint. You want to think about that before you turn everyone else against you.'

'I'd better go,' Sarah murmured, exhausted by the suffocating emotions fogging the room.

'No! Stay for a brew,' Karen said. 'Please . . . I really want to talk to you.'

'It ain't your house,' Maggie muttered, her voice barely audible now. 'You can't go round offering brews out whenever you feel like it.'

'I can when *I* buy the tea bags and pay the electric,' Karen countered frostily.

'No, really, I can't,' Sarah said. 'Thanks for asking, though.'

'I'll let you out,' Karen said, throwing a glare at Maggie as she wrenched the door open. 'Hope you're satisfied, you miserable old bitch!'

Following her sister out, Sarah paused in the doorway and looked back at her mother. She'd been prepared to forgive

and forget when she came here today, but finding out that
the bitch had known the truth all these years and had never
tried to put things right hardened her. She wasn't going to
waste any more time yearning for Maggie's love.

'Have a nice death,' she said, closing the door on the
deafening silence of her mother's response.

'I'm so sorry,' Karen said when Sarah joined her at the
front door. 'I knew she'd be off with you, but that was just
plain nasty.'

'Don't worry about it.' Sarah shrugged. 'I expected it.'

'Doesn't make it right, though.'

'I really don't care. It was you I wanted to see. It always
was.'

'Really?' Karen peered at her doubtfully. 'After what I did?
You must have known all along.'

'It doesn't matter.' Sarah smiled reassuringly. 'We're not
kids any more. I came to terms with all that a long time
ago.'

'Well, you're better than me,' Karen said. 'If it had been
the other way round I would have hated you.'

'Yeah, well, I don't hate you. Anyway, forget all that. When
am I going to see you again?'

'You really want to?'

'Wouldn't ask if I didn't.' Sarah smiled. 'Anyway, you've
got to meet your niece.'

'My *niece*?' Karen repeated, her eyes widening. 'Wow!
You've got a kid?'

'Yeah. She's called Kimmy, and she's gorgeous. You'll
love her.'

'Bloody hell!' Karen laughed. '*Me* an aunt. I can't believe
it.'

'Yeah, and *her* a gran!' Sarah hissed, jerking her thumb
back towards the living room. 'But I'm not telling her. She
doesn't deserve it. Anyway, look, I've really got to go. I

was only supposed to be leaving her for an hour. Let's swap numbers so we can set something up for you to meet Kimmy.'

'Brilliant!' Karen yelped, hugging her sister tightly. 'I can't wait! Just let me get a pen and paper.'

Sarah was smiling all the way to Hannah's house. She felt as if she had found a missing piece in her life – and put another firmly in the bin where it belonged. Shame that she and Karen hadn't had a chance to talk. She had so much to find out about her. But they had the rest of their lives to make up for the time they had lost.

Vinnie was on the couch when Sarah brought Kimmy home. Seeing him there, Sarah smiled, pleased to see him, eager to tell him her news.

'Hello, you!' she said, taking Kimmy's coat off. 'Haven't been waiting long, have you?'

'Since about three,' he murmured, frowning as he flicked the ash from his cigarette onto his knee and rubbed it in.

Sarah told Kimmy to go and play in the bedroom for a while. There was something wrong. Vinnie would never spoil his clothes like that otherwise.

'What's the matter?' she asked when they were alone. 'Has something happened?'

Looking up at her, Vinnie sighed heavily. She was so beautiful. He had missed her so much last night. His bed hadn't felt right. He'd spent too many nights in hers, in her arms.

'I've been thinking,' he said. 'That's all.'

'Oh? What about?'

'Us.' His voice was grave. 'I've been thinking about it all night.'

Sitting down, a knot of apprehension tightening her gut

now, Sarah said, 'What about us? Have you had enough, or something?'

'God, no!' Vinnie gazed into her fearful eyes. 'It's nothing like that. It's the opposite, if anything.' Breathing deeply, he sat forward. Then, suddenly, he dropped onto one knee.

'What are you doing?' she asked, a bemused smile twitching her lips.

Looking up at her, his eyes dark, he said, 'Will you marry me, Sarah?'

Gasping, she drew back from him, her free hand lifting unconsciously to her breast. Had he really just said that?

'Well?' He smiled uncertainly. 'I know it's not long since Pete – you know. But we don't have to do it right away. We can wait till you're ready . . . Say something.'

'I don't know what to say.'

'How about yes?'

'Oh, Vinnie, it's not that easy. There's Kimmy to think about.'

'What about her? She loves me. That's why we got together in the first place. Well, not *why*, but it was that conversation that sparked it all off. She wanted me to be her daddy, remember?'

'Yeah, I know, but . . . It's just so soon.'

'I said we could wait,' Vinnie persisted, squeezing her hands. 'At least say yes, so we know we're gonna do it *sometime*.'

Sarah saw the sincerity in his eyes and knew that he really wanted this. And was it so wrong? He'd be a wonderful father, and she had no doubt he'd be an amazing husband. He'd been a model boyfriend so far, treating her with respect and affection.

'Okay,' she said, coming to a decision. 'Yes, I will.'

'Really?' He could hardly believe it. 'Do you mean it?'

'Yes.' She laughed softly. 'But not yet.'

Peering deep into her eyes, he said, 'I told you a long time ago that I could be patient.'

'You did, didn't you?' Tipping her head to the side, Sarah smiled. 'I can't believe you remembered that.'

'I never forget anything,' Vinnie murmured. 'So don't think I'll forget that you just agreed to marry me.'

Lifting her left hand, he gazed for a moment at the rings still adorning her third finger. Then he slid them off and put them on the table.

Sarah felt a thrill of panic. They were the rings that Pete had given her, and letting Vinnie remove them was like a betrayal. It felt wrong.

'You don't need them any more,' he told her, stroking her cheek gently. 'That's the past. *This* is the future.'

Taking a small black velvet box from his pocket, he opened it and plucked a two-carat solitaire diamond ring from the groove within. Slipping it onto her naked finger, he raised her hand to his lips and kissed it.

'From now on,' Vinnie promised, 'everything you wear will be the best that money can buy.'

Lying beside Vinnie in bed that night, listening to his soft snores and watching the flickering of his eyes behind the long lashes, Sarah twisted the engagement ring around and around on her finger, and gradually came to terms with the decision she had made.

Mrs Walker. Her third surname. No, make that her fourth. Her father's name had been Bell, which made that her real maiden name – morally, if not legally.

But what about Kimmy's surname? Vinnie wanted Sarah to change it when they got married but she didn't know if it was the right thing to do. It seemed wrong to deny Kimmy her real father's name – as she herself had been denied.

Still, she would decide that nearer the time. Right now, she had more immediate things to consider. Like moving into Vinnie's flat. It was the one thing he had been adamant about. He would give her time for everything else, but he would *not* continue sleeping in Pete's bed. And she could see his point. *She* wouldn't like it if the situation were reversed.

Whatever she decided in the end, she would make sure that Kimmy was all right with it. This was the only home the child had ever known and Sarah wasn't about to traumatize her even more than she already had been.

Sarah needn't have worried. Kimmy was absolutely thrilled when they sat her down and told her about the move the next morning. But it wasn't just the prospect of moving into Vinnie's flat that made her jump up and down, it was the thought of being a bridesmaid at their wedding.

Sarah hadn't wanted to tell her that particular news just yet, but Vinnie hadn't been able to contain himself and had blurted it out. Seeing the joy on both of their faces as they discussed pretty dresses, shoes and flowers, Sarah finally relinquished the last of her reserve.

'I'll start packing this afternoon,' she announced. 'But you'll have to go and get me some boxes. And I suppose you'd better give me some money, as well.'

'Oh?' Vinnie grinned up at her from where he was playing with Kimmy on the floor.

'Well, I'll need a wedding dress, won't I?' she said, laughing when he immediately leaped up and swept her off her feet.

'When?' he asked, gazing lovingly into her eyes.

'How about six months from now?'

'Really?'

'Yes, really. Fifteenth of June okay?'

'My birthday!' Kimmy squealed, clapping her hands excitedly.

'Fifteenth of June it is, then,' Vinnie said, scooping Kimmy up and bringing her into the circle.

Finally, he had exactly what he wanted.

PART FOUR

2003

35

———◆◆◆———

'Wake up, Harry . . . Climb the steps into the light . . . Now, I'll count down from ten, and when I reach one I'll snap my fingers and you'll be awake and refreshed.

'Ten . . . nine . . . eight . . .'

Harry's eyes snapped open at the sound of clicking fingers and he gazed blearily up at the smiling moon face hovering above him, the spectacles barely hanging on to the tip of the long thin nose, the eyes as inquisitive and bright as a mouse's.

'How are you feeling?' Dr Bandera asked, taking a linen handkerchief from his pocket and dabbing his bald pate with it. It had been an intense session.

'Fine.' Harry stretched languidly. 'Like I've slept for a week. How was it?'

'We'll listen to the tape in a moment.' Dr Bandera scribbled something in his notepad and snapped it shut. Pressing the rewind button on his tape recorder, he rubbed his hands together. 'Cup of tea?'

'That'd be great. Thanks.'

Yawning long and hard when the doctor left the comfortable plant-infested office, Harry got up and stretched his legs. This had been a good session, he could feel it. Maybe it hadn't been such a crazy idea after all.

He had scoffed when his father had suggested hypnotherapy. He didn't need it, he'd said – he was doing just fine with his locked-in-memory syndrome, thank you very much. But his father had insisted, reminding him that people who were doing just fine didn't suffer nightmares and panic attacks, and didn't go into slumps of depression for weeks afterwards.

One thing was for sure. Whether the mumbo-jumbo was phoney-baloney or not, Dr Bandera sure was good at relaxation therapy. Harry hadn't felt this rested in months.

'Here we are.' Dr Bandera was beaming as he carried the cups in. Harry was a most pleasant and intriguing patient. 'Now, we'll just take a minute to talk before you listen to the tape. Smoke, if you wish.'

'Er, thanks.' Harry frowned bemusedly. 'No smoking' was Dr Bandera's strictest rule. There must be something big in store. Lighting up, he waited.

'You know what we discussed when you first came for treatment?' Dr Bandera said, opening the window. 'How memories can be so deeply buried that we need extreme measures to bring them to the surface. Well, I think we made a terrific breakthrough today. You see, the memories you've been harbouring are now in here.' Reaching out, he patted the tape recorder. 'Now, it can be incredibly disturbing when you come face to face with your darkest fears, so before we move on I need to ask if you think you're ready to face yours?'

'I think so,' Harry replied.

Dr Bandera looked at him for a while then nodded decisively. Harry was intelligent and level-headed, and he'd obviously had enough of living under this terrible shadow.

'You can't *lose* a memory,' he said, settling back in his seat and crossing his legs. 'Anything that happens to us stays for ever within our psyche. We *forget* most things because the information is too insignificant. Truly monumental things, however, we can bring to the fore with ease, because we enjoyed them greatly or were hugely moved by them. But we lock horrendous experiences away so that they can't torture our waking mind. We *leak* particles from time to time, allowing ourselves to come to terms in a gradual way with the associated *feelings* – the fear, the pain, and what have you. But our psyche prevents us from recalling the *details* because it fears that we could not survive reliving the event. Do you understand?'

'Mm-hm.'

'Well, *your* psyche has tried very hard to protect you, Harry. It has resisted several sessions thus far, and that is no mean feat. But at last we have made it see reason.'

Smiling at the doctor's choice of words, Harry sat up a little straighter. 'Does that mean what I think it means?'

'It means,' Dr Bandera said, leaning forward now, a serious expression on his face, 'that your tremendous brain has finally relinquished its hold on those memories. When you hear the tape, you will know everything. Are you ready?'

Harry took a deep breath. He was strong now. Whatever had happened to him as a child, the man he was now could cope.

'Let's do it,' he said, lighting another cigarette.

'How old are you, Harry?'
   'Ten.'
   'Where do you live?'
   'At Starlight.'
   'Do you like it there?'
   'No. The big boys pick on me and call me names.'
   'Have you got any special friends?'
   'No.'
   'What about Sarah?'
   'S-Sarah doesn't like me any more.'
   'Why not?'

*   *   *

'Relax, Harry. Let's move forward to the last night you stayed at Starlight. Where are you?'

'In bed.'

'Is it bedtime?'

'No. I'm upset because they won't let me see Sarah.'

'Who won't let you see her?'

'Dandi and Mr Chambers. They said she made a mistake.'

'And did she?'

'Yes.'

'How do you know it was a mistake, Harry?'

'V-Vinnie . . . Vinnie s-said . . .'

'Calm down, Harry. No one can hurt you now. You're quite safe. What did Vinnie say?'

'He – he said he was p-punishing me for lying to him, just like he'd punished S-Sarah for ignoring him. He said – he said he was glad Chambers got the blame, and he was going to make sure Chambers got the blame for me as well . . .'

Sitting in his car outside the consultation rooms, Bill Clark tapped his fingernails agitatedly on the steering wheel. Harry was taking far longer than usual and Bill was beginning to feel apprehensive – and guilty, it had to be said. He had forced Harry into this, so sure that he knew what he was talking about because he had read a couple of leaflets and visited some vague websites. He would never forgive himself if he had contributed to making Harry suffer even more than he already had.

The breath caught in his throat when Harry came out. He looked so troubled, his face as pale as it had ever been.

'What happened?' Bill probed gently when Harry climbed in beside him.

Shaking his head, Harry said, 'I don't really want to talk about it, Dad. Would you mind if we just go home? I'll explain when I've had a chance to think it through.'

'Sure.' Starting the car, Bill drove home in silence.

Dora Clark rushed to the door when she heard the car. Like her husband, she had become anxious about the length of time that Harry had spent at this appointment. He was usually out much earlier than this. She hoped that nothing bad had happened.

'You took so long,' she said when Harry stepped out onto the path. 'Are you all right?'

'I'm fine, Mum.' Bending, he kissed her cheek. 'I wish you'd both stop worrying.'

Dora glanced at her husband. He shook his head, telling her to leave it for now. Harry would come to them when he was ready.

Going up to his room, Harry snatched up his guitar and carried it to the window seat. Playing softly, he gazed out across the garden. There was no better view in the world, and it never failed to relax him. Trees and flowers everywhere. And the fish pond that he and his dad had created, complete with a walk-across bridge, always made him feel tranquil and calm.

His mum came into view after a while, carrying a large basket of washing. Watching as she pegged each item on the line, pausing now and then to rub at the small of her back, Harry sighed deeply. He made more than enough money to hire a housekeeper to do all these chores for her, but his mother was a stubborn old girl. If she wasn't doing something for the men in her life, she felt as if she were failing in her duties. And Harry and Bill humoured her, because they both knew she thrived on it. She had waited so long for a child of her own, and when poor, damaged Harry had come into her life she had made it her mission to heal his pain. And, for the most part, she had succeeded. If it hadn't been for her and Bill's gentle, caring ways, Harry knew that he might never have become who he was today. And, against all the odds, he knew he was someone worth knowing.

Not handsome in the traditional sense, Harry was reasonably good-looking. Age had stretched his ugly features so that his nose no longer seemed too large for his face, his mouth no longer too wide. He could even get a tan these days. And, with the progress in hair-colouring products, he'd had highlights put into his rich red hair, taking the words 'ginger nut' out of the equation.

But it wasn't just his looks that had improved. Everything about his life was a million times better than he had ever dreamed possible. Everything he had, everything he was, he truly owed to Bill and Dora. Just as he owed them an explanation now. They were so patient that they would wait for ever for him to tell them what they were bursting to know. But they deserved to be put out of their misery.

Putting the guitar down, Harry made his way downstairs and called his parents into the kitchen. Sitting them down at the table, he told them what he had learned today – and what he had decided to do about it.

36

<hr>

Replacing the phone in its cradle, the desk sergeant, Janice Webb, looked up at the sound of the door opening and tutted when she saw DI West entering.

'Trust you to turn up a second after you're wanted,' she scolded, releasing the inner door to let him behind the desk.

'I'm always in demand,' West muttered, shuffling sideways through the door to avoid dropping either the papers tucked under his arm or the hot lidded drink in his hand. 'Who requires the great man's genius this time?'

Janice handed him the name and phone number she had jotted down. 'Here. It's the third time he's rung, and he wants you to ring back as soon as. Sounded pretty desperate.'

'Who is it?' West grunted, gazing blankly at the name. 'Don't know any Mr Clarks.'

'Me neither.' Janice inspected a nail she had just chipped. 'Asked for *PC* West, if that's any help?'

'Bloody hell!' He drew his head back, a deep frown crinkling his brow. 'It's years since I was in uniform. What did he want?'

'What am I?' She arched an eyebrow. 'Madam Zelda the mind-reader?'

'No, Janice the bloody useless secretary,' he retorted. 'If you're gonna take messages, make sure you know what they're about, eh?'

'All he said was to tell you to ring him urgently. Oh, and

to say it's about "Starlight".' She shrugged. 'Don't ask me. He said you'd know what that meant.'

West's frown intensified. Starlight. That was a name he hadn't heard in a long time. Last he'd heard the Council had closed them down, relocating all the inmates and selling the property off at a huge loss for a quick sale. It had been an old folks' home last time he'd driven by.

Peering at the name again, he dredged his memory for any Mr Clarks he had come across in connection with Starlight. Drawing a blank, he wandered through to his office at the rear of the station, ignoring Janice's sarcastic call of 'You're welcome!'

Dropping the papers into an untidy heap on the floor, West sat down at the desk and rooted through the mess for the phone. Finding it, he dropped into his chair and hooked the receiver beneath his chin. Dialling the number, he flipped the lid off his drink with his thumb.

'Mr West?'

'Shit!' Jumping at the speed with which the call was answered, West spilled tea onto his hand, scalding himself. 'Yeah, this is *DI* West,' he snapped, recovering his composure and wiping his hand on his trousers. 'You wanted to talk to me? What's up?'

'I, er, don't really want to go into it over the phone. Would it be possible to meet up?'

'Depends who you are and what you want,' West said gruffly. 'I don't recognize the name.'

'Oh, of course, sorry, I should have thought. It was changed when I was adopted. It was Shaw when I saw you last. Harry Shaw. I don't suppose you remember me?'

'I do, as it happens.' West's eyebrow had risen to a sharp inverted V of surprise. 'Bloody hell, it's been some time, hasn't it? What can I do for you, son?'

'I've got some information about what happened,' Harry

told him cagily, unwilling to elaborate over the phone. 'Do you think it would be possible to meet up?' he asked again.

'Can't really see the point,' West said, sipping the tea. 'The case was closed way back. We got him, he did his time, end of story.'

'But that's just it,' Harry persisted. 'It's not. Look, I really can't go into it like this. I'm staying at La Granta. Do you think you could come and see me here?'

West was more than a little impressed. La Granta was an expensive hotel in the town centre. The kid must be doing all right for himself to be staying there.

'I know it's an imposition,' Harry went on. 'But if you could come tonight we could have a meal, or just drinks if you'd prefer? Please. This is really important.'

West's stomach rumbled at the mention of food. Glancing at his watch, he ran a hand over the stubble plaguing his chin. Ever since he'd turned grey, the damn stuff was growing thicker and faster than ever.

'All right, I'll be there at six,' he said, figuring that would give him time to get home, take a shower, have a shave and get changed.

'Thanks.' Harry breathed an audible sigh of relief.

'Don't thank me till you know if I'm interested in what you've got to say,' West growled. 'I'm retiring soon. I might decide it isn't worth the hassle.'

Walking into the foyer of the plush hotel two hours later, West whistled through his teeth. It was the kind of place that made you feel like a tramp if you hadn't blown your nose.

'May I be of assistance, sir?'

Turning at the sound of the haughty voice, West saw a man in full red, black and gold livery. He almost laughed, but he pulled his badge out instead – perversely pleased by the scandalized expression he received in return. Visits from the police obviously lowered the cultured tone that this clown held so dear.

'I'm looking for Harry Clark,' he said. 'Let him know I'm here, will you?'

'Certainly, sir.'

Shaking his head when the man bowed and walked away, West wandered across the foyer to read the gold-edged menu pinned to the wall beside the dining room. The descriptions were foreign, but the prices were pure English – and looked like you'd need to take out a mortgage to pay them.

'DI West?' It was Harry.

Turning, West gazed at him blankly for a moment. He almost didn't recognize him. At least six feet tall now, Harry Shaw was a man who held himself with a confidence that West had never thought to see in him.

'Thanks for coming.' Harry extended his hand.

Taking it, West smiled. 'Bloody hell, you've shot up a bit, haven't you? I wouldn't have known you in a million years.'

'I recognized you straight away,' Harry said, his eyes twinkling as he stopped himself from adding: *Despite the vast difference in age, weight and hair colour since I last saw you.* 'Would you like to eat?'

'As long as it's only a piece of bread.' West motioned towards the menu. 'About all I could afford off of that.'

'I'm paying,' Harry said. 'It's the least I can do.'

'Oh, well, if you insist.' Chuckling, West patted his belly. 'As you can probably tell, I never turn down a free meal.'

'Drink?' Harry asked, leading West to a table in the dining room.

'Scotch,' West said, glancing around at their snotty-looking fellow diners. He wouldn't have been at all surprised to see them wearing full ball gowns and tuxedos, given the poncey atmosphere of the place.

Harry called the waiter over. 'Two whiskies, please. Doubles.' Lighting a cigarette then, he offered the pack to West.

Taking one, West said, 'Thought they didn't like this sort of thing in these places?'

'When you're paying as much as they charge here, they tend to overlook it,' Harry said, finishing the coffee that he'd been drinking while he waited.

Chuckling, West shook his head. He'd never have envisioned Harry Shaw turning out like this – so confident and sure of his place in the world.

'So, what do you do?' he asked. 'Computers, I'd bet?'

Smiling modestly, Harry said, 'Websites, actually. I started in my dad's company, and . . . well, let's just say I outgrew it.'

'Oh, yeah?' West's tone was teasing now. 'I've heard about those websites. One of those Internet millionaires, are you?'

'Something like that.' Blushing, Harry looked down at his cigarette.

'I'm impressed,' West said, sensing that the lad was uncomfortable. 'Seriously. You were so fucked-up last time we saw you, me and my partner didn't think you'd make it. I'm pleased you're doing so well.'

'Thanks,' Harry said, knowing that West meant it by the tone of his voice. 'I was worried people who knew me before would resent me.'

'Never envy what you haven't got the sense to earn,' West remarked sagely. Taking his drink from the returning waiter, he sipped it and sighed. 'Now that's *nice*.'

'Would you care to order now?' the waiter asked.

'Can't even *read* most of it,' West snorted. 'What you having, Harry?'

'Steak.'

'Same for me.' West closed his menu with a snap. 'And make sure it ain't singing.' Seeing the waiter's blank expression, he said, 'No *blood*. I want it dead and buried.'

'Medium rare for me.' Harry handed the menus back. 'And a bottle of chilled white.'

Looking bemused when the waiter bowed and backed away, West said, 'So, what was so urgent that you had to drag me over here?'

'Well, as I said earlier,' Harry began, leaning his elbows on the table and resting his chin on his clasped fists, 'I've got information about what happened to me at Starlight. The problem is, if I'd told you over the phone *how* I came by it you'd have dismissed it out of hand. Which is why I invited you to dinner.' He gave a wry smile. 'I thought I'd trap you behind a plate so that you'd *have* to hear me out.'

Rocking back in his chair, West snorted softly. 'Remember what I said about retiring and not wanting hassle? Well, I meant it. So I'll listen while I eat, but if it's bullshit I'll get straight up and leave when I've finished. Are we clear on that?'

'Absolutely,' Harry agreed.

Pushing his plate back half an hour later, West burped loudly and wiped his mouth on a napkin.

'Lovely, that. Shame they can't give proper portions, but I suppose it'll stop my belt busting.'

'Glad you liked it,' Harry said, a little impatiently. 'So, what do you think?'

'Truth?' West paused to light a cigarette. 'It's bullshit. Hypnosis is a stage act. Haven't you seen those American shows where they give a bloke a sweeping brush and make him think he's dancing with Madonna?'

'I used to think it was like that,' Harry admitted. 'But now I've done it, I know it's not. It's not about making suggestions, it's about unlocking what's already there. I regressed to being ten years old in that session. I sounded exactly like I did when I was a kid. It was eerie as hell, but it was *real*.'

West peered at him for a long, silent moment. He wanted to help the lad lay his demons to rest, but it was all so ridiculous, and he was so close to getting out of the force.

'You do know there's not a snowball in hell's chance of this going anywhere, don't you?' he said at last. 'There's not a copper, a lawyer, or a judge in the world who would take it seriously. And even if you got lucky and someone *did* believe you, there's nothing to back it up but the ramblings of your hypnotized mind. And that, my friend, ain't admissible.'

'Granted it's hard to swallow, but I'm not trying to take this to court. I just want a chance to talk to Sarah about it. To try and put things right.'

'If you're thinking about putting it right with Chambers, forget it. He's done his time.'

'I wish I was wrong about this,' Harry murmured guiltily. 'At least then I'd know he hadn't served all that time for nothing.'

'I think you *are* wrong, if it's any consolation,' West told him. 'The evidence was pretty conclusive.'

'Anyone with an atom of cunning can set an innocent person up,' Harry argued. 'Don't tell me you've never seen it done.'

Shrugging, West said, 'Maybe so, but you're going purely on the basis of this hypnosis session and, to be honest, you haven't got a clue what this Dr Banderooney bloke said while you were out of it. He could have fed you all sorts of nonsense. I've seen it before, kid. It's called false-memory syndrome, and it's always got some whacked-out therapist at the heart of it.'

Sighing deeply, Harry looked down at his hands. 'I know it sounds ridiculous, but I just want to know she's all right. She looked out for me when I had no one, and I can't bear to think of her suffering like I was before the sessions. All I'm asking for is help to find her, and you're the only one I could think of.'

'With your knowledge of the Internet, I would have thought you could find her in a heartbeat.'

'I've tried, but it's impossible if the person you're looking for hasn't put themselves out there at some point.'

'All right.' West came to a decision. 'I'll try and find her for you, but only 'cos I'm kind of interested to see how she turned out. And it might take a while, so don't build your hopes up. When are you going home?'

'I'm not. I'm staying till I've seen her.'

'Here?' West raised an eyebrow. 'That'll set you back a bit, won't it?'

'I can afford it,' Harry said modestly. 'Anyway, I'll be doing business as usual from my room, so I won't lose out. Will you let me know when you hear anything?'

'*If*,' West corrected him. 'Yeah, I will – as long as it doesn't overrun my retirement date. After that . . .' He shrugged. 'You'll be on your own.'

Back at home a short while later, West made himself a cup of tea and carried it through to his study. Sitting at the desk, he thought over what Harry Shaw had told him.

There was no way it could go on record when there wasn't a bollock's hair of evidence. The kid had been so convinced that West had wanted to believe him, but that wasn't why he had agreed to look for Sarah. It was sheer curiosity that had pulled him on board Harry Shaw's loco express. Seeing the monumental change in Harry, he was intrigued to see how well Sarah had fared.

Picking up the phone, he dialled the station, expecting the amenable night sergeant, Gordon Lightfoot, to answer. He was surprised to hear Janice Webb's voice.

'What are you still doing there?' he asked. 'Haven't you got a home to go to?'

'For your information,' she snapped, 'some of us have to

take all the overtime we can get. We're not all on detective's pay, you know. What do you want?'

'Well, I *was* going to ask Gordon to do me a favour.'

'Won't I do?'

'Suppose so.' He took a noisy slurp of the too-hot tea. 'I need the whereabouts of a Sarah Mullen, last known address Demesne Road, Moss Side.'

'How far back are we talking?'

'Ten years-ish.'

'You'll be lucky!' Janice snorted. Then, 'All right, give me ten minutes while I have a look. Where are you?'

'Home.'

'I'll ring you back.'

'Thanks. You're a babe.'

Putting the phone down, West opened the desk drawer and rooted through the papers inside. Finding the tatty old address book he was looking for, he laid it on the desk and flipped it open.

He chuckled as he went through it. There were names and numbers in there of people he hadn't seen or heard of in years – snouts, mainly, and the occasional trustworthy hooker. He hadn't even thought about most of them, losing interest as he rose through the ranks and no longer needed them.

Jenny was listed under 'M' for massage. Jotting her number down in his notepad, he carried on flipping through the book of memories.

Snatching up the phone when it rang, he said, 'Did you get it?'

'No.' There was a hint of apology beneath Janice's brusque tone. She liked West. He was one of the few detectives she would put herself out for but she never let it be known. People tended to take advantage if you went all soft on them.

'Oh, well.' He sighed. 'Thanks for looking.'

Lowering her voice, she said, 'Look, how urgent is it?

Only, there's a few other avenues you can try if it's not life or death.'

'Such as?'

'The new link-up to the Central Register. This Sarah Mullen's bound to have seen a GP or dentist in the last ten years, even if she's off paper in every other respect.'

'Oh, yeah, I'd forgotten that. I don't suppose . . . ?'

'You must be joking!' Janice whispered harshly. 'I haven't got the foggiest how to use it, and even if I did I couldn't. Not tonight, anyway. The super's got visitors from the Met. You know how much trouble I could get into if he caught me playing with his precious new program?'

'All right, keep your knickers on. What are the Met doing there, anyhow?'

'Planning your retirement party, but you're not invited 'cos it's just for brass – to celebrate getting rid of you at long last.'

'Oh, ha ha! You're in the wrong job, Jan. You should be doing stand-up down the mess.'

'Certainly get enough material from you, don't I? Anyhow, piss off back to your cocoa, or whatever you're doing, and let me get back to looking like I'm doing something useful.'

'Don't strain yourself.'

'I won't . . . Oops! Gotta go!'

West smiled when Janice hung up abruptly. Replacing the receiver, he gazed at Jenny's number for a while then delved into his drawer once again. Finding the small photograph that Jenny had given to him a long, long time ago, he ran his thumb across the dusty face and smiled at the infectious grin, the happy eyes squinting in the sunlight. It wouldn't hurt to give her a ring, would it? It might yield fruit, but even if it didn't it'd be nice to talk to her again. It had been a good few years since their brief fling.

For a moment, he couldn't recall why they had called it off. Then it came to him. Oh, yeah. His ex-partner Kay Porter – or

Kay Ewing as she was now, having married one of her poncey Cheshire colleagues in the meantime – had turned up.

West had dumped Jenny without a second thought, sure that Kay had realized her mistake and come back to him. He'd soon realized that the mistake was all his. He was just a convenience while Kay did a two-month refresher course. As soon as that was over, so were they, and she legged it back to her big-shot detective husband, leaving West with nothing but a sour taste in his mouth and a desire for revenge. Not the hurt-em kind – the show-'em-what-you're-made-of-and-do-better-than-them kind. The very next day he had put himself forward for promotion. Now, several years on, he was a rank above both Kay *and* her hubby, and it felt good.

Even if it would all be over in a couple of weeks.

West had never contacted Jenny again. It hadn't seemed right, somehow. But she wasn't the sort to bear grudges, and he was sure she would tell him if she knew anything about Sarah.

Dialling the number, he lit a cigarette and sat back with a prickle of nervous anticipation, wondering how it would feel to hear her voice again after all this time. Getting no answer after a couple of minutes, he gave up. She was probably working. He would try again in the morning.

Going into the lounge, West switched on the TV and flopped into his armchair. Swinging his feet up onto the coffee table, he groaned as pain shot through his legs. Too many years on the beat followed by too many sitting in cramped cars had taken its toll. If he'd had any sense he'd have retired years ago while he still had a social life.

Frowning, he told himself to pack in the maudlin nonsense. He was only fifty-two years old. Was he seriously going to relegate himself to the past-it pile without a fight? Was he buggery!

So, Jenny hadn't answered her phone. He'd just go and look

for her instead. It was only eleven. The night was still young
– even if he wasn't.

Swinging his feet down, he grabbed his coat and headed
into town.

Molten Gold was the fifth place that West tried. It was on
Princess Street between a nightclub and a restaurant and he
felt conspicuous having to press the clearly labelled intercom
button with pissed-up clubbers and curious diners strolling by
within earshot. It had been all right when he'd been in uniform
but now he was plain-clothed they obviously thought he was a
punter.

Inside, Jenny watched him on the CCTV screen and smiled
at his obvious discomfort. It served him right, the two-timing
swine! Making him wait, she took the opportunity to look him
over. He'd put on a lot of weight since she'd last seen him, and
his hair was undeniably silver, but he still looked good. He
always had. Something about his aura had always attracted
her. He was so strong and positive. And he'd been a mighty
fine lover, too – for the brief time that she'd had the pleasure.
Bastard!

Flipping the switch at last, she said, 'Good evening, sir.
How may I help you?'

Recognizing her voice, he hissed, 'Jenny? It's me, Tony.'

'Tony?' She repeated the name loudly. 'Are you a regular
client, Tony?'

Glaring at a sniggering couple, he said, 'You know damn
well I'm not. Now quit messing about and let me in.'

'Business or personal?'

'Come on, Jen.' He looked pleadingly into the tiny camera
lens. 'I feel like a right plonker standing here. I'm getting
weird looks.'

'Serves you right.'

'*Jenny!*'

'All right, keep your hair on.' Relenting, she pressed the door release. 'Second floor.'

She was waiting for him in the corridor. Leaning against the wall, arms folded, legs crossed, she watched as he came towards her, a bemused smile playing on her lips.

'Long time no see, Tony. You haven't changed a bit.'

'Yeah, right,' he grunted, noticing that she actually hadn't. She looked better, if anything. Age suited her. What was she now? Forty-two? She looked thirty. Her figure was still trim, her face unlined, and her hair was shorter and gleaming with golden highlights. She looked great.

'Come to the office.' Jenny waved him in through the main door. 'Do you want a coffee, or something?'

'Something,' he said, eyeing the reception area, one eyebrow raised. 'Hey, this is nice. You've moved up in the world.'

'It's still Bernie Silva's place,' she said, leading him into a plush office. 'Difference is, I'm the manager now so I get to choose the décor.'

'Not bad,' he said, settling into a comfortable swivel chair. 'So you've been promoted, have you?'

'A while back, yeah.' She handed him a glass of Scotch. 'I hear you were as well. DI now, isn't it?'

'Where did you hear that?' West was intrigued that she should have kept up on where he was at.

'I have my sources.' Jenny smiled mysteriously. 'Let's just say we have a few of your lads in for . . . *stress* relief, and mouths tend to loosen along with muscles. But you wouldn't know that, would you?'

'Never went in for being mauled, myself,' he sniffed, sipping the drink.

'Not what you said when I was doing the mauling.'

'Ah, but you weren't a stranger.' Smiling, West raised his glass. 'You're looking good, kid.'

'I'd return the compliment, but it wouldn't be true.' She gave a claws-out smile. 'You look like crap. Sorry to hear about *Kay*, by the way. The dumper dumped, eh? Now, what is it they call that? Oh, yes . . . Karma. Or should that be poetic justice? Or maybe just the shit getting the shit he deserves?'

'All right, bring it on . . . I deserve it.'

'Too bloody right you do!' Jenny snapped. Then, taking a deep breath, 'But, no . . . I vowed I wouldn't do this if I ever clapped eyes on your ugly mush again. I'm better than that. I can be compassionate.' Feigning sympathy now, she said, 'Must have been hard to lose her like that?'

'Not really.' West shrugged. 'It made me go for promotion, so I guess she did me a favour.' Pausing, he smiled a little sadly. 'I shouldn't have done that to you, though. You deserved better.'

'Yes, I did, but never mind. We live and learn.'

'We do indeed,' he agreed, mentally kicking himself for letting her go. Jenny had a tongue on her, but it was infinitely better than listening to the silence he faced whenever he went home. 'Anyway, I didn't come to talk over old times. I need your help. I'm looking for Sarah Mullen.'

'Bloody hell,' she exclaimed, chuckling. 'Are you serious?'

'Yeah, why? What's so funny?'

'Nothing. Only that's how we met in the first place. Bit ironic, don't you think?'

'Suppose so. Do you know where she is, then, or what?'

'Still a charmer, I see?' she teased. 'I want an answer and I want it now! You make everything sound like an interrogation.'

'Sorry.' West ran a hand through his hair. 'I'm guess I'm a bit impatient.'

'You always were,' Jenny chided. 'Anyway, no, I don't know where Sarah Mullen is. Last time I saw her she was funny with me. I think she was still blaming me for losing her job. I told her she should thank your mate for that, but she was still a bit miffed.'

'Bob Vine? What did he have to do with it?'

'He was the one who grassed her to Bernie. Don't say you didn't know.'

'I didn't, as it happens. He never said anything.'

'Didn't *I* tell you when we were – you know?'

'No.' He gave a sheepish half-grin. 'But I don't think we had too many deep discussions back then, did we?'

'Complaining?'

'Not at all.' He shook his head. 'But it might have been nice to – I don't know – *talk* now and then.'

'My, my, we are getting old,' she murmured. 'Is this the all-action hero speaking?'

'All right, take the piss if you want, I deserve it. Anyway, what about Sarah?'

'Oh, she was fine.' Jenny flapped a hand. 'She was married, actually. Some guy from that home she was in.'

'Really?' West frowned. 'Don't suppose you'd know his name?'

'She didn't say.'

'Great. How am I supposed to track her down if I don't know her surname?'

'Can't you get a list of all the kids' names from Social Services, or something?' Jenny suggested helpfully.

'Nah.' He shook his head. 'The place was closed down years ago, and I doubt they kept the records. Anyway, this is unofficial. I can't go poking my nose into confidential files.'

'Unofficial?' She raised an eyebrow. 'What's it all about, Tone?'

'You don't want to know.' He chuckled. 'Let's just say one of her old friends had a . . . *spiritual* awakening and wants to make sure she's okay.'

'Spiritual, eh?' She gave him a cynical lopsided smile. 'And you're going along with it *because* . . . ?'

Shrugging, he said, 'Curiosity? Boredom?'

'Boredom? *You*?'

'I'm retiring soon.' West sounded suddenly weary. 'Your mind goes a bit funny, and you start reflecting on shit you've done – and shit you haven't. Sarah's unfinished business, I suppose. I'm just interested to know how she turned out.'

Jenny peered at him thoughtfully. Teasing aside, she couldn't believe his spirit was so low. It wasn't like him at all. The thought of retirement obviously wasn't sitting too comfortably with him.

Finishing his drink, West stood up. 'Oh, well, I suppose I'd best go and let you get back to your work. It was nice seeing you.'

Jenny felt a cold hand grip her insides. She couldn't let him go like this. Never mind Sarah, *they* were the unfinished business in her book.

'I don't suppose you'd fancy meeting up sometime?' she blurted out as he made his way to the door. 'For a drink, or something.'

West turned back, his brow puckered with suspicion. Was she just being polite because he'd moaned about retiring, or did she genuinely want to see him again?

'I won't be offended if you say no,' she went on. 'But we always got along pretty well, didn't we?'

'That's true,' he agreed, cocking his head.

'Yeah, well, I'd really like to see you again.' Jenny was almost blushing now. 'I thought about you a lot after we split up, and, well, there's been no one else. No one serious, anyway.'

'Come off it.' He narrowed his eyes.

'It's true.' She gave an embarrassed laugh. 'I'm not easy, you know. I'm actually pretty choosy. Anyway, my mother gave everyone such a hard time after you, none of them stuck around for too long.'

'Really?' West was doubtful. He'd met Jenny's mother a couple of times, and she'd been nothing but rude on both occasions.

Laughing, Jenny said, 'Yeah, she really liked you for some unfathomable reason. I think it was the uniform that clinched it. She was a bit of a rum old bugger under all that frosting. She blamed *me* for us breaking up. Didn't talk to me for weeks after.'

'Well, well . . .' Chuckling, West shook his head. 'Who'd have thought it? How is she, anyway?'

'Dead, thank God,' Jenny told him without malice. 'It was the best thing all round. She wasn't happy being such a moody old cow, and I sure as hell wasn't happy having to live with her after she moved in for good. Anyway, that's all water under the bridge now.' She flapped her hand. 'What are you saying about this date? Are we on, or what?'

West drew himself up to his full height. He'd spent too long shuffling around like an old man of late. If this lovely young woman still had time for him, wasn't it time he stopped dust-to-dusting himself?

'Yeah, that'd be great. Give me your number, I'll give you a call.'

'Oh, no you don't!' She laughed. 'I know you. You'll find something better to do. You give me yours.'

West was grinning all the way home. He should never have let Jenny go in the first place, and now that he had a second shot at . . . What? *Love?* He didn't know if that was what he would call what he felt for her, but whatever it was, it beat the hell out of the future he had been facing when he got out of bed that morning.

The answerphone's red light was flickering when he let

himself into the house. It was so rare for anyone to call him at home that it almost didn't register – a sad indictment of the fact that he had no life. Pressing *play*, he smiled when he heard Janice Webb's hushed whispers.

'Tony? It's me . . . Janice . . . pick up if you're there!' Pause. Tut. 'Oh, great, you're asleep! Oh, well . . . you'll get this in the morning.' Rustle of paper. 'Don't know if this is what you're after, but I did another quick check and came up with a few more Mullens in a two-mile radius of Demesne Road. Two men, and two women – unrelated. Well, the women are related, actually. Mother and daughter: Margaret and Karen. I'll just give you their address for now. Let me know if you want the blokes' as well. Got a pen?' Another pause. 'Right, it's 32 Hartnell Road, Rusholme. Let me know how you get on, and I'll keep looking for the other one. See ya!'

'You little darlin',' West murmured, grinning broadly as he copied the address down.

The machine beeped and the second message began. It was Jenny.

'Hi there . . . Just thought I'd try out the number – make sure you weren't pulling a fast one. Anyway, it was really good seeing you again, so, I'll, er . . . see you soon. Bye.'

As the automated voice told him there were no more messages, the mobile began to ring in his pocket. West grinned. Bloody hell, he was in demand tonight!

'Hello, Mr West.' It was Harry. 'Sorry to disturb you so late, but I forgot to give you my mobile number when you gave me yours, and I thought you'd best have it in case you tried to ring me when I was in the shower, or something.'

'Jeezus, kid,' West laughed. 'You been at the whizz, or something? Slow down.'

'Sorry,' Harry apologized. 'It's just that being here, and talking to you . . . It's all kind of brought it home that I might actually see Sarah again.'

'Yeah, well, you might be interested to know I could have a lead on her.'

'*Really*? My God, that was fast! Where is she? What's she—'

'Don't get too excited,' West interrupted. 'It's nothing much, but I'll be checking it out tomorrow. I'll let you know if anything comes of it. Try and get some sleep. You sound like you need it.'

'I'll try,' Harry agreed. 'But I doubt I'll manage it. Anyway, my mobile number . . . Have you got a pen?'

Hanging up when he'd taken the number, West shook his head. The boy was obsessed. But there was nothing wrong in caring for your friends. The world would be a better place if more people tried it.

Picking up the house phone again on this thought, he dialled the station.

'Janice? Hi, it's me. I got your message and it's a great help. The Mullen women are my girl's mother and sister – so, well done. I'll treat you to a takeaway next time our shifts cross.'

'No problem.' Janice sounded pleased. 'Anyway, you've got me interested now. Gonna tell me what it's all about?'

'Maybe when I've found her. See you soon.'

37

W est scowled with disgust as he pushed his way through the bushes straggling over Maggie Mullen's gate the following morning. After the best sleep in months, he'd made a real effort with his appearance and didn't appreciate getting covered in leaf shite.

Swiping at the slimy whatevers leeching to the arms of his jacket, he forced the scowl from his face as he rapped on the door. Maggie wasn't the most cooperative of people at the best of times. If he wanted her to talk, he'd have to play it cool.

Almost a full minute passed before a man opened the door.

'Morning, sir.' West flashed his badge. 'Mrs Mullen in?'

'Maggie?' The man's eyes swivelled nervously. 'Er, why? What's up?'

'She in, or not?' West adopted an officious tone.

'Who is it, Rob?' Maggie's raucous voice rang out from the back of the house.

'Guess that answers my question – *Rob*.' Smiling tightly, West moved forward, forcing Rob to step back. 'Through there, is she?' Nodding towards the living-room door, he walked straight through.

'Who is it?' Maggie struggled to turn her head.

'Coo-ee,' West said, popping his head around the door. 'Long time no see, Maggie. Been keeping out of trouble, have we?'

'Who're you?' she grunted narkily. 'What d'y' want? I've got no money if you're after ripping me off.'

West drew his head back and walked into the room with a mock-offended look on his face.

'Don't tell me you don't recognize me? I haven't changed that much. I'm still the same gorgeous old me. Not come to you yet?'

'Oh, it's you,' she said, recognizing him at last. 'What d'y' want?'

'Fine way to greet an old mate.' He tut-tutted. 'No cup of tea? No "Have a seat, Mr West"?'

'Fuck off!' Maggie lit a cigarette with shaky fingers. 'I'll do you for harassment, if you don't watch it. I'm disabled, me.'

'I can see that.' He shook his head in mock concern. 'Sad how life stamps us into the shit when we've never done anything wrong, isn't it, Maggie? I mean, you tried your best, didn't you?'

'Yeah, I bleedin' did, you sarky bastard.'

'I'm not being sarky,' West protested innocently. 'I mean it. The way you looked out for your kids, for example . . . How are they, by the way? Sarah and Karen, wasn't it?'

'Yeah, so?'

'Just asking. Nice-looking kids from what I remember. How old would they be now? Twenty-something?'

'Dunno. I don't keep count. What's with all the questions? What you after?'

'I'm off, Maggie,' Rob interrupted, eyeing West nervously. 'See you later.'

'Oi!' she squawked as he scuttled out. 'Get back here, you cunt! I need me bottle!'

'Oh, dear,' West said when the front door clicked shut. 'Have I chased your friend out?'

'Get to fuck, you bastard!' Maggie yelled at him furiously. 'Coming round here sticking your nose into stuff that don't concern you! Piss off! Go on . . . Get your stinking arse out of me house!'

'Keep your knickers on,' West chuckled, pulling a cigarette from his pack and lighting it. 'What you so upset about?'

'Me vodka!' she yelled. 'I'll get sick now, thanks to you. Happy now?'

'Knocked the gear on the head, have you?'

'Yeah. Fuckin' had to, didn't I?' Maggie snapped, searching beneath her quilt for her inhaler. 'That friggin' judge sent me to rehab. That or nick, he said, so I went for it. If I'd known they was gonna give me one of them things what makes you puke your lungs up if you so much as get a sniff of the smack, I'd have gone for lock-up any time!' Finding the inhaler, she took several puffs then relit her smoke.

'Christ, you *are* in a bad way, aren't you?' West affected sympathy. 'How's about I go and get your booze?'

'Yeah?' Narrowing her eyes, Maggie peered at him with suspicion. 'What's in it for you?'

'We're mates, aren't we?' he lied smoothly. 'Us coppers can't help but respect you street girls, you know. Especially ones like you who try your best for your kids.'

'I did, an' all,' she muttered self-pityingly. 'You wouldn't think it, though, the thanks I get. Our Karen only comes round to have a go. And as for the other bitch, I thought I'd seen the back of her.'

'Sarah?' He tried to sound casual. 'You've seen her lately then, have you?'

'Yeah, the other week. Nasty cow only turns up telling all her lies and turning my Karen against me!'

'That must have been a shock for you. What's she doing these days?'

'Fucked if I know. And I don't wanna know, neither. Getting all kissy-arse with our Karen after what she did! She can rot in hell for all I care.'

'How is your Karen?' West decided to try a different route. 'You say she comes round to look after you?'

'Yeah, she's good like that. Moans too bleedin' much about me drinking, but at least she cares. The other one would see me starve as soon as look at me.' Looking up at him now, Maggie licked her lips. 'You gonna get us that bottle, then?'

Smiling down at her, West shook his head. 'Nah. I don't think I should. Not if your Karen doesn't like it.'

'You bastard!' she screeched when she realized he meant it. 'You sly fuckin' bastard! Get out! Go on . . . get out of my house!'

'What's all the shouting?' Karen demanded, rushing into the room just then. 'Who are you?' She glared at West. 'What've you done to her?'

'Get him out, Karen!' Maggie demanded. 'He's dibble, and he's harassing me.'

'Detective Inspector West.' West flashed his badge. 'I wonder if we could have a quiet word?'

'About what?' Karen snapped, folding her arms. 'My mother hasn't moved off that couch in months, so I know she hasn't done anything wrong. Now, if you don't mind, I'd like you to leave.'

'You tell him!' Maggie tugged on the back of Karen's tight skirt.

Slapping her hand away, Karen opened the door and waited for West to go through it. Following him into the hall, she reached past him to open the front door. Sticking a hand out, holding it shut, West looked down into her angry eyes.

'I haven't seen you since you were five,' he told her quietly, 'so I'm not surprised you don't recognize me. But I assure you I know your mother very well. And what you heard when you came in, that was her getting mad because I wouldn't go and get her a bottle of vodka.'

'I see,' Karen replied coolly. 'Well, thanks for that, but I'd still like you to leave.'

'I'm looking for your sister,' West continued unperturbed. 'Your mum reckons she came round the other week.'

Narrowing her eyes, Karen said, 'What do you want with Sarah?'

'I just need to talk to her.'

'Is she in trouble?'

Frowning, West considered how best to proceed. He couldn't make out that he was here on official business. Karen was hostile enough already and she looked the kind to make a complaint, in which case she'd find out he wasn't authorized to be asking questions. And she was unlikely to respond too well to the story he had to tell – which, in all honesty, wasn't her business.

'So she's not,' Karen said, taking his silence as an affirmative. 'Bye, then.'

'Okay, I'm going. But could you tell Sarah I'd like to speak to her?' Pulling a contact card from his pocket West handed it to her. 'If you'd give her this, she can always leave a message and I'll get back to her.'

'And what should I tell her it's about?' Karen asked, snatching the card.

'I'm not really at liberty to say. But if you could give her that, I'd be grateful.' Opening the door now, he left.

Closing the door, Karen looked at the card in her hand, then slipped it into her pocket, instantly forgetting about it when her mother shouted: 'Karen . . . I need a dump. Bring us the pot, will you?'

Tutting with disgust at the pathetic wheedling tone of her mother's voice, Karen hung her coat on the banister and rolled her sleeves up. The bitch was going to be putting it on for England now, playing on Karen's sympathies for all she was worth. Just what she needed with a potentially life-changing appointment to attend when she finally got away.

Climbing into his car, West tutted. He should have said something to give Sarah a clue about why he was asking after her. The kid's name, or something. He had been intrigued enough to return Harry's call without knowing who he was just because he'd heard the name Starlight. But he couldn't go back now. The sister probably wouldn't answer the door.

Lighting a cigarette, he crunched the car into gear and headed home. He was on duty, but he needed to decontaminate himself after spending time in Maggie's filthy hovel. Anyway, nothing he was working on was so desperate that it couldn't wait. Retirement was good for that. You got handed all the short-term cases so that you wouldn't end up leaving halfway through something major and giving someone else a headache when they had to make sense of all the scattered pieces you'd left behind.

Going into his bedroom with a towel around his waist a short while later, West heard his mobile ringing. Locating it in his jacket pocket, he tried to sound busy when he answered it, in case it was his Super trying to catch him skiving. He was surprised to hear Harry's hopeful voice.

'Have you got anything yet?'

'Not really,' West told him, amused by his eagerness. 'I've only just come back from seeing her mother and sister as it happens, but they weren't too forthcoming. Oh, but there is something you can help me with while you're there. I saw an old friend of mine and Sarah's last night and she mentioned that she'd seen her a few years back. Thing is, she reckoned Sarah was married to someone from Starlight, so I need to know as many names as you can remember.'

'Christ. I didn't think she'd want anything to do with that lot again,' Harry murmured.

'Yeah, well, she obviously changed her mind.'

'I guess she did. Well, I'm not sure what names to give you. It could be someone she knew from before I got there. I was only there for her last year.'

'Whatever you remember.' West pulled a notepad and pen from the bedside drawer. 'Probably best to stick to the relevant ages, though. I doubt she'd have gone for anyone more than a couple of years younger.'

'No, she wouldn't,' Harry agreed quietly. Then, sighing, he pulled himself together. 'Right, names . . . Well, there's *Vinnie*.' He spat the name out. 'And his mates – Ollie, Pete, Rob, Jimmy and Ade.'

'Surnames?'

'Now you're asking. Vinnie's is Walker, as you know. And I know Ollie's was Ford and Pete's was Owens. But I'm not sure about the others. One might have been Johnson, but I'm not sure.'

'These will give me something to go on,' West said, jotting them down. 'It might take a while if they haven't got records, though. There's a new system that'd tell me when they had their last fart, but it's impossible to get into, so I'll have to do it the good old-fashioned way. Let's hope I find something in the next couple of weeks, eh?'

Harry was quiet for a moment, then said, 'I don't know if I should be telling you this, but I can probably access that system you're talking about.'

'No chance,' West snorted. 'You might be a whiz, but this is absolutely foolproof. There's all sorts of access codes and passwords.'

Scenting the kind of challenge that he couldn't resist, Harry said, 'You'd be surprised, Mr West. All I need is the program name. *Please*? It'd stop me ringing you every two minutes.'

West chuckled. He liked this kid. He was nothing if not determined, and he was respectful without being toadying. But there was no way he could share that kind of information with him. He'd be bollocksed for a pension if anyone found out. They were a vengeful lot, the police.

'Sorry, but I can't do it,' he said. 'You stick to what you do best, and let me get on with this, eh?'

'No one would ever find out that I'd hacked into it,' Harry persisted. 'I guarantee it. Ever heard of Com-Knox?'

'Yeah, course. It's uncrackable. And it's applied to the thing we're talking about.'

'Thought it might be,' Harry said. 'And it *is* uncrackable – to everyone but me. I designed it.'

'You're sending me up, right?'

'No, it's true.'

'Wow!' West gave a respectful whistle. 'That's some achievement.'

'Thanks. So, now do you want to help me out?'

'Can't,' West said, almost regretfully. 'Even if I wanted to, I wouldn't have the foggiest where to start. And I seriously wouldn't advise you to start messing about. There's no telling what tracers they've got on it.'

'Don't worry, Mr West,' Harry said, understanding West's predicament. 'I won't do anything to jeopardize you, I promise.'

'Good,' West said. 'And do me a favour, will you? Call me Tony. It doesn't feel right being called mister by a genius.'

Putting the 'Do Not Disturb' sign on his door handle when West had rung off, Harry made sure it was safely locked. Then he set up his laptop on the bureau. Linking it up to his mobile to keep it off the hotel bill, he lit the first of a full pack of cigarettes he would get through in the next few hours and set to work.

38

Carina got home at just gone two. She was nervous as she let herself into the house, having just had it confirmed that she was pregnant. She had no idea whose it was. She was still sleeping with both Glen and Vinnie. Less frequently with Vinnie, admittedly, but still regularly enough for it to be his.

She was torn over who she actually *wanted* to be the father. On the one hand, she relished the idea of having Vinnie's child. It would be a very bonny baby with their combined looks. But what could she realistically expect of him when he'd made it clear that he was only out for a good time? He liked screwing her, yeah, but he seemed to have no intention of taking it further – yet. Glen, on the other hand, would be the better father by far. He not only had the money and the power, he was also a committed family man. But was that enough when it was Vinnie who made her heart sing? And who knew . . . Vinnie might do a complete turnaround if he knew she was carrying his child.

Whatever she decided, she didn't have too long to deliberate. She would start to show in a few weeks and then she wouldn't be able to hide it from either of them.

Carina was hanging her coat up when Glen came barrelling down the stairs, bare-chested and reeking of aftershave.

'Where's my blue shirt?' he demanded.

'Have you looked in the wardrobe?' she asked.

'Course I have.' He marched past her into the dining room.

'Bet you've shoved it in the wash with your stuff. It'll be fucking pink by now!'

Going calmly upstairs, Carina checked the wardrobe. Finding the shirt, she shouted to Glen and threw it down to him. Forcing herself to smile, she leaned her elbows on the banister rail and watched as he inspected the shirt's collar. If she didn't know him better, she'd swear he had another tart on the go. But there was no way she was going to accuse him and risk getting her head blasted off. He was getting more and more moody of late, and his temper was no pleasurable sight to behold – much less be on the receiving end of. Anyway, it was more likely the coke that was getting to him than another woman. He'd only done it at parties to start with, but it had become just about every day since that business with Dex Lewis in London. He'd brought so much of the shit home with him that no matter how much he shoved up his nose it never seemed to dent the amount he had left. She would have to have a serious word with him about it before this baby was born.

'Are you going out, babe?' she asked now, thinking a nice quiet night in might be just what they needed.

'Yeah. I've got a couple of new places to check out.'

'Will you be long?'

'What is this?' Glen peered irritably up at her. 'Since when have you kept tabs on me?'

'I'm only asking. I just thought you might stay in for a change. Watch a film. Get an early night.'

Sighing, Glen ran a hand through his hair. He didn't mean to be so snappy, and he knew he was neglecting her, but it pissed him off when she questioned him. It was like living with his ex-wife again.

'Maybe tomorrow, eh? I've got a lot of shit to sort out today.'

'It's okay. It's not urgent.'

Wandering back into the bedroom, Carina peered at her reflection in the dressing-table mirror, looking for signs of impending motherhood. Her eyes did look clearer, and her skin definitely had a sort of iridescent glow. It could just be the lotions she used religiously night and morning, but she believed it was more than that. Turning sideways, she ran her hands over her still-flat stomach, envisioning what it would look like with a bump. She was dreading it, but at the same time she could hardly wait.

'Got any fags?' Glen shouted up the stairs.

'In my coat pocket,' she called back. 'Do you want me to iron your shirt?'

'No, thanks. I've already done it.'

Hearing his footsteps thundering up the stairs seconds later, Carina sat down on the bed and composed her face into a carefree smile. It slipped as soon as he barged through the door.

'What the fuck are these?' Glen thrust the business cards he'd found in her pocket into her face. 'What've you been doing? Screwing all the travelling fucking salesmen in fucking England behind my back? Luigi's fucking Hair Design!' He read one scornfully. 'Peter fucking Hernandez, Interior Decorator! I bet I know what kind of interior decorating *he*'s been doing, you slag!'

'Glen!' she protested, shocked by his tone. It wasn't the first time he had raised his voice to her, but it was the first time she'd felt physically threatened. 'They were supposed to be a surprise. I was going to have a make-over and get the house done up. And there's one from the doctor. I was going to tell you—'

'You lying *bitch*!' He swiped the cards across her cheek. 'Doctors don't give out business cards! You think I'm fucking *thick* or something?'

Carina raised a hand to her stinging cheek, her eyes wide

with fear now as Glen loomed over her, shoulders hunched, his face as livid as she had ever seen it.

'Babe, I swear it's the truth,' she croaked. 'I went for—'

'Shut your fucking *mouth*!' he roared, raising his fist, his eyes blazing. 'Don't you *ever* lie to me!'

'I'm not!' she yelped, cringing back. 'I swear it on my life, Glen! It was just—'

'Get up,' he snarled, foam bubbling at the corners of his mouth as he struggled to restrain himself. 'Just get up and get the fuck away from me before I do something I shouldn't! *NOW*!'

Leaping up, Carina fled to the safety of the bathroom. Locking the door, she ran to the toilet and threw up. Collapsing to the floor in a gasping heap when she heard the front door slam behind Glen seconds later, she sobbed with relief. That had been truly terrifying. And if he could kick off like that over some innocent business cards, what the hell would he do if he found out about her and Vinnie? No wonder Vinnie had been so adamant that she should keep her mouth shut.

What was she going to do now? She couldn't pretend everything was normal after that outburst, and how was she supposed to tell him her news if he thought she was being unfaithful?

Getting up after a while, Carina splashed her face with cold water and stared at her weepy-eyed reflection in the mirror. At least he hadn't hit her, that was something. He'd just frightened the life out of her instead. But people did that when they were under pressure. He could have deals going wrong left, right and centre. His business could even be under threat again, for all she knew. And the drugs wouldn't be helping. She knew for a fact that they made you go paranoid if you did enough. And some people even got schizophrenia from them, didn't they?

Down below, the doorbell rang. Taking a deep breath, she

patted her face with the towel and went to answer it. It was Vinnie.

'Where's Glen?' He walked straight in, a frown of irritation puckering his brow. 'I'm supposed to be picking him up, but his car's not outside. He's not gone out again, has he?'

'Yeah.' She closed the door. 'But I don't know where. He didn't say.'

'Great,' Vinnie muttered, glancing at his watch. 'He could have said. He's getting a bit fond of taking off and leaving me stranded.'

'He probably just forgot you were coming,' Carina said, waving towards the dining room. 'I'll make you a brew if you want to wait.'

'No, I'm getting off. I've got better things to do than sit around here drinking tea. Tell him to ring me if he wants me.'

Opening the door, Vinnie turned to say goodbye and noticed Carina's red-rimmed eyes for the first time. 'What's wrong?' he asked.

Chin wobbling, she flapped her hands. 'Nothing. Don't worry about it. I'm just feeling a bit run-down.'

Frowning, Vinnie hesitated. He couldn't just walk out and leave her like this. She was obviously upset about something and while they weren't as full-on now that Sarah was on the scene he owed her an ear, if nothing else. And she *was* looking pretty tasty today. He was sure he could squeeze a quick one in.

'What's going on?' he asked, closing the door and going to her. 'Come on, tell Uncle Vinnie all about it.'

Falling against him, Carina let him push her up against the wall and pull her skirt up around her waist. She clutched at him as he unzipped his fly and thrust himself into her.

'Will you run away with me?' she blurted out as his rhythm quickened for the final leg.

'You what?' Pushing himself away from her, he peered down at her as if she'd gone crazy.

'Will you, Vinnie?'

'Don't talk rubbish,' he snapped, zipping himself up. 'Why say something stupid like that? I thought you knew the score? I thought we had an understanding? Tell me you're not thinking of telling Glen!'

'Never!' Gripping his sleeves now, she said, 'I know what you meant about him now. I've seen it for myself.'

'What's he done?' Apprehension gripped Vinnie's throat like a stranglehold. 'You haven't told him? He hasn't hit you, has he?'

'No.' Carina shook her head. 'But he wanted to. I've never seen him like that, Vinnie. I was really frightened. Can't you take me away? He'd never have to know we were together. We could just disappear, and—'

'Pack it in!' he barked, yanking his arms free. 'It ain't gonna happen – none of it. I'm not going on the run for *you*. Are you mad? Glen's one of my best mates!'

'Shag *all* of your mates' women, do you?' she screamed, her face distorting with anger and rejection.

'Not that again,' Vinnie groaned, running a weary hand over his eyes. 'Look, behave yourself, Carina. I don't want you like that. I never have. You're just an easy lay. That's it.'

Tears streaming down her cheeks, Carina bunched her hands into fists and hammered his chest. 'I'm pregnant, you bastard! And it's probably yours, so *now* what have you got to say?'

Throwing her up against the wall, Vinnie grabbed her by the throat. 'Don't even *try* that one on me. You're on the Pill. You told me you were.'

'Yeah, I am, but it's not infallible.'

'Bullshit! You're pulling a fast one.'

'I'm not, Vinnie. I swear it. The doctor told me today. He said the type of Pill I'm on is only eighty-odd per cent.'

'So why didn't you tell me that in the first place? I would have made double sure. You couldn't seriously think I'd want a bastard with *you*?'

'Don't, Vinnie. You're being really cruel.'

'Cruel?' Vinnie snorted. 'Come off it, Carina. I'm not playing games here. You can mess up your own life as much as you want, but you ain't taking me down with you.'

Peering up into his eyes, Carina felt the pain turn to stone-cold anger.

'Who is she, Vinnie?' she asked, as calmly as if they had been discussing the weather. 'Come on . . . You can't keep denying it. It's obvious. Who is this bitch you'd turn your back on your own child for?'

'Whatever's growing inside you is *nothing* to do with me,' he hissed, lowering his face until their noses were almost touching. 'And if you tell Glen any different, I'll kill you. Do you understand me?'

Laughing bitterly, she said, 'Two threats in less than an hour. How lucky am I?'

'You *are* lucky,' he told her venomously. 'Lucky I'm not putting an end to all this bullshit right now. I could, you know? And I'd get away with it, too. My jeep's right outside the door. I could snap your neck, wrap you in a blanket and carry you away, without a single person seeing me.'

Instinctively knowing that he was capable of doing exactly that, Carina dropped her gaze.

Peering at her for a few more seconds, Vinnie pushed himself away and straightened his clothes.

'Don't ever say anything like that again,' he said, calmer now. 'Right?'

'Right,' she murmured, holding her throat between her hands.

Without another word, Vinnie stalked out.

Sliding down the wall, Carina thought about what he'd said and felt the anger return. Why the hell should he get to walk away from this without a care in the world while everything collapsed around her head? It wasn't right. And she wasn't going to let it happen.

Hauling herself up, she ran upstairs and repaired the damage that the two men in her life had inflicted. Covering the puffy skin around her eyes and the redness of her nose with foundation, she lined her eyes and slicked a fresh coat of tinted gloss onto her lips.

Snatching up her keys, Carina headed out with revenge in mind.

Sarah jumped when Vinnie came in with a murderous scowl on his face. He hadn't long gone out and she hadn't expected him back for hours. Putting down the magazine she was reading, she said, 'What's the matter? Has something happened?'

'Nothing,' he snapped, throwing his jacket over the back of the couch and slumping down.

Frowning, she got up and hung the garment on the coatstand. There must be something wrong for him to throw his clothes around like that. Vinnie hated things to be out of place.

'Can't you make Kimmy eat her biscuits at the table?' he complained, fussily picking a crumb off the couch cushion. 'You know I can't stand mess on the furniture.'

Sarah felt immediately guilty. She *had* given Kimmy two biscuits a couple of hours earlier. She had cleaned up after her, but obviously not well enough.

'Sorry,' she apologized. 'I didn't realize she'd made a mess.'

'I'm not asking much,' he went on tetchily. 'I just want a clean house.'

'Yes, I know. It won't happen again. Coffee?' Smiling, she went towards the kitchen.

'Just a minute.' Vinnie called her back. 'I want a word.'

Coming to sit beside him on the couch, Sarah looked at him expectantly.

'I want us to have a baby,' he announced.

'Pardon?' She drew her head back.

'I want us to have a baby,' he repeated. 'One of our own.'

A warning bell clanged in Sarah's head.

'But I thought you loved Kimmy?'

'I do, but it's not the same as having your own flesh and blood, is it?'

'I know. But I wasn't thinking of having any more just yet.'

'Don't be so fucking selfish!' He glared at her, his eyes colder than she ever remembered seeing them. 'This isn't for you, it's for *me*. You've had yours, now I want mine.'

'Vinnie!' She was shocked. 'Don't talk to me like that. We've only been together a couple of months – don't you think it's a bit soon?'

Getting up, Vinnie snatched his jacket off the stand and pulled it on. Wrenching the door open, he said, 'Let me know when you've decided.' Then he marched out.

Sarah sat and looked at the door long after he'd gone. Where the hell had that come from? And where did he get off talking to her like that?

This was not turning out the way she had envisioned at all. And it wasn't only Vinnie's attitude just now, or his complaints about her lack of housewife skills. She was seeing far less of him than she had when he had been visiting her at her flat, and when he did come home he was getting more and more uptight. She knew that his work was important to him, but she had wondered if his frequent absences were a symptom of discontent. Maybe he was regretting his decision to open his immaculate bachelor pad to a woman and child? But why, then, would he want a second child to further disrupt his life if that was the case?

Sarah might not have been quite so averse to the idea if Vinnie hadn't approached it so aggressively, but she found it disturbing that he had said he wanted one of his own. Not just one that hadn't been fathered by another man but one that was separate from her as well.

Not for you, for me . . . You've had yours, I want mine.

Getting up, she wandered into the kitchen to find something to do. She needed to occupy herself otherwise she would drive herself crazy with ifs and buts.

Opening every cupboard, she removed all the tins and bottles and set about cleaning the shelves.

Was she being paranoid, Sarah wondered as she scrubbed, or had Vinnie really meant it the way it had sounded? Still, whether or not he intended to cut her out of the picture, she would have to seriously think about this bolshie new attitude of his before she put on the white suit hanging in her wardrobe and agreed to honour and obey. There was no way she was going to let *any* man obliterate her right to decide what she did with her own body, no matter how much she loved him.

Carina's car idled up to the kerb. Vinnie's jeep wasn't here, so he obviously hadn't come straight home after leaving her. She decided to hang around for a while, hoping she might get lucky and see his mystery woman.

Leaning across the passenger seat, she gazed at the windows of Vinnie's ground-floor flat, looking for signs of movement within. Not seeing any after a few minutes, she threw the car into gear and headed home. She longed to march inside, bang on the door and set the bitch straight, but she couldn't risk it. She'd have to show ID to the security guard, and Vinnie would find out she had been there. He would go ballistic.

But that didn't mean Carina was going to give up. She would just come back later. Or tomorrow. Or every day, until she'd done what she needed to do. If this baby she was carrying *was* Vinnie's there was no way he was walking off into the sunset with his new woman and playing happy families.

39

West rang Jenny as soon as he got home after work. He'd been thinking about her all day, couldn't wait to see her again.

'That date,' he said when she answered. 'How does tonight grab you? I can be ready by eight. I'll pick you up and take you to this great restaurant I know in—'

'Sorry, babe,' Jenny interrupted. 'I'm working.'

'What, again?'

'Yes, again. It's pretty regular, this manager lark. Can't just take time off whenever you feel like it, you know. I'm off on Sunday, if you think you can wait that long.'

'Looks like I'll have to, doesn't it?' he grumbled.

'You can always call in and see me at work,' she suggested.

'What, and have everyone think I'm after a bit of the other?' he snorted. 'I don't think so.'

'Oh, well, we'll just have to do it the old-fashioned way then, won't we? Over the phone.'

'I'm retiring soon, don't forget. It'll take more than a few phone calls to keep my blood flowing.'

'Better start thinking of ways to fill your time, then, hadn't you?' Jenny teased. 'I'm an independent woman with a very busy schedule. Subject of which, babe, sorry to rush you, but I'm going to have to go. I was just on my way out of the door when you rang. There's a staff meeting tonight, and I've got loads to do after that. Are we on for Sunday?'

West smiled. 'We're on.'

At a loose end, having been blown out – in the nicest possible way – by Jenny, West showered for the third time that day and headed over to Harry's hotel, as eager now as Harry himself to find Sarah. He was still labelling it as curiosity, but he knew it was more than that. It was the excitement of the hunt. And after several dull months, thanks to the recent truce between the rival gun gangs, he needed all the excitement he could get.

Bypassing the receptionist, he inspected himself in the elevator's mirrored walls as he travelled up to the third floor. He thought he looked younger than usual. Maybe retirement wasn't such a bad idea after all.

Harry opened the door when he knocked and pulled him inside. Rushing back to his seat, he said, 'This program is amazing.'

'Christ,' West muttered worriedly, following him across the room. 'Don't tell me you've got into it? I thought I told you to forget that.'

'Sorry, I'm a bit deaf.'

'A bit fucking stupid more like,' West snapped. Peering over Harry's shoulder, he saw that the kid had not only hacked into the supposedly impregnable program, he had also managed to split the screen into four windows, each showing a different category of highly restricted information. 'Oh, shit,' he muttered. 'What have you done? We're gonna get hammered. *I'm* gonna get hammered!'

'No, you're not,' Harry murmured without looking up. 'I've put a block on it. Even if anyone picked up a signal of any sort, they'd never find out where it's coming from.'

'I can't take the risk,' West said. 'Come on, lad. Pack it up.'

'All right,' Harry agreed. 'Just give me a minute to get out of the application.'

Thinking that Harry was disconnecting, West breathed a loud sigh of relief. 'You're a bloody genius, I'll give you that,' he said, taking a wander around the suite. 'You should come and work for my lot. You'd have every criminal on record stitched up in no time.'

'Think they'd pay what I earn now?' Harry grinned wryly over his shoulder.

'You've got a point there,' West conceded. 'Probably wouldn't earn enough in a lifetime to afford a week in this joint.' Looking around now at the plush couches arranged as a sort of informal conference area, the enormous, comfortable-looking bed just visible through a dividing door, the not-so-mini bar, he whistled through his teeth. 'I didn't know they *had* places like this in Manchester.'

'It is nice, isn't it?' Harry said, his eyes still riveted to the screen. 'I had to get the best to keep my mother from freaking out. She thinks Manchester's some kind of slum where the rats and the people coexist in perfect harmony.'

'It is,' West chuckled.

'Got it!' Harry exclaimed suddenly. 'Look, Mr – *Tony*.'

'What d'y' mean, "got it"?' West demanded, hurrying back to Harry and peering at the screen. Single-view now, it was the opening page of the Central Health Register. West felt a thrill of pure panic. 'Oh, for fuck's sake, Harry, I thought you were turning it off.'

'I will – in a minute. But we're in now, we might as well have a quick look.'

'Make it quicker than quick,' West scolded, intrigued despite himself.

Tapping in *Mullen*, Harry added *Walker/Ford/Owens/Johnson*, then *Manchester: Central, sex: female, age: twenty-seven*. Pressing *enter*, he almost cheered when the information they had been looking for appeared as if by magic.

Name: Sarah Louise Mullen. Born: St Mary's Maternity Hospital,Manchester.08.10.77.Mother:MargaretLinda Mullen—Spinster.Father:Unknown.Address:12Corbett Street, Longsight, Manchester.

'Get to the latest entry,' West ordered, desperate to get disconnected before the SAS came flying through the window.

'She's not seen a doctor this year,' Harry said, scrolling back. 'Ah, here we are. Last medical information logged in February 2003. Missed appointment with a bereavement counsellor.' He looked up at West questioningly. 'Wonder what that's all about?'

'No details?'

'Well, I could get into the records of the GP who put her forward for it, but I don't really want to intrude on her personal files unless we absolutely have to.'

'Yeah, whatever.' West flapped an impatient hand at the screen. 'What else?'

'July 2000,' Harry read. 'Appointment at an ante-natal clinic – one month check-up of her daughter, Kimberley Marie Owens.' Sighing, he rested his elbows on the bureau and brought his hands up to his mouth. Seeing in black and white that Sarah was a mother had made him feel peculiar. Pulling himself together after a moment, he cleared his throat. 'Well, I guess it's clear what her name is now. She obviously married Pete.'

'Pete? He was one of the gang, wasn't he?'

'Yeah. Vinnie's best mate.'

Shaking his head, West said, 'Wonder what attracted her to one of your tormentors?'

'He wasn't the worst,' Harry murmured, squashing down the feeling of betrayal. 'He always just seemed to be going along with whatever Vinnie wanted, but I got the impression he wasn't particularly comfortable when it got vicious. Maybe he changed when he got free of Vinnie? Stranger things have happened.'

'They have that,' West agreed, putting a fatherly hand on Harry's shoulder. The lad was obviously suffering. 'Is there an address?'

'Flat three, Danika Court, Hulme.'

'Phone number?'

'Yeah. It's . . .'

Jotting it and the address down, West repocketed his notepad. 'Right, turn it off,' he said, sighing with relief when the screen immediately went blank. 'And don't ever do that to me again, you little shit. I'm too old for that kind of malarkey.'

Pulling up outside Danika Court a short while later, West unclipped his seat belt.

'Come on, let's go see if she's in.'

'I don't think I should come.' Harry peered out at the flats, his heart sinking at the thought of his lovely Sarah spending her days and nights within those drab walls. 'It might be better if you speak to her on your own. Pete might get annoyed if I turn up accusing his best mate of all sorts.'

'Okay, wait here, then. I'll try and get her alone, tell her you want to see her. If she wants to discuss it with hubby afterwards, that's her business. Won't be long.'

Harry watched until West had disappeared through the flats' communal door. Letting his gaze wander, he tutted with disapproval at a gang of kids throwing bricks at an abandoned car on a patch of waste ground. This wouldn't happen in Surrey's leafy suburbs. The police would have rounded them up and prosecuted the parents by now.

He was just wondering how he could have become so far

removed from this kind of normality after spending his first ten years living exactly like this when the car door was yanked open. His heart catapulted into his throat.

'Shit!' he squawked when West jumped in. 'You scared the bloody life out of me! I thought someone was hijacking the car.'

'This shit-heap?' West chuckled. 'I don't think so. It's all Beemers and Porsches with this lot. She's not here.'

'Oh?' Harry was disappointed. 'Did you speak to the neighbours? She might be having coffee with a friend or something.'

'More likely a beer and a spliff round here. But it's not that. She's moved. A month ago, according to the woman next door – not long after her husband died.'

'Pete's *dead*?'

'Yup.' West started the car and pulled away. 'Crushed by a train. Oh, shit!' He slapped a hand down on the steering wheel. 'I remember that. Pete Owens. Yeah. He drove onto the tracks, doped himself up with smack and alcohol, then just waited for the train to do the rest.'

'Suicide?'

'Well, *yeah*.'

'Christ. That's awful. No wonder Sarah needed counselling.'

'Obviously she didn't, seeing as she missed the appointment,' West reminded him. 'Anyway, it looks like she might be getting a different kind of comfort.'

'Oh?' Harry sensed that he wasn't going to like what he was about to hear. He was right.

'Seems she had a fella coming round after hubby snuffed it. Apparently, he started staying over a few weeks after the funeral. Then, about a month back, Sarah and the kiddie moved out and the new bloke helped take her stuff away – what she didn't leave or give away, that is. Looks like she did a complete clear-out. Only took clothes and toys, and a couple of personal bits.'

'Think she moved into a furnished place?'

'More likely in with lover boy, and he didn't want reminders of his predecessor.'

'Not likely to forget if he's got to look at the guy's daughter every day.'

'Shouldn't be a problem if he's a decent bloke.'

'What's his name?'

'No idea. Seems our Sarah's as reserved as ever. She didn't tell the neighbours anything. First they knew was when they saw her taking the boxes out.'

'So what do we do now?'

'The neighbour reckons Sarah's best mate might know where she's gone.'

'Oh, right,' Harry murmured, feeling a sharp twinge of jealousy. He had always thought of himself as her best mate. Still did, even after all these years.

'Whatever he's done, I'm not interested,' Hannah said when West flashed his badge. 'I haven't seen hide nor hair of him for three days, so you're wasting your time asking me where he is. What's he done, anyway?' she asked then, folding her arms.

Smiling, West said, 'I wouldn't know, love. I don't know who you're talking about.'

'You're not looking for Steve?' She narrowed her eyes.

'Not unless he's the one Sarah Owens went off with.'

'Sarah!' She snorted. 'With my Steve? You *must* be joking. He wouldn't go near her if I was dead and buried.'

Harry felt himself bristle.

'I thought you were supposed to be her best mate?' West said.

'Yeah, I am. I love the girl. It's just my Steve ain't too fond. He thinks she's stuck-up.'

'Ah, I see . . . Would it be possible to come in for a moment and have a little chat about her?'

'If you're not gonna be long.' Hannah stepped back. 'Only I've got to go and pick my little one up from the youthy in fifteen minutes.'

'Shouldn't take long.' Smiling, West went inside and took a seat at the kitchen table. 'Bigger than they look, these houses, aren't they?' he commented, looking around. 'Couldn't fillet a fish in my place.' It was a lie, but he knew the women in these areas liked to think they were a step up the ladder. And feeding their egos tended to loosen their glued-shut mouths.

'I like it.' Hannah sounded proud. 'Especially since the Direct Works put the new units in. I got to choose for the whole block, so I got the best. See that?' She pointed at a tall free-standing unit. 'They threw that in extra. None of the others have got one. Only me.'

'It's really nice.' West nodded approvingly. 'Classy.'

'Cup of tea?' Hannah offered, suddenly in no hurry to get rid of them. The beauty of her new units hadn't quite worn off yet and she still enjoyed showing them off. But, more importantly, she wanted to hear what West had to say about Sarah. No one had heard from her since she'd left, and Hannah couldn't wait to spread the gossip.

'That'd be nice, thanks. Harry?'

'Er, yeah, thanks,' Harry muttered, sitting down. He thought the units were cheap crap. And if she made another crack about Sarah, he'd tell her.

'So, what's Sarah been up to?' Hannah asked, handing the teas out and plonking herself down at the table with a greedy gleam in her eye.

'She hasn't done anything wrong,' West said, disappointing her. 'We just need to talk to her, and her neighbour said you might know where to find her.'

'Well, I don't,' she told him gloomily. 'She never even said she was going till the day itself, and then she didn't say where, She just said she'd get in touch.'

'And has she?'

'Not yet, no. But she will. We were like that, me and her.' Hannah showed them her crossed fingers. 'It was me who helped her through it all when Pete died, you know? Poor cow didn't know if she was coming or going, so I had to take over most of the arrangements. I went to the inquest with her, an' all. Right joke, that was.'

'Oh?' West raised an eyebrow. 'What happened?'

'The judge making out like Pete was a junkie.' She pursed her lips disapprovingly and reached for a cigarette. 'He wasn't, and I said as much to your lot, but they were dead set.'

'As I recall,' said West, 'the autopsy revealed he'd taken heroin before the crash.'

'So they said, but I know he didn't,' Hannah stated authoritatively. 'But would they listen to me? Would they buggery. I reckon he was spiked, and I stand by that. I knew Pete. Drink and dope, yeah. But smack? No way!'

'What did Sarah think?'

'Same as me, to start with. But she changed her mind once she heard the autopsy report. She got real pissed-off with Pete after that, said he'd taken the easy way out and dumped all his shit on her and Kimmy.'

'Pretty typical reaction,' West remarked, lighting a cigarette. 'Especially after a suicide.'

'Yeah, but it wasn't, was it? And if Sarah was any kind of wife, she wouldn't have been so quick to condemn him like that. He might have been a waste of space, but what man isn't? He had nowt on my Steve when it came to being a shit. She should have thought herself lucky.'

'So they weren't too happy?'

'They were okay. No better or worse than anyone else. Not bad enough for him to do what they said he did, I'll tell you that for nothing.'

'Sounds like you don't think too much of her?' Harry interjected, trying not to let his disapproval show.

'It's not that, love.' Hannah looked at him for the first time. 'I just don't agree with how she handled things. She's my best mate and I do care about her, but I wish she'd done better by Pete after he died. She did her best when he was alive, bless her, but carrying on with his mate straight after like that . . .' Leaving the rest unsaid, she shook her head and dragged deeply on the cigarette.

'His mate?' West cast a glance at Harry.

'Yeah, *Vinnie*.' She spat the name out. 'Sarah fetched him round one time when she come to get Kimmy. I'd had the kid for a couple of days, you see – giving Sarah a bit of space to get her head together. Anyhow, she turns up this night with *him*, and suddenly she's all fine.'

'You say his name was Vinnie?'

'Yeah. Said he was an old friend of hers and Pete's and he was looking after her.' Snorting softly, Hannah flicked her cigarette aggressively. 'That's what I didn't agree with. It wasn't decent so soon after Pete. But you can't tell Sarah nowt once she's made her mind up.'

'Is she still seeing him?' West asked, feeling the emotions coming off Harry in waves.

'Pfft! It's him she's gone to live with.' Hannah rolled her eyes. 'Not right, that. Shouldn't do it to the kiddie. She's only just lost her daddy, and all of a sudden she's got a new one. Poor little thing hasn't got a clue, she's just all excited about being a bridesmaid.'

'Bridesmaid?' West's eyebrows rose sharply. 'They're getting married?'

'So she says. I told her she was being an idiot rushing into it like that, but she reckoned they was going to wait a few months.'

'Have they set a date?'

'Yeah, Kimmy's birthday. But I couldn't tell you when that is. Round summer, I think.'

'June,' Harry murmured, remembering the date of the one-month check-up.

'Yeah, somewhere in the middle,' Hannah said. Then, catching sight of the time: 'Oh, sugar! I'm gonna be late.'

West stood up. 'Sorry for keeping you so long. Can we drop you off somewhere?'

'No, thanks.' She yanked her coat on. 'I don't want to be seen in a car with a pair of five-Os. People round here can smell you lot a mile off. They'd think I was a grass or something. No offence.'

'None taken.' West smiled. 'One last thing . . . I don't suppose you'd know where Vinnie lives?'

'Never asked.' Hannah opened the back door and stepped outside, waiting for them to follow so that she could lock up. 'Didn't like him, so I wasn't exactly planning on visiting.'

'Been invited to the wedding?'

'Have I buggery, and I doubt he'd let her ask me even if she wanted to. You could see in his eyes he couldn't stand me. Couldn't wait to get her away that time they came for Kimmy. If she had any sense, she'd run a mile and never look back.'

'Oh?' West held the gate open to let Hannah out of the garden.

'If you ask me, he's not right,' she said, her voice and face clearly displaying her dislike of the man. 'Looking down his nose at me and Steve like we was dirt. And I thought it was weird how he thanked me for looking after her, like I'd done *him* a favour. I said she was my mate, so course I'm gonna look after her, but you could still tell he was trying to cut me out of the picture. Anyhow, don't suppose it's much help, but he was driving a right flash black jeep when he brought her round that time. Proper shiny it was, with blacked-out windows and that.'

'Don't suppose you'd know the registration?' West asked, thinking the chances were zero.

'I do, as it happens.' Hannah was smug. 'VW One-One. Said to my Steve at the time how it should have been on a Volkswagen not a jeep.'

Shaking his head approvingly, West said, 'You are a true star, Mrs . . . ?'

'Hannah will do,' she said, buttoning her tent-like coat. 'You lot and last names always spells trouble in my book.'

Climbing into the car, West and Harry watched until Hannah had waddled out of view.

'You can say what you like about the people round here,' West remarked, 'but they're not short of nous. Looks like she had your mate sussed from the off.'

'He's no mate of mine,' Harry muttered darkly.

Picking up on his distress, West said, 'I know it's a shock, son, but Sarah's not stupid. If she thinks she's in danger, she'll get herself out of it.'

'What if she doesn't realize?' Harry's face was pale and troubled. 'And what if we don't find her?'

'Don't panic.' West started the car. 'It'll be a piece of piss tracking him down with a number plate like that.'

40

———◆◆◆———

Vinnie still hadn't come home by eight but Sarah wasn't overly concerned. He quite often got back a lot later than this. And after his tantrum earlier, she wouldn't be surprised if he went for a drink or five before coming back with his tail between his legs.

She'd just put Kimmy to bed when she heard his mobile phone ringing. Smiling, she went through to the living room, glad that he'd decided to come back early after all. They'd be able to clear the air now and still have enough of the night left to crack a bottle of wine and watch a nice romantic film before making up properly.

Vinnie wasn't there, but the phone was still ringing. Following the sound, she traced it to the floor behind the couch where it had fallen when he threw his jacket there. Picking it up just as it stopped ringing, she frowned at the name displayed on the screen: Carina.

Who the hell was *Carina*?

Sarah sat down heavily, her heart hammering in her chest. Could this be the reason he'd been so distant lately? Did he have another woman?

Course not! she scolded herself. He was distant because he was working all hours, that was all. He loved her deeply. He always had. Anyway, men who were cheating didn't beg to get married. They didn't make love with the passion that she and Vinnie shared almost every night. Didn't act so possessively, not wanting to share their secret treasure with anyone else. And they certainly didn't want to have babies with the woman they were cheating on.

She stared at the name, sure that she had heard it some-where. Then it came to her. Pam – Vinnie's boss's mother. She had said it when Sarah met her that time. Carina was *Glen*'s girlfriend.

Sarah's racing heart began to slow. Okay, that was accept-able. But it was still a bit weird. Why would she be ringing Vinnie if he was at work?

She jumped when it began to ring again. And again the display read *Carina*. Forcing the paranoia aside, she answered it.

'Hello?'

Getting no answer, she turned and walked towards the win-dow, thinking that maybe the signal wasn't getting through.

'Hello . . . ? Can you hear me? Okay, well, just in case you can, Vinnie's not home. I think he's still working.'

Still no reply, but Sarah knew that the call hadn't been disconnected – which, she assumed, meant that her message had been received.

'Sorry about that,' she went on, a little awkwardly now. 'Nice to speak to you, anyway. Bye, then.'

It felt weird hanging up. For all she knew, Carina could have been in the middle of saying something. But she would realize what had happened if she thought about it.

Outside, the tears streamed down Carina's cheeks as she stared at the silhouette of the woman standing at Vinnie's window. So it *was* true. She had known all along that it was, but seeing it with her own eyes . . . Hearing the voice . . .

She knew for sure now, but she still didn't *want* to believe it. She wanted things to be back the way they had been.

Snapping the phone shut when the figure moved away from

the window, Carina rested her head back and wiped her eyes roughly. No more tears. From now on, she would spend her energy on preparing for the battle ahead.

And there *would* be a battle when this all came out. If the baby looked anything like Vinnie, Glen was sure to demand a blood test and she'd have no choice but to agree. If it came back that he wasn't the father, she had little doubt about the methods he would use to get the name of whoever *was* out of her. And the way she was feeling right now, she would gladly tell him before he so much as raised his voice, because there was no way that she was putting her neck on the line to protect Vinnie if he didn't even have the decency to be honest with her.

Jumping when a car pulled in behind her, its headlights glaring at her in the rear-view mirror, Carina fumbled with the keys and started the engine. Shit! That could have been Vinnie. She had to stop being so careless.

Pulling away with a screech, she drove around the corner, her legs shaking so much that the car kangarooed, then stalled. Opening the door, she threw up on the ground. Flopping back, she ran a hand over her clammy face. This was doing her no good. She couldn't deal with this alone.

Killing the lights, West leaned towards Harry and looked up at the flats.

'Bloody hell, these look expensive,' he said. 'They're new as well. This used to be the probation office when I was on the beat.'

'Sounds about right,' Harry muttered scathingly. 'He wouldn't want to go too far off his usual course, would he?'

'Settle down,' West said, peering at the main door. 'Staying here, I take it?'

'Yeah.' Harry's jaw muscles were working overtime. 'I might kill him if I see him.'

West's mobile trilled just then, signalling that a text message had come in. Flipping it open, West grinned when he saw the name.

'Important?' Harry asked, frowning, hoping it was nothing that would delay them.

'Jenny,' West told him. 'Remember her?'

Drawing his head back, Harry peered at him. 'Should I?'

'I thought you would,' West said, taking another look at the flats. 'It was because of you that I met her – in a roundabout way. Remember when you ran away and I came looking for you?'

'When I was hiding out at Sarah's.'

West turned to look at him now. 'So you *were* inside, you little shit! You said you'd slept in the shed.'

'Oh, yeah, I did, didn't I?' Harry grinned. 'Sorry about that, but I didn't want to get her into trouble.'

'I felt sorry for you,' West went on, his tone accusing even as his eyes twinkled. 'Jeez! I never thought I'd be duped by a couple of kids.'

'A couple of *smart* kids.'

'Couple of smart-*arses*, more like. Well, anyway, it was that night I met her. She was working with Sarah.'

'Oh, that's right.' Harry nodded. 'I remember Sarah telling me about her.'

'Yeah, well, *she* lied to cover for Sarah as well, and I wasn't best pleased at the time. But I fancied the tits off her, so I got in touch a few weeks later.'

'And you've been seeing her ever since? Wow.'

'Not exactly, no. We had a bit of a thing for a while, but we sort of split a few months later and I haven't seen her since.' Pausing, West smiled fondly. 'Not until you turned up and made me go looking for Sarah, that is. To cut a long story short, I traipsed halfway across Manchester looking for her 'cos I thought she might know where Sarah is, and when I found her, she jumped me.'

'Really?' Harry laughed.

'Well, not literally,' West admitted. 'But it was *her* idea to meet up again. And I think we'll be all right this time.'

'Well, well.' Harry shook his head. 'Talk about vicious circles.'

'There's nothing vicious about Jenny,' West said. 'Or you and Sarah.'

'Just Vinnie,' Harry muttered. 'Anyway, have you thought what you're going to say when you get inside?'

'Nope.' West shrugged. 'I'll decide when I see her.' Climbing out, he shook his trousers down then leaned back in. 'Give us two blasts on the horn if anyone turns up. I'll be as quick as I can.'

Sarah was running a hot bubble bath. Hearing her own mobile phone ringing in the living room, she ran to it and snatched it up. 'Hello?'

'Sarah? Is that you?'

'Karen?' Smiling when she heard her sister's voice, Sarah sat down. 'How are you? I'm sorry I haven't rung, but you wouldn't believe what's been happening since—'

'I need to see you,' Karen interrupted, a distinct hitch in her voice. 'Can I come round?'

'What's the matter?' Sarah asked, sure that her sister was crying. 'What's happened? It's not Mam, is it? She's not . . . ?'

'It's nothing to do with her. It's just . . . Oh, Sarah, I don't know what to do. I thought I had everything worked out, but it's all a mess, and you're the only one I trust. I know we haven't seen each other for years, but you're still my big sister.'

Frowning when the doorbell rang, Sarah said, 'Look, someone's at the door, Karen. Just let me deal with it and I'll ring you right back, okay?'

'Okay,' Karen agreed, sniffling. 'You won't be long though, will you?'

'No, I promise. You'll be all right for a few minutes, won't you?'

'Yeah, I'll be fine. Hurry up, though, Sarah.'

Cutting the call, Sarah went to answer the door. She didn't recognize the man and, assuming it was one of Vinnie's workmates, was about to tell him that Vinnie was out, when he said,

'Hello, Sarah . . . Remember me?'

Frowning, she peered at him, then gasped with surprise. 'The copper!'

'The detective inspector now, if you don't mind,' he corrected her. Stepping back, he looked her over approvingly. 'Wow, you look great. How old are you now? Eighteen, nineteen?'

'Twenty-six!' She laughed, knowing that he was complimenting her. 'Come in,' she said then, regretting it almost as soon as the words left her mouth. Vinnie wouldn't be too pleased if he came home and found her entertaining a policeman. She didn't know the details of what Vinnie did for a living, but she did know that he kept a gun in his jeep, so it couldn't be entirely legitimate.

'I'd best not.' West flicked a quick glance back along the communal corridor. 'I only came to ask if you'd agree to meet up with a mutual friend sometime soon.'

'Oh?' Sarah folded her arms and gave him a bemused smile. 'Who? . . . Oh, God, it's not Dandi, is it?'

'Dandi?' He frowned. Then, putting a face to the name, 'No, no, it's not her. It's Harry Clark.'

'Harry Clark?' It was Sarah's turn to frown now. 'Are you sure it's me you're looking for?'

Slapping his forehead, West said, 'Not Clark, *Shaw*! Harry Shaw, as was, now Clark.'

Sarah's eyes widened with astonishment. 'Harry? *My* Harry? Where is he?'

'In the car.' West felt a lump forming in his throat as her beautiful eyes flooded with tears. 'He, erm, doesn't want to see you here, though.'

'Why? What's wrong? Has something happened? He's not had a terrible accident, has he?'

'Nothing like that,' West assured her, wondering if he had ever engendered such love and concern in one of *his* friends – and sincerely doubting it. 'It's a bit complicated, but he's got something to discuss with you and, under the circumstances,' he nodded through the front door, 'we think it might be best to meet up somewhere a bit more private.'

'When?'

'Er, how about tomorrow?' He was amazed that she had agreed so readily. 'You can bring your daughter, if you want. I'm sure I could occupy her for a few minutes while you and Harry catch up and whatnot.'

'Fine.' Sarah dabbed at an escaping tear. 'Where?'

'He's staying at a hotel in town. La Granta. Do you know it?'

'No, but I'll find it. What time?'

'Ten all right?'

'Ten's fine.'

'Great. I'll meet you in the lobby and take you up. Well, I'll see you then. Oh, just one thing . . . Do you think you could keep this to yourself? I know you're living with someone, but I'd really appreciate it if you didn't mention this to him. Not until you've had a chance to speak to Harry, anyway.'

'I won't say a word,' she assured him. And she wouldn't, even if Vinnie *did* come home tonight – which was looking increasingly unlikely. 'Oh, God!' she yelped, remembering that she had left the bath running. 'I've got to go. The bath . . .'

Waving, West backed away.

Closing the door, Sarah ran into the bathroom and turned the taps off. Then, grinning from ear to ear, she undressed and slipped into the chin-high bubbles. She was going to see Harry tomorrow! She couldn't believe it. She'd thought about him so many times over the years, wondering if he was all right – if he was alive, even. And now she was going to see him. She could hardly wait!

Sarah didn't hear her phone ringing and ringing on the living-room table.

41

Feeling sicker than he'd ever felt in his life before, Harry paced the floor, riddled with doubts over what he was about to do. Learning that Sarah was planning to marry Vinnie had completely mashed his head. What would he say to her? Would she believe him?

Taking a deeper than deep breath when he heard West's distinctive rap at the door, he wrenched it open.

'Hello, Harry.' Sarah tipped her head to the side. 'Remember me?'

He gazed at her mutely. How could he *not* remember her? She had been his whole world for ever.

'I'd kiss your head like I used to,' she went on, 'but I don't think I could reach that high. When did you get so *big*?'

Pulling himself together, Harry moved towards her and gave her a hug. 'Oh my God, Sarah, I can't believe you're here.'

'Well, I am.' She laughed to cover her tears. 'And I've only got a few hours, so are you going to let me in, or what?'

Letting her go, he said, 'Sorry. Course, yeah. Come in. Where's your daughter?' he asked then. 'I thought you were bringing her with you?'

'I decided to take her to the nursery,' Sarah explained, wiping her eyes with a tissue. 'I thought it best not to confuse her. Mr West said you didn't want me to mention this to

Vinnie, and she wouldn't understand if I said she had to lie about where we'd been.'

'Good thinking.' West nodded. 'Sorry for putting you in an awkward position.'

'No, it's fine.' Sarah flapped a hand. 'She likes nursery, anyway.'

'Can I get you anything?' Harry hadn't taken his gaze off her since he'd opened the door. 'Coffee? Tea?'

'Coffee would be nice.'

Tearing his stare from her at last, Harry rang down for room service. Then he came to sit beside her on the couch, watching her raptly as she made small talk with West about the changes in the city centre.

Turning to him at last, Sarah took his hand and squeezed it. 'God, you've changed.'

Blushing, he said, 'For the better, I hope?'

'You were always gorgeous to me,' she mock-scolded. 'But look at you now. You're such a . . . *man*.'

'*Am* I?' Harry gazed down at himself with mock alarm.

'Pack it in!' Slapping his arm, she turned to West. 'See why I had to look out for him? He's an idiot!'

Smiling, West glanced at his watch and stood up. 'Look, I'm gonna head down to make fun of the waiters while you two have a chat. I'll come back in half an hour – is that enough time?'

'Yeah.' Harry nodded. 'Should be. Thanks, Tony.'

'Not necessary.' Flipping his new friend a wink, West headed for the door.

Seeing him out, Harry saw the maid coming out of the lift. Waiting, he took the trolley from her, then slipped the 'Do Not Disturb' sign on the door handle. His hand shook when he poured the coffees. This was the hardest thing he would ever have to do.

Watching him, Sarah hoped that he wasn't going to tell

her something awful – like he only had a month to live, or something. Reaching out, she brushed an out-of-place hair back behind his ear.

'You look great, Harry. And I can't get over how big you are. I was expecting my old Harry – you know? That little kid with the smart mouth.'

'You haven't changed,' he said, handing a cup to her. 'You're even more beautiful, if anything. And softer . . . like you've found yourself and you're comfortable with who you are.'

'I am.' Sarah smiled. 'Being a mum helps. You lose all the anger that was eating you up when you look into the eyes of your own baby.'

'Does she look like you or Pete?'

'Me.' Sarah looked down at the cup in her hand. 'I suppose you heard what happened?'

'Yeah. It must have been terrible.'

'It was,' she agreed, unconsciously turning the engagement ring around with her thumb. 'But I had to keep it together for Kimmy's sake. Vinnie helped.'

'Mmm,' Harry murmured disapprovingly.

'What's wrong?' Sarah gazed at him. 'You're not upset with me for being with him, are you? . . . Shit! Stupid question. Of course you are. But he's different now.'

'Sarah . . .' Harry turned towards her, his eyes dark. 'I really need to talk to you about Vinnie. And not just about the things you know about. There's other stuff, too . . . Stuff I've only just found out.'

'What stuff?' She frowned, not liking the sound of this. 'What are you talking about?'

Putting his cup down, Harry took her hand in his and sighed heavily, wondering how best to start.

'When I came looking for you,' he said at last, 'I didn't know what I was going to tell you. I just wanted to make sure you were all right – that you weren't a mess, like I was before I found out. But now I know you're going to marry Vinnie, I've got to tell you.'

Sarah stiffened. 'If you're going to tell me what a terrible person he is, I want you to stop right now, because—'

'Sarah,' Harry interrupted sadly. 'The last thing I want to do is hurt you, but if I let you go ahead and marry Vinnie without telling you what I know, I'd never forgive myself. All I ask is that you remember how much I love you and that I wouldn't be doing this unless I absolutely had to.'

'I'll listen.' She slipped her hand free. 'But I warn you now, I won't be pleased if it's all the same old rubbish. He's changed – a lot.'

'I'm sure you think so,' Harry murmured. 'But you might think differently when you know the whole story.'

'I doubt it.'

Harry wanted to be gentle, but there was no easy way of saying what he had to say, so he came right out with it. Sarah couldn't have been more shocked if he had slapped her in the face. Standing up when he'd finished, she glared down at him.

'You know what I've been through, but instead of being happy that I've finally got a chance of a good life, you'd rather tell me all this crap about my fiancé, just because he used to *pick* on you when we were kids. Big wow, Harry! Like you were the only kid who ever got bullied. Get over it!'

'Sarah, please . . .'

'Save it!' Storming to the door, Sarah wrenched it open. 'I thought you were special, but you're no friend of mine. Goodbye, Harry.'

'Where is she?' West asked when he got back to the room and found Harry alone.

'Gone,' Harry muttered, flopping back down into his seat.

'Did she hear you out?'

'Oh, yeah, she listened. Didn't believe a single word of it, but at least she let me get it all out.'

'Well, that's something.' Going to the bar, West poured two stiff drinks. 'She'll be thinking it over now. Have faith, son. She isn't stupid.'

'I'm worried what *he*'ll do if she goes back and tells him,' Harry said. 'There's no telling how he'll react, and we already know what he's capable of. Well, *I* do. I know you're still not convinced.'

'Not a hundred per cent,' West admitted. 'But even if you're wrong, I do know he's a bad lot. I saw what you wrote about him in your diary.'

'Diary?' Harry looked up, a frown of confusion creasing his brow.

'Yeah, my partner and me found it under your bed the night you ran away to Sarah's.'

'Oh, my God,' Harry murmured as the memory fell into place. 'I thought someone had pinched that. I stayed out of everyone's way for ages after that. I thought someone would kill me for what I'd written about them.'

'Sorry.' West smiled tightly. 'But that's why my mate took it. He didn't want to risk someone else finding it and taking it out on you when you got back. He meant well,' he went on quietly. 'I thought he was a bit of a clown when I got landed with him, but he was all there.'

'Was?'

'Yeah, he got killed in a hit-and-run a few years back.'

'Oh, I'm sorry.'

'So was I. Anyway, never mind that. I've been thinking. Maybe we'd best leave Sarah for a day or two. Give her a chance to calm down and think things through. She knows where you are if she wants to contact you.'

'Suppose so,' Harry murmured, hoping West was right to be so unconcerned. He had a terrible feeling that Sarah was going to tell Vinnie everything and put herself in real danger.

42

Sarah's mind was working overtime as she drove home. Harry had really pissed her off. Okay, so he was jealous that she'd decided to marry Vinnie after everything that had happened when they were kids, but where the hell had he come up with a story like that? How could you just 'remember' something like that – and under hypnosis, of all things? It was too ludicrous for words. He *knew* it was Chambers, but if he wanted to make-believe the man was innocent after everything she had told him – *and* after Chambers had been caught and convicted of doing that to *him* – then he was a bigger fool than she would ever have imagined.

Whatever Vinnie *had* done in the past, she knew him too well to believe he would do the things that Harry had accused him of. He was gentle and affectionate – when he was home. And Kimmy adored him. There was no way she was going to jeopardize all that on the strength of these ravings.

Pulling up outside the flats, Sarah saw that Vinnie's jeep still wasn't there. He hadn't come home the night before, and she had rushed out this morning without leaving a note. She hoped he hadn't come back in the meantime and gone off again in a huff. That would be all she needed after the terrible morning she'd had.

Just as she was reaching out to open the security door, she heard someone calling her name in a harsh whisper. Turning, she peered all around.

'*Sarah!*' It came again. '*Over here!*'

Spotting her sister waving from behind a car on the opposite side of the road, she remembered the phone call the previous night and felt a rush of guilt. She had promised to get straight back to her, but she'd been so busy thinking about Harry that she'd completely forgotten.

Running across to her, she said, 'Oh, God, Karen, I'm sorry! You must think I'm a complete bitch.'

'It doesn't matter,' Karen said, still semi-crouching, watching the flats. 'What are you doing here?'

Squatting beside her, Sarah said, 'I live here. Weren't you waiting for me?'

'No. I'm looking for someone.'

'Oh?' Sarah was intrigued. 'Who? I might be able to help.'

'No one can help me,' Karen muttered, hugging her stomach. 'I'm pregnant.'

'Really?' Sarah frowned sympathetically. 'Is that why you were so upset last night? Are you having problems with the dad?'

'One of them,' Karen admitted, her gaze still riveted on the flats through the car windows. 'The other one doesn't even know yet, and he isn't gonna be too pleased when he finds out.' Pausing, she gave a weary sigh. 'That's why I rang you last night. I was going to ask if I could stay at yours till it's sorted, but this is a bit too close for comfort.'

'Does one of them live here?'

'Yeah. The one who knows. I told him yesterday and he wasn't exactly thrilled. I'm just waiting to see the bitch he's shacked up with so I can tell her what kind of a loser he is.'

'Who is she? I might have seen her.'

'No idea, but she's bound to be some ugly slag,' Karen sneered. 'There must be *something* wrong with her if he won't even admit he's going with her. He must be ashamed of her.'

Sarah laughed out loud. 'Well, I don't think I've seen any deformed slags over there. What about him?'

'Him!' Karen snorted. 'Now there's a question.' Pausing, she bit her lip, struggling to keep her emotions in check.

'You all right?' Sarah asked, shifting to ease the pressure in her legs. 'You really like him, don't you?'

'Yeah,' Karen said, the breath catching in her throat and coming out as a sob. 'But I don't know why. He was such a bastard when I told him. All he could say was how he'd kill me if I told Glen.'

Sarah went cold.

'Glen?'

'Yeah.' Karen wiped her nose in the back of her hand. 'My boyfriend. He's the one who doesn't know yet.'

'And the other one?'

'What?'

'What's the other one's name?' Sarah felt dizzy now.

'Vinnie – why?' Karen peered at her with concern. 'Are you all right? What's . . .' She left the rest of the question hanging as realization slammed home. 'Oh, my God! Not you? Please tell me it's not you!'

Sarah didn't know whether to hit her sister or comfort her. She didn't know anything any more. 'But her name's Carina,' she murmured. 'Glen's girlfriend. His mum told me.'

Karen stared at her in disbelief. 'You've met Pam?'

'Yeah. Vinnie took me round the day before we got engaged.'

'Engaged?' Karen gasped, her face as drained of colour now as Sarah's. 'No . . . You can't be.'

'Well, I am.' Sarah showed her the ring. 'It was the day I came round to Mam's. He was waiting when I got home, and he asked me then.'

'You're lying,' Karen hissed, pain overriding reason. 'That's from your husband. You're just trying to hurt me.'

'No, I'm not.' Sarah was becoming angry now. *She* was Vinnie's fiancée. Karen had her own man. If she'd messed about with Vinnie before he got together with Sarah and had got herself pregnant, that was her problem. But there was no way Karen was taking Vinnie just because her own man wasn't interested.

'Mam was right about you.' Karen's eyes sparked with malice. 'She always said you were a slag, and she was spot on. The best thing she ever did was shove you in that home. Why didn't you just stay there?'

'Grow up!' Sarah snapped, shocked by the vehemence of the words.

'I mean it,' Karen continued, all the hatred she'd been storing up for Vinnie's mystery woman pouring out in a rush. 'Vinnie was mine long before you came on the scene, and he still is!'

'Vinnie was thirteen when I met him,' Sarah spat back. 'Are you trying to tell me you'd already had him then? 'Cos if you are, *you're* the slag here, not me!'

'What are you talking about? He wasn't in a home.'

'Oh, yeah? Don't know him as well as you think, then, do you?'

'All right, so I might not have known about that,' Karen admitted defensively. 'But I do know *him*. We were going together for ages before I met Glen. And I know for a fact he wasn't seeing *you*.'

Sarah inhaled deeply, trying to calm down. This wasn't resolving anything.

'How many months gone are you?' she asked.

'Four,' Karen muttered unhappily.

'Are you sure?'

'Positive. The doctor did all the tests yesterday, and it matches my dates.'

'Well, it can't be Vinnie's,' Sarah said. 'We've been together for longer than that and I know he hasn't been seeing anyone else. Your dates must be wrong.'

'They're not. And for your information, we're still seeing each other.'

Sarah felt her world sliding out from under her. 'When *was* the last time?'

'Yesterday,' Karen told her triumphantly. 'Vinnie came to pick Glen up but he'd already gone out. If you don't believe me, he was wearing his black Gucci jeans, his grey jumper and his black Nikes. Oh, and he had the dark grey Calvins on, the ones with three little buttons.'

Sarah knew she was telling the truth. There was no way she could have known about his boxers otherwise – the boxers that Sarah had bought *after* moving in with him. The ones she had seen him putting on yesterday.

Karen gazed at her sister's pale face and felt a hint of regret for having delivered the news so bluntly.

'Look, I'm sorry it turned out like this,' she said, reaching a hand out to touch Sarah's arm. 'And I shouldn't have said that stuff about Mam. You didn't know what was going on.'

'No,' Sarah muttered, shrugging her hand off. 'But *you* did.'

'Only that he had a woman. If I'd known it was you . . .' Pausing, Karen sighed deeply.

'Well, now we know, what are we going to do about it?' Sarah asked, her voice as calm as she could manage under the circumstances.

Karen shrugged morosely.

'This isn't helping anything,' Sarah said, standing up. 'Let's go get a coffee.'

'Okay,' Karen agreed. 'But not in there. We'll go to a café.'

Karen ordered a pot of coffee. Pouring two cups, she pushed

one across the table. Sarah stirred a sugar into it then took her cigarettes from her pocket. Lighting one, she slid the pack across to Karen.

'What do you want to do?' she asked, when they both felt safe enough behind the dividing wall of smoke to speak. 'Are you planning to tell Glen it might not be his?'

'I don't know,' Karen admitted. 'He went a bit funny on me yesterday. He got jealous 'cos he found some stupid business cards in my pocket. There was one for you actually, but I can't give it to you because he ripped them up. It was off some copper who came to Mam's looking for you.'

'Don't worry about it,' Sarah told her. 'This is more important. Look, you probably won't appreciate me saying this, but can't you just make a clean break until you've sorted yourself out?'

'I'm not giving everything up without a fight,' Karen said, looking at her as if she were crazy for suggesting it. 'Glen will snap out of his mood when he realizes how stupid he's been. He won't want to lose me.'

Frowning at her sister's see-sawing logic, Sarah said, 'And where does Vinnie fit into this? I thought you wanted *him*?'

'Yeah, I do, but he's scared of what Glen would do if he found out. I'm not risking losing Glen until I know what Vinnie's doing.'

'You already know.' Sarah's voice was cool. 'He's with me.'

'*And* me,' Karen said defensively. 'I just wanted to put you straight.'

'Well, now you have, so what next? Are you planning to tell him you've seen me? Do you think he'll be so relieved it's all out in the open that he'll suddenly realize it's you he's wanted all along, or something?'

'He might.'

'Bollocks! He doesn't even know who you really are. He thinks your name's Carina, for God's sake.'

'So? You *are* allowed to change your name, you know.'

'I take it you've done it legally then, 'cos it's gonna be a bit awkward explaining it when you get married. You have to take your birth certificate, you know.'

'I'll tell him nearer the time.'

'Which *him*?' Sarah held her gaze.

Karen pursed her lips, but didn't answer.

'You haven't got a clue what you want, have you?' Sarah said, beginning to realize how confused Karen actually was. She didn't want to let Glen go and risk losing everything if Vinnie didn't want her. But she refused to let Vinnie go if there was the slimmest chance of him committing to her in the future – however far off that might be.

'If everyone would just stop interfering it would be easy,' Karen mumbled. Dipping her spoon into the sugar bowl, she stirred it until grains began to spill over the side. Reaching across the table, Sarah stilled her hand.

'I'm not your enemy, Karen, I'm your sister, and believe it or not, I'm trying to help you.'

'If you really want to help, walk away. I'm pregnant with Vinnie's baby. You're not. Can't you just leave him and give me a chance?'

'If it was just me stopping him from being with you, I probably would,' Sarah replied. 'But it's not, is it? What did he say when you told him you were pregnant?'

'Nothing.'

'Don't lie. You said he wasn't too thrilled.'

'All right, so he got a bit rough.'

'How so?'

'Pushed me up against the wall and threatened what he'd do if I told Glen,' Karen admitted reluctantly. 'Said it'd be really easy to just snap my neck and put me in his jeep and get rid.'

'Did you believe him?'

'Kind of.' Karen looked down miserably into her coffee, embarrassed to admit that the man she loved had treated her so badly. 'I know he wouldn't hurt me really,' she went on. 'He's just worried about Glen. He doesn't want to get on the wrong side of him. I said we could run away, but—'

'What did he say?' Sarah interrupted, sick to her stomach that Vinnie had even discussed something like this with another woman.

'That we'd never escape Glen,' Karen told her glumly. 'I know he's right, but I just wanted him to say something positive like he would if he could, or something. Anyway, that's when I asked who *you* were. Said I wanted to know who this bitch was that he was putting before me and the baby. That's when he got heavy. He said the baby was nothing to do with him, and if I said anything to Glen he'd . . . Well, you know the rest.'

'That's why,' Sarah murmured.

'Why what?'

'Why he came home in such a mood yesterday, demanding to try for a baby.'

'He didn't?' Karen's face had gone pale again.

Sarah nodded slowly.

'Bastard!' Karen hissed. 'What's he playing at?'

'I don't know,' Sarah muttered coldly. 'But he's not playing it with *me*, that's for sure.'

'I can't believe he did that.' Karen shook her head. 'Not wanting me to tell Glen, yeah. But saying he wants to get *you* pregnant, with all this going on. You're not going to, are you?' she asked then, a spark of genuine panic in her eyes. 'You're going to dump him, right?'

Looking at her, Sarah knew that that was exactly what Karen wanted. No matter what had been said, or how hurt they both were, Karen would jump feet first into Sarah's vacated place if Sarah left Vinnie. And much as she herself didn't want him now that she knew the truth, Sarah wasn't about to give Karen the satisfaction of thinking that the younger sister was walking away with the prize.

'I want to hear what Vinnie's got to say for himself first,' Sarah said, pushing her cup aside. 'Can you take me back now? I need to get Kimmy.'

They didn't speak a word during the drive back to the flats. Getting out at the corner, Sarah watched until Karen's car was out of view, then climbed into her own car and set off for the nursery.

Despite what she'd said about hearing Vinnie's side of things, she had no intention of staying with him now. He had messed everything up. He hadn't changed at all. He was still the same cocky, no-good little bastard he'd always been. How the hell had she fallen for it?

Vinnie's jeep was parked up when Sarah got back and she felt the anger churning in her stomach. She forced it down. Not yet – and definitely not in front of Kimmy.

Under normal circumstances she would storm inside, pack her stuff and leave. But she had to put Kimmy's needs first, and if that meant playing the game for another few hours, so be it. With any luck, Vinnie wouldn't be around for long and she'd have a chance to pack in peace.

Kimmy had fallen asleep. Lifting her out of the child-seat, Sarah carried her inside and laid her down on her bed. Easing her daughter's coat and shoes off, Sarah covered her with the quilt. Then she went into the living room.

Vinnie was sitting on the couch, a dark scowl on his face, his eyes narrowed to slits as he followed her progress across the floor. 'Got something to tell me?' he asked, his voice low and mean.

'No.' Sarah kept her cool. 'Want a drink?'

'No, I don't want a fucking drink,' he snarled. 'I want to know what the fuck you think you're playing at. Where have you been all day?'

'Out,' she said, fighting the urge to demand to know where the hell *he* had been all night. 'I dropped Kimmy off at nursery and went into town.'

'Where's the shopping?'

'Pardon?'

'I said where's the shopping?' He was raising his voice now. 'If you've been to town, where's the fucking *shopping*?'

'Stop shouting!' she hissed. 'Kimmy's asleep. I went bloody window-shopping, if you must know – for wedding shoes! What the hell's the matter with you?'

Glaring at her, Vinnie didn't say anything, but Sarah could see him chewing this over. Finally, he sat back, seeming to accept her explanation.

'Why have you been in such a bad mood for the past couple of days?' she asked, sitting down and lighting a cigarette. 'Have I done something to upset you?'

'It's not you,' he muttered, drumming his fingernails on the couch arm. 'There's loads of shit going off at work, that's all.'

'Oh?' Raising an eyebrow, she looked at him as if she was really interested. 'Like what?'

'Nothing to concern you. I think I will have that drink now.'

'Sure.' Standing, Sarah went into the kitchen. 'Brandy?'

'Yeah. And did you think about what I said yesterday, about us having a baby?'

Sarah gritted her teeth. He had some gall!

'I thought we should get started as soon as,' he went on, coming into the doorway now and grinning at her. 'You say Kimmy's asleep?'

'Yeah, but she's only napping. She could get up any time.'

She handed him his drink. 'Anyway, I said not yet. If I get pregnant now, my suit won't fit.'

'You can buy another nearer the time.'

'It wouldn't feel right.' Sipping her drink, she smiled. 'Think about it . . . They'd all be saying that's *why* we're getting married.'

'I don't care what anyone says,' Vinnie snapped. 'It's no one else's business. Anyway, who's going to know?'

No one, Sarah thought bitterly, *seeing as you wouldn't let me invite my friends.*

Quite a few things had changed since she'd moved in with him, she was beginning to realize. He'd made it more than clear that none of her old friends were good enough now that she had moved up in the world – his phrase, not hers. But how was she supposed to make new friends when he wouldn't introduce her to *his*, and didn't like her talking to the neighbours?

And then there was the matter of her clothes. Vinnie had made her throw away almost everything she had, and had gone out and bought her a load of designer gear to replace it: long skirts, jeans, polo-neck jumpers, and button-up-to-the-eyebrows blouses. At the time, Sarah had accepted his smiling explanation that he just wanted to treat her to stuff she had never been able to afford, but the more she thought about it, the more she knew that he just wanted to cover her up.

Yes, there were lots of things that she would be glad to escape. But she had to tread carefully if she hoped to get herself and Kimmy out in one piece.

'I hope you're not trying to fob me off,' Vinnie was saying now, his eyes taking on the same cold glint she had seen the day before. 'You didn't take your Pill this morning, did you?'

'Yeah. Why?'

'Because I've told you what I want.' His voice was mean again. 'And I said it last night, so you've got no excuse.'

'And I said I didn't want any more just yet,' she replied quietly, not liking the way this was going.

'Where are they?' Downing his drink, Vinnie slammed his glass down on the ledge. 'The pills – where are they? In your bag?' Turning, he looked for it.

Frowning, Sarah said, 'No, they're in the bathroom cabinet where they always are.' Following him as he strode from the room, she said, 'Vinnie . . . What do you think you're doing?'

'What you should have done last night,' he said, snatching her contraceptive pills off the cabinet shelf. 'Flushing these down the bog.'

Sarah was furious. How dare he do this! It was as if she no longer had control over *anything*. Pete would never have treated her like this in a million years. And neither would the Vinnie who had talked her into giving up everything she owned to be with him.

The lying, cheating bastard!

'What the hell do you think you're playing at?' she demanded, glaring at him as he popped each tablet into the toilet. 'You can't *force* me to have a baby.'

'I can do what the hell I want!' he shot back at her.

'No way!' She shook her head angrily. 'You're not treating me like this.'

Sneering, Vinnie thrust his face into hers. 'Oh no? And how are you gonna stop me?'

'Well, I won't be sleeping with you, for a start,' Sarah hissed, standing her ground.

'Is that right?' Grabbing her by the throat, he propelled her out of the door and across the hall into their bedroom. 'Put that to the test, shall we?' Throwing her down on the bed, he unzipped himself and then went for the button on her jeans.

'Stop it!' she gasped, struggling to push him away. 'Pack it in, Vinnie! What the hell's got into you?'

'I'm sick of being treated like an idiot, that's what!' he yelled, slapping her hard across the face. 'Everyone thinking they can take a fucking piece of me whenever they want! It's a fucking joke!'

'*You're* the fucking joke,' she screamed, kicking now, and tearing at his shirt. 'You think you can do whatever you want and everyone's just got to lie down and take it! Well, you're wrong, Vinnie! You're not pushing *me* around! And if you think I'm having your fucking baby after this, you can think again! I'm *never* having one with you! Pete would kill you if he knew what you were doing!'

'What did you say?' Pulling back, Vinnie stared at her, his eyes bright and manic.

'You fucking heard,' Sarah hissed, wanting to tell him exactly what she knew about him but forcing herself to bite back the words. Hurt as she was, it wasn't fair to bring her sister and Harry into this craziness.

'Think Pete *loved* you, do you?' he sneered. 'Shall I tell you how much he loved you, eh? . . . So much that the pathetic cunt was willing to take *my* money to dig him out of the hole he'd dug himself into! So much he *lied* to you to go out on a job with me!'

'I don't believe you,' she snarled, still trying to kick him. 'He was a better man than you *any* day!'

'Oh, yeah? So where did he say he was going the night he died? Bet he didn't say he was meeting me, did he? Didn't tell you how he was so greedy he drank all my booze and smoked the whole spliff himself? Such a good fucking man, wasn't he? Such a good husband and father?'

'Yeah, he *was*!' she screamed, missing the implication of what he was saying as she fought to get him off her. 'You're a *bastard*, Vinnie – always were, always will be!'

'*This*,' he gripped her face in his hand and squeezed it hard, contorting it, 'is why I had to punish you first time round. You don't know when to keep that foul mouth *shut*!'

The punch came so fast that Sarah didn't see it until it connected with her eye. The pain was instant and blinding. Slipping into unconsciousness, she didn't feel the next punch, or the hair being torn from her scalp as he dragged her onto the floor, or the kicks that followed.

Or the jeans being torn from her legs . . .

Vinnie was holding her when she came round, sitting on the floor with his arms around her, rocking her as the tears streamed down his face.

'Oh, my baby, I'm so sorry,' he sobbed, kissing her swollen face. 'So, so sorry . . . I never meant to do it . . . Please forgive me. I'll never touch you again, I swear it . . . Sarah, my Sarah . . .'

With pain racking every inch of her body, and an icy draught crawling over her bare thighs, Sarah knew exactly what he'd done – and what he had said immediately before – and she was shocked to the core. But she knew that she had to keep her wits about her now more than ever in her life before. Not just for herself – for Kimmy. If he was capable of doing this to the woman he professed to love, what would he do to a defenceless child?

'You're awake,' he sobbed when he saw that her eyes were open. 'Oh, thank God you're all right!'

'I'm okay,' she mumbled, tasting blood. 'Kimmy . . . ?'

'Sshhh, she's fine.' He stroked her hair. 'She didn't hear anything, I promise.'

Sarah tried to sit up. 'I – I need to get cleaned up before she sees me.'

'Don't struggle,' he said, lifting her. 'I'll do it.'

Carrying her into the bathroom, Vinnie placed her gently

on the toilet seat then ran warm water into the sink. Soaking the sponge, he kneeled in front of her, his eyes warm and compassionate as he dabbed at the drying blood like a father tending his precious child.

And Sarah let him do it, even though every fibre of her being was screaming at her to get out of there.

'Your face is swollen,' he said when he'd finished, smiling conspiratorially – in this together now. 'We'll have to say you fell down the stairs, or something.'

'What stairs?' she slurred, wincing at the pain from her split lip.

'Oh, yeah, that's a point. Well, you slipped getting out of the bath, then. Smacked your face on the sink.'

'Yeah, whatever,' she murmured, standing painfully. 'I need to check on Kimmy.'

'Why?' His face darkened in an instant. 'Do you think I'd hurt my child, or something?'

'Of course not.' Sarah forced herself to reach out and stroke his cheek. 'I know you'd never do that. I just want to make sure she didn't hear anything.'

Holding on to her hand, Vinnie said, 'She didn't, Sarah. I swear it. Oh, God . . . I'm so sorry. Will you forgive me? Can we put this behind us and start again? You know I love you more than life.'

'I know.' She slipped her hand free. 'Just let me check her, then I'm going to have a lie-down.'

'Yeah, you do that.' Standing, he helped her from the room. 'I'll get you something to eat. What do you want? A butty . . . ?'

'No.' She shook her head. 'I couldn't eat anything, my – my mouth is too sore.'

'Oh, shit, yeah. That was stupid. Soup, then. Want some soup?'

'No, nothing.'

'Coffee?'

Sighing, she said, 'Yeah, fine.'

Kimmy was still fast asleep. Gazing down at her, Sarah felt the tears welling up in her eyes and thanked God that she hadn't woken up and seen what had happened. Why hadn't she just have kept her mouth shut? She could have replaced the pills tomorrow.

'She's so beautiful,' Vinnie whispered, slipping his arms around Sarah's waist and gazing down at Kimmy. 'Just like her mummy. But I think she's got a look of me as well. Around her mouth. Can you see it? How she kind of purses her lips when she's thinking things over. I think her nose is a bit like mine as well.'

Sarah forced her body not to respond to the thrill of genuine fear coursing through her. He was talking as if he was Kimmy's natural father, and it was just too crazy. If nothing else told her how desperately she had to get away from him, this was the final nail in the coffin. The first chance she got, she was out of there.

Glen was unsuccessfully hiding an enormous bunch of flowers behind his back when he came home later that night. Dropping to his knees in front of the chair Carina was curled up on, he grinned sheepishly and brought them out with a flourish. 'Ta-da!'

Frowning, she said, 'What are they for?'

'To say sorry for being such a moody bastard.' He peered up at her with hangdog eyes. 'Forgive me?'

Carina considered playing on his guilt for a while but decided against it. She was in enough of a mess right now – she'd better take what she could get while the going was good. Grinning, she held out her arms.

'Course I forgive you, you idiot. Come here.'

'I know you'd never cheat on me,' Glen murmured, stroking

her hair. 'But I can't help getting jealous. You're so beautiful. I just don't want to lose you.'

Closing her eyes, she took a deep breath. It was now or never.

'I'm pregnant, Glen. Those cards you found, one was from the doctor I'd just been to see.'

Pushing her back, he peered at her face. 'Really?'

'Yeah.' She was nervous now. 'You're not mad, are you?'

Shaking his head slowly, he pulled her back into his arms and held her tight. 'How could I be mad about that? I'm made up. Christ!' He laughed. 'Wait till I tell me mother she's going to be a granny again!'

Carina sighed into his shoulder. If anyone was going to suss her out when this baby was born, it was Pam. She might be old and knackered, but she was sharp as a whip. With any luck, she'd be dead and buried by the time the kid was born.

Moving back, Glen looked at her, his eyes still gleaming. 'Seeing as you're having my baby, I think it's time we thought about making an honest woman of you. What d'y' think? You wanna get married?'

Nodding, she threw her arms around his neck. It was the answer to everything. Once Glen's ring was on her finger and his name was on the birth certificate, she'd be safe to do whatever she wanted to do. She'd just have to let the dust settle a little, then, when she was safely married, she and Vinnie would get together again and no one would be any the wiser.

As for Sarah . . . That bitch would be long gone. She was stupid for thinking that Vinnie loved her. She obviously didn't know him half as well as she thought she did, or she'd know that he had it bad for her own little sister.

43

Vinnie didn't let Sarah out of his sight for three full days. Having told Glen that he had come down with flu, he followed her from room to room, watching her like a hawk, refusing to let her do anything. He cleaned up the flat, fed Kimmy and played with her – telling her to let Mummy get some rest because she had hurt herself. And he waited on Sarah hand and foot, spoon-feeding her soup until her swollen mouth could open enough to take solid food.

Sarah was becoming desperate by the time Glen rang and demanded that Vinnie get his arse back to work. She'd been so sure she was never going to escape, she almost cried with relief when Vinnie said he would be there in twenty minutes.

'I'll be back as soon as I can,' he told her, tucking in the quilt he had wrapped around her where she lay on the couch. 'Shall I drop Kimmy at nursery?'

'No.' She shook her head. 'Leave her. I'll be all right. Anyway, you might not be able to pick her up again.'

'I could send a taxi for her.'

'No, really,' Sarah insisted. 'They won't let just anyone take them out.' Forcing herself to smile, she said, 'Anyway, if she can't be with you, I don't trust anyone else to look after her.'

The lie worked as planned. Smiling, Vinnie leaned down to kiss her.

'I love you so much, babe. We're gonna be a great family,

you'll see. And we'll bring the wedding forward. As soon as the bruises have gone, I'll go to the registry office and change the date.'

'You do that,' she said, maintaining the doe-eyed smile.

As soon as she heard his jeep start up and drive away, she threw the quilt aside and hobbled into the bedroom. Swallowing a couple of painkillers dry, she pulled her suitcase from the back of the wardrobe and opened it up on the bed.

'What are you doing, Mammy?' Kimmy asked, coming into the room.

'Playing a game,' Sarah told her. 'Now I want you to run into your room and grab some clothes and toys, then we're going to go out and pretend we've gone on holiday.'

'What about Daddy?'

'*Vinnie!*' Sarah corrected her sharply, annoyed at Vinnie's latest tool of control: making the child call him that. 'Anyway,' she tempered her tone, 'he's the reason we're playing the game. I want him to come home and look for us. It'll be really good fun.'

'Like hide-and-seek?'

'Exactly.' Reaching down, Sarah gave Kimmy a quick hug. 'Go on, now. We've got to be really quick or he'll come back and catch us.'

Throwing the bare essentials into the case when Kimmy ran to her own room, Sarah dressed as quickly as possible. She hadn't been joking about Vinnie coming back. She was sure he would find any excuse to get away from Glen and come and check up on her. And she intended to be long gone when he did.

When they were ready she tried to ring a taxi, but the phone was dead. Thinking Vinnie must have unplugged it before he went out, she checked the connection box, only to find that he had ripped the end off the wire.

She looked around for her mobile phone then but couldn't

find it. The last time she remembered having it was when Karen had called. She'd forgotten to take it with her in her rush to see Harry the following morning, and she hadn't seen it since.

Realizing that Vinnie must have taken it, she gritted her teeth and checked her handbag. Her keys were gone, and so was her purse and her bank card. She had nothing, but she was determined not to let this hamper her escape. Harry would help her out until she had a chance to get to the bank.

Sarah just prayed that Harry hadn't checked out of the hotel yet. If he had, she was in serious trouble. She didn't know how to get hold of Jenny or West, and she doubted Hannah would have the money to pay the taxi fare she would have racked up by then – or the inclination to help, seeing as Sarah hadn't been in touch for so long.

Taking Kimmy's hand, she picked up the case and went to the door. It was locked. She almost lost it then. How *dare* he lock them in? What if there had been a fire? They would have burned to death. The bastard!

Storming back into the living room, she tried the window but it too was locked – as they all were. Getting a knife from the kitchen drawer, she attacked the lock. If Vinnie wanted to play games, he would just have to foot the bill for whatever damage she caused.

Breaking the lock at last, Sarah pushed the window wide and threw the case out through it. Lifting Kimmy up, she lowered the child to the grass outside then climbed out after her – grateful that it was a ground-floor flat. If it had been a floor up, they'd have been trapped for ever.

Pushing the window to, she reached for Kimmy's hand and, looking all around to make sure that Vinnie wasn't hiding somewhere nearby, ran towards the main road. Flagging down a black cab, she directed it to take her to the hotel.

★   ★   ★

Harry and West were just coming out of the elevator when Sarah burst through the hotel's main door. Spotting her, Harry ran to greet her. The smile slid off his face when he saw the bruises covering hers.

'Oh, my God, Sarah, what happened?'

'I need help,' she mumbled. 'Can you pay the taxi? My daughter . . .'

'Where is she? She's not with Vinnie?'

'No . . . In the t-taxi. Please . . .' Bursting into tears, she fell against him.

Taking her to West, Harry said, 'Look after her while I get Kimmy.'

Harry came back a couple of minutes later, carrying Sarah's case and holding Kimmy's hand.

'I'm sorry for landing this on you,' Sarah murmured guiltily. 'I'll pay you back as soon as I can get to the bank.'

'I don't want it,' he told her quietly. 'Come on, let's get you upstairs.'

In the elevator, Harry and West tried to avoid looking at Sarah's battered face, but it was difficult with mirrors all around. Everywhere they looked they saw the damage from a different angle. The journey took only a few seconds but it felt like hours before they reached the third floor.

'Do you need anything?' Harry asked Sarah when they were in the suite. 'An ice pack, or something?'

'No, I'm fine,' she assured him. 'It's nowhere near as bad as it was.'

'Jeezus!' he hissed, shaking his head, his eyes filled with pain and anger. 'I didn't think he'd do this. I'm so sorry I interfered.'

'It's not your fault,' she told him in a whisper. 'Really. It wasn't about you. There's other things going on, but I don't want to talk about it in front of Kimmy. She needs a nap. Is there somewhere she can lie down?'

'Yeah, sure. The bed's just through there.' Harry pointed through a door into the bedroom.

'Right, let's talk,' West said when Sarah had settled Kimmy into bed. Sitting down, he handed her a cigarette while Harry ordered coffee from room service. 'Did you tell Vinnie what Harry told you?' he asked, leaning towards her to give her a light.

Sarah shook her head. 'I didn't get a chance. When I got home my sister was there. That's what this is all about.' Taking a deep breath, she told them what had happened.

'Bloody hell,' Harry said when she had finished. 'He really is a bastard. So the whole time he's been seeing you he's been sleeping with your sister? And now she's pregnant, and it might be his?'

'And he thinks he'll make it all go away by getting *you* pregnant,' West joined in, shaking his head with disgust. 'That's low.'

'Did he . . . hurt you?' Harry asked.

'No,' she murmured, unable to meet his pained gaze. 'I was unconscious.'

Harry's eyebrows rose, but he didn't say the words that were on the tip of his tongue – that history had repeated itself.

'Can I make a suggestion?' West ventured gently. 'Get yourself to a clinic and get yourself checked out.'

Frowning, Sarah gazed up at him, not understanding.

'Diseases,' he explained gently. 'I know it's not something you want to think about, but under the circumstances you can't be taking any chances.'

Sarah wrapped her arms around herself as a shudder passed through her. Looking at Harry, she said, 'You know all that stuff you said about him. It was true, wasn't it? You weren't just saying it to make him look worse?'

'It was true,' he replied quietly. 'I know it sounds strange, the hypnosis and everything, but I've had flashbacks since I heard the tape and I've actually remembered a lot more.'

Fetching the coffee in when it arrived, West poured three cups and handed them round.

'I don't know what you make of it,' he told Sarah. 'I didn't believe it myself when Harry first approached me, but I've spent the past few days with him and I've changed my mind.'

'I don't just *think* it's true,' Harry said. 'I *know* it is. I can even remember the smell of his breath when he was saying it.'

'What exactly *did* he say?' Sarah needed to hear the words again – to solidify the hatred growing within her heart.

'That he was punishing me for lying about your address – just like he'd punished *you* for treating him like dirt. And he was glad you thought it was Chambers because you'd belong to him one day, and you'd be grateful to him for protecting you.'

'I don't understand why he told you anything.' Sarah frowned. 'He must have known you'd tell.'

'I think he meant to kill him,' West interjected. 'Harry was barely breathing when we got to him. The bastard had forced a couple of pills down his throat. He knew that Harry wouldn't remember anything if he survived.'

'I still don't understand why he admitted it. It doesn't make any sense.'

'Because he's a psychopath,' West said. 'Not full-blown or he'd have no fear, but this is typical borderline behaviour. They have a compulsion to see the results of their handiwork, but they're smart enough not to say anything that would land them in it. It was probably eating away at him that he couldn't tell *you* that he'd had you. Watching you suffer was obviously enough for a while, but when you pulled that knife on him you probably turned him on and made him want you again. That's the only thing they respect, you see – danger.'

'Which is why he likes working for Glen,' Sarah murmured, beginning to understand. 'Karen reckons he won't admit to the baby because he's so scared of him.'

'Actually,' West said, 'I think it's more likely that he just doesn't want her. He's fixated on you. She'll have been a convenience – a dangerous one given that she's Glen's woman, but that will be the kick that kept him going back for more. And now she's threatening to blow his cover it's not fun any more. Did you tell him you knew about her, by the way?'

'No.' Sarah shook her head. 'I wanted to protect her.'

'Good job, considering what he did to you. But I think you should warn her, just in case. He's not going to be pleased when he realizes you've escaped. It might be a good idea to get her over here and let her see what she's messing with.'

'Can we trust her not to say anything?' Harry asked. 'I don't want to risk having Vinnie follow her and get his hands on Sarah again.'

'I don't think she'd say anything if I asked her not to,' Sarah said. 'But I don't know her number. It's in my phone, and Vinnie took it.'

'All the more reason to warn her.' West's tone was dark. 'If he goes through your numbers and recognizes hers, he'll put two and two together. Can't you remember it?'

'No.' Sarah shook her head. 'Oh, hang on,' she said then, getting up and going to her case. 'She wrote it down for me. It should still be in my jeans pocket.'

'Ring her,' West urged when she found it. 'If she hasn't told Glen yet, she should agree to meet you here without telling them anything.'

'Use this.' Harry tossed his mobile to her. 'My number doesn't show. It'll be safer.'

Taking a deep breath, Sarah tapped in Karen's number.

'Karen?' she said when it was answered. 'It's me. Are you on your own? . . . Good. I need to speak to you, and it's urgent. Can you get away? . . . No, it's got to be right now. I'll, er, meet you in town. Do you know the coach station? Well, I'll be there in half an hour. Please don't tell *anyone*. I'll explain everything when I see you.'

Karen frowned when she didn't see Sarah. Parking her car she walked around the coach station three times, glancing at her watch every few seconds. If this was a wind-up she wouldn't be too pleased.

'Karen?' a man said just when she was about to give up.

Turning, she saw that it was the policeman who had called at her mother's house looking for Sarah.

'Not you again,' she snapped. 'Are you following me or something? I've already told you I don't know where she is, so just bog off and leave me alone.'

'You mightn't know where she is,' he said, taking her arm. 'But I do. She's waiting for you. Come on.'

'Get off me,' Karen hissed, refusing to move. 'Do you want me to start screaming? I will, you know!'

'I bet you would as well,' he chuckled, taking his mobile from his pocket and ringing Harry's number. 'It's me,' he said when it was answered. 'Put her on for a minute, will you?' Handing the phone to Karen then, he waited while she spoke to Sarah.

Handing the phone back, Karen glared at him. 'All right, I'll come with you.'

'Good girl.'

Karen was a little shocked by Sarah's battered condition, but she didn't let it show. She was actually quite pleased. It certainly threw doubt onto the so-called love that Sarah claimed Vinnie felt for her. He would never have done something like this if he felt that much for her. Yeah, he had gripped Karen by the throat and threatened her, but that was nothing compared to this. It was perfectly obvious who he felt the most for.

'Know what I think?' Karen said when Sarah had told her everything. 'I think you just can't admit that you were wrong about him. He doesn't care about you, so you're trying to turn *me* against him.'

'Did you see him today?' Sarah asked.

'Yeah, why?' Settling back, Karen lit a cigarette and casually crossed her long legs.

'Didn't he say anything?'

'About what? *You?*'

'I take it you haven't told him about me, then?'

'I presume you told him yourself, hoping to put him off me.' Karen gave a small triumphant smile. 'Looks like it backfired, though, doesn't it?'

Shaking his head, West went to the bar to pour himself a stiff drink. This girl was a piece of work. It amazed him that she shared Sarah's blood.

Sarah sighed wearily. 'Vinnie didn't do this because of you, Karen. He did it because I said I'd *never* have his baby. He threw my pills away to force me, but I got mad and pushed him too far. If he could do this to me, what do you think he'd do to you if you pissed him off?'

'He doesn't love you,' Karen retorted smugly. 'So that argument doesn't work.'

'Yes, he does,' Harry cut in authoritatively. 'He always has, and he always will. And I should know. He used to beat me black and blue until Sarah agreed to meet up with him after she left the home. She didn't get in touch for *six* months, but he *still* left me alone because he was waiting for her. Doesn't that tell you how much he wants her?'

'No, it just tells me they were kids, but he's grown up now.'

'And progressed from childish thuggery to man-sized violence,' West snapped, pointing at Sarah. 'You think that's acceptable? He beats your sister to a pulp and locks her in a flat so that she has to lower her child out of a window to escape, and you think it's all right because, in your twisted head, you think it means he loves *you*.'

'She doesn't know what he's really like.' Sarah jumped to her sister's defence. 'He's a real sweet-talker when he wants to be.'

'Sure she knows.' West cast Karen a dirty look. 'He's already told her he doesn't want her, but she's willing to trade off your misery for whatever little piece of him she can get. She's out for herself, all the way down the line.'

'Hey, I don't have to justify myself to you,' Karen yelled.

'Can we please stop arguing and sort this out?' Sarah cut in. 'Karen, I don't care *who* Vinnie goes with, but he's too dangerous for you. He killed my husband.'

'Prove it.'

'Unless he says it again, I can't. But that doesn't mean I don't believe it. And you should too. You said yourself that you thought he meant it when he threatened you.'

Karen couldn't argue with that, but she wasn't about to admit it.

'You know it's the truth.' Sarah reached for her hand. 'Why don't you let us help you before he ruins your life like he's ruined mine? And what about Glen? Have you told him yet?'

'I have, actually.' Karen gazed at her sister coolly. 'He asked me to marry him and I said yes, so I don't need your help, do I?'

'And what about Vinnie?'

'I love him.'

'Oh, for God's sake, this is ridiculous,' Sarah snapped. 'You keep changing your mind from one minute to the next. You've just said you're going to marry Glen, so where does Vinnie fit in?'

'Why don't you just keep your fucking nose out of my business?' Karen yelled. 'Everything would be all right if you hadn't turned up! You've left him now, so stop acting like this has got anything to do with you.'

'It's got *everything* to do with me,' Sarah yelled back. 'Look at me, Karen. Look what he did to me.'

'You asked for it.'

'*What?*'

'You heard me,' Karen hissed spitefully. 'You always had a nasty streak, didn't you? And you said it yourself – you pushed him too far. Well, that's what you get, isn't it? Maybe it'll teach you to keep your big mouth shut for a change.'

'You're not seriously saying this is my fault?'

'That's *exactly* what I'm saying. You just couldn't take it that he loves me, not you, so you tried to poison him against me. But that didn't work, so now you're trying to turn me against him. Well, forget it! Me and Vinnie love each other and nothing you say is going to change that. Just stay out of my life from now on.'

Gazing back at her coldly, Sarah said, 'If that's what you want.'

'It is.' Getting up, Karen stalked to the door.

'Sorry I made things worse for you,' Sarah called after her. 'I won't bother you again.'

'Good!'

'Bitch!' West hissed when Karen walked out without a backward glance.

'We've got to get Sarah out of here,' Harry said. 'If Karen tells Vinnie where she is, he'll come after her.'

'You're right,' West agreed. 'Best book her into another hotel.'

'I'll ring around,' Harry said, getting up and going to the bureau for the phone book.

'No, wait.' West slapped his forehead. 'What am I thinking of? She can stay with me – you both can. I've got loads of room, and it'll be safer. He'd only track you down if you booked in somewhere else.'

'No.' Sarah shook her head. 'Thanks for the offer, but this isn't your problem. It's me he'll come after. It's best if I just take Kimmy away.'

'Where to?' Harry demanded, offended that she was shutting him out. 'Have you got the money to start up somewhere else?'

'Not really, but I'll manage. I always do.'

'I won't let you do it.' Harry was adamant. 'You're my best friend, Sarah. And friends don't turn their backs when the going gets tough, they stick together and help each other out.'

'I agree,' West chipped in, folding his arms. 'Like it or not, Sarah, we're all involved. And if you're too proud to take help for yourself, you'd better have a good hard think about that little girl of yours. Are you going to force *her* to have a shit life, running from town to town, with you always looking over your shoulder just because you've got something to prove?'

They were harsh words, but they hit Sarah where it mattered most.

'All right,' she conceded. 'But I'm not happy about dragging you into this. And if he finds out where we are, I'm going – and I won't be telling you where.'

Glen and the guys were lounging around in the living room when Karen got home. Smiling, she went across to the couch and sat beside Glen, waiting for an opportunity to have a quiet word with Vinnie.

It was almost an hour before Glen ran upstairs to have a quick shower before going out for the night. Getting up, Karen asked Vinnie to help carry the dirty glasses into the kitchen.

'I know about Sarah,' she said when they were alone. 'It's a long story, but I'll tell you everything later. Make an excuse to go home early, then give me a ring and I'll come round.'

'Not to mine, you won't.' He looked horrified by the suggestion. 'And what do you mean, you know about Sarah?'

'She's gone,' Karen told him, running water into the sink to cover their voices. 'And she isn't coming back. I was talking to her just before I came home.'

'How?' Vinnie demanded belligerently. 'You'd best not have been round there saying anything to her.'

'No, I haven't.'

'What do you mean, she's gone?'

'Look, just wait till I've told you everything before you go jumping in at the deep end.'

'Where is she?' Vinnie's face was livid now as he crossed to Karen and grabbed her arm in a steely grip. 'Tell me, or I swear I'm gonna hurt you!'

'Get off me!' Karen hissed, fear creeping in now as she gazed up into his rage-filled eyes.

'I'll *kill* you if you've said anything to turn her against me,' he hissed back, his voice so low that it was barely audible.

'Don't threaten me,' she retorted icily, injured pride making her turn nasty. 'Unless you want me to shout for Glen? I'll scream my head off and tell him you were trying it on with me. Try me if you don't believe me,' she went on, blinking rapidly now, bringing tears to her eyes. 'Look, I'll be crying in a second, *and* I've got marks on my arm where you've been forcing me up against the sink. Who do *you* think he'll believe?'

'You fucking bitch!' Vinnie tossed her arm aside. 'I'll make you pay for this.'

'I don't see how,' she snarled. 'I'm having his baby. Do you really think he'll take your word over mine?'

'You said it was mine.'

'Well, it's not. I got the dates wrong. It's Glen's.'

'What kind of game are you playing?' Vinnie demanded, glaring at her confusedly. 'What are you trying to achieve?'

Leaning back against the ledge, Karen shook her head slowly as she rubbed her arm. 'I really don't know, Vinnie. Maybe I just needed to see what you would say if you knew about Sarah.'

'This isn't finished,' he hissed, pointing a warning finger at her. 'Not by a long shot. If she's gone when I get home, I'll be coming after you. You'll never dare tell Glen what we've done, and I won't give you a chance to drop me in it with him. You won't know what's hit you.'

Smiling sweetly when Glen called him just then, Karen said, 'Run along, there's a good boy.'

Vinnie bit down on the anger surging through him. He couldn't afford to leave it like this. He'd been stupid to get into this kind of argument with her with Glen so close. If she opened her mouth, he was dead.

'Look, I'm sorry,' he murmured, turning on the sincere eyes.

'Pardon?' Karen gazed back at him uncertainly. She wanted to be angry, but he had *never* apologized to her before. Not for any of his cruel words, not for any of the times when he had hurt her deeply.

'I said I'm sorry,' Vinnie whispered, taking a step towards her, his stare burning into her soul. 'It was just the shock of it all. But it could be for the best – her leaving, I mean. It wasn't really working out. My heart wasn't really in it.'

Karen was melting, her heart quickening at the nearness of him.

'You'd best go before Glen comes looking for you,' she whispered, touching a hand to his chest.

Closing his eyes, Vinnie inhaled slowly as if her touch had scorched him and he couldn't bear to tear himself away.

'Okay, I'll go,' he said huskily. 'I'll call you, soon. We need to sort this mess out once and for all. I need to do right by you. I can see that now.'

Leaning back against the sink when he had gone, Karen exhaled shakily. She hoped with all her heart that he meant what he'd said. She was more than willing to give him a chance to prove himself, but she didn't know if she could take it if he rejected her again.

44

West was embarrassed when he showed Sarah and Harry into his house. He had lived alone for far too long and hadn't noticed how badly he had neglected the big old semi. Their presence made him see it through fresh eyes and he was appalled by the layer of dust coating everything in sight, the piles of papers, the heaps of clothes he had failed to carry upstairs after washing them . . . the smell of decaying food emanating from the kitchen.

'Sorry about the mess,' he said, going into the kitchen and opening the window. 'I don't spend that much time here.'

'Don't worry about it,' Sarah told him. 'It's only a bit of dust. It'll give me something to do.'

'Where shall I put these?' Harry asked, struggling in with his and Sarah's suitcases.

'First and third rooms.' West pointed up the stairs. 'Put Sarah and Kimmy in the back one, there's two singles in there. Coffee, Sarah?'

'That would be great.' She gave him a grateful smile.

Noticing how weary she looked, he showed her into the living room and told her to make herself at home. Carrying the drinks in a few minutes later, he smiled to see mother and child fast asleep on the couch. Drawing the curtains, he left them in peace. Given what they had been through over the past few days, he had no doubt that they could use all the sleep they could get right now.

Going into the study, he called Jenny to let her know what was happening. He figured that Sarah would appreciate having another woman to talk to, and he knew how much Jenny wanted to see her. But if he were honest, it was also a ploy to get Jenny round here. He'd always known she was conscientious about her job, but he hadn't realized quite how committed to it she was. Since hooking up with her again, he'd only actually seen her three times. The rest of their communication had been by phone because their shifts conflicted perfectly. When he was working she was sleeping, when he was free she was working. He couldn't wait to retire and spend a full, uninterrupted day with her.

Jenny broke her golden rule and called in sick. She hated taking time off work, especially now she was the boss, but the thought of seeing Sarah was too tempting to resist.

'Where is she?' she asked, giving West a cursory peck on the cheek as she barrelled through his front door less than an hour after receiving his call.

'Living room,' he told her, standing where she had left him with his arms spread. 'Is that all I get?'

'You'll get the rest later,' she called back over her shoulder.

Awake now, Sarah jumped when the door flew open. Turning, she was shocked to see her old friend standing there. Getting up, she said, 'My God, Jenny! What are you doing here?'

Rushing to her, Jenny hugged her tight, then pushed her back and looked her over. 'Look at you. All grown up and twice as gorgeous.'

'With these bruises, I don't think so,' Sarah snorted softly. 'How did you find out I was here?'

'Tony told me, how d'y' think?'

'*Tony*?' Sarah shook her head bemusedly. 'But how? . . . What's going on?'

'Don't tell me he hasn't told you?' Jenny turned to give West a scolding look.

'Didn't get much of a chance,' West said, shrugging his jacket on. 'Anyway, I'm sure you'll bring her up to speed while me and Harry go to the takeaway. Hope everyone likes Chinese. See you in a bit.'

'Well?' Sarah demanded when they were alone. 'What's going on?'

'I'll tell you later,' Jenny said, kneeling down beside Kimmy who was still sleeping. 'I want to have a look at this little girl of yours.'

'She's wiped out.' Sitting down, Sarah gazed sadly down at her daughter's face. 'She hasn't said anything, but I know she's freaked out about the state of me. I had to tell her I fell down some stairs. I suppose you know what's been going on?'

'Yeah, Tony told me.' Jenny exhaled noisily. 'I didn't expect you to look this bad, though. The bastard really did a job on you, didn't he?'

'Doesn't matter now,' Sarah said. 'Kimmy's safe. That's all I'm bothered about.'

'Yeah, well, just make sure you *stay* safe.' Looking up at her, Jenny frowned. 'Tony said you weren't too happy about coming here. Said you were all for taking off and trying to make do by yourself. So what's the deal with that?'

'I just said it's not their problem.' Sarah was defensive. 'I got myself into it, so why should they suffer?'

'Because they're your friends,' Jenny told her. 'We all are, and I thought you of all people would know the value of that. Look what you did for Harry when he needed you. Don't you think he deserves a chance to pay you back?'

'I hadn't thought of it like that.'

'Well, maybe it's time you did. I've only met him once, but I know he's a belter. And he's really worried about the two of you.' She nodded down at Kimmy. 'Why don't you put him out of his misery and let him look after you, just till it blows over with the dickhead who did this to you? You can't tell me you're not happy to see him again.'

'Yeah, course I am,' Sarah agreed.

'Well, then,' Jenny said, as if that concluded it. Gazing down at Kimmy, she smiled wistfully. 'She's an angel, Sarah. You don't know how lucky you are.'

'Oh, I do,' Sarah murmured. 'Believe me, I do.'

The house came alive over the following week and West couldn't believe the change that living, breathing people brought to the atmosphere. Sarah had cleaned the place from top to bottom, and Harry had turned out to be a dab hand in the kitchen. West was soon feeling the benefits of cutting out the burgers, pizzas and takeaways that had made up his diet for the past too many years.

Jenny was still working nights, but her days were her own, and she liked nothing better than to spend them with her friends. Especially Kimmy, with whom she had formed a strong bond. Any excuse she got, she took the child out for walks, or whisked her off to the shopping centre to spoil her. It filled the childless space in her heart, and gave Kimmy a break from the house – and the others a chance for adult talk.

Winding his outstanding cases down in preparation for leaving in three days' time, West was in the radio room checking out an address when the report came in of a car sticking boot-up out of the River Medlock. He wasn't paying particular attention when the controller took the registration number, but his blood ran cold when she relayed the owner's name. Dropping everything when he heard that the divers had recovered a body, he ran outside and jumped into his car.

Arriving at the scene some ten minutes later, he ducked

beneath the tape and made his way over to where the body had been laid out on the grass.

Gazing down at Karen Mullen, her pretty face bloated and grey, her unseeing eyes bulging from their sockets, West felt something snap inside him. She hadn't been the nicest of people but he wouldn't have wished this terrible death on her.

Shaking his head, he approached the attending pathologist who was writing a scene report on the bonnet of his car. 'What's the verdict, George?'

'At a glance, accidental,' George Smedley told him, brushing his glasses back onto his nose with the back of a still-gloved hand. 'She went out of control on the road back there, crashed through the fence and went in off the embankment, judging by the skid marks.' He pointed across to the muddy slope on the far side of the water, where two deep grooves were clear to see all the way down to the water's edge. 'Did you know her?' he asked then, wondering at West's more than usual concern. Detectives were usually the least affected of all the attending bodies at scenes such as this, and West was hardier than most.

'No,' West lied. 'It just winds me up when youngsters die like this. It's so fucking pointless.' Exhaling noisily, he glanced at his watch. 'Best get on, I suppose. I only stopped to have a nosy. See you later.'

Making his way back up the slope, he climbed into his car and drove home to tell Sarah the awful news.

'That's *it*!' Sarah cried when she heard. 'That's the last fucking thing he's getting away with!'

'Calm down, Sarah.' Harry held her as she sobbed. 'We don't know it was anything to do with Vinnie. Tony's already told you it was an accident.'

'No, it wasn't!' she yelled, jumping to her feet and pacing

the room. 'I know it was him, I just know it! She was pregnant, Harry – with *his child*. How could he do that?'

'Because he's an evil bastard,' he murmured. 'But there's still no proof he's involved. We're just going to have to wait until the autopsy.'

Going to the window, Sarah hugged herself and stared out at the garden. It was pointless waiting for the autopsy report. It was bound to come back with a verdict of accidental death, just as Pete's killing had been classed as suicide. Whatever had happened with Karen, Vinnie was behind it, and Sarah had to put a stop to him – once and for all. But this time she really would have to keep Harry and West out of it.

'Where are you going?' Harry asked when she suddenly turned and stalked into the hall.

'For a drive,' she told him, her voice deadly calm as she pulled her coat on. 'Don't mind if I borrow your car, do you, Tony?'

'Where you going?' Harry asked, concern growing within him. 'I'll come with you.'

'No.' Gazing into his eyes, she shook her head. 'I just need a bit of time alone. Will you look after Kimmy for me?'

'Of course, but . . .'

'I don't think you should be alone just now, Sarah.' West came into the hall. 'You've had a nasty shock. Why don't you come and sit down? I'll get you a drink.'

'I don't need a drink,' she told him, forcing herself to give them a tight smile. 'I'm fine, honestly. Don't worry. I won't be long.'

Walking out then, her back rigid, her head high, Sarah climbed into West's car. It was time to set the final phase of her association with Vinnie Walker into motion.

It wasn't Vinnie's day to visit Pam, but Sarah wasn't taking any chances. Parking up out of sight, she settled back to watch the bungalow.

After half an hour a woman came out and closed the door without locking it. Realizing that it must be the carer who, according to Vinnie, left about an hour before the men began their rota, Sarah waited until the woman had driven away. Then she slipped out of the car and walked quickly across the road.

Letting herself into the bungalow, she locked the door and crept along the corridor. Pressing her ear against the bedroom door, she listened hard. The only sounds inside were the tinny voices of a chat-show host and his guests. Sure that Pam was alone, she tapped gently, then pushed the door open.

Pam was peering at her suspiciously as she came into the room.

'Hello,' Sarah said. 'I'm, er, sorry to disturb you. I don't know if you remember me?'

'I remember you,' Pam said, frowning now. 'What are you sneaking about for?'

'I needed to talk to you, and I didn't want anyone to see me.'

Pam waved at the chair beside her bed and flipped the TV off with the remote. 'You haven't got long if you don't want to see no one,' she said. 'My Glen's due soon, and he ain't best pleased today, so he might be a bit off with you if you're still here. Girlfriends!' Tutting, she rolled her eyes. 'Good as gold till they get their hooks in, then *whoosh*! They're off all over the place, doing all sorts. Do us a favour, love.' She pointed across to the dressing table. 'Pass us me fags. That carer thinks she's a clever bitch putting 'em out of reach.'

Sarah's hands were shaking when she brought the cigarettes over. Peering at her concernedly, Pam said, 'Get it off your chest, pet. I can see you're upset about something. Is it your mam?'

Sarah burst into tears before she could stop herself. Patting her shoulder, Pam let her cry herself out. Lighting two cigarettes then, she passed one to her, saying, 'Right, what's the bitch done?'

'It's not her,' Sarah said. 'It's – it's my s-sister.'

'Your sister?' Pam prompted gently.

'Her name's Karen.' Sarah continued shakily. 'But you know her as Carina.'

'Carina? . . . My Glen's Carina?'

'Yes.'

'Your sister? Well, I never. And her name's Karen?'

Sarah nodded. 'I didn't know she was calling herself Carina. Not for a while. I only saw her for the first time since we were kids the day after I saw you. She – she was at my mam's. She looks after her, you see, because she's really ill.'

'Maggie is?'

'Yeah. She's got all sorts wrong with her and Karen goes round every day to see to her, and that.'

'Well, I'm gobsmacked.' Pam shook her head. 'All this time I'd thought she was pissing off to see her fancy man, and she's been doing that. I wonder if Glen knows? I'd best ring him and put him out of his misery. Daft sod's been ringing all over the place looking for her 'cos she stopped out last night.'

'She's *deeead . . .*' Sarah wailed, exploding into a fresh burst of tears.

'You what?' Pam drew her head back and stared at Sarah. 'Are you sure?'

Making a concerted effort to pull herself together, Sarah nodded. 'Her car went off the road. The police pulled her out of the river this morning.'

'Bleedin' hell!' Pam murmured, shocked. 'It'll break Glen's heart, this. She was carrying his baby, you know. He only told me the other day. Proud as punch, he was. I never reckoned much to her, to be honest, but she's been sweet as a peach since he told me the news. Aw, this is awful.' Frowning with genuine sadness now, she shook her head.

'I'm sorry,' Sarah said, taking a tissue from her pocket and wiping her nose. 'I didn't mean to upset you.'

'Don't worry about me,' Pam told her, squeezing her hand. 'She was your sister, you must be shattered. What's she been calling herself Carina for, though, if her name's Karen? I don't get that.'

'She wanted to change herself when she got away from Mam,' Sarah explained. 'She was going to tell Glen before they got married.'

'Is that what you've come round for? To tell me, so I can tell him?'

'Not exactly, no. It's really hard to know where to start, but there's something he should know. About Vinnie.'

'What about him?'

Raising her face, Sarah looked the old woman straight in the eye. This was going to be difficult. Pam loved Vinnie – she wouldn't want to believe what Sarah was about to say.

'I know you think the world of him,' she said. 'So did I, till I found out what he's really like.'

Narrowing her eyes, Pam nodded. 'You're good with make-up,' she said, referring to the bruising that Sarah had tried to conceal. 'I take it he did that?'

Nodding, Sarah said, 'He tried to force me to have his baby, but I said I'd never have one with him and he went berserk. I'd just found out that he'd raped me when we were younger, you see.'

'Go on,' Pam urged when Sarah paused for a little too long. 'How does this fit in with Glen and your sister?'

Sarah really didn't want to tell Pam that Karen had been having an affair with Vinnie. Glen couldn't hurt Karen now, but she still felt a need to protect her.

'I wasn't the only one he raped,' she said at last. 'Remember when you were in hospital? Well, he did it to Karen, too.'

'For real?' Pam asked quietly.

'Yes.' Sarah forced herself not to look away. 'She was waiting for me when I got home the other week. She was going to warn Vinnie's girlfriend what he was really like, but she didn't know it was me. We both got a shock.'

'I bet you did,' Pam muttered, believing her. Not only because she instinctively liked her, but also because she remembered how quiet Carina had been when she'd visited the hospital the day after the stroke. She'd looked really peaky. The poor cow must have been going through hell.

'Just tell me one thing,' she said. 'The babby . . . ?'

'It was Glen's,' Sarah told her quickly. 'She was absolutely sure about that. And she was so happy about it, but it was breaking her heart that she couldn't tell him about Vinnie because she thought he wouldn't believe her.'

'Little bastard,' Pam snarled, shaking her head. 'She should have told Glen, though. He might have a temper, but he adored that girl. He'd have slaughtered Vinnie for that.'

Peering at her, Sarah wondered at the ease with which she had accepted Vinnie's guilt. But then she thought about Kimmy, and knew that she would take *her* word over anyone's, no matter how much she had previously liked them. Blood was blood. And the same way she was putting Karen before Vinnie despite everything Karen had done to hurt her, Pam would put Glen before him, too.

'Is that all?' Pam asked, wearying now.

'No,' Sarah admitted. She opened her mouth to say more, but was stopped by the door opening.

'How come the door was locked, mother?' Glen asked. Pausing when he spotted Sarah, he said, 'Oh, sorry. Didn't realize you had a visitor.'

Sarah's heart was in her mouth. Glen Noble was a huge bruiser of a man, and his eyes were sharper than any she had ever seen. She was suddenly very afraid.

Looking from Sarah to his mother, Glen narrowed his eyes

as he sensed that this was no ordinary visit. 'What's going on?' he demanded.

'Sit down, son,' Pam told him quietly. Waiting until he'd pulled a chair up to the other side of the bed, she said, 'Now, whatever you think when you hear what you're about to hear, you'd better stay in that seat till I say you can get up. D'y' hear me?'

'Don't play games,' he replied irritably. 'Just tell me what's going on.'

'I'm not playing,' his mother scolded him sharply. 'Now stay put, or else.'

'Fine,' he muttered, folding his arms.

'Good. Are you on your own?'

'Joe dropped me off, but he'll be back in a bit. Why?'

'Vinnie's not with him?'

'No.' Glen frowned darkly. 'You're pissing me off now, mother. Get on with it. I've not found Carina yet and you're wasting my time.'

'I'll think you'll find I'm not,' Pam said quietly. 'Now button it, and listen. This is Sarah.'

Glancing back at Sarah, Glen nodded.

'She's the daughter of a very old friend of mine,' Pam went on. 'So you just keep that in mind. Now, she's got something to tell you, and you're going to listen until she's finished. Right?'

'Yes.' Tipping his head to the side, Glen gazed at Sarah with pained resignation.

Feeling as though she were walking into a very bad place from which there was no way out, Sarah told him what she had already told Pam. Reaching the same point she'd been at when he interrupted her, she took a very deep breath before saying, 'I think Vinnie killed Karen.'

'Why would you think that?' Pam asked, keeping Glen pinned in his seat with a stern look.

'Because he said he would if she told Glen, and she was about to,' Sarah replied, keeping her own gaze on Glen, in fear of him making a dive for her. 'The day you found those business cards, Glen. She said you got really mad and had a go at her. She'd been crying when Vinnie turned up and he thought she'd told you. He said he could snap her neck and put her in his jeep and no one would ever know. She was terrified.'

Glen still hadn't spoken. His chest was heaving, his nostrils flaring as he listened, his unblinking eyes riveted to Sarah's face.

'When he attacked me,' Sarah went on, 'he as good as admitted that he'd killed my husband. I believed him. And Karen believed he would kill *her*. She wanted to tell you, but she loved you so much she couldn't bear the thought of hurting you. And she didn't want to risk losing you, either. I know she was flashy, but you were her world. All she wanted was to get married and have your baby. That's all she *ever* wanted.'

Tears had begun to stream from Glen's eyes, but he still hadn't spoken. Then, just when Sarah thought he never would, he said, 'He's a dead man.'

It was so calm and flat, it almost didn't register that he had said it. Then Sarah felt the icy trickle of relief down her spine. He believed her, and he wasn't going to cross-examine her. She didn't know if she'd have been able to stand up under that.

Patting his hand, Pam said, 'You do what you have to do, son.'

Looking at Sarah now, completely unashamed of the tears, he said, 'No doubt the police will release her body to you?'

'I suppose so,' she murmured numbly. It hadn't even occurred to her.

'Well, I'll pay,' he said. 'For everything.'

'He means it,' Pam told her. 'Anything you want, you just ask, yeah?'

Embarrassed, Sarah looked down at the tissue she had been shredding. 'I'd appreciate your help with the funeral,' she said after a moment. 'But that's not what I came for. There's something I want to do, but I need your help.'

'Name it,' Glen said, sniffing loudly as he rubbed his eyes with the heels of his palms.

45

Vinnie got out of the shower and strolled naked into the bedroom to get ready for a night that he was really looking forward to.

Glen had called that morning, telling him to come to a meet later that evening. He was to leave his jeep behind the old cottages in Styal Woods, then walk to the watermill on the other side of the timbered area and wait to be picked up.

It sounded shady and he was buzzing, sure that some sort of promotion must be on the cards if they were letting him in on the action. Maybe he was about to get his own crew to run, at long last.

Dressing in dark clothes as directed, he splashed his face with cologne and looked himself over. Perfect.

Switching off the lights, he set the alarm, locked up and went outside.

It was a warm night and the moon was hiding behind a murky orange haze, making the streets dark and anonymous. The perfect setting for a hit.

Vinnie was whistling as he strolled to his jeep, feeling better than he had in ages. Life was definitely on the up now that Carina – or Karen, or whatever the stupid cunt's name was – was sorted, and there was no danger of Glen hearing things he didn't need to know.

It had been so easy getting her to tell him everything. All he'd had to do was lay on the charm and she'd been putty in his hands. He'd had no problem getting Carina to drive out to meet him. She was literally begging for it when he slipped her the last shag she would ever have in the back of her car, and getting her to smoke the smack-spiked spliff straight after was a piece of piss. She'd been so high already – buoyed by Vinnie's promises of running away to start a new life with her and the baby.

She'd been wrecked after the spliff, but not so much that she wasn't convinced she was capable of driving. Following her – to make sure she got home in one piece, he'd said – he'd kept a watchful eye out as she slewed across the road markings. Fortunately, he'd chosen the perfect spot for their rendezvous, and they hadn't seen a single civilian, let alone police car on the way. His timing was spot on when he nudged her through the fence and down the embankment. And once again he was in the clear.

And he had all the information he needed to get his woman and child back since Carina had told him where they were and who they were with. As soon as this job was out of the way, he would go to that hotel and take back what was rightfully his. And maybe he'd teach Harry Shaw another little lesson in the process.

Arriving at the woods, Vinnie killed his lights and parked up. Lighting a cigarette, he used the flare of his lighter to peer around in the pitch dark. There was nothing to see, and nothing to hear but the slight breeze whispering through the ancient trees, the occasional owl hoot, and the rustling of small animals going about their business in the undergrowth.

Finishing the smoke, he ground it out underfoot and made his way through the wood to the watermill. Under cover of the swooshing waters rushing by beneath the bridge, he walked across the gravel path leading out to the road.

Emerging from the shadows cast by the trees, Vinnie spotted Glen's car parked up ahead. Adrenalin began to course through his veins as he approached it, but he kept his cool.

Joe was in the driving seat, Glen beside him in the front, and Al in the back. Climbing in beside Al, Vinnie was grinning as he greeted them all. But he quickly settled down when he picked up on the tense atmosphere. Whatever they were doing tonight, it was heavy.

Joe started the car and eased out onto the road. Gazing out of the window, Vinnie realized they were heading back towards Manchester. Breaking the cardinal 'no question' rule, he dared ask why.

'Are we meeting the others somewhere—'

Al's fist connected with Vinnie's nose before the words had completely left his mouth. Doubling over as the pain tore through his face, Vinnie felt his first flush of true, unadulterated fear. Then Glen reached across the back of the seat and grabbed Vinnie's lapels with both hands. Yanking him forward, Glen sank his teeth into his ear and shook his head like a pit bull in battle.

Vinnie screamed until he blacked out.

46

Sarah was shivering. She was freezing, and she felt dizzy and nauseous. She didn't know if it was regret at having got herself into this or fear of it all going wrong. She just wanted to get it over with.

Wrapping the coat that Glen's man Freddie had given her tighter around herself, she peered around the old swimming baths. She had passed it many times throughout her life, but had never been inside before. It had been closed down way before she was born and no one had ever bothered to do anything with the place. It had been boarded up for as long as she could remember, but it felt eerily inhabited, as if the ghosts of its former patrons were watching from the dressing stalls that were no longer there. Sarah almost imagined she could hear their whispers, but it was only the faint leaking-in of passing traffic.

Freddie took a small silver hip flask from his pocket. Taking a swig, he offered the flask to Sarah. She shook her head. She wanted to be as clear-headed and sober as humanly possible when the others arrived.

Her heart catapulted into her mouth when she heard the metallic clang of the outer door-covering being wrenched back a short time later. She glanced at Freddie wide-eyed, gripped by the sudden fear that Vinnie might have escaped and beaten Glen here. If he walked through that door, gun in hand, that awful smile on his face, she wouldn't wait for him to kill her – she would kill herself.

'Steady,' Freddie murmured, stepping in front of her, his hugeness shielding her as he drew a sawn-off from beneath his coat and aimed it firmly at the jagged spears of metal jutting down over the doorway. Dropping his aim when Glen ducked beneath them and stepped inside, he turned to Sarah and gave her a reassuring wink.

'Fuck a duck, it's colder than a friggin' abattoir in here,' Glen said, clapping his hands against his arms. 'You all right, Sarah? Freddie been taking good care of you?'

'Yes, thanks.' She was acutely aware of how utterly ludicrous such politeness was in these surroundings, under these circumstances.

She gasped out loud when Joe and Al came through the door dragging Vinnie between them. In the faint beams of light filtering in through the gaps in the boards covering the windows, she could see that his nose was broken and the left side of his face was dark with blood.

'Don't worry,' Glen told her, putting an arm around her shoulders as he walked her towards the deep end where the others had dragged Vinnie. 'We didn't do too much damage. Just enough to let him know we ain't messing – and give me a bit of satisfaction. The rest is yours. Do you still wanna go through with it?'

Sarah inhaled deeply, desperately trying to draw oxygen from the air. She felt as if she were hyperventilating, and she wasn't sure she could stand up, breathe, *and* do what she had to do.

'You can leave it to us if you want to call it off,' Glen told her, peering down at her concernedly. 'It's gonna happen whatever, but you don't have to watch if you can't stomach it.'

Gritting her teeth, Sarah shook her head and forced herself to look at Vinnie. Sitting where Joe and Al had propped him beneath the diving board, he was staring straight at her as they bound his hands and feet with rope.

Freddie climbed the wrought-iron steps to the top of the board and attached another rope to the handrail. Al caught the noose end when Freddie dropped it down and looped it around Vinnie's neck.

'Don't let them do this, Sarah.' Vinnie spoke for the first time.

'Belt up, dickhead,' Joe snarled, kicking him in the stomach.

Sarah steeled herself. This wasn't a game she could stop at any time. It was revenge – for every terrible thing this man had done to her and to the people she loved.

'Sarah?' Glen said, conscious of the length of time they had already been here. 'You're gonna have to make your mind up.'

'I'll do it,' she told him. 'But I want to do it alone.'

He peered down at her for a moment, then nodded. 'All right, but we're right outside if you need us.'

Looking up then to Freddie, who was crouching at the head of the board like a huge bear about to leap off a cliff, Glen said, 'Reel him up till he's on his toes, then come down.'

Motioning the men out of the room when they were done, he handed Sarah a small handgun. 'This ain't to kill him, it's to hurt him. We'll finish it, you just get what you need in the meantime. Remember what I told you?'

'Yeah.' She nodded.

'Gloves on?' He checked her hands. 'Hair back? Got them boots I give you? Good girl.' Smiling at her now, he turned to Vinnie and mimed aiming a gun at his head. Making a slow *BOOM!* sound, he walked out, laughing.

Alone now, Sarah took a step back, the irrational fear that Vinnie would somehow spring forward, miraculously unshackled, and attack her all too real in her mind.

'Sarah, please,' he implored, his voice a whisper. 'You don't have to get involved in this. It's not about you. Glen's got it all wrong. Untie me, babe. We'll find a way out of here. Please, Sarah. I love you.'

'No, you don't.' Sarah was shaking from head to foot. 'You don't know what love is. You wouldn't have hurt me if you did.'

'I never meant to. You've got to believe me.'

'Fuck you!' she hissed. 'You're a filthy bastard liar, Vinnie! I know all about you now, and I hate you with all my heart – just like I always did!'

Realizing that she wasn't going to help him, Vinnie felt the anger course through him. After everything he had done for her, this was how she was going to repay him? He would kill her with his bare hands! Bucking against the rope around his neck, he laughed when she almost fell over with fright.

'What's the matter, Sarah?' he sneered. 'Scared?'

'Not at all.' She forced herself to calm down. 'If anyone should be scared, it's you, you sick bastard.'

'Oh, tut tut,' he hissed, his eyes flashing with impotent anger. 'That's not very nice, is it? Feel brave with your friends behind you, do you? Think I won't get out of this and hunt you down?'

'Big words,' Sarah spat back at him. 'Coming from the man who's all tied up and helpless. How does it feel, Vinnie? To know you're at my mercy now? Aren't you going to try and sweet-talk your way out of it? Aren't you going to beg me to save you?'

'Vinnie Walker don't beg, darlin'!'

'Did my sister beg?' Sarah's voice was deathly calm now.

Vinnie laughed, a strange, strangled, nasty sound. 'Oh, she begged, all right. She was always begging, that one. Begging for my *dick* like the whore she was!'

Raising the gun, Sarah held it between both hands and aimed at one of Vinnie's knees.

'Don't talk about her like that,' she warned. 'Karen was innocent compared to you.'

'Come off it,' he sneered, goading her, convinced that she would never have the nerve to pull the trigger. 'She was a ten-quid slag with a cunt like the fucking Channel Tunnel!'

Glaring at him, Sarah stepped as close as she dared and pulled the trigger. The recoil wrenched her shoulder and threw her back, but she hit her mark. Roaring with pain, Vinnie bucked and jerked on his rope as the pain tore through his leg.

'*Cunt!*' he snarled, when it subsided to mere agony. 'You'd better finish me off, bitch, 'cos I'm gonna rip your heart out when this is over.'

'Why did you do it, Vinnie?' She felt strangely detached now that she had begun. 'Why did you have to kill her? That's all I want to know.'

'Because she deserved it,' he hissed. 'And I don't know why you care 'cos she *hated* you, you stupid bitch.'

'And did I deserve what you did to me?'

'Which bit? The *birthday* fuck? Or the fuck to plant my seed in you? Missed your period yet?'

'Oh, don't worry about that.' Sarah smiled nastily. 'I made sure *that* didn't get a chance to grow. I told you I wasn't having *your* bastard. Didn't you believe me?'

'Bitch!' he spat, swinging his feet out to kick her, almost hanging himself in the process.

'Calm down, Vinnie,' she told him, shaking her head. 'I was a bit late for the morning-after pill seeing as you kept me prisoner for so long, but they can do wonders these days at getting rid of trash.'

'Just like I got rid of your *husband*,' he hit back.

'Now that wasn't nice, was it?' she said, her tone facetious. 'There was just no need for that. What did he ever do to you?'

'Don't try and fuck with my head.'

'Why not? You fucked with mine. This is payback. For me . . . for Harry . . . for Karen. Say bye-bye to your other knee, Vinnie. Then say bye-bye to me, because I'm gonna walk out of here and get on with my life. And guess what? . . . You ain't gonna be part of it *ever* again.'

Stepping towards him then, Sarah aimed the gun at his other knee. Missing first time, she calmly straightened up and tried again. Gazing on dispassionately as his face contorted with pain, she shook her head.

'You're really not that good-looking when you get right down to it, are you? Looking at you like this, I remember why I wanted Pete instead of you. He was *so* handsome. Oh, and that reminds me. You haven't seen Harry Shaw lately, have you? He's *really* changed, Vinnie, and he loves me as much as ever.'

Pausing, she narrowed her eyes and licked her lips before delivering the killer blow.

'And Kimmy *adores* him. She's with him right now. In fact, you know what I think I'll do when I leave you here, Vinnie? I think I'll go home and marry him. Give Kimmy a *real* daddy.'

Laughing at Vinnie's screams of rage and frustration, Sarah turned her back and walked out of his miserable, soon-to-be-over life.

EPILOGUE

A year later

S arah heard the car tyres crunching gravel and ran to the window.

'Oh, God! The limo's here! I'm not ready.'

'You look fantastic,' Jenny told her, reaching up to clip a stray ringlet back in place. 'Perfect.'

Looking at each other, they giggled. They had already drunk three-quarters of the champagne but they decided to finish the bottle. Pouring two glasses, Jenny handed one to Sarah.

'What a year,' she said, sighing loudly. 'I can't believe we made it this far after everything that's happened.'

'Me neither,' Sarah agreed. 'But I'm glad we did. It's been brilliant, hasn't it?'

'It sure has,' Jenny grinned. 'And it's gonna get better and better. To you.' She raised her glass.

'And you,' Sarah replied, clinking hers against Jenny's.

'Ready?' Jenny asked when they had drained their glasses.

Exhaling nervously, Sarah nodded.

Kimmy was waiting on the church step, a vision in peach frills, her glossy ringlets held back by a pearl tiara, a beribboned basket of flower petals in her hand.

Harry was waiting at the gates. He stepped forward when the limo pulled up and opened the door. Helping Sarah and Jenny out, he shook his head, his eyes misty with emotion.

'Oh, my God, you both look absolutely beautiful.'

'You don't look so bad yourself,' Jenny teased, fiddling with his bow tie. 'What do you think, Sarah?'

'He knows what I think,' Sarah murmured, reaching up to kiss him. 'He's gorgeous.'

Smiling, Harry cocked his elbows. The two women took an arm each and the trio walked up the path to the church door. Gazing down at Kimmy when they reached her, Jenny's chin began to wobble.

'Oh, look at you,' she said, bending to give her a hug. 'You look so lovely.'

'Ready, babe?' Sarah asked.

'Yeah.' Kimmy nodded.

'Off you go, then.' Sarah pushed her gently towards the door.

'This is it,' Jenny murmured, turning to Sarah.

'Yes, it is,' Sarah agreed, her eyes filling with tears as she hugged her friend. 'Come on. Let's get it over with.'

Opening the doors, Harry motioned to the organist to begin the Wedding March. Waiting until Sarah and Jenny were behind him, he led them down the petal-strewn aisle.

'Who gives the bride away?' the vicar asked when they were in place.

'I do.' Taking Jenny's hand, Harry brought her forward to stand beside West. Stepping back then, he smiled at Sarah, mouthing, 'Me and you next?'

Blushing as she realized what he had said, she nodded quickly.

MANDASUE HELLER

The Front

Sometimes it's wise to scratch beneath the surface before you make your move.

When old school friends Lee, Mal, Ged and Sam decided to make some easy money, nothing could have prepared them for the catalogue of disasters that was soon to follow.

Robbing a supermarket should have been an easy job, nothing could possibly go wrong – but it did. With one of them wounded and a dead body on their hands, could matters have got any worse?

They should have known that a small supermarket on a Manchester estate wouldn't make that much money, and they had no idea that as small fish they had unwittingly plunged into a very big pond and were now swimming with the 'great whites' of the criminal underworld.

The shop they robbed, their ticket to an easy life, was merely THE FRONT for something bigger than they could ever have imagined.

CORONET BOOKS
Hodder & Stoughton

MANDASUE HELLER

Forget Me Not

A killer has made Manchester's Westy Lane his local hunting ground, leaving the police a very special gift – a tiny forget me not flower placed delicately in his victim's entrails.

Lisa Noone is twelve years old and wise beyond her years. Pat Noone is her mother, a fearsome woman who just happens to be a member of the oldest profession in the book. Together their lives are far from perfect, but they will always have each other. Or will they?

One night after a youth club disco, Benny arrives in Lisa's life. He is tall, dark and in Lisa's eyes the most gorgeous man she's ever seen. But Benny is not all he seems. And whilst Lisa savours true love she is totally unaware of his real intentions.

Benny wants more from Lisa than she will ever know.

'A cracking page-turner.' *Manchester Evening News*

CORONET BOOKS
Hodder & Stoughton